A
PARTIAL
HISTORY
OF
LOST
CAUSES

A
PARTIAL
HISTORY
OF
LOST
CAUSES

a novel

JENNIFER DUBOIS

THE DIAL PRESS NEW YORK

Published in the United States by The Dial Press,
an imprint of The Random House Publishing Group,
a division of Random House, Inc., New York.

DIAL PRESS is a registered trademark of Random House, Inc.,
and the colophon is a trademark of Random House, Inc.

LIBRARY OF CONGRESS CATALOGING-IN-PUBLICATION DATA
DuBois, Jennifer.
A partial history of lost causes / by Jennifer duBois.
p. cm.
ISBN 978-1-4000-6977-4
eBook ISBN 978-0-679-60474-7
1. Chess players—Russia (Federation)—Fiction. I. Title.
PS3604.U258P37 2011
813'.6—dc22   2011006057

Printed in the United States of America on acid-free paper

www.dialpress.com

2 4 6 8 9 7 5 3 1

FIRST EDITION

Book design by Casey Hampton

To Richard du Bois, who knew how to love life;

And to Carolyn du Bois, who knows how to live it.

We are all doomed, but some are more doomed than others.

—Vladimir Nabokov, *Ada, or Ardor*

And if in this wide world I die, then I'll die from joy that I'm alive.

— Yevgeny Yevtushenko

PART ONE

1

ALEKSANDR

Leningrad, Russia, 1979

When Aleksandr finally arrived in Leningrad, he was stunned by the great gray span of the Neva. The river was a churning organ in the city's center—not its heart, surely, something more practical and less sentimental but just as necessary. The amygdala, maybe, or both kidneys. It had been six days from Okha—on a boat and then a train—and out the window he'd seen the entire country: first the teetering spires of Sakhalin's drilling rigs, as familiar to Aleksandr as his own dreams; then the abandoned green train at the port, melting into the sand ever since the war with the Japanese; then the ten thousand salmon rotting in the sun on the eastern shore, waiting for Moscow to telegram permission for their loading; then the curling stems of smoke above the villages that were impossibly far apart (he never knew he'd been living in a country this enormous all along). He saw deconsecrated cathedrals, miners with faces black and hard as their coal, great shoals of stunted grass and bleached sky. By the time he arrived at Moskovsky Vokzal, he thought he'd just about seen enough. He knew he should be grateful. The trip to Leningrad had required months of bureaucratic maneuvering, papers acquired and signed and lost, attempts and reattempts and bribes from Andronov, the man who would be Aleksandr's trainer at the academy. Finally, one day, Aleksandr's entry visa had arrived—with all the randomness of a June snowstorm or a plague of falling frogs—and that was the bottom line, he often thought: not that you could be sure that nothing would work, but that you could be sure you would never, never know what would.

And on the tracks—amid the screeches of braking trains and departing lovers, and the coiling smells of grease and cigarettes and cooking oil and acrid cologne—he almost lost his nerve. He almost wanted to drop his luggage on the track and ride the train all the way back to the Pacific, although his only chess set was in his rucksack and he was nearly out of bribe money. As the train had pulled into the station, the man next to him announced to the entire car that today was Stalin's centenary. Everybody around looked quickly away. But here was the evidence: Sinopskaya Naberezhnaya was overrun with police, their uniforms striking red and gold against the horrible white sun. They were there to make sure nobody got too mouthy or too festive.

"Papers?" A policeman was behind him; his tone suggested that Aleksandr had already ruined his day. Aleksandr drew his hand against his eyes, and delicate grains of soot fell from his eyebrows. Just over one of the policeman's gargantuan shoulders, Aleksandr caught snatches of the green-gray Neva. Its stark and sturdy arm put the city in a headlock, he thought, or held it up like an osteoporotic backbone.

"Papers?" the policeman said again. His chinstrap was digging into his prodigious neck, and his gilt cockade flashed in the sun. Aleksandr rifled in his rucksack. When he produced his papers, the policeman appraised them with a sour look and tapped his nightstick against his thigh.

"Sakhalin?" he said. "Did you take the wrong train?"

And Aleksandr thought: It's a real possibility.

"No? Do you talk? Never mind. I don't care. Go on. I'm sure you know what day it is."

Aleksandr did know. And he was starting to decide about the Neva, too: really, it was the brain. Not the part of the brain that thinks up sonnets or show-offy chess moves; not the part that sighs sorrowfully in corners and reads Solzhenitsyn and wonders what it all can mean.

It was the part that tells you to fuck, to run from things, to live, even when your better nature tells you not to.

———

Years later, after Aleksandr stopped playing chess and started playing politics, the city would become something altogether different. Bored women with absent eyebrows in Turkish silk bobbed in the lines outside nightclubs, pouring vodka of insane expense into the snow and laughing. Enormous billboards and neon signs made stamps of light against the sky, advertising dreams and attitudes and lifestyles of varying degrees of attainability. Leningrad became St. Petersburg, and St. Petersburg became a place to make and blow loads of cash—there were businesses and ladies enough for industrious men to conquer. Eventually, chess became something different also—once Aleksandr became the world champion and his brilliance was remarked upon so often that it became tedious. This was how somebody with some kind of unusual beauty—enchanting mismatched eyes, impossibly red hair—must feel: after a while, receiving extra credit for something so arbitrary becomes a burden. Chess was a part of him, no different from his poor posture or homely face. And chess became a humiliation and an indictment in the end—after he'd lost the title and his better moments were forgotten but his one best moment, that one best game, still hung over him, preceded him always, like a leper's bell. He was very good for a while, and then something else was better.

But when he was young, he'd had a whole life to imagine.

Stumbling out into the day from the train station felt like emerging from imprisonment only to be lined up against the wall and shot. Aleksandr made his way to his kommunalka first, picking through throngs of stern-looking people, and several small children tried to steal from him before he even made it out onto the street. He followed his careful directions to himself and kept a dumb, hyper-focused attention on his papers. The number of people here was staggering, and more people than lived in the entirety of Okha stepped on Aleksandr's feet before he made it to his new building.

The building was three stories tall and looked, from a distance, like a pile of cinders. In the packed brown snow of the front yard, a very young man stood next to an overturned trunk. The trunk's lid was unhinged like a half-open jaw, and its contents were splattered across the yard; clearly, it had recently been thrown down the blocky staircase. On the stoop stood a gray-curled old lady in a red housecoat. From the way she was shaking her fist at the young man, Aleksandr figured she was the steward. Up close, he could see that the front door—formerly red, he thought—was splintering. The windows above it were welded shut.

"Excuse me," said Aleksandr. "I'm moving in today."

The steward ignored him. "Go away," she said to the young man with the trunk. "Go away and never come back."

And Aleksandr thought: Maybe it's not too late.

The steward handed Aleksandr his keys. In the kitchen, the rusty communal sink smelled of urine. An older woman in a bathrobe, her hair piled implausibly into a towel, was making toast underneath the exposed piping. On the other side of the kitchen hung decadent skeins of ladies' panty hose. On the bathroom shower curtain, bright green frogs frolicked between patches of black mold. In the hallway, a sign admonished the tenants not to hang up their underwear outside.

Aleksandr's room contained a bed bolted to the floor, a chitinous desk, and an urn-shaped samovar, presumably left over from the previous tenant. Near the ceiling, the laths were showing through the plaster. Raggedy strips of light filtered through the tiny fortochka above the bed, and Aleksandr went to lie in them. The exposed mattress was vaguely moist against his skin. He stretched out his legs. In Okha, he'd shared a bed with his two kicking little sisters, and they'd thrashed all night like dying fish.

He stared at the crescent-shaped fungal smear on the wall; he gazed through the latticework of frost on the windowpane. He tried to sleep. At the end of the week on the train, he'd been so desperate for sleep that he'd tried briefly to sleep in the bathroom—balanced precariously above the hole that emptied onto the tracks—until someone had yelled at him to get the fuck out, idiot. But in bed, he found that he missed the oceanic rumble of the train. He found that he was restless with the energy of being somewhere new when, his whole life, he'd only ever been somewhere old. He found he didn't feel like taking off his shoes yet.

He thought of the policemen down at the train station. He wondered if, out in the city somewhere, anybody was dumb enough to be celebrating.

He wrestled his map from his pocket, picked up his rucksack, and headed down the stairs. In the kitchen, he passed a woman who was using a filthy spatula to scrape the remains of an egg off a pan. She looked at Aleksandr darkly and did not speak. Outside, the cold was settling into itself—announcing its scope, the way pain does after a moment or two—and the cold, along with the accumulated fatigue of six days on a train (two of them spent standing up), was making Aleksandr dizzy. All around him, buildings were painted blue only up to height level, and Aleksandr felt as though he were trapped in the mural of a child who had grown bored and wandered away. The wind kicked up.

Nevsky Prospekt was beautiful: the friezes and columns looked like ancient Rome, and the half-buried stores and bright orange signs and illuminated cinemas looked like the center of the very modern universe. Aleksandr recognized the rally by a beaming poster of Stalin, held high above the crowd like a grandfatherly, mustached god. The crowd was small—desultory and damp, ringed by nervous-looking police. As he approached, Aleksandr saw that the Stalins were everywhere: out of one photo, Stalin glowered menacingly; out of another, Stalin stared with an expression of stern benevolence. Into a microphone, a man droned dully about the Battle of Stalingrad. At the edge of the crowd lurked a small group of men with skunk-striped Mohawks and plaid shirts. Aleksandr leaned against a telephone pole and tried to listen. He was exhausted, he realized, and here—in this last pocket of stingy sun, with the wind breaking at the buildings behind him and the monotone buzz of military accomplishment in his ears— he thought he could probably fall asleep standing up. He pulled his cap tighter over his head. His gaze faltered. His head started to fall forward.

"Enjoying the show?" A man was talking to him. Aleksandr lifted his earflaps and looked. The man was tall and thin; when he moved, it looked like his joints were locking and unlocking and painfully rearranging themselves. He was holding a glass bottle of Pepsi and wearing no gloves. Next to him stood two other men. One was notably pale, even for here, and had eyes the color of kopecks. The other was short, scarred, and writing furiously in a notebook. His mouth moved as if he was chewing something, even though Aleksandr somehow felt sure that he was not. All three of them were dressed in striped sailor shirts and quilted jackets and sodden flapped hats. The tall one wore a small silver medallion around his neck.

"Indeed," said Aleksandr. "Quite a sight."

"To think Koba would be one hundred," said the tall man. His voice was flatter than irony. "What a pity he is not here to enjoy the party."

"True," said Aleksandr. "It's evidently true."

"His reforms were truly adequate to the task of modernization, am I right?"

"Very adequate. More than adequate."

"And that mustache," said the pale one. "That mustache was quite an achievement, yes? Koba had more hair in that mustache than some men have on their entire heads."

Aleksandr turned to look at him. There was something about this one's face that made Aleksandr not want to look at it straight: a hag-gardness underneath the eyes that raised uncomfortable questions about life in Leningrad. "Yes," said Aleksandr, staring balefully at the ground. "An impressive feat."

The tall man looked at Aleksandr with some amusement then. When he leaned in, his voice was lower. "Did you know he was five feet four?" he said. "He was. He was five feet four and had a bad arm. They never showed it in pictures. They never showed him standing next to anybody. He's sitting in all the pictures with other dignitaries."

"I didn't know that," said Aleksandr carefully. "I was given to be-lieve that Comrade Stalin was a man of some stature."

Aleksandr did not understand how things had gone so wrong so fast, so he turned to the short man, whose scars looked as if they might have just as easily been from fights as from some debilitating skin dis-ease, and stuck out his hand. "Hello," he said. "I'm Aleksandr Kimo-vich Bezetov. I just moved here." He cast a bright smile, because in Okha, old women had always responded well to his smile. The men shot glances at one another and seemed to experience some collective facial twitching. It wasn't eye-rolling, precisely, but Aleksandr was seized by a frozen feeling that it meant something similar. He looked at the men and squinted. He tried to see in them signs of trouble, but they just looked like everyone else he'd seen on his way from the train station—underslept and vaguely hostile. The tall one was thin, but the other two looked simultaneously chubby and wanly malnourished, as though they'd had enough to eat of only one kind of food. The shortest one crouched down to the ground, revealing the haunches of a mustelid.

"I'm Ivan Dmietrivich Bobrikov," said the thin one. "This is Nikolai Sergeyevich Chernov."

"A pleasure," said Nikolai from the ground.

"The sovok here is Mikhail Andreyevich Solovyov," said Ivan. "Where are you from?"

"Okha," said Aleksandr. "In the east."

"We know where Okha is," said Nikolai. "We're students of geography."

"Geography?" said Aleksandr politely.

"Well, history," said Ivan. He cracked his knuckles.

"Real history," said Mikhail.

"Shut up, Misha," said Ivan. He winked at Aleksandr as though they were adults looking over the head of a child. Aleksandr didn't know what would be communicated by winking back, so he didn't. "And why are you here, tovarish?" said Ivan.

In the center of the crowd, a man was offering a tender eulogy for Stalin. His voice buckled and his nose turned bright red with emotion.

"To play chess," said Aleksandr. "I have a place at the academy. I'm working with Andronov."

"Oh yes? And what is a boy from Okha doing at the academy with Andronov?"

Aleksandr scratched his nose. "I was in his correspondence course first."

"I see," said Ivan. "You have a favorite player, then? You like Spassky?"

"He's all right. He let himself be psychologically outmaneuvered by Fischer, though, in '72. All the nonsense with the money and the late arrival."

"That match was rigged by the Americans, though, am I right? They were controlling Spassky via chemical and electronic devices, yes?"

Aleksandr stared at Ivan. He had no idea what he was supposed to say to this. "No," he said slowly. "No, I don't think so."

"And Rusayev? You're an admirer, surely, of Rusayev?"

"He's a bore."

"A bore!"

"He would've lost to Fischer, too, if Fischer hadn't gone crazy."

"The Americans should still have the World Championship, you're saying?"

"Well, I don't know about should. I'm just saying they would."

"Hm," said Ivan. "Interesting ideas you have. Is that all you brought with you?" He eyed Aleksandr's bag. "Meager possessions. The sign of a strong commitment to the Party."

Aleksandr didn't like that Nikolai was still crouching; it made him look as if he was about to pounce.

"I have some other things in my building," said Aleksandr. "But I'm committed to the Party." It was nice to say a familiar phrase in a strange city.

"I'll bet," said Ivan, producing a piece of paper and a pen from somewhere inside his enormous black coat. He held the pen's cap between his teeth and wrote something down. "Here." He handed Aleksandr a piece of paper, and Aleksandr squinted at it. "Café Saigon," said Ivan. "Maybe you've heard of it?"

"No," said Aleksandr apologetically. He was forever having to confess to not having heard of things, not having known things, not having done things. It was tiresome.

"It's on the corner of Nevsky and Vladimirsky. It's the building that always looks like it's under construction. We're pretty much always there, since our flat really doesn't have heat. Stop by sometime, if you like. Everyone else there is always talking about music, but we can talk geography."

Aleksandr stared at him. "Isn't geography sort of a settled field?"

"Less than you might think, turns out."

"Well," said Aleksandr. "All right." He awkwardly held the paper in one hand and his small backpack in the other. In the square, a tinny recording of the national anthem was starting to play. Aleksandr tried to turn to face it, but Ivan caught him by the shoulder.

"By the way," said Ivan. "Are you any good? At chess, I mean."

"Oh. Yes. I'm maybe starting to be."

"You came to Leningrad to find out?" said Nikolai.

"Yes." This was embarrassing: something about admitting out loud that he'd moved across the continent to determine his skill level at a game seemed outlandishly childish, as though he'd told them that he'd run away to find something he saw in a dream.

"Good," Nikolai said. In the waning light, his spotted face looked like some sort of environmental catastrophe. "That's good. Leningrad is where you find out what you are made of, yes? What you can stand."

The men laughed. "Yes," said Misha. "That's true. Tell me, tovarish, what can you stand?"

Aleksandr twisted the paper in his hands. "I don't know." The anthem was reaching its bombastic conclusion now, and lyrics about scarlet banners and deathless ideals went sailing over Aleksandr's head.

"Don't worry," Ivan said, putting his pen back in his pocket. "You'll find out."

———

And Aleksandr did find out. He could stand, it turned out, quite a lot: he wasn't particularly bothered by the communal bathrooms, the thin walls, the lack of privacy. He had nothing to guard: no lovers, no secrets, no deviations from the politically acceptable. In Okha, he'd lived with a mother and little sisters who took no interest in him; here, he sometimes dreamed of having a dark, mysterious question at the center of his life. The kommunalki were designed to collapse families, flatten out intimacies, make everybody the keeper of each other's secrets until those secrets became shallow and harmless. Soon Aleksandr knew far more about his neighbors than he cared to—if the door handle was turned down, the neighbor was out; if the slippers were gone, he was in for the night; if a man came back to his wife after an absence, it was expected that the neighbors would take the children. Everybody walked around half dressed—the women with their pale legs slipping in and out of their bathrobes, the men wearing stained undershirts as they boiled potatoes. Everybody stole one another's food—gelid and anonymous items left on the stove would be quickly, quietly consumed—and during the month without hot water, the women took to setting pots to boil in the kitchen and bathing right there without closing the door. Aleksandr heard even more than he saw—the crying of infants and drunks and lovers and widows—and sometimes he wanted to make some noise back: make people stop their screaming for a moment and wonder at what was going on in *there*. But his evenings were silent. He drank tea and read his chess books and chopped time into little tolerable increments until he thought he might be able to sleep.

Days were not much better. He registered at the chess academy and started work with Andronov, the instructor who'd heard of Aleksandr from his eastern scouts and summoned him across the continent, making the trip possible through contacts and bribes and veiled threats. In the months before his departure, Aleksandr and his family had taken to regarding Andronov as a terrible destroying angel who'd capriciously chosen Aleksandr for an awesome, elevating, all-consuming challenge. So it was nearly heretical to admit that Andronov was a disappointment: he was a short man with a thick neck, as it turned out, and he spat involuntarily when he spoke. At registration, Andronov took a perfunctory glance at Aleksandr, a slightly longer look at his papers, and said, "You may go. You will play number eleven." Aleksandr took his damp papers and went where Andronov pointed. Number 11 was a surly, pimply-faced youth from Irkutsk. Number 11's pimples encouraged Aleksandr to think that he might also need a friend, but that was a mistake. Aleksandr's questions after their first match were met with withering thirty-second silences followed by monosyllabic answers. Aleksandr found he did not need friends so badly.

A few weeks into the term, Andronov stopped by to watch Aleksandr play. Aleksandr beat his opponent that day—in fact, he'd beaten everybody he'd played so far, and he would beat all of his opponents at the academy during his time there, and Andronov himself, eventually—but Andronov only sniffed and said, "Not bad, considering."

Aleksandr's days, then, were spent in chilly, high-ceilinged rooms, across tables from men and boys who seemed dreadfully unhappy to be there. At first they treated him with indifference; then, as his winning streak grew noticeable, they treated him with a simmering resentment so understated that it amounted, basically, to more indifference. After a while Andronov started treating Aleksandr a bit differently—never warmly, though he watched his matches with more interest and gave him extra gruff attention and advice. He seemed to regard Aleksandr as a prize horse who merited careful monitoring but would be shot like the others if his leg was broken.

Still, Aleksandr's days were bearable. The breaks were interminable and awkward, but the matches seemed to exist outside of time—he fell into them as though he'd been knocked unconscious, and he never grew accustomed to the strange feeling of coming out of them and realizing that hours had passed without him.

Nights were worse. His mother phoned him occasionally, and he would tramp down the hall in his slippers, trying to avoid the gray stains on the floor. His mother would warble about his sisters and their schooling and ask him when he might be able to send money. Other people would need the phone for more pressing concerns: illnesses, money transfers, semi-secret arrangements and negotiations. They would crowd Aleksandr off the phone with their scrutiny, their calculated proximity. "No, Mamenchka," he'd say. "I can't send any money yet." Then he would tramp back down the hall to his dark room, light a candle, turn on the samovar for tea, and close his eyes until he could almost hear his former Pacific Ocean out the window.

There weren't friends, exactly, at the kommunalka, but he did come to know the characters there with as much depth as he probably knew anyone. On one side of him lived a small family—a couple and their toddling, very dirty baby—and he began to understand that the man beat the woman, and that the woman pinched the baby, and that the baby had a different cry depending on who was being beaten or pinched. On another side was an old muttering woman who was in constant conversation with nobody, as far as Aleksandr could tell. There was a long-haired elfin man who brought home other men; he had a post at the university, and halfway through the year he was found out and fired and had to leave the city. Everybody watched while he left, picking up his matted fuzzy slippers and carefully banging them against the doorframe while the steward held his keys. There was a drunk who would drink your cologne or dandruff shampoo if you left any in the bathroom. There was a pair of young girls who slept days and took calls in the nights and disappeared. The rustlings and comings and goings of everybody around him made Aleksandr feel as though he lived at the center of a panting organism—an organism without an inner monologue, that ran through the forest in syncopated, unknowing movements, looking for something.

At night Aleksandr lay in bed and pressed his eyes closed so hard that he saw stark designs against his eyelids and imagined the lives of the people around him. He saw the night girls, Elizabeta and Sonya, reclining across their beds, legs tangled together with the unnatural ease women seemed to have with each other's bodies. Their room would have the faint smell of lilac, cold and mild. They would have a parakeet, and they would devote a tragic amount of attention to it. They would come home on winter nights and turn on the samovar, wipe off their eye makeup carefully, and laugh about the bodies and idiosyncrasies and preferences of their men. They were, as Aleksandr imagined them, not entirely unhappy.

The old woman, Aleksandr decided, was talking to her dead husband. In early versions, he imagined for them a love story so beautiful that he'd have to stop thinking about the old woman sometimes—when the wind sliced through the side of the building like razor through cotton, and the enormous coldness of his solitude made him somehow afraid, as though he'd been cast into outer space—and he'd have to go to his chess books to recover. The old woman and her husband had been the unusual kind of people who wanted more than anything to love somebody, and they'd been lucky enough to find each other, and once they did, they were happy together—not grudgingly so, not with resigned resentful contentment, but really, really happy—forever. He was arrested for anti-Soviet activities and sent to the gulag for ten years, and when amnesty came, the old woman waited and waited and worked to find him but couldn't. So she sat nights, looking out the north-facing window, talking to him, trying to lead him back to her, muttering to him her secrets and stories and permanent love.

This early version was too maudlin, thought Aleksandr—especially as the frost of October hardened into the deep ice of November, and the summer and Okha became a long time ago, and the chess institute yielded illumination and high praise and absolutely no friends—so he amended it: the old woman had hated her husband, who'd been a fat Party official with soft hands and pampered tastes and no loyalties to anybody. He'd sold out friends for almost nothing; he was motivated not by a genuine commitment to perfect social equity but by a shallow desire to be stroked and rewarded by superiors. She'd run away from him because the bitter indifference of the lonesome city was preferable to his petty attentions and cruelties. She cursed him all day long, every day, warding him away with her churning, self-sustaining hate. The hate rose from their building like steam and hardened into a charm that kept her safe—and she could never stop her muttering, no matter how crazy it made her look, no matter how the young people avoided her in the hallways.

Looking back, Aleksandr was embarrassed to admit, it wasn't the humiliations and the moral compromises and the general undermining of humanity that most bothered him. In those days, he followed the papers only as much as the papers followed chess—which was some— so big important lapses on other subjects did not concern him, though it was true that incompetence in running a city turned out to be several degrees worse than incompetence in running a village. The trash piled up in Leningrad as in Okha, but Leningrad produced more trash. In Okha the roads turned to lakes of mud that stuck so savagely that some trucks, every year, had to be left until things dried out in July, and the ice went unattended everywhere—but in Leningrad there was so much ice that the streets were impossible even for walking, forget driving, and Aleksandr quickly bent an ankle that turned black before it got better. But it was not terrible. He had a roof, at least, and there was always some kind of food at the market, even if it wasn't the kind you were looking for. He didn't care for the billboards and didn't believe in the slogans, but nobody else did, either. He regarded Communism as a kind of collective benign lie, like the universal agreement among human beings to rarely discuss the fact that everybody would one day die.

What bothered him most, actually, was the cold. The cold seeped into his bones in October and stayed there. His fingers and toes took on a deep reptilian blue that was difficult to shake, no matter how much he pinched them or stood covering himself in the lukewarm communal shower. It had been nearly this cold in Okha, he figured, but cold was different when you lived alone. His arms and neck ached from the tension of constant low-grade shivering; he slept fitfully, curling into himself and breathing into his pillow to catch snatches of warmth that soon turned moist and chilled. By January he almost could not remember what it felt like to be warm, to let his shoulders and jaw slacken, to take a breath in the fresh air that didn't nearly choke him with cold. This, he thought, this could drive a man crazy—it was like constant semi-starvation, or sleep deprivation, or whatever else they did to men in Siberia. If he had any secrets to reveal, he would confess them all for an hour by the summer sea, asleep in a ray of sun. He dreamed about warmth, he later thought, the way incarcerated men must dream about women.

And so it was not principle that finally drove him to the café on Nevsky and Vladimirsky. Later, journalists would want to know what impelled him to first start meeting with the other unsatisfied youth in Leningrad; what moral outrage finally pushed him over the edge and into the waiting arms of the dissident movement. And for a while he would tell them lies—about the constraints to his free and far-ranging ideas, to his literary appetites, to his pride—and they would nod appreciatively and respect him all the more. Until one day, long after his career in chess had peaked—he would always recall it was the year when he first lost to a computer, a much noted event that prompted worldwide speculation about the triumph of technology and the obsolescence of human beings, generally—he leaned in and told a writer from a small Azerbaijani newspaper the truth: that he'd started going to the cafés, at first, because they were the only place in that first forbidding winter where he could, for a moment, get warm. That was why he went the first time.

And for other reasons, he kept going.

2

I beat my father at chess for the first time when I was twelve, and at first I thought it meant that I was brilliant. I danced around the kitchen, skidding in my socks, taunting him with his fallen king, and it seemed unlike him not to laugh. My mother poked her head in to see what the yelling was about, and I said gleefully, "I beat Dad at chess."

My mother looked at my father, who was poring over the chessboard, his cheeks sucked in, his eyebrows clenched.

"Did you let her win, Frank?"

"Did you, Dad?" I said, insulted. I sat down at the table and fiddled with the knights. They were my favorite, because they were best for sneak attacks. "You didn't, did you?"

"No," my father said, packing up the pawns, settling them in their foam for what turned out to be forever. "No, I would never do something like that."

———

But how many of us would want somebody posthumously sifting through our past, looking for the first misstep? In retrospect, anybody's eccentricities, charms, and mistakes can take on a darker dimension and become foreshadowing. All we can know is that my father's mind was gone, by anyone's standards, by the time he was forty. So I do not think my projections for myself are overly pessimistic.

If you're interested in stories about what can be done in a short lifetime, the history of chess is not a bad place to look—it's populated almost entirely by people who were at their best when they were barely out of adolescence. There's Bobby Fischer, of course, though that story ends badly (with lunacy, exile in Iceland, and anti-Semitism) and Alexander Alexandrovich Alekhine, though that story ends badly, too (with alcoholism, erratic behavior, and more anti-Semitism). Then there's Aleksandr Kimovich Bezetov, who was the USSR chess champion by the time he was nineteen, and the world chess champion by the time he was twenty-two. His is a sad story, too, in some ways, although I didn't know that when I ran away to Russia to find him.

Before Huntington's caught up with my father, he was as captivated by the Soviet Union as he was by chess. I grew up during the gasping tail end of the Cold War, and armchair speculating on geopolitics was something of a national pastime. For my father, though, it seemed to hold a particular meaning—it was his evening hobby after coming home from his days of teaching music to college students. He'd puzzle about the ironies of a regime that censored the fact of censorship. He'd spend dinner parties debating whether Brezhnev's Soviet Union was totalitarian or merely authoritarian. One day when I was about seven, I caught him on the floor of his study poring over photographs of Soviet parade order. "What are you doing?" I said.

It wasn't unusual to find him doing odd things. My father had a healthy disregard for social conventions: he once let me paint the house windows in rainbows with my watercolor set, to my mother's horror, and he'd clap for trees that he thought were doing a good job of exploding into red during the fall. When I couldn't sleep, he'd let me sit up and watch Johnny Carson and drink ginger ale. When I spilled purple ink on the brand-new white sofa, he helped me turn the pillows over so my mother wouldn't find out. One time he took me out to watch a meteor shower at midnight on a school night—and I remember the chill of the wind and the subversion of learning that the universe still existed at night when you couldn't see it, or weren't supposed to.

"Trying to figure out who's really in charge over there," he said. "Who do you think?"

I looked. In the photographs were grim men, their faces framed by mustaches and furry hats. None of it looked like a parade, in my understanding of the word. I pointed at one of the men with my toe. "Ah," my father said. "Chebrikov. A very educated guess. You should go into government."

"I'm going to be a marine biologist," I said, even though it turned out I wouldn't be.

"Very well," my father said solemnly. "If you must, you must. But do you know how else they try to find out who's in charge?"

"No, how?"

"They look at the portrait order on the walls."

"Like, the most important portrait would be on top?"

"Exactly right."

"That's weird."

"Exactly right again, Irina."

I don't know what all that was about for him. He was a pianist and a professor of music, and during the life in which I briefly knew him, he was happiest at his piano, composing his songs, or sitting at a table, playing a game. It was a good life, as far as I could tell. But perhaps it was not the only one he might have wanted.

When we played, he'd reverentially remove the pieces from his box—he had an old and enormous set with wooden pieces the size of my palm—and lean forward. "With these," he'd say—quoting Charles the First, I later learned, though at the time I thought it was his own private phrase—"ruler and subject strive without bloodshed." So maybe that's it: all the sublimated war impulses, the breathless following of geopolitics, were a desperate craning of the neck down a road decidedly not taken.

But these are not questions that a child thinks to ask, and by the time I knew to ask them, there were no answers forthcoming.

It was too bad my father never got to see how the Cold War ended; he would have been tickled beyond belief that our CIA never saw it coming. ("Do you know how many people are getting outrageous salaries to try to read Chernenko's body language, Irina?" he'd say to me.

"They get fifty bucks every time he sneezes. I tell you, kid, it's nice work if you can get it.") He would have loved the coup attempt in '91 (he loved nothing better than a good coup attempt). He would have loved to see the falling of the Berlin Wall. My father had a limitless capacity to be touched by the histories of other nations, the fates of other people—and more than that, he loved the intricate ballet of advance and retreat. He loved it all in real life as much as on the chessboard. Like Lear—like anyone—he wanted to see who won and who lost. He wanted to see how things would turn out.

And if I'm honest, that's a good part of my own grief these days. Not a majority—that's composed of good old-fashioned fear, the animal will to survive tangling with the cold pronouncements of medical science. But a fairly significant amount—maybe 15 percent or so—is just sorry that I don't get to see the end.

So I wish my father, the dedicated Russophile, had been able to watch these things. Although in a way, I suppose he did. He was in the same room as it all. In '89, when the Wall came down, he was still at home, and he spent most of his days in darkened rooms, the lunar light of the television flickering across his eyes. That Christmas, Ceauşescu was executed along with his wife, their pale corpses paraded across Romanian state television for the viewers' satisfaction. My father sat with a bib, trying to bring stewed carrots to his cheek and missing. In '91 came the footage of Yeltsin bellowing at a tank: by then my father was in a nursing home, his mouth agog, his eyes glazed, his hands waving and reaching at things just beyond his reach. The Cold War had ended, and its terminal images were flashed across the television for the smug first world to see. And though my father was, by that point, fairly indifferent to these events, I suppose it's right to say that he technically lived long enough to see them.

————

Everyone is their brain, of course—and in my callous worldview, everyone is only their brain. But my father was somehow *especially* his brain. His sense of self came from brilliant inferences, razor-sharp memories, a sense of humor that cut you off at the knees and left you unsure what had happened until you tried to walk away. Some people have other elements at their core that can sustain some brain damage—a silliness or a sweetness or a faith—and Huntington's can take quite a while to completely unravel them. Some people die with gentleness intact, and there is room to believe that they are still in there somewhere, if you're the kind of person who likes to believe those things. With my father, it was not like that. He was a mind, first and foremost, and a mind is an elaborate system of pulleys and levers and delicate balances. And when one piece is missing, the whole system has lost its integrity.

Early in the disease, the minor disorientations and lapses that happen to everyone occasionally started happening to him all the time. Then his sense of causality went—moments existed outside of consequence or context. He sat at the piano, but he no longer played. His personality dulled into a crude, distorted version of itself. He grew younger, in terms of preoccupations and anxieties. Then his memory started to erase from the present backward. I disappeared. Then, eventually, my mother did.

In the very beginning of his illness—in those bewildering few months after I beat him at chess for the first time—people always assumed he was drunk. At nine in the morning, on Tuesday nights, in grocery stores and in libraries and once, horribly, at my school play, people looked and whispered and shifted their weight. My mother would keep her eyes straight forward, so she couldn't see them be embarrassed for her. I would twist in my seat and roll my eyes and think I might absolutely die of mortification. I spent most of my teenage years convinced that my genetic status was irrelevant, since I wouldn't survive the sheer raw humiliations of adolescence anyway.

Later, my father started to look like a caricature of someone who was sick, and occasionally people would think that he was making a tasteless joke with his exaggerated movements, his rhythmic jerking, the little oppositional gestures he made to overcompensate. People who saw him from behind would sometimes go quiet in disapproval until they saw his pale, gaunt face and eyes that seemed to have receded too far into his skull. Then they'd stay quiet.

At the end, his arms went wild in great loping movements, his fingers twisting. My mother fed him with an incredible ease and tenderness, opening her mouth wide at him the way you do with an infant to get him to eat. I fed him sometimes when I was home on college vacation, and I always felt slightly awkward and embarrassed to be doing it—as if he were going to snap out of it at any moment and look at me sharply and ask me what the hell I was doing.

Do not let anyone tell you the psyche goes quiet into that good night. It writhes, gropes for meaning, until the last. He unfurled nonsense with the same jittering repetitiveness as his interminable string of nucleotides. At the end he was choking on his own saliva. It is not a way to die.

————

The day I got my results, it was windy. I walked out in the street after talking with the geneticist—even though I wasn't supposed to be alone, Claire had known from the look I gave her that I would murder her with my own two still-functional hands if she tried to follow me. Skeletal leaves scraped the sides of buildings; the T shuddered past the Mass General Hospital stop, and an army of medical students got out; the Charles River was dull and polluted all of a sudden, speckled with a few halfhearted red sailboats. The sky looked nauseous. And I was struck by two thoughts—one, that all of this had already lost something for me. And two, what an unoriginal thought that was.

I threw up in an alley. People passed by me, startled—was I a cancer patient, sick from chemotherapy? Was I about to terminate an unwanted pregnancy? Was I on drugs? It was the beginning of this kind of looking and questioning: exactly how much pity, in the end, did I deserve? How was it best meted out, if at all?

It had been ten years since I beat my father at chess for the first time. Inheriting from the paternal line makes for a younger onset. In the office, they'd told me that my CAG number—my number of clotted chromosomal nucleotides—was 50, corresponding to an average onset of thirty-two years of age. Half of the people with a CAG number of 50 become symptomatic earlier than thirty-two, half become symptomatic later. That is what an average is.

The doctors gave me this information on a helpful chart where CAG numbers are plotted against average onsets—like looking up the healthy weight for your height, or the appropriate benchmarks for your infant's psychological development.

I walked out of the alley and Claire was standing there, holding my coat for me. I had vomit on my shoes. She put the coat around me and held it around my shoulders on the T. I sat shaking, and Harvard students gave me dark looks on their way back from the internships that would propel them into the great wide world. We watched the smoky gray clouds in the pink sky across the river. We counted the sailboats. We went home and drank and swore for three days straight.

———

I was still in college then. There had been much agonizing over whether to give me my results so young, but I convinced everyone that it was the responsible thing—so I could plan whether to have children, so I could set the kind of short-term attainable goals that terminal people are so fond of. I employed depths of maturity and bullshit I didn't even know I had at the time, talked philosophically and stoically, pretended to have a faith in God and a good attitude (of which I have neither). I met with a psychologist, and I said things like "I'm not going to let this thing beat me" and "It's in the hands of the Lord." Afterward, I collapsed and drew in on myself and fell into the dark depression I'd promised everyone I would avoid.

Claire and I were living in a big gray two-story near Somerville that year. I was, I fear, very difficult. I stopped doing schoolwork. Claire dragged me through my Formal Logic problem sets. I stopped going to campus or eating. Claire brought me bagels and left them outside my door. I moped. I skulked. I monopolized our shower for hours, running all the hot water and using all the grapefruit shampoo, because it was the only place in the house where nobody could hear me crying.

I started bringing home different men every weekend, and all Claire did was ask me to bring home cuter ones. "I know you're having a breakdown, and I respect that," she said. "I just think you could be doing better in this department."

Now, of course, it's very different, and I look back on that time with a sort of bemused chagrin. It's a wonder that I escaped college without an unwanted pregnancy at the very least—full-blown AIDS at the worst. Somebody asked me about it once—a frat boy, strangely enough—as I was shrugging off the condom he dangled before me. "Don't you worry about AIDS?" he said. And out loud I said no, not really, but in my head I thought, Please, please, please let me get AIDS so I can die of pneumonia, so my brain is the last thing out the door, so that when I die, it is actually me dying and not somebody else.

———

I graduated somehow, barely. I majored in philosophy. A false premise yielding a false conclusion is logically valid, as I recall. Then I went for my doctorate in comparative literature. I studied Nabokov.

Other people laugh about staying in academia their whole lives: spending an eternity earning a Ph.D., gathering up knowledge they can't hope to practically employ, studying the countless refracted interpretations of a world they've never experienced. Being a perpetual academic is living in a potential energy that never becomes kinetic. I have trouble laughing about this.

After college I calmed down considerably. I'm not out much, but very occasionally—once or twice in the past five years, let's say—I'll meet someone interesting, with a dry sense of humor and a dark intelligence, and I'll know objectively that this is the kind of person whom, in another lifetime, I would want. I can see this other lifetime sometimes, if I squint, but I don't particularly resent it. It's like looking at other people's vacation photos. And if there is an actual sense of loneliness or longing, it's like feeling a human hand touch you through gauze—removed and almost unrecognizable.

———

I began playing chess Saturdays in Harvard Square, against the old wizened men who charge you a dollar to lose to them. I did not grow up to be a chess prodigy—or any other kind, for that matter. But I find something compelling in the game's choreography, the way one move implies the next. The kings are an apt metaphor for human beings: utterly constrained by the rules of the game, defenseless against bombardment from all sides, able only to temporarily dodge disaster by moving one step in any direction.

The chess men emerged without comment in early March, sitting in the stoic steam of their coffees, waiting for the rest of the world to catch up with them and become alive again. The chess men came back before the street performers—the live statues that locked and unlocked themselves for loose change, silvery-black-skinned men who beat on overturned plastic buckets, wild-eyed prophets who described in lurid detail the end of the world. The chess men came back before the academic tours of ambitious young people started to create big traffic blocks, before the college students stripped down to only their unnatural tans and fanned languidly across the Square, before all of Cambridge roused itself sufficiently to once again protest the foreign policy disaster of the moment. My favorite opponent was a man named Lars, who stationed himself at the chess sets with such fierce commitment that I'd forget he could, if he wanted to, get up and walk away. The first day I met him he took one look at me and said, "You look like somebody who feels sorrier for yourself than is strictly necessary."

I'd been out wandering, as I often did in those days. It was two years after I'd gotten my results, and I was halfway through my dissertation on trilingual wordplay in *Ada, or Ardor*. I liked the bitter cold the best; it narrowed the meandering, self-indulgent courses of my mind into a focused dissatisfaction with what was right in front of me. This, I'll be the first to admit, was an improvement.

I sat down, and Lars promptly decimated me at chess, then told me exactly what was wrong with my game and with me, more generally. After that, we were friends.

Lars told me a lot of other things eventually, though there was no way that all of it was true. He'd been born in Stockholm, he said, the son of shipping magnates, descended from Swedish royalty. His family had lost everything during the embargoes of 1979. He'd been homeless in Philadelphia, spent a year in Hong Kong, been dishonorably discharged from the Swedish military for reasons he would not discuss. There were conflicts in his stories, mysteries, great gaping holes in time and space, but Lars did not respond to challenges on these fronts except by starting to beat me faster when I asked nosy questions. So I learned not to. Lars lived off of bluffs, wild claims that were never, ever verifiable. He'd worked in a mine on the Black Sea, he said. He'd jumped trains in Moldova, he'd learned to recite the Qur'an from Pakistani immigrants in London. And who could say with absolute certainty that he had not?

There's an intimacy in listening to somebody's lies, I've always thought—you learn more about someone from the things they wish were true than from the things that actually are. Sometimes, though, there were intentional provocations—allusions to bastard children, assassination attempts, that sort of thing. Or worse, advice. Analyses. Witty aphorisms. "You know what your problem is?" he asked me more than once. And even though I always told him that I did know what my problem was—that it had been revealed to me via the best genetic testing science could offer—he invariably gave his own interpretation. "Too much thinking" or "Not enough sex" or "Not enough thinking about sex," he would say. These assessments were typically followed by instructive tales from his own life, in which having sex or avoiding thinking saved the day.

The last time I saw him before he stopped talking, Lars told me about being shot at in Turkey. It was the end of March, the time of year in New England when you feel yourself regaining the will to live. The sky was a weak white, and the people floated through Harvard Square like brightly colored aquarium fish of all different shapes and origins. I'd bought us both coffees. Lars put five sugars in his, then sent me back into the coffee shop for more. When I returned and looked disapproving, he said, "You know what your problem is? You're afraid to have any fun."

"I have fun," I said, taking a sip of coffee and spilling some on my coat. The board between us was still a blank slate. There were limitless ways for either of us to win or lose, although we could both be pretty sure which way it would go. "I have all kinds of fun," I said. "Fun such as you could not imagine."

"I'll bet," he said. "You look just like the kind of girl with a secret life of fun."

I opened by advancing my king's knight. Lars mirrored me. "You can't even imagine the fun," I said. "You don't even *want* to."

"I, however," he said, "have had a life full of adventure. I have narrowly cheated death many times. I have earned the right to a little sugar in my coffee now and then."

"Okay," I said.

"Did I ever happen to mention the time I was almost killed in Turkey?"

I was not allowed to ask him what he'd been doing in Turkey in the first place; this would be viewed as unforgivably intrusive and rude. The rules of the game were long established.

"It was a few hours outside Ankara," he told me. There was a flurry of pawn movement, the debut introduction of the bishops. Lars's attitude toward chess was the same as his general attitude toward life: you can't be squeamish about it. You have to embrace it, fuck with it a little, see what it will do to you. Excessive calculation leads to paralysis, which leads to death.

"Wait, when was this?" I said, which I knew would irritate him. Irritating Lars was a tactic of mine. I advanced my bishop's pawn and planned to advance my queen's pawn next, in order to consolidate a pawn center and finally, for once, perhaps, drive Lars away.

"The seventies. Who can remember, exactly? Before you were born."

"I'm thirty."

"Please." He made a face and introduced his queen. It was early for her, though the move was technically aboveboard. She wasn't vulnerable to attack, and he was only trying to maintain his hold on the center. I flattered myself that this meant he was worried. "It is not classy for a woman to admit her age," he said.

I squinted at the board. Lars had folded his king protectively behind his queen and her knight. In the center of the board, my bishop and pawns were lined up as if before a firing squad.

"Anyway," Lars said. "I was with a friend. A woman friend." Most of Lars's stories featured a woman friend—always different, like Bond girls, entering the narration long enough to be seductive and saved and exiting without a fuss. Lars told me again and again how beautiful he was in his youth. When I knew him, he had streaked and matted gray hair and always dressed in plaid, but there was a certain impish quality to his blue eyes that I suppose somebody could have found attractive

once, although I don't pretend to be an expert on these things. Of all
the stories Lars told me, the ones about his beauty are the ones I think
he most wanted to be true.

"Okay," I said. "Carry on." I swiped one of Lars's pawns out of
sheer spite.

"So we find this lovely river hours outside the city. We think, A nice
place to have a picnic, have a little rest, you understand."

"I understand," I said. The pawn capture, I saw now, had been a
mistake. I'd opened up a diagonal onto my king. Lars was hemming
me in with his usual bored calculation, letting me make my own mistakes.

"We are thinking to lie down for a while and get to know each
other a little better," he said. Lars took my pawn with his knight. I took
his offending knight with my knight, who was prompty captured by
Lars's queen.

"Yes," I said. "I get it." I castled. Lars sacrificed a bishop, breaking
up my pawn center.

"We are going to fuck in the grass."

"Okay," I said. "I know." I don't know if it was a translation issue or
some kind of elaborate cross-cultural mockery, but Lars always treated
me as though I had no idea what he was getting at—and he was always getting at something. "For Christ's sake," I would say, "my brain
hasn't melted yet. You will probably be the first to know when it does."
"What do you know?" he would respond. "You've spent your whole
life at university. When's the last time you were with a man?" And that
would usually end the conversation.

"And so we are in the grass. The river is so blue. An insane green-
blue such as we do not find in nature. What is this called?"

"Turquoise, maybe. Aquamarine. Cerulean."

"You have more words than you need," he said. He said this to me
once a day, at least.

"Maybe," I said.

"And so we fuck like muskrats," Lars said grandly.

"Rabbits, maybe."

"What?" He frowned at me, his bushy gray eyebrows twitching.

"I think you . . . fuck . . . like rabbits. You know. Copiously and in public?"

He frowned. "In Sweden, this is a problem with muskrats."

"Okay," I said. "Anyway."

"And it was lovely," he roared. "We hear much about the politics of the Kurdish people, but not so much about the beauty of their women."

"This is true," I said. Lars swung his queen regally toward my cowering king. She was imperious, immune. I scowled.

"And when we rise—this is many hours later—Sinbil jumps. Something has landed at her feet, making puffs of dust. 'Lars,' she says, 'I think somebody is throwing rocks at us?' "

"You, of course, know they are not rocks."

"Of course I know they are not rocks. 'Sinbil,' I say, 'those are not rocks. Run!' " Lars took my bishop with his queen. " 'Zig-zag,' I tell her! 'Zig and zag your way up the hill!' Check your king, by the way."

I moved my king into the rook's old spot, where he huddled, looking fragile and deposed. I yawned, which is my cover for everything.

"The hill which had taken us a half an hour to pick down, suddenly we are atop of it after only moments. This is what being shot at will do to you."

I stared into my coffee and tried to discern what percentage of Lars's statements, in this case, were bullshit. In my experience, he was an unusual breed of liar. He half-believed his own lies, but he wasn't an outright lunatic, much as it pained me to admit it. He didn't lie for gain, either, or to manipulate others, or for self-promotion. He lied, it seemed to me, to make his life larger. He started with a true thing, and then he exploded it—blew it up in all directions, made it crazier and more colorful and more disastrous. He told things not the way they had happened but the way they should have happened.

"We make it to the car only just in time," he continued. "I swear at those bastards in Turkish. We race away back toward the city, but it takes us hours. Just think, if one of us had been shot, we would have been really, really dead before we reach civilization. The rental car company says, 'Oh yes, there are thieves in the hills, did we not tell you not to take the car out to the hills without your bodyguard?' But I know better."

He was starting to coast, which meant that he'd seen exactly how he was going to win. He always relaxed a little bit at that point. His talk, which never stopped or wavered, grew even more abundant and luxurious. He smiled. He asked rhetorical questions.

"What do you think I knew? Well, I knew that this was an unlikely explanation. Why would the thieves have been after us, two lowly travelers of modest means, not even Americans? Why would they be waiting out in the hills if they had not followed us there first? Why not just stay in the city and steal money the easy way?"

I looked longingly at my own queen, rendered impotent by all the material that I'd never managed to properly launch—a knight, a castle, the black bishop. All wasted.

"No, all that was far too simple, too suspicious. Thieves? Please. Do not insult me." He lowered his voice. "It was Turkish intelligence."

"Oh, come on," I said, stalling for time even though I knew that this kind of talk was mostly useless. "What would Turkish intelligence want with you? What would anyone want with you except your passport?"

"Shh," he said, looking at me sternly. "You think they do not have agents here even now? They tried to kill me once. Are you trying get me murdered? This is not an honorable way to try to avoid losing. Check your king again, by the way."

Lars's queen had taken a straggling pawn, and I moved my king back to his previous square. Lars advanced his knight for backup, which seemed, at that point, excessive. I brought my own knight over to the action, but it was far too late. The queen could not be taken; she stalked my king with an attention that felt like mockery. Then a waiting bishop swept in from nowhere and took my very last defending pawn. I knocked over my own king.

"Okay," I said. "That's it."

"An object lesson in what happens once the pawn wall in front of the castled king is breached," Lars sniffed. "But next time, next time. You are getting better. I was fearful for several moments." He always said this, too. It was annoying. I would truly love to beat Lars at chess before I die.

After my results came in and my Ph.D. was earned and while my father was still dying—my father had been dying for so long that it was hard for me to remember sometimes that he ever hadn't been—my life fell into a sort of sorry, isolated routine. On Saturdays I'd play chess with Lars. On Sundays I would visit my father, who had been relegated to a nursing home once he no longer knew who or where he was. I'd stroke his arm and feed him pharmacy-bought chocolates and uphold perky one-sided conversations. During the weeks, I taught Introduction to Composition at a technical college in the South End. My students were alternately insipid or adorable, depending on my mood. Most of them were listless, their opinions half formed and loosely held. This always mystified me, since when I was their age, I had a very serious relationship with my own opinions. I'd stay late at the office long after my colleagues had trickled home to commitments of some kind. Not children and families, usually, since they were mostly my age and younger. But they'd go back to live-in boyfriends and girlfriends, Pilates classes, cats, potted plants. Prerecorded television programs, Spanish conversation groups, tango lessons. I could have had any or all—or most—of those things, I suppose, but my major character flaw is an inability to invest in lost causes. When you are the lost cause, this makes for a lonely life.

At home, I'd usually find a stream of voice-mail messages from my mother. They were often about antioxidants, with which she was obsessed. They've been proven to do something against Alzheimer's, I guess, and certain kinds of cancers, but there's no suggestion that they do anything about Huntington's. Still, my mother's life was made possible by a forced, carefully calibrated optimism—the kind that finds something to appreciate when things go badly slower than expected. She'd send me packages full of dark chocolates, fancy dried blueberries, instructions to go out and *immediately* purchase a specific genre of spinach—along with newspaper clippings about people pulling through adversity. My mother wasn't loopy or delusional; she didn't buy into crystals or fortune-telling or anything like that. She got through my father's death with the pragmatism of a World War I amputee nurse. But she believed that lives can be better or worse, and that deaths can be better or worse, and that much of how you live and die is actually up to you—which I, of course, found a terrifying concept.

After we placed my father in the nursing home, my mother moved to Sedona, Arizona, to find out if there was anything left for her in this life. She took up jewelry-making. She found a profoundly tan boyfriend. She got some sleep. She thought of it as her brief entr'acte between tragedies, I suspect. I know she always planned to come back for me when the time came. I did not relish the thought of summoning her back from her barely begun new life to ask her for another two decades of spoon-feeding. The poor woman deserved better.

I didn't have many friends. I could chalk it up to general orneriness, and surely it was partly that. But there was also this: it's isolating when absolutely no one will discuss the thing at the very center of your life. My father went completely unmentioned for years by the people whom I considered my friends, and even his death, when it finally came, was substantially ignored. My own genetic status was assiduously avoided in conversation, as though it was a horrible facial deformity and everyone I knew was a stranger. People who haven't lost anyone think that to speak of grief is to summon it. People who haven't grappled with their own mortality think that to speak of death is to make it real. And in my teens and twenties, most of my friends had never buried anybody who wasn't a grandparent or a dog. So nobody asked after my father. Nobody asked after me. And sadness, forever unacknowledged, eventually becomes resentment.

―――――

My father must have felt his share of isolation and resentment, too, in the years preceding his final declension. Maybe that was what made him come to view Aleksandr Bezetov as some kind of kindred spirit. Or maybe it was something else—the idea of youth trumping obsolescence or intellect trumping entropy. My father was a man who loved his own mind and knew that one day he would lose it. That's what made Aleksandr his hero, perhaps—here was a person whose neurological circuitry was so luminescent that it shone through seven time zones and a Cold War. Here was a person who knew the value of his own intelligence, and the shortness of its reign.

One winter night when I was seven, I had a fever so high that the shadows became animals against the wall and the room spun slowly around me. It was snowing, and the snowflakes caught the streetlight and turned red, and I was filled with the vague generalized anxiety of being sick and a child. I went downstairs, and my father was sitting with a glass of bourbon. Through the television static, two dark, angry-looking men were playing chess at a table.

"Dad?" I said, shivering uncontrollably through my fever.

"Look at this," he said. "Come here."

I sat on his lap, sweating into his lapel with my fevered head. The men on the television were hard to make out through the snow—they were gray and amorphous, crackling with every move, the ghosted relics of another universe.

"Where are they?"

"Russia. That's very far away. It's a huge country east of Europe."

"They look far away," I said. "Is it cold there?" The room the men were in had a cold light to it. There was a silence between them that felt full and fierce, as though if you listened carefully enough, you might hear in the static silent taunts and dares and ruminations. The younger of the two men scratched his chin and sacrificed a bishop.

"Look at him," my father said, putting his finger right on the television, in violation of a rule of my mother's. "He's twenty-two, you know." The man he touched had a face that was gray and gaunt but also tautly intelligent. He touched the pieces with a furious energy that bordered on recklessness. His opponent handled his pieces carefully, nearly caressing the bishops before moving them, letting his fingers linger for a split second on the move he had just made. The young man scratched his head vigorously, moved his queen with an offhand impatience. "He's going to be the youngest chess champion in the world," my father said wonderingly.

The muted men stared at each other, and we stared at them. My father stroked my forehead and I felt tired, but I wanted to stay awake so I could remember whatever it was my father wanted me to remember. Time seemed to collapse. The only sound was the crackle of the static, and we watched for what must have become a very long time—until the final moves were made, the tipping point beyond which all was inevitable. I've since studied this game: how Aleksandr sacrificed his black rook, which was consumed almost greedily by Rusayev's white knight, and then swung his other rook—which had been lurking idly on the other end of the board, huddled like a creature, forgotten by the audience and, presumably, the old man—down to the end of the board. At the time, all I knew was that my father was rapt. He leaned forward slightly. In the monochromatic Eastern light, Aleksandr cracked his knuckles. His opponent's king lay sideways on the black tiling, dead. Maybe there was the faintest rustle of a gasp in the audience. Or maybe I'm imagining that part. But I know what my father said afterward, even though I still wonder whether he was telling me the truth.

"You see," he said, turning off the television with a flash that made bright spots in my eyes. The red snowflakes kept coming, slower and slower. My father spoke so quietly that I wasn't sure whether he was talking to himself or to me. "You see," he said, and I shivered again. "You can do a lot before you are thirty."

3

ALEKSANDR

Leningrad, 1980

The first time Aleksandr went to the café, Ivan and Nikolai didn't recognize him. Aleksandr had grown thinner that winter, since his mother wasn't around to make unpalatable food endurable, and he was paler. The relentless cold had given him a wild-eyed look of defeat. It made him move awkwardly, too—with all his limbs straight, his shoulders making tense bunches at his ears, every muscle trying to burrow farther into his body. He didn't look like himself anymore, and he hadn't looked like much to start with. So when he showed up at the Saigon on a snowy black night in January, Ivan and Nikolai stared at him with bald suspicion. They were sitting at a table in a corner with tiny clear shots of vodka before them and an enormous bricklike ashtray between them. The curtains around their table were a dark green that had been dulled by proximity to smoke and conspiracy. Ivan was cradling a cigarette between his two long fingers and talking; Nikolai was nodding vigorously and taking notes. Aleksandr stood over them, not wanting to interrupt.

"What do you want?" said Ivan. He was wearing a frayed Sex Pistols T-shirt and the same silver medallion he'd had at the centenary. Aleksandr pulled off his hat and let some snow fall onto the table.

"Goddammit," said Nikolai. A clump of snow disturbed his vodka. "Who the hell are you?"

"I'm sure he's just about to tell us," said Ivan.

Aleksandr looked around the smoky café. It was labyrinthine and dark, though slanting red light illuminated corners here and there—a man and a woman without rings talked with their faces very close together; several groups of young men spoke in rustles and spurts and eruptions of laughter; a man in a wheelchair sat alone, rocking back and forth, the edge of his cigarette a rotating satellite as he gestured. Aleksandr closed his eyes for a moment and let the voices make a mosaic around him. They were relaxed, he decided, in their joking or raving or romance. They sounded like people talking in a bedroom, not a public place. Later, he realized that what he was hearing was the sound of people not lying.

"Sir?" said Ivan sternly. "Have you lost your way?"

"I'm Aleksandr Kimovich," said Aleksandr. "We met at the centenary. You were taking notes. I just moved here."

"What?" said Nikolai. His disastrously splotched face was carved into a parody of concern; he looked like a social realist painting, thought Aleksandr—*The Insolence of the Youthful Alarm and Worry!*

"You gave me this address," said Aleksandr, feeling immediately stupid. "You wrote it down for me and said to stop by."

"When was this?" said Nikolai. The snow in his vodka was starting to melt. Aleksandr had a sinking feeling and remembered a time in grade school when he'd been passed a note to meet one of the girls under the pine tree at noon, and he went and waited and didn't understand.

"I remember," said Ivan. He flecked ash into the tray. "You're the chess prodigy, right?"

Aleksandr turned his face to the side. "I'm just at the academy."

"I read about you some," Ivan said. "You've been doing well."

"Thank you," said Aleksandr, then didn't know what else to say. He didn't want it to seem as though he had come only to be congratulated on his success.

"Please, please, sit down," said Ivan. "Join us. Nikolai Sergeyevich, would you be so kind as to order the young man some vodka?" Nikolai gave Aleksandr a long, appraising look and disappeared into the smoky hallway, leering mildly at a few young women at the next table on his way out. "So. Aleksandr Kimovich. You're liking the city so far?" Ivan smiled as though he were a Soviet ambassador trying to win over the dictator of a third-world socialist state.

"It's very nice," said Aleksandr.

At this, Ivan laughed. When he sucked his cigarette, his face turned to glinting angles and sharp edges. He raised his eyebrow. "Your apartment gives you no trouble?"

"No," said Aleksandr, although he sometimes wished it did. He sometimes wished that the steward or one of the other tenants would burst into his damp room, with its flickering and tenuous light, to see what he was doing. The winter had been so lonely that the encroachment of anybody, for any reason, would have been welcome.

"Where's the other one?" said Aleksandr. He remembered the third in Ivan's trio, the one who looked the scruffiest, who'd said that they liked to study real history.

"Misha." Ivan stopped and ticked his long fingers against his chin. "You have a very good memory to remember poor Misha."

"Thank you," said Aleksandr. He did have a very good memory, though, as Andronov always told him, his greatest strength in chess was in forgetting what he'd remembered and doing something else altogether.

Nikolai returned with a tray of Stoli, swirling and crystalline in the light. Aleksandr thanked him, and Nikolai said nothing. Ivan raised his glass and clinked it against Nikolai's. "To Misha," said Ivan.

Nikolai drank without toasting. Aleksandr picked up his vodka and examined it. In the glass, the light made chords of blue rainbows.

"What?" said Ivan. "Do you not have this in the east? It's to drink."

"I realize." It tasted acerbic; Aleksandr pressed his lips together and swallowed some water. Ivan scoffed.

"What do you do with your time there?" said Nikolai.

"It's not as cold there. There are other things to do." Aleksandr gulped the rest of the shot to show them that he could, and Ivan handed him another.

"Our friend Misha," said Ivan, "has unfortunately gotten himself into a little bit of trouble."

"I'm sorry to hear that," said Aleksandr. The tendons in his neck were starting to unfurl slightly, and he wanted to look around the café some more. The ceiling was high and cavelike, strung with glowing lightbulbs the color of absinthe. Above the bar, bottles glinted with fish-belly silvers. The man in the wheelchair was still ranting to himself, puncturing the air with his cigarette tip.

"Who is that man?" said Aleksandr. "Who is he talking to?"

"You're odd," said Ivan. "Your priorities are odd."

"Alcohol isn't good for my game," said Aleksandr. He was starting to be sorry he'd come. "It makes me fuzzy. It dulls my memory. Chess is all memory. Memory and imagination."

"Memory and imagination are both technically illegal," said Ivan. "Do you want us to order you a beer, then?"

"The beer is water," said Nikolai. "Don't insult the man. The beer's not suitable for infants."

They passed another shot glass to Aleksandr, and he rolled it between his fingers. The glass felt clean, and when it was full, it was just about the weight of a king in a good set. Nikolai produced a cigar from his pocket and lit it with a Saigon Café matchbook. The cigar made sweet swirls in the air. Aleksandr's head felt as if it were attached by a string connected to the ceiling and was dangling above his torso, moving in tandem with his gestures, manipulated by an unseen puppeteer.

"What happened to Misha?" said Aleksandr. It was hard to form words. He was coursing with a silly relaxation, a pleasant absence of energy that left only a few things thinkable: taking deep gulps of the cinnamon smell of the cigar, watching the green lights bob like buoys on a dark ocean.

"Well," said Ivan. "Misha got stupid, Aleksandr Kimovich. And I'm going to tell you this so you don't get stupid, too."

"Okay," said Aleksandr stupidly. His tongue was clumsy in his mouth.

"Because, to tell you the truth, you don't seem like the sharpest individual," said Ivan.

"No," said Nikolai. "He doesn't."

"I know you're a brilliant chess mind," said Ivan. "This is what the newspapers tell me. And I believe what the newspapers tell me, always."

"Always," said Nikolai.

"But you can be good at one thing and not so good at other things," said Ivan.

"Or you can be good at one thing and not so good at any other thing," said Nikolai.

"Misha got stupid," said Ivan. "He got stupid. He disseminated falsehood. He made statements that are not officially recognized as truth."

"He circulated defamatory statements about the Soviet state and system," said Nikolai.

"Oh?"

"He signed a petition," said Ivan, "and he's been thrown in a psikhushka. We don't know when he'll be back." He rubbed his temples, his fingers fluttering against his dark hair.

"He's an idiot," said Nikolai. When he turned toward the light, his scars became aubergine thumbprints across his face.

"The point is," said Ivan, "in seriousness, there is something of that in you, I think, and I hope you won't mind me saying so. Don't do what people ask you, unless they are from the competent organs. Don't violate the traffic laws."

"I don't have a car," said Aleksandr.

"Don't grant favors. Don't make assumptions. I trust you were in the Komsomol?"

Aleksandr shook his head. "You don't really have to in Okha. It's such a tiny town. Why, were you?"

"Everybody was," said Ivan curtly. He raised his eyebrows at Aleksandr and pulled his mouth into a tight line. "All the decent students."

"I see," said Aleksandr. His head was starting to clear, and the green lamps were becoming dull orbs that pulsed against the inside of his eyelids. Nikolai and Ivan started talking about music, and then about women, and then about the invasion of Afghanistan and how many months it might take the Soviet army to subdue its dusty, uncultivated landscape and people. Aleksandr hadn't been following

the story much, although he'd glimpsed headlines as he flipped his way
to the chess coverage—an "interventionist duty," it was called, and "an
invitation from the socialist brethren of Afghanistan"—and he bobbed
in and out of listening. He was thinking about Misha, in psychiatric
prison for having bad luck. He thought of the countless incomprehensible papers he'd encountered in his efforts to get to Leningrad, how
many he'd signed without reading, without understanding. He went
to find the bathroom.

Near the door, the man in the wheelchair was still talking to himself.
"Motherfuckers," he was saying, punching the air with his cigarette.
His head was down against his chest, as though he were telling secrets
to his breastbone. The man's legs were shriveled and mostly missing,
and his face had an odd flatness to it. When he lifted his head into the
light, Aleksandr could see that he was missing teeth, too, which wasn't
unusual but which contributed to the man's overall look of unnerving
concavity. He looked like a person who'd been taken apart entirely
and then put back together wrong. "Fucking motherfuckers," the man
said again, and looked straight at Aleksandr. "Don't trust them." The
green café lights gave him a radioactive glow.

"Who are motherfuckers?" Aleksandr realized that he really
wanted to know.

The man crooked a finger at Aleksandr and beckoned for him to
come closer. Aleksandr did so, bringing his cheek down to the man's,
inhaling his smell of rust and alcohol and something else that made
Aleksandr sad, even though he didn't understand why.

"Who?" Aleksandr said again. "Who are motherfuckers?"

"They all are," whispered the man, then laughed a choking, startling laugh. He gestured with his cigarette, ashing onto Aleksandr's
shoes, grandly implicating all the people in his field of vision. "Everyone."

When Aleksandr stumbled out into the ice-wrecked streets several
hours later, there was a shred of ash in the eastern sky. The light looked
as though it had been filtered through dirty gauze; the clumps of snow
were beginning to take on the fuzzy shape of mold. A tattered ad warn-

ing against the evils of Demon Vodka stuck under Aleksandr's shoe, and he kicked it away. The air was sharp with the gasoline of idling Zhigulis. Leningrad was gearing up for another day, and the illegal street vendors were organizing themselves in dark corners: men in brown layers setting up carts of vegetables, the gray beets and cabbages turning to colors in the breaking sun. A woman stood shivering with her fish, their tongue-colored bellies slick in the light. Boys in wool caps crouched watching for the police, ready to alert their families and collapse the wood stalls and vanish. They could disappear as quickly as the cockroaches in the kommunalka could scatter from the cold light, as quickly as a person could evaporate into a car and never come back.

Aleksandr walked down Nevsky Prospekt, past the Museum of the History of Atheism and Religion. Leningrad was such a difference from the mangled wreck of Okha, a city that nobody had planned for or intended. Leningrad was all stately foresight and clean geometry, indisputable proof that Russians, too, could think more than one generation ahead. It was a beautiful city if you could open your eyes against the wind long enough to really see it. But Aleksandr didn't look around much on his trip home after his first night out with Ivan and Nikolai. There was a new menace for him here, he thought, subtler and more nefarious than KGB in white Volgas. Back in Okha, he'd understood the nature of the game; he'd walked the parameters of his life over and over until he couldn't even dream his way out of them. He'd known everyone there, and he'd known everyone's grandparents and pockmarks and slimy vegetable gardens, and if there had been other-thinking people among them, he'd have known that, too.

In Leningrad, he could tell, it was going to be different. He'd never thought to be scared before of old people pushing papers. He'd never been scared of the women who stood in the street and sold roses.

When Aleksandr returned to his building, one of the night girls was standing in the corridor, the snow of her boots making turpentine-colored pools at her feet. She was knocking on the steward's door vigorously, which Aleksandr had never seen anybody do. He stood and watched her and wondered what would happen.

"What are you looking at?" said the girl. She was the darker-haired of the two girls, and Aleksandr knew her for her swearing in the hallways. The father of the family next door to him had complained about it one time, leaning over to spit into the sink next to Aleksandr. "I don't like trying to raise a child next door to blyadi," said the man. "It's going to make him ask questions, and the fewer questions he asks, the better for him."

The girl snapped her fingers in front of Aleksandr's face. "What?" she said. "Do you talk, by the way?"

"I talk."

"Oh." She looked disappointed. "I had a bet."

"What are you doing?" he said. "I don't think the old woman comes to her door in the mornings."

"She'll come this morning. I don't care how bad her hangover is. Worms came out of the faucet. This is a problem."

"What kind of worms?"

"What kind of worms? What the fuck does it matter what kind? I go to turn on the hot water. I'm used to no hot water. No hot water does not surprise me. I know we don't know each other very well, tovarish, but *little* surprises me. But worms seem, you know, excessive, I think." Her brown hair was flying all around her face, and she swiped it from her eyes so hard that Aleksandr wanted to reach out and gently protect her from herself.

"Yes," he said. "Certainly excessive."

"So, I don't know, I thought I might ask the old woman about this." She resumed pounding, making her knocks sharp and arrhythmic for maximum annoyance. "It's just that I'm coming back from a long night, you know? I work nights."

"I know."

"You know," she said, then knocked again, harder. "Yes, I suppose you do know. Just like I know that you are the chess prodigy from Siberia—"

"Sakhalin."

"Yes," she said.

Aleksandr was struck, still, by her careening indignation. Her knocking was the knocking of a person who had been terribly wronged. It was pretty bad, the worms in the faucet. But it could not possibly have been the worst thing.

"Which one are you?" he said.

"What?" She turned to face him, and when she moved, he heard clicks and clinks, the unidentifiable feminine shifting of heels and various bits of jewelry. She was dressed in black, although he thought there might be multiple components to her outfit—a shirt, and a short jacket, and a skirt, maybe? Her face was pretty, but maybe not pretty enough to sustain the attention that came from wearing only black. The outfit was like a drum roll.

"Are you Sonya, or are you the other one?" said Aleksandr. He couldn't remember the other one's name, and he couldn't remember, either, which of the things he thought he knew about them were true and which he'd made up himself. They really were prostitutes, he thought. He wasn't sure about the parakeet.

"I'm the other one. Elizabeta Nazarovna." She rested her head forlornly on the door. "I think she's not home."

"I'm Aleksandr Kimovich Bezetov."

"Okay," she said, not taking his hand. She lowered her voice and started muttering cruelties at the door. "You tramp. You ape. You dirty, double-crossing, overcharging, collaborative bitch." She stopped, and Aleksandr wondered if she was out of insults.

"Do you think maybe you should try not to make her mad at you?" he said. She could kick Elizabeta out, probably, or throw all her things out the front door, like she'd done with the university lecturer. He thought of Elizabeta's things scattered across the bare front yard: books and perfume bottles; black indistinguishable garments; flecks of silver jewelry.

"Please. She sells winter things out of the basement every year. I know because all my mittens are from her. She's like a spider. She's more afraid of us than we are of her." She turned again to the door. "And like a spider," she hissed, "you lurk in the dark even in the daytime, you are unpleasant to look at, and you are universally reviled. Hey." She turned back to Aleksandr. "Do you smoke?"

"Cigarettes?"

"Yes." Now he would have to start.

She nodded. "Well, pretty much all Sonya and I do is smoke and tell lies. So if you ever want to come over for that, feel free. I know you don't really do anything."

"I do things. I'm busy. I go to the academy, you know. I have a trainer," he said. He'd never tried to impress anybody with his game, and he was aware of how very poor he was at bragging, even when he wanted to. He cleared his throat and gazed at a spot above Elizabeta's head and tried to look intellectual and preoccupied and haunted. "Chess absorbs most of my time."

"Yes, well," she said. "If you get a moment, then." There was a rustling sound from within the apartment, vague cross murmuring and shuffling. Hideous bright light bled underneath the door and through its cracks. The old woman had stirred.

"Finally, you wretched she-beast," muttered Elizabeta, and then in a high false voice, she said, "Babushka? Puzhalsta? Please, dear grandmother, it's your tenant Elizabeta here with a question for you. I might find a few rubles for you if you answer the door."

At this, the steward appeared, her graying whiskered face looking pinched and poisonous. Her hair was wrapped up in a dirty maroon scarf, and she gave off a faint smell of cheap tea and restless sleeping.

"What?" she said, looking at Aleksandr, who moved away from Elizabeta. "In God's name, what?"

"Worms in the faucet, babushka," said Elizabeta. "Please forgive me for bothering you. I know you're very busy." She winked at Aleksandr.

"Honestly," said the old woman, who retreated into her apartment again, presumably to retrieve the tools necessary for handling worms.

Elizabeta smiled and shrugged. "Remember," she whispered to Aleksandr. "Apartment nine, if you want some smokes and general hilarity. Thank you so much, babushka," she called. "I so appreciate your help."

"Okay," said Aleksandr, and left her calling out bright lies to the steward, marveling at how expertly she could pretend to feel something she didn't.

After a cold shower—avoiding even attempting the hot water faucet—and a day of dry, peeling fatigue and clumsy mistakes at the academy, Aleksandr came back and lay in bed. It was only five P.M., although dark again, as always, and his bed felt colder than usual from having lain unmade and unoccupied for so many hours. He thought briefly about Elizabeta in apartment nine, getting ready for her night of work, and he wondered if he should stop by to say hello and borrow a cigarette and see whether the worm situation had sorted itself out. Maybe he'd sit on Elizabeta's bed, which would be unmade, like his, and they'd split a cigarette. Prostitutes, like chess students, probably needed to economize. Maybe her roommate, Sonya, would be there, too, and he'd tell them stories about his night out. "Café Saigon?" he'd say casually. "Ever heard of it?" And if they had, terrific, and if they hadn't, all the better. "How do you stay so brilliant with no sleep?" they'd ask him, concerned. And he would smile and take a long puff from his cigarette, and he would not cough, and he would wink and say, "Practice."

His bed was growing a little warmer, and he pulled his hands into his sleeves and rubbed them together. On second thought, maybe he wouldn't go over there. He thought about Misha, wincing in the cold rooms of a psikhushka because he'd done something for a stranger. He thought about the legless man and about his assertion that everyone, *everyone,* was a motherfucker. He thought he could believe it. Aleksandr rolled over and rubbed his feet together and tried to remember everything he could about his mother's house in Okha. He thought of his little sisters, who looked like him and swung between scorn and laughter with the suddenness of heat lightning. He thought of his mother, who sat up long nights thinking unknowable thoughts and singing sad songs. It was just as well that he wouldn't go to apartment nine. It was remembering that he was good at, remembering and imagining. And whether or not these were useful skills for Soviet life, they were things you could do quietly, upstairs in a boardinghouse, alone.

4

IRINA

Cambridge, Mass., 2006

I was playing chess with Lars one day in early spring when the man who turned out to be Jonathan stopped by to watch us. I don't really know why; his later claims about what drew him over were not ones that I could quite bring myself to believe. Lars and I made an odd pair, I suppose—an impish old man and an unnervingly pale young woman, grimacing at each other over an unimaginative position—and at first I thought that the man had a bet with himself about the outcome of the game. I skimmed my bishop along the board until it was eyeball to plastic eyeball with one of Lars's knights. The knight was defended, and this move was not really going to get me anywhere. But for some reason, I wanted the man to see me do something dramatic.

"There's a man watching us," Lars said loudly.

The man coughed. "I hope you don't mind."

"Fine," said Lars. "But you better not cough again."

That first moment has taken on some mythic contours for me now, I suppose. I'm both impious and clinically self-absorbed, so it makes sense that I look hardest for meaning in my own memories. The man kept standing there. At the time, it was probably vaguely uncomfortable—this man watching us, his scarf whipping out behind him in the wind, his eyes growing stung and watery in the cold. He was passably attractive but not arrestingly beautiful. Still, I wonder if I felt a sense of particularity, of unique rightness, in his face even then— in the curl of his hair and the slight crag of his chin and the pencil shavings of stubble across his cheek, in the way his eyes were tired and snappishly intelligent at the same time. It's possible that his face felt familiar to me, but it's also possible that this is a quality conferred only in retrospect. I tried not to look at him.

"Can I play the winner?" he said.

"One dollar," said Lars.

"How much do I pay you?" he said to me.

"I don't charge," I said. I still wasn't looking at him. "I also don't win."

"She doesn't." Lars sniffed. "If you're playing the winner, you're playing me."

"I'll take my chances."

He watched us play. People talk about being able to feel a gaze, and I never believed that until I had to squirm through this game. I think even my arms were blushing.

"Are you letting him win?" said the man.

Lars harrumphed and looked insulted.

"No," I said. "I never let anybody win."

"At anything?"

I was confused as to what we were talking about. "Not if I can help it," I said. I was aware that this made no sense, since I was losing to Lars—as usual—and it came out as a weird sort of inverted brag.

"Which she never can," said Lars. "She never can. She always loses." He was trying to get this point through the man's head, though I don't know why. There was a dollar to be made, after all.

We played. My fingers felt self-conscious in the way they grabbed my knight, in the way they lingered when they put the knight down. I felt them fluttering in my lap. I felt myself twirling my hair (I am not traditionally a twirler of hair). Good Christ, I thought. What the hell is this?

I lost, more quickly than usual.

"He's all yours," I said to the man. I stood up too fast. I could feel the air between us, which was suddenly too dense and too thin at the same time. I felt that somehow there would never be a distance between this man and me that would be acceptable, no matter what; that closeness and farness both were going to be forever unendurable. I was standing up then, and he was sitting down. There was a whirring in my ears like an oncoming train.

"You should stay," said the man. "To see how it's really done."

They played, and the man was terrible, far worse than I am. He barely knew the rules—he seemed to think it was checkers—and he lost dramatically, with flourish and good humor. Lars seemed increasingly agitated, despite the coming dollar. He seemed to know that this game had stakes that weren't really about chess, and I could tell that this annoyed him. He respected the game and didn't like to see it used for sillier ends. He didn't shake the man's proffered hand at the conclusion of the game.

"This isn't Parcheesi," said Lars.

"I realize that," said the man.

"Don't come back until you've studied some," said Lars. "I'm a busy man."

"I appreciate your indulgence."

"Must have been bad luck this time," I said as the man stood up.

"Very bad luck," he said. "I'm usually a menace on the chessboard."

"I don't doubt it," I said.

"I'm Jonathan," he said. "Maybe sometime I could give you some pointers?"

———

I don't know. I don't know. He was funny, sure, and smart, but there were plenty of men in Boston who were funny and smart—Boston's major export is people who are funny and smart, who have advanced degrees, who read on public transportation. And I don't want to go too much into the gruesome details. Personally, I find other people's witty banter disgusting. Whenever the kids in the office started in on it, I'd plug my headphones in to an episode of *Frontline* on the computer.

But I will say this: it unfolded with the inevitability of a fatally flawed chess game. We met for the first coffee, which led to the art show, which led to the sex—and that was the first time in a long time. He brushed his lips along my neck, and multicolored constellations exploded behind my eyelids, and I was struck by the unfamiliar feeling of not being furious at my body. Afterward, I traced my fingers along his perfect form, the sturdy convexity of his perfect brain—perfect because it wasn't doomed, or at least not any more doomed than is typical—and I realized that I didn't resent it, not really, for its normalcy. And that, I'm afraid, was that.

———

It was a good spring. Leaving Boston has cast it with a bittersweet sheen, which makes everything seem poignant. But at the time, it wasn't. Jonathan and I drank coffee and talked and had lulls in our talking. We walked through the red rain-soaked bricks of Cambridge. We watched the Citgo sign reorganize its colors against the night sky. Sooner or later, we started talking in hypothetical about the relatively short-term future. And that was when I realized—or maybe remembered—that I had a problem.

I stopped calling him. I let his calls go to voice mail, even though I didn't like the thought of my stupid voice-mail voice—overly solicitous and frightfully high-pitched, like a chipmunk prostitute—talking into his ear over and over and over.

Before I'd started dating Jonathan by accident, I'd been careful to avoid romantic relationships. This ban of mine was not an affectation, nor was it the outgrowth of a willful and baseless social isolation. It was my attempt to carve out for myself some space to manage without anyone else watching too closely. It was my attempt at sanity. And— let it not be forgotten—it was also my slim, feeble, selfish attempt at selflessness.

I thought about the day I beat my father at chess. It's too much to say that this was the day I stopped knowing him, but it was certainly the day I started to stop. I wondered what my equivalent day would be, what my corresponding departing gesture might look like. I wondered if I wanted Jonathan to be the one to see it.

I started fantasizing about running away. I saw myself walking through cobblestoned streets in generic European capitals; I saw myself riding a camel against a bright blue desert sky. I tried to think of a way out of this—some bargain that would mean I could stay with Jonathan, and call him back, and love him without worrying about the day when the person who loved him would stop being me, because there was no me anymore, in any meaningful sense.

I still hadn't told him.

———

In the end, I couldn't tell him, so I had to show him. I took him to meet my father.

In the car, I explained. I told him that my father's and my shared fate was in no way unique—in fact, it might be the only thing that's truly universal. Death, anyway, is universal. And even losing our minds doesn't really set us apart—we all lose our minds, after all, it's just that some of us lose them with death, and some of us lose them a bit before. All we miss, really, is thirty to forty years. When you think of the time we spend alive versus the incredible amount of time we spend dead, thirty to forty years doesn't amount to that much. But when that time is filled with the particular events of your own life, one finds it does take on an inordinate significance.

I told him about the nucleotides, the genetic test, the prognosis. I told him that atrophying of basal ganglia starts years before symptoms present, and that right now—in this car, in this moment—parts of my brain were dying, parts that I didn't know I needed, but parts that I would never, never be able to get back. I told him that there wasn't an emotion or an impulse or a stumble that I could completely trust; I told him that one day—if I let it—everything I did and said and thought would be nothing more than the entropic implosion of a condemned building or a dying star.

He listened. He held my hand lightly. I don't know if I can call that understanding.

The nursing home smelled, as it always did, of stewed carrots and antimicrobial cleansers and the singed coffee that the first shift had made and not had time to drink. There was a part of me that didn't like showing my father off like this, as though he were a scientific exhibition and not a former person. At the same time, if there was a way to make Jonathan see what I looked at when I looked in the mirror, then this was it. You could talk about the degradation of cortex tissue forever. But real understanding was in the inverted mouth, the yellow concavity of the face. The dark eyes that shone like those of a prisoner who knew he'd be executed at dawn, though I tried not to sentimentalize. I didn't think my father really knew his fate anymore. This, for him, was the easy part.

We went to him. I rubbed my father's thin shoulders. I gave him a chocolate. He looked somewhere beyond us. He gummed his mouth and made cork-popping sounds. His fingers forked like the shriveled arms of a dinosaur, and he pressed them so fiercely into the table that they turned white.

"Hello, Mr. Ellison," said Jonathan. My father, of course, said nothing back.

"Genetics," I said.

"Will that be you?"

"Not if I can help it."

In the car on the way back, we were quiet. I let Jonathan drive my car. Route 2 broke into a view of the city, silver buildings catching the receding light, the Prudential Building flashing palely in the murk. I opened the window and thought about my father. Like most people, I was not my best self at twelve. And it bothered me sometimes to think of this version of myself as the last vision my father had of me before his mind went—as if this made any sense. As if he was standing on the opposite end of some magic beam of rainbow light, remembering me in my youth, carrying around a smudged mental snapshot of who I used to be. Really, it was the other way around. But in weak, sentimental moments, I wanted to tell him: look. I grew up with a sense of humor, anyway. You would have liked me if you didn't already.

All this by way of saying that it matters to me how I am remembered.

————

My father died in April. It was quiet, and strange, and unreal in the way that anything you long for long enough gets to be. It was not horrifying. It was calm, morphined, inevitable. In some ways, it was the only thing that had gone right for my father in the better part of two decades. I kept my hand on his head the whole time, and he turned cold before his pulse stopped. He turned yellow, too—this was from his liver giving out—and it did seem like a process, a natural compulsion, a source of some secular comfort, if only you discounted the eighteen years that had preceded this moment. My mother and I stood there, our tears strangled somewhere back in our throats because we breathed only when he did. And he died sometime after that last breath, sometime after that last pulse, though it would be hard to say precisely when. Dying for two decades takes something away from life, but it takes something away from death, too. Death itself becomes a dim asymptote, ever approaching, ever unreachable. Until, at long last, it is reached.

I thought of Jonathan—I thought him of pointing to my father, to his skittering hands and carved-out eyes. He asked if that would be me, and I'd said no, not if I could help it. Which reminded me of Lars's saying, "But she never can, she never can."

———

Jonathan came to the funeral, and he held my hand and bowed his head with the appropriate amount of sober reflection. Still, even then, I was starting to feel a chasm between us, crumbling into enormity. It's true that we are all mortal, but maybe it's also true that some of us are more mortal than others. The cemetery was almost lovely—full of the mild green of new buds and grass shyly beginning to assert itself, the cool wind blowing the trees' shadows across the graves in a way that was a little beautiful and a little unnerving. And Jonathan regarded everything—the coffin, the grave, the green Astroturf laid out to conceal the exposed dirt—with the expression of a spectator.

I look back now, and I tell myself that in this, as in all things, there are advantages. So we don't marry, have children, grow old together. This is what we miss. We also don't stop sleeping together, divorce, come to see each other as strangers, look back in bewildered grief to these early days and try to unravel how it all went so wrong. Those days—that last spring in Boston—were the only days. There is something to be grateful for in this, I think.

But at the time, I wasn't grateful yet. I looked at the sky; I looked at the ground. Everything was fragile and raw and acute. I looked at Jonathan. We are not the same, I thought. And you would not wish for us to be.

A few weeks after my father's death, I went to clean out the house, and that was when I found the box. My mother had kept the house through my father's illness—partly because she wanted a place to stay when she returned for semiannual visits, partly because it was the only asset that the state couldn't claim after we relinquished my father and his savings to a publicly funded facility. After the death, my mother was free to sell the house, and she'd asked me to handle the posthumous categorizing and cataloging and investigating that comes with a completed life. I was given an afternoon to reduce my father to the elements we would most want to remember him by: the wittiest letters, the loveliest souvenirs, the most flattering photographs. Everything else would be thrown out.

The box was in my father's study, shoved between a stack of withered postcards and his creaky, outdated globe. When I looked inside, I found a mess of snarled newspaper clippings, curling from age and multiple handlings, and I nearly stepped away, closed the box, and left the mystery alone.

Actually, that's not true. I didn't nearly close the box. I am not the kind of person who would close the box. I kept the box open, and I started to riffle. And inside the box I found pictures and clippings of Aleksandr Bezetov, the chess champion.

The first clipping was a 1980 article from *Literaturnaya Gazeta,* detailing an early success of Aleksandr's at that unpronounceable Leningrad chess academy of his. In the picture, he's heartrendingly young and nondescript—he never did look like a person who'd amount to much, even when he already had—and he appears slightly chagrined at being photographed. The clippings then follow him to regional and nationwide victories in Russia to international triumph at some tournament in Reykjavík. In the earlier pictures, he is gaunt and grumpy; his gestures are all hard angles; he has an expression of low-grade exasperation. The eighties begin. The reporting about him has a breathless quality; his youth is much remarked upon, as is his brilliance. He has a subversive manner of play, it is said. He has an attitude. There are reports on disputes with the FIDE. He stops meeting the camera's eye when he's photographed. He fills out some. He starts to look older.

He plays Rusayev interminably. The match is halted. The match is resumed. The last game is played. This was the game I had watched with my father, and the ferocity of Bezetov's expression put me in mind of that night—the delirious rotating of shadow against wall, the slow-falling snow turning the color of dying fire. Bezetov wins. In the picture with his trophy, he appears clinically depressed. The clippings seem shakily cut now, as we move into the late eighties and the first stirring of my father's Huntington's. All documentation stops fairly soon after my father's symptoms present, though not as soon as I might have imagined. After 1990, there's nothing—nothing about Bezetov's book, his much mourned loss to an IBM computer, his entry into post–Cold War politics. My father missed all that. My father missed a lot.

It was a strange thing, this chronicling of another man's life. It isn't what you expect to find in a secret reliquary hidden in your father's study. In my narcissism, I'd imagined school pictures, honor roll announcements, pinecone Christmas ornaments; in my conspiracy-mindedness, I'd imagined love letters, mysterious sets of keys, government correspondence. Instead, what we had was the grim and thorough documentation of the career of a Soviet chess player—a man my father had never met and whose story he never got to finish. It was unexpected. But I can't say it was terribly surprising, and not just because of my father's love of chess and the Soviets, generally, and this Soviet chessman, specifically. I remembered the night of the snowstorm and my father's glassy-eyed rapture over the unexpected turns in a faraway game. To my father, Aleksandr Bezetov wasn't just a precocious young sportsman. He was the personification of order over anarchy. He was the embodiment of facing down near-certain doom with a degree of panache. Most important, perhaps, he was the representation of the possibility of unlikely events, which I'm sure my father was already starting to be interested in by the time he sat me on his lap and showed me some of the things one could do in a very short time.

In the bottom of the box was a letter. I let myself pretend for a self-congratulatory moment that I wouldn't read it. And then I did.

The letter was photocopied, undated, and written entirely in Russian. Back then, before I came to St. Petersburg, my Russian was weaker than my father's had been, even though mine had come from my Ph.D., and his was primarily self-taught. It took me three reads to get the full scope of the letter, and even now that my Russian is fairly good, I wonder if there are elements I miss or misunderstand. Roughly, this is what it said:

Dear Mr. Bezetov,

You may find it strange to receive a fan letter from an American. Then again, you might get many a day, for all I know. There's a lot to admire about your career, generally—the originality and radicalism of your strategy, your perseverance in the face of almost certain defeat, your remarkable intelligence. All of this is especially captivating for a person who has spent many years paying close attention to the significance of opening gestures; one suspects that you will go far. I feel a certain affinity with you, I suppose, because I'm fighting my own complicated match these days—and am, I fear, nearing the bitterest of losses. And I'm wondering if there's a question you might find time to answer for me.

You wouldn't be where you are if you weren't mostly a winner— a winner, that is, at those matches that have counted the most. And yet there have been games, matches, tournaments that you've lost. And among these, surely, are games, matches, tournaments that you've known all along you were losing. Surely there are those that have been lost from the start, those in which your intellect proved itself to be the limited and temporary and mortal intellect that it does not always seem to be. When you find yourself playing such a game or match or tournament, what is the proper way to proceed? What story do you tell yourself when that enormous certainty is upon you and you scrape up against the edges of your own self?

Please forgive the oddity of the questions. Chalk it up to the sentimentality or the lunacy—or perhaps, charitably, the clarity—that comes from leaving too much, too soon.

With appreciation,
Prof. Frank Ellison

I read it over once more and sat down on the radiator for a long minute. It's possible that I cried the slightest bit. And then I read it again. I was struck by the formality of the tone. The bit about "opening gestures" was my approximation of a phrase that was somewhat difficult to translate—literally, I think it was "the commencing gambit"— a reference to the early signs of my father's illness, no question, but an odd phrase for him to use. And even post-translation, the whole letter was written in a different idiolect than I remembered as my father's— though the vocabulary he used with me, I had to remind myself, was inevitably that which one uses with a child. My father had never spoken to me as an adult because he had never known me as an adult. So it's wrong for me to say whether any particular tone, any particular language, was or wasn't typical for my father. The truth is, I did not know.

Similarly, I did not know what this letter meant to my father, what kind of feature it was in the misty landscape of his life. Perhaps it was strange, or perhaps it was wholly singular, or perhaps his life had been full of letters of this kind—to chess champions, to squash players, to noted economists, to circus performers. Maybe this letter, this affinity, was one of many. Then I read it again and decided I didn't think so.

He knew he was going, and maybe that gave him some particular insight—some inexplicable knowledge that this, *this,* was the proper way to exit, the proper narrative to follow. I am approaching my own end now and am still awaiting that particular bolt of understanding, but that's not the point. If my father found it, then I'm happy for him.

I thought about his questions. Clearly, he must have been thinking a lot about fate when he wrote the letter, and he wanted Aleksandr Bezetov to offer some authoritative comment on the issue. My father was not a religious man—or if he was, he hid it very well—and I don't think he saw fate as a preordained ending invented by some cruel, self-amused deity. When my father wrote about fate—which might as easily have been meant as destiny or even, perhaps, future—I think he was writing about the reality that is, when there are so many other realities that could have been. When one is afflicted with a genetic disaster that one has a 50 percent chance of escaping, this kind of thinking becomes prominent. One feels like a special kind of loser to lose at fifty-fifty odds.

I wondered if my father ever received an answer. The fact that the letter was photocopied suggested that he'd sent the original. But perhaps not—maybe he'd been overtaken by embarrassment, second-guessing, time, distraction, and finally, illness.

I rifled through the papers twice but found no response from Aleksandr. There was, however, a brief note from somebody else.

Dear Prof. Ellison,

Thank you for your letter. Unfortunately, Mr. Bezetov isn't able to respond to your queries at this time. I wish you all the best with finding your answers.

Best,

Elizabeta Nazarovna

I read the note again. She was a secretary, most likely, though there was something a little wistful about the phrasing, as though she'd read my father's letter in a capacity that went beyond purely official duties. I stared at the box for a long time, listening to the silence reverberate around the house and wondering. It was clear that my father never got his answers from Aleksandr Bezetov. And that seemed an unjust thing for a person who got so little else.

Maybe that was when I first thought of going. I was already looking for a graceful exit from Jonathan's life, and—I'm not above admitting it—I was already looking for a last adventure. I did not want to put my mother through something she'd barely survived the first time. The thought of running to look for answers to my father's questions had an alluring symmetry. Like a chess move, this move was an iteration of preexisting realities. Though it's true that such a move was in no way inevitable, and finding answers—or, indeed, Bezetov himself—would be nothing short of miraculous.

But as Nabokov's loathed Dostoyevsky pointed out, miracles never bother a realist.

5

ALEKSANDR

Leningrad, 1980

Aleksandr kept going to the Saigon every week for the rest of the winter, and his visits there became the dull smudge of dawn against the bleak, interminable horizons of his days. It was not a warm dawn, rosy and flooded with sunshine and hope—Nikolai was rude, and Ivan was pompous, and Aleksandr quickly grew to understand that neither of them particularly liked him—but it was fundamentally better than nighttime. On Saturday mornings, when there were fewer police out, Ivan and Nikolai would take him downtown to the banned-book market, which moved every week. At night they'd sometimes go to see underground art shows at the culture club of the Kirov plant, or go to see Sankt-Peterburg play at the Saigon and then drunkenly debate the band's purported monarchist leanings. Sundays Aleksandr spent holed up in his room, poring over sloppy translations of Kurt Vonnegut and Iris Murdoch, which interested him more than the jaunty stories about intrepid boys in challenging natural circumstances that he'd read at school in Okha. Weekdays he spent at the academy, or in the bright gymnasiums of universities, beating everybody, hitting the timers with his thumb. Passage of time seemed a product of Aleksandr's own sheer will, as though he were exerting all his best strategy against the days, forcing them to relent and eventually disappear.

At first Aleksandr was universally dismissed—dismissed because he was so young, and eastern, and fierce-faced; dismissed, he finally decided, because people found themselves wanting to believe he was stupid, and this desire sometimes outlasted evidence to the contrary. But slowly, the world began to take notice—first within the academy, where his amassed collection of wins, and the startling ways he'd acquired them, began to elicit attention, then suspicion, then hatred—and then outside the academy, via a moderately sized profile in *Literaturnaya Gazeta*. It wouldn't be long, he could only figure, before word of his greatness bled out completely onto the streets and became widely known. The profile was just the beginning. Once things really got going, he would have to learn to be self-abnegating and funny about it all. It was best to be modest when one's life changed. And he loved to think about how his life would change. The steward might bring him tea and saiki in the mornings. She might brag about him to new tenants as though he were a selling point of the building, along with the location and the indoor plumbing. Some bitter night he might hear Elizabeta mention him to someone outside his door, her voice like the whisper of dried flower petals falling to the floor. "That's where he lives," she'd say. "Aleksandr. The chess prodigy." He'd settle back into his dreams then, and in his head the cerulean sea would turn to black-and-white blocks that he'd skate across to the edge of the earth.

It was only a matter of time, he'd known, until he'd play Andronov. The certainty of this was something of a standing joke among the other boys. If he tried something new or bizarre, the boys would say, "Are you going to try that on Andronov?" If he made a mistake—rarely, rarely, though it did happen—the boys would shriek and yell that Andronov would not let him get away with *that*. But when Andronov grabbed him by the ear one day and pulled him into the back office, Aleksandr was surprised. "Am I in trouble?" he said. He'd been playing Oleg, a bright white boy who seemed to make a game of how little he could speak.

"Come with me," said Andronov.

Aleksandr shrugged at Oleg, who started to put away his pieces.

Aleksandr followed Andronov down the hall to his office, where Andronov plopped into a chair. "Sit," he said. Aleksandr did.

Between them was Andronov's antediluvian desk, overrun with wedges of chess books and creaking antique sets. Under different circumstances, it would have been interesting to explore Andronov's office—in particular, it would have been interesting to see what breathlessly admiring notes about Aleksandr were contained in Andronov's vast collection of papers. But today was not the day, and Aleksandr was beginning to understand, as he vainly tried to get Andronov to look at him, that there might never be one.

Andronov threw a copy of *Literaturnaya Gazeta* toward Aleksandr. "So," he said. "I see you've been talking to the press."

"Well, technically, the press was talking to me."

"I see you offer some opinions about the skill level of your peers here at the academy."

"They asked me!"

Andronov shoved a wheezing set toward Aleksandr. "Play," he said.

"I'm white?"

"Play."

Aleksandr opened with a sedate Nimzo-Indian Defense. A ritualized, bloodless exchange of pieces soon followed. Andronov hemmed; his hands grew inky and his forehead shiny, and Aleksandr saw that he was not committing to a pawn structure. Occasionally, he muttered tensely into the game, as though it were the chessboard's audacious attitude that he'd found fault with, not Aleksandr's.

"After this," said Andronov at last. "Where will you go?"

"Go? What are you talking about?" Aleksandr felt a dry contraction in his throat that squeezed its way down his body. If he pretended not to understand, maybe he wouldn't have to. They were headed for a draw here, he figured.

Andronov positioned his fat elbows on the books, where their dimples winked at Aleksandr menacingly. "After you beat me, where will you go? You think you can stay here after this? You think we'll participate in a farce like that?"

"Oh," said Aleksandr. "Do you think I'll beat you?" But he was starting to worry. Andronov had sailed his bishop to h2, ignoring that Aleksandr could trap the bishop—he'd corner it between pawns, and its power would be squandered for the duration.

"Could I, I don't know," said Aleksandr. "Could I help, maybe?" He flicked his pawn to g3, buttressing Andronov's bishop in its own prison.

"Help? With what? The cleaning? You want to do the laundry? You want to be our washerwoman?" He drew his h pawn forward, harnessing small arms.

"I mean maybe I could teach?"

At this, Andronov's elbows descended onto the table with a meaty crash. "Teach? You want to teach here? You see, tovarish, that's exactly what I'm talking about. That arrogance. Nobody can stand it. Nobody could stand it before, and nobody can stand it now."

Aleksandr backtracked his king diagonally before he spoke. "I'm not trying to be arrogant," he said. "It's just that I don't really have anywhere else to go during the days."

"Find somewhere, if you're so smart." Andronov advanced his pawn once more. He was hoping to secure the bishop's release. Aleksandr could see damp swirls of sweat coursing down his neck.

Aleksandr realized then that he was angry. He usually didn't realize he was angry until it was too late, but today he was making a note of it as it was happening. Andronov seemed to tremble in his vision, and he heard the sound of an animal crashing through the forest somewhere in the very back of his head. He moved his king laterally. It breathed down the neck of Andronov's bishop.

"I thought being successful was a good thing," he said. He was keeping his voice neutral. He was making declarative statements. "I thought it would reflect well on the school. I thought you'd be— pleased." He'd almost said "proud."

"Pleased? No, tovarish." Andronov pulled at his temples, took off his glasses, and looked up at Aleksandr for the first time, maybe ever. His eyes were like little pearls in the endless nude folds of an oyster. "I'm neither pleased nor displeased by the successes or failures of my students. I'm here only to run an efficient chess academy, and your presence is not conducive to that." Andronov's bishop retreated by one square, futilely, and Aleksandr realized for the first time how badly Andronov had not wanted to lose.

"I see," said Aleksandr. He took Andronov's bishop with his king.

"Good," said Andronov. "Then we're in agreement. You will be gone by this afternoon." He gave a nod, disturbing his chins. The game, it seemed, was at an end.

Aleksandr walked out into the hallway and looked up at the high arching ceiling. Stingy, dirty-looking light streamed in through the great windows, giving the room a constant feeling of impending indoor rain. It was true he hadn't really learned anything here. But he'd liked the feeling of doing what he came to Leningrad for; he'd liked, too, the anesthetizing psychic disappearance he experienced when he beat the other men. He hadn't woken up excited to go to the academy, but at least he'd woken up knowing where he would go. He could not imagine a life in Leningrad without it. He could not understand what it would look like, how his days would organize themselves, what would prompt him to get out of bed or how anybody would know whether he was alive or what would keep him here at all, come to think of it. Surely there would be other tournaments, other successes ahead, but without the academy, there was nothing concrete tethering him to Leningrad. He could float away—into outer space, up into the hoary slopes of the forbidding north, back to Okha to kill the chickens for his mother. There was nothing keeping him here or anywhere. And in the absence of an excuse to be elsewhere, Aleksandr found himself heading to the bar across the street.

——

After an hour of drinking and self-pity, Aleksandr realized that the man sitting next to him was staring. Aleksandr pretended to crack his neck so as to get a look at him. When he turned, he caught the man's eye. His gaze was patient, and Aleksandr wondered how long he had been sitting there. "Cigarette?" said the man.

He was well groomed, though his nails were stained with cataracts of yellow nicotine, and his breath, when he leaned close, reminded Aleksandr of his own mortality. The man was an apparatchik.

"I don't smoke," said Aleksandr, moving slightly away.

The man stared at Aleksandr bemusedly for a moment. His nose was running in a way that made Aleksandr nervous. "You don't smoke," he said. "Of course you don't smoke. I feel I've read this about you."

For a buoyant moment, Aleksandr flattered himself that the man meant he'd read this about Aleksandr in the paper. But of course not.

"In my file," said Aleksandr. He'd known he probably had a file—it was even a little gratifying; it meant something about his game. But to hear it mentioned in public was startling. Its existence was understood but indecent, like the mechanics of human reproduction.

"Myself, I don't drink," said the man cheerfully. "So we're both deviant."

"You don't drink?"

"Not on the job, anyway. Even that's unusual enough, though." He leaned back; the miserly neon bar light made a corona around his head. "You drink, for example."

"I'm starting to need to."

"Alcoholism is a disease of capitalism." The man stubbed out his cigarette. "Anyway, you're young."

"I'm nineteen."

"That's gruesomely young."

"This is what they tell me."

At this, the man laughed, as though somebody had told him that Aleksandr was going to try very hard to be funny and that it was best to humor him. He made a show of dragging his arm along his eyes, as though wiping away tears of mirth. "Forgive me," he said, offering his hand and identification. "I haven't introduced myself. I'm Petr Pavlovich Nikitin. I'm something of a liaison between the Party and the game."

The ID confirmed him as a CPSU man, though his heavy suit and his manicured hands had already announced him. In the card's photograph, Petr Pavlovich was younger and thinner, looking startled and proud, his epaulettes too big for his shoulders. At the time, he must have been thrilled and shy and aghast to be given such a job.

Aleksandr took the man's hand, furious with himself for his own pathological niceness. The man's hands felt as velvety as they looked; the coarse buildup of nicotine on his nails was an incongruity, like scar tissue from some long-ago wound. Aleksandr realized that Ivan had warned him about this exact conversation.

"We understand you're finished at the academy," said Petr Pavlovich. "We understand you beat Andronov."

"That was quick. Did he call you himself?"

"Now, now. We're going to be good friends, you and I, as long as you don't ask direct questions."

"Was it Oleg? I didn't even know he could talk."

"Let's start over," said Petr Pavlovich. He ordered another round of shots, then produced a lighter from his pocket and gazed at the flame a moment too long before he lit up. When he smoked, his lips made a little spanking sound around the cigarette. "Let's start over. I've been unclear. A player like you, you're a credit to the Soviet Union. You remind the world who the best chess players are."

Aleksandr took the first of his two shots. He didn't usually drink Stoli, but all the state-produced vodka tasted the same. He wanted to tell the man to fuck off, though it would be a shame to give up his career when it was just starting to take off. Anyway, Aleksandr had never told anybody to fuck off. Politeness was his paralysis, and he would have to abandon it someday. But not, he thought, just yet. "Thank you," he said.

"I notice that you haven't yet joined the Party."

Aleksandr rotated his shot glass between his fingers. He looked at the reflection of his thumb in the alcohol, lumpy and distorted. "No," he said. "I guess I haven't."

"An oversight due to youth, no doubt." Petr Pavlovich, still smoking too loudly for comfort, smacked his lips in satisfaction at this pronouncement.

Aleksandr said nothing, which was—along with chess—one of his great strengths in life.

"You live in the kommunalka, am I correct?"

"Yes."

"Crowded there, I'd suppose. Plumbing issues, I'd imagine."

Aleksandr thought of the worms in the faucet. "Some."

"You'd probably like a private apartment, I'd think?"

"I have my own room."

"That is indeed very fortunate," said Petr Pavlovich grandly. "But surely you'd like a little more privacy? A little more space? You have, what? Eight meters? Nine?"

Aleksandr thought of his room. He thought of its cramped dampness, the infrequent hissing of its atavistic radiator. He thought of his piles of chess magazines and how he was always sleeping on them by accident.

"A young man like you," said Petr Pavlovich, "you probably have a special woman in your life. You're probably thinking about starting a family."

Aleksandr said nothing. If only the man knew how inappropriate this particular approach was.

"Or maybe I'm getting it wrong," said Petr Pavlovich. "Maybe not one special woman but several? Even so, more space would be nice. More privacy, undoubtedly. A nice little dacha out in the woods, maybe. A gorgeous view and wildflowers in the summer. A place to play chess with designated visitors. Holidays on the Volga. Sound nice?"

Aleksandr embarked mournfully on his second shot of vodka.

"They said you were quiet," said Petr Pavlovich. "But you're practically catatonic. I'll make a note of it in your file."

"I'm quite content in my room."

"I highly doubt that. But even if you are, you know there's a lot else we can do for you. Travel. Exit visas for vacations. You can shop at the Party stores. Better meat, maybe? You like food? You like women? You like anything?"

Aleksandr thought of the mustard-yellow tins of stringy reserve beef at the state store; he thought of the bruised eggplants, rotting on the side that didn't show through the packaging. He thought of the air of the kommunalka, stale with the smells of old cooking and feet wrapped in too many socks. Then he thought of a dacha in a shady woods during a cool summer; he thought of caviar and wine and fresh produce, all laid out on a table under a gently heaving tree. He thought of beautiful women who were the perfect inversions of Elizabeta— they'd be blond, where she was dark; they'd be fawning, where she was indifferent; they'd be generically interchangeable, where she was stubbornly singular.

"You understand me, I think," said Petr Pavlovich. "You're a magnificent chess player. But you can be better. You can be a credit to the Party, and we can be a credit to you."

Aleksandr contemplated his empty shot glasses. "I don't know that that's the case."

"Listen," said Petr Pavlovich abruptly, and all of a sudden Aleksandr could feel the man's energy shift gears. "You should probably stop hanging around with that Ivan Dmietrivich."

Aleksandr put down his glass too loudly. "What?"

"Another, sir." Petr Pavlovich tapped the bar, and Aleksandr downed another shot. His eyes watered shamefully. The lozenges of light coming through the window looked fatalistic. Petr Pavlovich stood up.

"Don't be foolish, Aleksandr. Don't get mixed up in all that."

Aleksandr stood up, too, shakily. He reached for his wallet, but Petr Pavlovich stopped him with a soft hand.

"Please, Aleksandr Kimovich," he said. "Think about what I've said. But the drink—accept it as a token of our hearty congratulations. It's on us."

———

Twenty minutes later, Aleksandr stumbled to the Saigon, where the bartender eyed him skeptically but said nothing. As usual, the café was filled to the rafters with smoke and conspiracy. The man in the wheelchair had positioned himself near the doorway this time; patrons picked their careful way around him and scurried past his dark pronouncements. When Aleksandr walked past, he saw that the man's hair was flecked sparsely with bits of bread. Nobody asked him to leave. It was an unjust world.

When he saw Aleksandr, the man turned gray with excitement and leaned close, opening the black globe of his mouth. "Leonid Ilyich is here, oh, God, he's here," he shrieked, and Aleksandr tried hard not to stumble in surprise. He'd been expecting a whisper, some secret insane confidence, not a shriek, and the man's shouting voice was unexpectedly shrill. It turned Aleksandr's heart inside out in the way of ancient, irrational fears—the sight of things that crawl and skitter, the feel of a presence behind your neck.

"What?" said Aleksandr. He tried elbowing past the man, who groped for Aleksandr's hands and missed. Aleksandr wondered momentarily whether the man could still see.

"Brezhnev. He's right there." The man gestured toward the depression in the wall where Ivan and Nikolai were sitting, their smoke unfurling into dust-colored fronds. "He's here. I promise you that. He's everywhere."

Aleksandr disentangled himself from the man's searching hands, from his long fingers that fluttered through the air as though playing an enormous pipe organ, and scrambled away in revulsion. At their usual table, Nikolai and Ivan were sitting with an enormous stack of newspapers between them. Blue overheard lights caught their vodka and splashed marine onto the table. Nikolai was scratching into an enormous notebook and laughing, his legume face contorting into strange creases. He was wearing a new leather jacket. Aleksandr was not sure he'd ever seen Nikolai laugh.

"That man," said Nikolai, gesturing to the man in the wheelchair, who still sat shrieking at his invisible audience, "is clinically insane."

"He's a prophet, maybe," said Ivan. "Descended from Rasputin. What say you, Aleksandr? Do you believe that stuff in the east?"

"Please," said Nikolai. "Give the boy a break. He's important now, you know." He stubbed his Iskra into the ashtray. It curled like a giardia against the others.

"In the great Soviet states," said Ivan, "no man is more important than another. So what's the story with you, Aleksandr? Aren't you famous yet? Shouldn't you be off knocking back shots with Party officials? Getting to know a better class of prostitute?"

"Okay," said Aleksandr. Fuck Andronov. Fuck, quite possibly, everybody. "I'll leave, then."

"Stay, stay," said Nikolai solicitously. "Ivan, you must be gentler with the boy."

"You're getting to be a pretty big deal, yes?" said Ivan blithely, ruffling the newspapers. "We just saw something about you. Nikolai, didn't we just see something? In *Literaturnaya Gazeta,* yes? Is that possible, Aleksandr?"

"I don't know," said Aleksandr. He hadn't meant to sound as

miserable as he felt. He found himself putting his head on the table, letting his forehead absorb the cool of the wood. He imagined the tree that the wood came from—in a great forest on the Black Sea, maybe, its roots strangled by salt water, its pale green leaves shifting savagely in the wind. Maybe it came from the north. Maybe it was a small tree, demented by the lacerations of tundra gales, standing shriveled and bent against the odds. Aleksandr squinted and saw the bottles above the bar make a smear of watery gemstones.

"Are you drunk?" said Nikolai. He turned to Ivan. "Is he drunk?"

"That would be unprecedented. He's clearly just lost his mind. Aleksandr, have you perhaps lost your mind?" In Ivan's voice, Aleksandr noted a certain hapless tenderness, as though Ivan were an awkward father trying to handle a sickly baby. Aleksandr could hear Nikolai's jowls stirring in curiosity.

"I got expelled from the academy," Alexandr whispered into the wood. He wanted to keep his face on the tabletop as long as he could. It was possible, he realized with horror, that he was crying.

"I told you," said Nikolai. He lowered his voice to a solemn baritone rasp. "I told you he was a bit unstable. I told you he didn't warrant confidences."

"I'm fine," said Aleksandr. "I am completely fine." But his neck felt unbearably heavy, as though filled with sand or guilt. Had he been arrogant? He hadn't thought so; he'd always been the one with an extended hand left out after his opponent had turned away in an odd swirl of disappointment and derision. But when he tried to think of going back to Okha—to live among his chickens and his sisters, to let Leningrad and chess become the ever fading memory of a dream or hallucination—he couldn't quite stand it. He had to admit to himself that he'd liked the feeling of winning. He'd liked having something to be humble and gracious about.

"I thought you didn't like the academy," said Ivan. "I thought you were bored by it."

Aleksandr dug his chin harder into the table. Above him, he could hear words mouthed and a head vigorously shaken. Finally, he felt an anonymous hand on his shoulder; from its fleshy coarseness, he figured that it had to be Nikolai's.

"I didn't, really," said Aleksandr. "I was bored." The wood was cooler now; its surface seemed to provoke small eddies in the air, and he could feel himself falling into a pleasing emptiness. "I just don't really know what I'm going to do now."

Another pause—filled with some sort of silent negotiation and punctuated by a guttural grunt from Nikolai—concluded with Ivan saying, "You'll come and work for us, I suppose."

Aleksandr's head filled back up, and he saw his life turn precariously on its axle and round a corner. Sprigs of sweat burst out on his skin, and he gulped hard at the redness consuming his throat. He was afraid to look up.

"Nikolai, honestly," said Ivan. "Please give this man your vodka."

———

Ivan and Nikolai, it turned out, wrote a monthly pamphlet, and they brought Aleksandr over to show it off to him. Ivan's room was tiny, the floor covered wall-to-wall with imbricate books and papers and bits of trash. In certain corners, Aleksandr caught the faintly arctic smell of mold. A typewriter sat atop a stack of books in the center of the room. Above the television, Brigitte Bardot gazed knowingly out of a poster, her midsection creased from multiple moves. Ivan had been a lecturer at a university before he'd been fired for anti-Soviet agitation—"the dissidents are the only unemployed in the Soviet Union," he said as he poured Aleksandr a tumbler of kvass. He'd only just moved into this apartment after five years of waiting for a propiska, and he was convinced that it wasn't bugged yet. Ivan had an enormous number of books, though the quotas meant he had to buy five political tracts for every one Turgenev. They stood in great multicolored stacks, arranged as carefully as tables and chairs. A one-eyed tortoiseshell cat stood among them, assailing them with nuzzles and purrs.

"That's Natasha," said Ivan, petting the cat with his toe. "My one true friend in this life." He set down a plate of shashlik on a stack of old *Sovetskaya Kultura* and winked at the cat. Nikolai crouched on the carpet and busied himself with the shashlik, and Aleksandr did the same. It was odd to see Nikolai and Ivan outside the café—in broad daylight, squatting, smacking their lips, eating sausage—when he'd only ever known them at the café, haloed by smoke and illegal ideas. Above them, the typewriter loomed. It seemed like the chassis on which the entire apartment was holding itself up.

"You do the pamphlet on the typewriter?" said Aleksandr.

"Right," said Ivan.

"You stole that from the university?"

"I bribed a customs official. The university has all the typewriters registered."

Aleksandr took a bite of shashlik, which was salty as blood, and looked around some more. There were fist-sized clumps of dust in the corners, and the glass that Aleksandr was drinking from, when he held it to the light, was pocked with remnants of milky drinks long gone.

"And you type up the pamphlet here?" said Aleksandr.

"That's the idea," said Ivan. "We get submissions from friends. Poetry, prose, accounting of arrests. The accounting of arrests is the most important part. No offense meant to the poets, of course. We type up the original and make carbon copies. You can only get about eight before the quality is too degraded to use. We do that a few more times until I'm out of ink or out of my mind. Each recipient is supposed to make a few more carbon copies and pass those along. With each iteration, a couple of people fall off the rails, but it gets respectably far that way."

"How often is this?"

"Every three weeks or so."

Aleksandr looked at Nikolai, who was staring out the window and gumming his shashlik meditatively. He wasn't paying attention, or perhaps he was pretending not to pay attention. He was still wearing the leather jacket, and Aleksandr wondered about that, fleetingly. It looked well-made, which meant foreign-made—Italian, perhaps—though that was impossible.

"Can I see it?" said Aleksandr to Ivan.

Ivan opened a drawer fast enough that Aleksandr knew he had been waiting to be asked. "Of course," he said, producing a pamphlet. "Here." When he leaned close, Aleksandr could smell the kvass—somehow acrid and dusty both—on his breath. Ivan flushed as he handed Aleksandr the journal. It was strange to see Ivan want something, and stranger still that the something should be Aleksandr's approval.

The cover was dull, with oddly small black font. It didn't look like the kind of journal a person would idly pick up; there was no promise that anything of interest lay within. In fact, the cover seemed to suggest that the contents might include an essay on metaphysics, or a survey of current breakthroughs in agricultural technology. Aleksandr opened it anyway. The first page was an anonymous introduction, clearly written by Ivan. ("Friends," it read. "We convene in these pages, once more, to take stock of our situation and ourselves. . . .") Then there was an oblique poem that Aleksandr read three times and still didn't understand, though it seemed to be dwelling on the subject of "capitulation" at some length. There was an essay about rereading Bulgakov for modern times. And then a grim report of arrests, detentions, searches around Leningrad in the past month. This was the longest section of the journal—pages and pages of dates and names and abuses, without comment, in tiny lettering. The section was called "A Partial History of Lost Causes," which was also the name of the journal.

"It's incomplete," said Ivan. "We don't even try to get it complete. It's just a sample, really. You get the general character of the month— what they were most interested in and what they got."

Aleksandr stared at the account. Here there were arrests for misuse of state machines (he thought of the ill-gotten typewriter lurking in the living room), and here there was a detention for "disseminating falsehood" (he thought of how the very line that accounted that detention might be considered officially false), and here there was an imprisonment for "malicious parasitism" (this meant unemployment, which Aleksandr was, by any measure, afflicted with), and here there was a midnight search on the grounds of conspiracy (he looked around at the contracting tendons of Ivan's neck as he swallowed hard, the inflamed stare of Nikolai as he looked at everything except Aleksandr, and wondered how much he trusted them). He put the pamphlet down. He leaned toward Ivan. "I got approached by an official tonight," he said. "They offered me a dacha."

Ivan nodded. "They want you to join."

"Yes."

"You have a file."

"Of course."

"And you said no to them?"

"Of *course*."

"There must be something very compelling about that building of yours."

"He told me not to hang around with you."

"Very sound advice."

"They know about this?"

"It's not a secret. Nothing is a secret. Maybe exactly who we are, what we're about, that might be a secret. Who our contributors are and who all of our subscribers are—those are secrets, too. The details are a secret. But the fact is not. We are not a secret. Your involvement, quickly, will not be a secret. KGB has asked you a question, and here you will be giving an answer."

Aleksandr remembered the silken hands of Petr Pavlovich, he remembered the admonishment not to be foolish. Not bad advice, all things considered.

"Even though we're not a secret," said Ivan, "you need to behave always as though we are. Crucially, you need not to be followed, because we don't want to let go of our details. You and me and Nikolai here, we're worthless bachelors, and who could care what happens to us." Aleksandr could not decide whether this level of indifference was something to admire or disdain or fear.

"But we have subscribers, we have contributors, with families," said Ivan. "We need to minimize their chances of arrest. Thus, we need to be as discreet as possible, all the while remembering that we're not kidding ourselves. Okay? Luckily, the KGB isn't as artful as you might think. Sometimes there will literally be a white Volga driving slowly around the city, waiting for you at corners." He took a swallow of kvass and grimaced slightly. "But sometimes it will be a bit subtler. The best you can do is zig and zag around the streets. Don't take the same route habitually, and never start coming here on a routine. Find plausible reasons to be wherever you're going—the culinary store, the footwear store. And if you think you're being followed, bore them to death."

"Okay," said Aleksandr slowly. He stared at his glass. Cloudy filaments drifted through the kvass like seaweed in a briny sea. "I'm pretty sure I can do that much."

"The bottom line is that you will be known. You will be noticed. It will go in your file. At the same time, you can never, never be followed, because we need to protect the others. You can never have any information on your person. No lists. No addresses. No maps. But this is no challenge for a man of such formidable memory, yes?"

"I think I can manage."

"You get called in for questioning, you're gone, okay? You think someone's followed you here, you go sit in the park for an hour, and then you get back on the metro and go home and never come back."

"You never come back," said Nikolai severely. "We won't be offended."

Aleksandr stared at Nikolai. "I like your jacket," he said.

Nikolai took a gulp of kvass and looked down.

"Aleksandr," said Ivan, twirling a tether of sausage on his bent fork, "you are blessed with a face and manner that nobody can recall. I'm too tall, and Nikolai's too ugly—forgive me, Nikolai—to blend in a crowd. You are anonymous. Not to the authorities, of course. But to the people they ask to describe you. If they harass a subscriber and ask him who brought the journal, what's he going to say? Oh, the man was not so tall, not so short, brown hair, plain face, two eyes, and a nose? It will make it difficult for them to figure out exactly what you are doing, exactly where you have been. And nobody around you will ever suspect you. You look too dumb to be up to anything."

"Okay," said Aleksandr. "Wonderful. It's nice to be appreciated."

"Indeed," said Ivan, returning his sausage to the plate without eating it. "Welcome to distribution."

Distribution meant waking up very early in the morning, following carefully memorized directions to obsessively confirmed addresses, and knocking. Aleksandr wore a heavy hat for this, which took on a rich animal smell in precipitation, and he tilted it forward so that it cast dark shadows over his dark face. This was in case anyone recognized him—in case anyone looked up from his paper one morning and wondered what Aleksandr Bezetov, subject of a small feature article in *Literaturnaya Gazeta,* was doing riding public transportation. But, as he learned from walking around the city anonymously in the afternoons—after his route was over and his hat was off and he turned his face up toward the wilting sun—it was probably an unnecessary precaution.

He met interesting people this way—the subscriber list was small but diverse and full of people Aleksandr never would have expected. There were women, for one thing, and older people, and one or two people who'd been forced to make public self-denunciations that year. He'd been provided with detailed descriptions of their physical appearance. If anybody else answered the door, he asked directions to the metro in his best approximation of broken Russian until that door was slammed. The client list was always under twenty people. Occasionally, a new person who'd gained the trust of Ivan and Nikolai at the Saigon might be added to the list; occasionally, somebody got paranoid or got a promotion and frantically, rudely told Aleksandr to please never, never come back. And so he didn't.

Some mornings he spent walking around the city, other mornings he spent taking the metro, and many mornings were a combination of both: riding the metro a few stops and then walking a mile only to reconnect with the metro again. This was Ivan's idea, and it was the way Aleksandr came to feel he owned and understood the city: the constant early-morning romping that brought him down into the elegant bowels of the station, ornate and ostentatious and reinforced against nuclear attack; then up into the weak white of a Leningrad dawn, trudging into the mist while the city around him became a phantom and then a specter and then a silhouette; then back down to the metro, where the men hurried and jostled and the lights dripped like the chandeliers on the *Titanic.*

It was on a metro morning in what was allegedly spring that Aleksandr saw Elizabeta at work. She was standing on a subway platform at five A.M., half hanging off the arm of an enormous man who looked like a dinosaur. She was at the very end of her night, Aleksandr figured. Her black attire that moved as though it were its own system, with its own provocative ideas, looked undone somehow; her face, still almost beautiful, looked older. There were bluish pits of fatigue under her eyes, and her makeup seemed miscalculated. The man's great forehead was like a shelf overhanging his face. He leaned close to Elizabeta and said something to her, and she laughed the same laugh she had used with the steward.

Aleksandr would tell himself later that he almost went to her. He thought about it. He really thought about it. He could go gather her up with him, bring him on his mission, pay the man back whatever he had spent on her, with interest, and then run laughing out into the street, leaving the man behind to shift his prehistoric mass in anger and confusion.

But there was work to do—for him and, he knew, for Elizabeta. And work, of course, was sacred. So he stopped watching and turned away and kept moving, up the enormous, unending staircase that led to the city and the day.

6

IRINA

MOSCOW, 2006

My flight landed at Sheremetyevo at night, but the line at customs was long. Angling over the landscape during our rickety descent, I'd watched the weak lights that Moscow cast up into the universe, and I was struck by how small they seemed in comparison to the rest of it: the enormity, the darkness. The flight had been long—the six hours over the churning Atlantic, the three hours chewing overpriced and mysterious British sandwiches at Heathrow, and the last restless, hiccuping leg of the journey to Russia. The flight attendants had been conspiratorial and hostile. I'd flipped through my Russian 3 book and tried to order a soda. They'd rolled their eyes and looked me up and down and asked me in English whether I might prefer a diet. I'd pressed my face against the cool window and looked out and asked myself: How? Why? For what?

———

What happened was Jonathan wanted me to move in with him. We were in love, I guess, and moving in together, in our culture, is part of the natural progression of that particular disease. I'd told him yes, and then I'd told him maybe, and then I'd told him I was leaving the country forever.

I knew that I could not move in with Jonathan. I knew—really, I knew—that we had been playacting. The sentiment was real enough, I suppose, but the rest was composed of gestures imitating the behavior of other people, people who had an entire future to love and fail each other. And there was something almost insulting in his asking—something patronizing at worst and willfully clueless at best. It was as though he had not been paying attention. I was thirty. I was in my last year or two of sound body and mind. I was not going to move in with Jonathan only to have him watch whatever things he'd improbably loved about me disappear. I don't sentimentalize love so much that I think it can endure such assault. It's one thing to love a person who is absent; it's quite another to love a person who is reduced and deformed and endlessly, endlessly present. I had loved my father once. Did I love the person he was when he died? I don't know. What person was that?

I was going to leave Jonathan. Once I'd decided that, it seemed only right to leave everything else.

The night after Jonathan asked me, I came home to my empty apartment alone. I took out the letter my father had sent to Aleksandr Bezetov, and the terse reply from Elizabeta Nazarovna. I thought again about my father having to live and die with all his best questions unanswered. I thought again about Aleksandr Bezetov. I couldn't help but hate him a little. All that energy and intelligence and, crucially, all that time—that whole average life expectancy—and he couldn't find it within himself to answer my poor dying father's few questions, abstract and intrusive though they were. It seemed like such a pittance for a man who had so much. It seemed so stingy to delegate a response— a nonresponse at that—to your secretary or whatever.

I looked again at the letter from the secretary. There was that vaguely sorry, vaguely sheepish tone, as though she knew that this was not the proper way of things. Elizabeta Nazarovna. Quite a mouthful, that.

I went to the computer. I typed in "Elizabeta Nazarovna" and "St. Petersburg." I squinted through the Cyrillic and sounded out words. There was a birth announcement for a baby born in 1998. There was a reference to a dissident poet who had died in the purges. There were pictures of a very young woman from a social networking site. She had perfectly manicured hair and the long furry arms of an anorexic, and in every single photo she held a different swirly, improbably colored cocktail. There was a woman running a store selling vintage Communist paraphernalia. I clicked through an interminable number of Elizabetas: old, newborn, implicated, expatriated. And then, to my everlasting chagrin, I began calling them.

I made rules for myself: I called only people who lived in Moscow or St. Petersburg (nobody who'd ever lived in Leningrad would go back to the country, I figured, not if they could help it). I ruled out people who were too old or too young. I ruled out people who'd had professions in the seventies or early eighties. I got mostly wrong numbers and dial tones and a coldhearted, impossibly fast-speaking operator who furiously chastised me for a transgression beyond my understanding. I reached a child Elizabeta. I reached an uncomprehending Elizabeta. I reached the widower of a dead Elizabeta. Finally, I reached an Elizabeta with a faint, strangely fragile voice that said, "Da? Da?"

This wasn't her, either, I didn't think. She sounded like a particularly technophobic grandmother, somebody who talked at the phone as though the person she was addressing was actually inside it. What the hell, I thought, was I doing?

"Zdrastvuytye," I said carefully. "Minya zavut Irina Ellison. Govorite po angielski?" Though I thought I could manage all of it in Russian, I figured it would be embarrassing enough in English. No need to make it worse, if that could be avoided.

There was a pause the length and temperature of the Cold War.

"Yes," she said at last in English. "What do you want?" She sounded like she thought I was selling something, which was a reasonable conclusion. I've found that most people are selling something, even if they don't always know what.

"This may sound odd," I said. "But my father was a correspondent of Aleksandr Bezetov. Do you remember him?" I tried to keep my voice gentle and supplicating, a posture I'm not particularly good at adopting. I waited. There was another glacial silence, and I worried that I'd offended her. She was probably old, probably forgetful, and who knew what her relationship to Bezetov had been, and here I was asking her to grope for Gorbachev-era memories. I started to imagine kind ways to disentangle myself from the conversation—confusion about inverted numbers, swapped identities. But through the haze of my discomfort, which was expanding rapidly, filling up the silence, came her voice again, stronger this time, more certain.

"Aleksandr Bezetov," she said, and I could hear her thawing out. Her voice had changed to clinking glass; behind it, I could hear the glinting echoes of laughter. "Yes. I believe I remember a thing or two about him. That dumb kid."

I'd never thought of the esteemed Aleksandr Bezetov as a kid, and I tried to think of the kind of woman who would. She'd have to be old, for one thing—older than I was ever going to be, anyway.

"You worked for him?" I said.

"Not exactly."

"But you knew him?"

Another pause. This one was fuller somehow—rife with silent memories that seemed to register in the crackles of the telephone wire.

"Yes."

I hung up the phone.

———

When you get ready to die, you look back over a lifetime and try to unravel its enduring questions. You retroactively assign meaning to chaos, you make coincidence into portent. You scan your past for moments that might have been road signs, and then you try to see which way they were pointing. It's an unrelenting striving for tenuous links, a dazed hunting for patterns that may or may not exist. You are a child looking for a lost thing in the sand, racing against the tide and the approaching darkness, trying desperately to remember where you might have buried it.

When I scanned my life, I found an alarming lack of loose ends. Bezetov, in a way, felt like a loose end.

So I thought about Russia: cold and vast, criminal and corrupt and possessed of an impossible language, hostile to foreigners and women traveling alone. Then I thought about trying to sort through what few mysteries remained to me.

I double-checked my savings account: large from a lifetime of modest pay but too responsible living. I double-checked my age: one year, four months until average age of onset. I double-checked Elizabeta Nazarovna's name and address.

It was logistically easy—almost too easy. I wasn't trying to disappear. I was just trying to wrap up. But the accumulated attachments and obligations of an entire abbreviated lifetime took, in the end, under a week to resolve. I found myself wishing to leave behind a somewhat messier life. I half hoped that something would come up—an unknown bastard child, or a court case, or a professional emergency—that would require my attention, that would grab at me with insistent hands and pull me back to Boston and my life. But nothing did. I'd lived a life of relative simplicity and organization. I'd lived a life with an eye to leaving it. And here I was, leaving it, just as tidily as a traveler who doesn't bother to unpack at the hotel room because she knows the time there is limited.

I withdrew my stocks and my savings. I submitted my final grades for my final cast of students, and then I submitted my resignation. I left three months' rent for my landlord. I spent some time on the Internet. I spent some time counting the number of whims indulged in a lifetime (none, discernibly, in my case). And then I spent some time saying goodbye—which, like everything, is easier if you've got a head start.

I told everybody—mother, doctor, college friends, co-workers—that I was going on a trip. It was going to be meandering, I said, and spontaneous and luxurious and self-indulgent and, most important, very long. I said that I wanted to see the world while I still could; I said that I wanted to have an adventure on my own while I could still do anything on my own. My co-workers were supportive. My mother, I am sure, was relieved. People who'd never spoken of my diagnosis, people who'd never asked about my father, were thrilled to have a concrete and explicable and ultimately positive way to obliquely reference it. They talked about what an important decision it was. They talked about what a self-actualizing trip it would be. If they secretly thought

I'd chosen an odd locale for my final vacation, they had the courtesy not to mention it.

I gave Jonathan the same line, more or less, though he understood me well enough to know that it probably was not true, that I was probably never coming back. He was disbelieving, of course, grief-stricken, angry, all that. He thought I was bluffing; he thought I was losing it. He wanted me to go to counseling.

I wasn't bluffing, although I probably wasn't at the most mentally stable moment of my entire life. But I wanted to say—and finally did during one of those last awful nights that I will spend the rest of my life trying not to remember—look: I am not the one who's delusional. I am not the one with a distorted vision of reality.

Ultimately, what could he do? I am an adult woman and a United States citizen; financially independent; capable of affording an expedited visa. He couldn't stop me, the way nobody can really stop anyone from leaving them, in the end.

———

A few days before I left, I went to play my last game with Lars. It was May, and the air was silky. It didn't feel like a day to play chess, but I wanted someone to talk to. This, however, was not to be. Lars raised his eyebrows at me and said nothing. "Hello, old man," I said when I sat down. "How've you been?" He shrugged and gestured beatifically to the chessboard.

"What?" I squinted. "Is something wrong with you?" Lars looked the same as usual—dishwater-gray hair, a sunburned nose, the personal presentation of a person who sleeps habitually under bridges—but his eyes shone with higher than usual spirits. He handed me a card.

In response to my recent detention by the FASCIST CAMBRIDGE POLICE, for disturbing the peace by singing, I have taken a vow of silence. Please support me in my endeavors to combat the FAS-CIST PIGS' attempts to abolish LIFE, ART, and FREEDOM in our hometown.

"You got arrested? For singing?" Lars's eyes flickered, and he pointed to the word "detention" in the note. "Detained? For *singing*?"

He nodded solemnly.

"Okay," I said. "I guess that's about right."

Then we sat quietly and began to play our usual game. My heart wasn't in it, so he went easy on me, I realize—I came closer to beating him that day than I probably ever had. But I did not win. And now, I suppose, I never will.

"You are almost no fun at all without language," I said halfway through the game. Lars stuck out his tongue, I guess to convey that he was at least a little bit fun without language.

"It's too bad that you don't want to talk," I said. "Because I have news."

He turned his face to the side and narrowed his eyes. Lars loves to gossip, and I knew it would bother him to have to abstain from gossiping, even in the service of his noble political objectives. He grabbed a pen and flipped his petition over. *What?* he wrote.

And so I began to talk. And talk. I rambled with uncharacteristic fluidity, unhinged and incoherent and even more self-absorbed than usual. What I was getting at, I guess, was that I was terrified, although I never would have come flat out and said so, to Lars or to anyone. Lars could tell, though—you don't achieve his heights of success in life without an instinctive ability to read people—and he watched me swirl my coffee, ignore my muffin, and knock over my pawns with an expression of mounting disgust. I was midway through a monologue about the relative merits of a quiet departure from Jonathan's life before he could see my brain break down, when Lars couldn't take it anymore. He nearly spat out his coffee and his five weeks of silence along with it.

"Oh, please," he said. "Don't you know that you *like* to feel this way? You like to brood. It is, I am afraid, your limited charm."

"You're talking."

"You drove me to it."

"I don't brood. I contemplate."

"What do you want me to say to you?" His eyebrows waggled mournfully, and he offered me his castle in despair. "You never listen. That's why you never get any better at chess."

"I've gotten better," I said, watching the castle, trying to catch sight of whatever gruesome trick he might be baiting me for. "Haven't I?"

"No," he said. "You haven't."

"Oh." I took the castle and waited—waited for the wire to be tripped, the world to crash down on me, a plague of bishops to fall on my besieged head. But nothing happened. He skimmed his knight over into the neighborhood of my queen. For now, at least for now, I had sustained a minor victory.

"Look, if you want to run away, run away. I'm not stopping you."

"Obviously."

"But maybe you should stay with this man for a little bit. He's probably very dull but unlikely to be any duller than you. You have some sex, you know? It will be good for you. Sex, yes? You've heard of it?"

"I can't remember."

"It will be good for you. It will make you smile. You are always so serious." He made a mock-serious face at me. His cheeks puffed out and his eyes shone earnestly.

"You look like Kim Jong Il."

"Or don't. Fine. You want to be sad and sorry, you go ahead. Probably better for your game this way."

"That's a primary concern of mine."

"Yes. I am sure. Check your king."

As I was on my way out of the game and the conversation, Lars actually grabbed my lapel and pulled me down, close to his graying face. He blinked at me reproachfully. "Look," he said. "Since I'm already talking, since you've already ruined my petition, I'll tell you something. You know what your problem is?"

"I daresay I do."

"You are afraid to have anything you care about leaving," he said victoriously, as though he'd just toppled my king for exactly the one thousandth time in a row—which, it's entirely possible, he already had.

"What?" I said. "There are a lot of things I care about leaving."

"No," said Lars, sitting back down on his concrete slab, his voice thickening into something deeper, more somber. Usually, his voice tripped lightly between stories and lies, advice and aphorism—the ongoing banter of a magician who is trying, ultimately, to keep you from seeing what he's doing. Now his voice dropped a register; his accent seemed to flatten slightly. "Right now," he said, "the only thing you can't stand to leave is yourself. Maybe there are other things you like. Maybe there are other people you enjoy. Your old pal Lars, for example. But the only thing you absolutely cannot bear to lose is your own—what? Self-knowledge?"

I squirmed in my seat. "Self-awareness, maybe."

"Self-awareness. You are in love with your own self-awareness."

"I am fond of my own self-awareness, sure," I said, trying to sound reasonable, nondefensive, restrained. "Isn't everyone, though?"

"Some of us more than others, maybe."

I scanned Harvard Square for a moment—the ebb and flow of multicolored humanity, the rotating courses of individuals with their competing agendas and dreams and plans for the day. The girls who marched through the square in business attire, making international phone calls, were starting to look heartbreakingly young to me. One of them stood still, holding a bouquet of flowers in one arm and her phone in the other, talking angrily in what I thought was Mandarin Chinese.

"Your life has been too quiet," Lars said decisively, and I drew my attention back to him. "Your life has been too lonely."

I looked into my coffee cup hard and noticed with some alarm that there was a shimmering sheen floating across the top.

"Well," I said, trying to fight down the minor seizure happening in my throat. "I'm thinking of going to Russia."

"To Russia?" He sat back. "Why? Your beloved old pedophile?" He meant Nabokov.

I shook my head. "No." I sucked in my cheeks and straightened up in my chair. "I want to meet Aleksandr Bezetov. The chess player."

"Ah," said Lars, looking at his nails with interest. "Thinking of challenging him to a game?"

"My father and he were correspondents, actually." I said this huffily, in the overly offhand way that people mention things they are desperately, embarrassingly proud of.

"Indeed?" he said. His eyes twinkled with an elfin merriment that might have been endearing were it not so self-satisfied. I waited for him to ask about the details but realized he wasn't going to. Lars's brush with political dissidence had made him patient, stoic.

"They were correspondents before my father was ill."

Lars's tufts of gray hair were starting to be backlit by the afternoon sun, and in silhouette they made his head look either haloed or horned. "You know," he said, "I drove across Soviet Russia in the eighties. Nasty place. The women, though. The women there are amazing." I waited for him to say more, but he didn't. With a wave of his hand, he relegated this trip, with whatever dangers and briberies it had involved or should have involved, to the vast vault of items deemed none of my business.

"Well, great," I said. "I don't trouble myself with countries possessed of substandard women." His face was taking on a sentimental look, arranging itself into a far-off gaze and a wistful smile, an expression worthy of double-edged regrets and state secrets. I was losing his attention. We were sinking back into the realm of the fictive—whatever shreds of reality just emerged were going to disappear under churning waves of sarcasm, speculation, and story. "Enough," I said. "Stop that right now." I stood up, and this time I meant it.

His face refocused slightly with the momentary clarity of a poker player who suddenly knows that his opponent isn't kidding around. "Irina," he said.

"Yes."

"It's good for you to have an adventure."

"I think so, too."

"You'll send me a postcard, won't you?"

"Sure."

"And," he said. "Just think of how many stories you'll have to tell me when you get back." He hugged me. He smelled of ash, with wilder undertones of coffee and sky and liquor before noon. And then he clapped me on the back, and I turned and walked down Mass Ave. I left him there, sitting on his block, reorganizing his pieces, and though I have no way of knowing for sure, I would imagine that he's sitting there still.

I shuffled forward in line at Sheremetyevo, squinting at the Cyrillic on the signs and mouthing words to myself. I proffered my papers and had them stamped glumly, suspiciously. I coursed through mobs of older, cabbage-scented women; younger women with clacking talons and color-leeched hair; shifty-eyed men who shuffled and cut the lines. Everybody seemed to know better than to complain.

"Business or pleasure?" said the customs official, his head cocked to one side, his expression an unlikely blend of paranoid suspicion and boredom.

I thought about it for a moment. Pleasure seemed absurd as I looked past the man and into the airport—at the fraying upholstery on the walls and the truncated skeletons of what must have, at one point, been chairs. The air was bizarrely cold. Forlorn old women squatted by the windows. Women my age manned kiosks, their gum snapping like rubber bands against skin. A dog with the size and grace of a hyena stalked one corner, and nothing in his manner suggested that he was employed by the airport.

"Business or pleasure, please?" the man said again, his tone suggesting that he might be offering me firing squad or lethal injection.

"Business." As soon as I said it, I knew it to be true.

The air outside was muggy and chilled at the same time. It was the kind of weird weather that creeps up on you, makes you sweat under your jacket and then makes your sweat turn to ice. A line of taxicabs lurked along the curb; the drivers had the fierce look of men who tamed wild things for a living. I hailed one and situated myself in its backseat. I produced from my pocket my hostel information and Elizabeta's phone number and address. My eyes were dry and feeling slightly dislodged. This whole thing was already feeling like a suspect undertaking.

"Maly Zlatoustinskiy, please," I said. We peeled out of the airport parking lot. Clouds were starting to clot along the horizon, and I watched bone-colored housing units begin to take shape beneath them. The outside of the city was as anonymous and dour as rural semi-civilization anywhere; when I rolled down the window and felt the dirty rain smack against my cheek, watched the bright yellow cellphone ads materialize, and smelled the exhaust, I felt as if I might have been in New Jersey. As we got closer to the city, though, I could feel foreignness start to accumulate like weather. Along the road were stands selling pastries, with hand-printed signs in Cyrillic, stark black lettering against cardboard. Small, scoured-looking trees squatted against the wind. The wind was different, too: it had an untrammeled quality, as though it had sailed without interruption across a country frighteningly vast. I thought of the map of my father's above the chess sets in his study: the chicken-fat-yellow USSR, hunched above the world like a jaguar in a tree, waiting to pounce. Even now, even reduced by history and one-third of its landmass, I thought I could feel something of its size as I looked out the window. The plains crashed into the white sky like an ocean on a flat earth.

Moscow was upon us in bits, incrementally visible through the murk. The traffic was horrendous, the graffiti multilayered and emphatic. The men were light-skinned and square-jawed, with the kind of bland good looks that have always made me feel slightly menaced. In the women you could see the jostling of the centuries. The old women were Tolstoyan and nearly toothless, with gnomic features and fiercely wrapped kerchiefs. The young women were as elaborately assembled as the women of the Upper West Side, although some were elegant (swept hair and dark clothes, sparse and gleaming bits of jewelry) and some were tacky (bejeweled bosoms, tricked-out hair, the ruffled pelts of various unidentifiable Siberian weasels). They moved through the streets like the competing emissaries of various historical periods. In front of a department store, a man sat on a box with a chained and collared chimpanzee. I watched everything in a daze, retroactively registering the miracle of air travel. I'd snapped my fingers, rashly spent some money, and here I was—across the universe in a forbidding country where I knew no one, with only a scrawled and suspect address to guide me. Nobody had stopped me. Only a few people had even noticed.

The taxi let me out in front of my hostel. I got out and buzzed the doorbell. On one wall of the hostel, SLUT INFLUX was spray-painted in big block letters. A noise that sounded like the honk of a monster indicated that the door had been unlocked. I climbed the creaking stairs and found myself at the top of the stairway, at the end of a hall, standing in a yellow orb of light. A young man with weirdly rockabilly hair sat at the front desk, tapping his foot. The reflection of the computer screen was cast onto the glass cabinet behind him, and I could see a green expanse with miniature numbers and playing cards along the bottom.

"Wait," he said in English without looking at me.

I waited. He clicked his mouse. I looked around the lobby. On the walls were fraying posters of various Russian landmarks—the Hermitage, St. Basil's, Lake Baikal. There was an incomprehensible map of Moscow, the subway system color-coded like nerves and capillaries in a medical textbook. There was an advertisement for an art show that had concluded in 2002. On the glass, a fifth shimmering card was overturned. The boy kicked the desk.

"Blyad," he said. He turned to me. "Name?"

"Irina Ellison," I said, producing my passport. He took it and flipped to my picture, which was outdated and silly—taken in college, before I'd gotten my results, when I was affecting a smile that I'd not yet realized looked affected. My hair was short, and the skin around my mouth was flat, and my eyes sat in my skull properly, without being surrounded by semicircles the color of weak tea. I looked, I saw with a start, young. And it's only when you see how young you once were that you become, in your own mind, old.

"Hm," he said, and snapped closed the passport. He filed it away for safekeeping and collateral and handed me a pair of keys and a map with our building circled on it. "Here is Moscow boardinghouse." He pointed with a marker. "Here is metro. Here is bar. You are thirteen." He pointed down the hallway, which curved around menacingly. Smoke hung visibly in the air, making the light look greasy.

I took the map and the keys and wound my way down the hall, my luggage thumping behind me as though I were being followed by a deformed dog. I'd splurged on a private room, and I found it much as I'd imagined it—dim and dark and cold but serviceable. I dropped my luggage to the floor. I turned the key and locked myself in. I was here, strange as it was to realize. In my wallet, I carried the letter my father had drafted to Bezetov. Tomorrow I would start tracking down the answers to his questions. But tonight all I wanted to do was curl up in a ball, turn my back to the wall, and fall asleep in my clothes. I lay on the bed and closed my eyes.

———

I woke up fourteen hours later, although it took me a while to figure that out. I'd had restless, shivering dreams that disappeared immediately from memory but left me unhinged. I looked out my window and tried to discern the hour, but the outdoors looked oddly timeless. A fine film of rain was filling the air like ambient noise. The sky was white. On the street churned a sluggish river of people, moving too slowly for business and too dully for pleasure. I looked at my watch and tried to think. It was nearly two in the afternoon.

In the light of day, I could give my room a more complete inspection. There were mysterious stains on the floor, and I soon found an apocalyptic toilet down the hall. In the shower, the smell of somebody's gardenia shampoo floated just above the smell of wet dirt. I walked down the hall and passed the rockabilly poker player, who was shuffling his iPod with his thumb. There was a horrific smell outside the hostel's entrance. I declined to investigate its source.

Downstairs I found a tabac selling tiny bear pins and bottled water. Candies of no discernible national origin sported nutrition information in fourteen tiny languages. Depressed-looking pornography was sold alongside gossip magazines, forbidding copies of *Pravda,* the international edition of *Time.* I bought some chocolate-covered banana jellies and sat on a park bench and thought, for the first time since landing, about what I was really doing here.

In the light of day, asking Bezetov to answer my father's letter—a letter he'd never even read, most likely—seemed presumptuous and a few degrees beyond odd. When I tried to understand what I'd get out of it, I felt weirdly stupid, like a person trying to do a math problem in a dream. It was true that my father had wanted these answers, but it was also true that he'd managed to die without getting them. Surely I could do the same. I wasn't sure how to approach Bezetov, even if I could find him. He was being constantly mauled by chess fans, I supposed, and maybe I could pretend that was what this was about. Maybe I could pretend that the whole undertaking was just the dying vanity project of a middle-class American—weren't other, richer people with more mainstream interests always doing things like this? They hired professional chefs to teach them about soufflés. They learned obsolete languages. Having grown weary of perfecting the commoner abilities in life, they sought to acquire more exotic ones—windsurfing, herb growing, flower arranging. I could pretend that this was like that. I could pretend that I was vainly, fitfully meeting the demands of my own ego.

But the fact remained: Bezetov was whom my father had written to when the hourglass was running, its sand hissing with the force of an arterial hemorrhage. Maybe there was something my father knew that I didn't yet. Maybe there was something he knew that I would need to know soon enough. I wasn't sure that looking for it was a sensible way to spend one's last twelve to twenty-four months. But it would have to be sufficient.

I took Elizabeta's number out of my pocket and ran my finger across her name and address. I called her again, and explained who I was, and reminded her of my quest for Bezetov.

"Oh," she said. "I remember you."

"I'm sorry for the broken connection the other day."

"I've been sitting here waiting by the phone ever since."

"I think there was some problem with the international calling."

There was silence that went on long enough to feel like skepticism.

"Are you a reporter?" she said finally.

"No," I said, wondering if I should have been a reporter.

"He'll talk to Western reporters. He loves to talk to Western reporters. But I don't like to. Talking to reporters is a young man's game, I find."

"I'm not a reporter," I said, sounding surer this time.

"Nobody's ever a reporter," she said cryptically. "What's your interest in him, then? Are you a chess fan?" Her voice was becoming businesslike, crisp, and I was starting to hear the faint sheen of British English over the staccato of her Russian accent.

"Yes. Sort of. Not avidly. A casual fan, you might say."

"Are you political?" I heard the faint click and hiss of a cigarette lighter, followed by light wheezing.

"Also casually."

"Nobody's political, either."

There was a pause filled with some minor puffing. Then, horribly, she coughed. The cough sounded tubercular and wrenching, as though all the delicate things in her chest were coming painfully undone. When she was finished, she said, "Look," which struck me as a strangely American thing to say. "You could try to talk to him yourself. But you have to be credentialed. You have to be from somewhere. You can't come out of nowhere."

I thought for a moment. "What about a university?"

"Maybe. Maybe a university would be okay," she said, and her voice became coy and a bit sneering. "Why? Are you from a university?"

"Yes," I said boldly, and told her the name of my school. My former school. "I'm doing research." What were they going to do—fire me? Have me killed? "I have a letter from you. My father wrote to Aleksandr, and you wrote him back."

"I don't remember."

"Could I come see you, do you think? I'll bring it."

"I don't know about that." Her voice was receding again, becoming brittle, like glass blown too thin. "Why are you here now to do your research? If you're not political?"

Something about telling a lie makes it easier to tell a hard truth. The truth feels hidden in plain sight, and you start to forget which things are true and which things you wish were true and which things you conjured from nowhere just to make a story sound better. "I'm probably dying this year," I told her.

"My dear," said Elizabeta, and she coughed again. "That's no great distinction."

7

And one night, at long last and against all odds, came a knock on the door. There was a glassy clinking and the breathy almost-sound of soft things shivering up against one another. And when Aleksandr pulled open the door, there was Elizabeta: summoned to his room at last by the magnetic draw of his imagining, over and over, this very moment.

He'd been doing his mending by candlelight, and on his bed were piles of torn trousers. He stood in the doorway with a needle in one hand, wearing his worst shirt. Elizabeta was in her usual complicated black, and her hair was flying everywhere and catching colors in the weak hall light. In her hand she held a sheaf of paper.

"I heard this was you," she said, thrusting it into his hands.

It was the most recent issue of the journal, open to a smeared black-and-white photo of a pained-looking man with a beard.

"That's not me," said Aleksandr. "That's Sharansky."

Elizabeta laughed then, a complicated, multidimensional laugh filled with genuine appreciation for a bad joke, as well as mild derision toward its badness and a faint undertone of self-reproach for laughing. It was the kind of laugh you could write a university thesis about.

"Where did you get that?" said Aleksandr. When she pressed the journal into his hands, he thought, her thumb lingered against his palm.

"Nowhere," she said. "It was passed on to me. It doesn't matter. Listen." Her hair was falling out of the clip; it seemed unlikely to Aleksandr that the clip was even trying to do its job. It was purely decorative—like her shirt, come to think of it, which seemed too thin to offer much protection against any kind of weather. He wanted to feel how thin her shirt was, to take its fabric between his fingers and gently pull. Just to see.

"Are you listening?" She'd wedged her shoulder against the door. "Can I come in?"

"Um," said Aleksandr, because there were the clumps of clothes on his bed, which wasn't made, and the candles had burned down, and his teacup was making a puddle on the table, but she was already in, running long fingers against the walls, brushing aside the clothes and sitting on the bed without asking.

"This is crazy," she said, pointing to the journal.

"Have you read it?"

"I did. It's very good. It's very smart. But what I'm wondering is, are you suicidal?"

"Not suicidal," said Aleksandr. "Just showing off."

And then, just like that, her mouth was on his, although he wasn't sure how. One moment he'd been speaking, and another moment the space between their mouths had disappeared. He drew one hand to her face, brought the other to feel the small instrument of her rib cage. Then she was drawing back, with each beat of his heart she was disappearing from his arms, and it seemed to him that he would always remember this: a sequence of snapshots of a woman, laughing with her eyes down, in each image a little farther away.

"Sorry," she said. "That was just in case you're going to be assassinated by KGB sometime soon."

"Oh," he said, and then he stopped because he couldn't think of anything smart to say. The back of his neck was running cold with the memory of Elizabeta's fingers there, and he felt his brain frozen into an idiocy he feared would be permanent. "Who told you this was me?"

"Nobody. I saw the chess essay, and I've been noticing your weird hours lately, and I just— But listen, Aleksandr, don't get stupid, okay? People have seen this. Party people have seen this."

"How have Party people seen this?"

Elizabeta shook her head. "I mean, they know everything."

"How do you *know* Party people have seen this?"

"Aleksandr," and now Elizabeta was twisting up her hair, cracking her neck so hard it made Aleksandr wince, and standing up. "You know I know a lot of different kinds of people. Anyway. I should go." She was in the doorway, and her eyes were looking somewhere beyond Aleksandr's. "I'm sorry I bothered you." But she spent another moment not leaving, biting her lip and looking oddly mournful.

"You didn't bother me," said Aleksandr, although he realized he felt bothered. He put his hand on her shoulder—self-consciously, fraternally. She plucked his hand with hers and started pulling his fingers, slowly and tenderly, until the knuckles cracked.

For a moment the only sounds in the room were shallow breathing, the popping of Aleksandr's joints, the hiss of candles burning down to the ceramic and then quietly, without a fuss, going out.

"Watch out, Aleksandr," said Elizabeta as she turned to leave. "That's all I really came to say."

———

It went like that for a little while, then. When Aleksandr looked back and counted, it added up to only six weeks, though somehow it felt like somewhere between a day and a half and his entire lonely life. She came in the evenings. At first there were pretexts—some new item she'd seen, some new warning she had—but soon enough she abandoned them. Soon enough she stopped knocking.

He'd slept with only one woman before Elizabeta—the daughter of the owner of Okha's sole petrol station, who was mostly silent and smelled of wool—and with Elizabeta it was a different thing: the inversion or recapitulation of what had before been a rather stern affair. With Elizabeta, it was all exuberant gymnastics and sudden right

turns. They'd lie end to end for a long time, and he'd get lost somewhere there—the room seemed to rotate, and time didn't seem quite
like itself. They bit each other's skinny shoulders. He tongued the
fingerprint-sized indentation above her navel. They fell off the bed
and laughed.

Then they'd lie together and tell each other things that made Aleksandr blush to think about—not because they were obscene but because
they were not. It seemed humiliating in later years to have shared so
much so quickly and for so little. The fucking was one thing—this was
something he later got good at, and there were many other women,
many other playful romps and beleaguered beds and high-end hair-
styles ruined. But all that talking. All those confidences. He shuddered
to think about it. At the time, though, he didn't know any better, and
he was filled with the gleeful lurching and teeth-chattering panic of
early and undiagnosed love. Elizabeta told him about her childhood in
Khabarovsk—about her father, drunken and stinking and apoplectic,
and her mother, drunken and silent and besieged—and how she did
not like her life in Leningrad but, truth be told, she'd liked her life
in Khabarovsk quite a bit less. And Aleksandr told her about arguing with his grandfather about Communism, and listening to Radio
Free Europe, and playing correspondence chess with the students at
Andronov's academy until he'd finally been summoned into his own
future. And he told her how chess was the only escape from loneliness, and how epic his loneliness had been here, all these months before
she'd knocked on his door.

She'd bring her slippers inside his room so that the neighbors didn't
notice her pair outside his door—though like most secrets in the building, it was no secret for long. The walls were thin. Aleksandr could
hear the neighbors sneeze and toss creakily on their beds. He tried
not to think about what they might have heard of him and Elizabeta,
though it was hard not to wonder when the steward glowered smugly
at Aleksandr in the hallway, when the man who didn't like living near
prostitutes clapped him manfully on the back. "Hope she's giving you
a discount, tovarish," the man said.

Aleksandr winced but didn't answer. He was too happy.

It was remarkable, truly startling, the way that he could be thinking about Elizabeta absolutely all the time. Other thoughts came and went, skimming along the surface of the vast reservoir of consciousness that was devoted always to her. He was surprised at his capacity to think of other things—of many other things—with some degree of intelligence and depth without ever ceasing to think about her. She'd set up a full-blown military occupation of his brain. This energized him, made him wittier and livelier around Ivan and Nikolai, made him try harder at everything, made him fix his buttons and comb his hair and pull on his pants with more attention than he ever had before. Ivan even remarked that Aleksandr seemed to have snapped out of it. By this he seemed to mean that Aleksandr had snapped out of his entire personality, which certainly felt true.

There was a physical sensation in his chest, an internal compression that felt pathological; he felt constantly on the verge of tears or mad laughter or cardiac arrest.

He'd never believed in any of it before, but there it was.

———

It was a few weeks later that Misha made his return to the Saigon. It was a rainy night in early April—the sky was unleashed, and all the effluvia of winter were running through the gutters and out into the Baltic—and when Aleksandr, Ivan, and Nikolai reached their usual table, they were surprised to find a man waiting for them. He was a man you had to get used to looking at. His face looked as though it had been turned inside out: red sores shone through his thin hair and linked down the sides of his face like sideburns; the lights of the café made small yellow pools in the shallows of his face. The skin below his eyes seemed to conceal permanent low-grade internal bleeding. "Shit, Misha," said Nikolai. "What the fuck happened to you?"

They'd been planning to talk about the next issue, but when they saw Misha at the table, Nikolai and Ivan fell to silence.

Aleksandr had met Misha only the once, so he wasn't entirely sure what the man usually looked like. He was sure, however, that nobody could usually look like this. The veins against his temples were an alarming blue; his eyes seemed to float a millimeter or more beyond his skull. He was thin enough to provide his own anatomy lessons. He sneered, which did further violence to his face. "Care to join me, fellows?" he said.

"Of course," said Nikolai, pulling out a chair with a murderous scrape and jostling the table by sitting down too quickly. Aleksandr followed suit. Ivan leaned toward Misha, deep inlets forming between his eyebrows.

Misha sat and said nothing for a long while. He looked profoundly weary and too undone by life to ever voluntarily engage it again. Ivan and Nikolai stayed quiet, and their silence started to seem like reverence—as though Misha were a deposed king coming home to reclaim his land, or a wronged god returning to survey his wrecked world.

"Well," said Misha after they'd all stared at him slightly longer than was decent. "How have you been occupying yourselves? In my absence?"

"Please," said Ivan. "What can we get you? Do you need something to eat? A drink, maybe?"

"Nothing to drink." Misha issued a cough that was thick and wounding. "The doctors tell me my internal organs are like tissue paper. A stiff drink could kill me here and now. Unless that's the idea?"

"Let me get you some bread, at any rate," said Nikolai. "You look like shit."

"Is that what you've been doing, then? Drinking? Eating bread? Having a merry old time?" Misha turned toward Aleksandr, who felt an electric bolt judder his spine. It was the way he felt when he looked at the half-formed man in the wheelchair, or when the white Volgas passed him on the street. "Who's this?" said Misha. "This is your new friend?" He extended his withered hand, and Aleksandr saw no choice but to take it. It felt dusty and shriveled, like an organic object buried for millennia in a desert.

"I'm Misha," said Misha, and stared. It was amazing how a man so weak and shrunken could diminish everyone around him just by staring.

"We've met." Aleksandr felt Misha's chicken-bone fingers curl in his palm.

"Have we? You'll forgive me. My memory is shot, I'm afraid. That's the funny thing about being involuntarily committed to an insane asylum when you're mentally sound. By the time you come out, you're not quite yourself anymore." Misha looked at Ivan, the whites of his eyes glinting like the abdomens of fish. Ivan, not historically a person who was easily lost for words, said nothing.

"So," said Misha brightly. "You're not going to tell me, then? What's new? Don't tell me you've all been sitting on your asses all year while your old pal Misha is suffering in a psychiatric prison?"

"We're doing a journal," said Aleksandr. Misha's tone was making him feel oddly defensive of Ivan and Nikolai. They'd spent months carbon-printing the journal until their fingers turned blue; they'd risked their lives and sanity delivering it around the city. There was no way to know for sure, but Ivan said they might have a few hundred readers now. This counted for something, and Aleksandr didn't know why Ivan and Nikolai sat with their heads slung low, twisting their napkins and ignoring their vodka and looking afraid.

"A journal?" Misha looked amused. "What kind of journal?" Ivan and Nikolai said nothing, so Aleksandr shrugged and opened his satchel. He fumbled with the zipper under Misha's wolfish half-smile, which was becoming more ironic by the moment, but he managed to produce a copy. He pushed the sheaves of paper across the table, drawing his hand back quickly in case Misha reached out.

"It's political opinion, mostly," said Aleksandr. "Also philosophy. Chess articles. Poetry. Some visual art."

Misha started thumbing through the tract, the little smile frozen on his face as if he were faking it for a photograph. *"A Partial History of Lost Causes?"* he said. He continued to flip, issuing small exhalations like a man having a nightmare. The flipping became faster and faster, and Ivan and Nikolai grew rigid, and finally, Misha reached the back cover of the journal and threw it back at Aleksandr with a force that was surprising, considering his arms seemed to be missing their tendons. "Partial, indeed. Do you have a cigarette, at least?"

Nikolai passed him a light. When Misha took a pull, his cheeks seemed to disappear entirely. Aleksandr could nearly hear Ivan and Nikolai thinking, and he was sure that if he looked up he'd see jet trails of reproach and recrimination passing between them over his head.

"You're doing this all wrong, you know," Misha said authoritatively at long last. He blew white smoke and issued another consumptive cough. "It's shit. You think—you really think—your drawings here are going to make a difference?"

Aleksandr looked down at his hands and absorbed himself in his peeling cuticles, the calloused edges of his fingertips. Ivan said quietly, "Maybe."

Misha leaned forward, and Aleksandr instinctively leaned back. Up close, Misha smelled of poison disguised as medicine. When he spoke around the cigarette, his voice sounded strangled and high, like a violin played wrong.

"I wonder if you know what they did to me there," said Misha. Ivan spread his long fingers out on the table one by one and turned up a palm. He shook his head. "They'd scrape the rust off of old needles and use them over and over. They gave me sulfur injections. They put electric cables on my temples."

Aleksandr winced. Misha's veins ran so close to the surface of his skin that his face looked like a map of underground rivers.

"They'd wrap me in sheets, then dunk me in a bathtub full of ice, then toss me near the radiator. When the sheets dried, they'd tear off my skin." Misha took another puff of his cigarette and blew out his smoke coolly, methodically, in the general direction of Ivan's face. Ivan coughed and turned aside and said nothing.

"They made me sleep in the same bed as a man who called me Stalin. At first I thought he was trying to insult me, but then I realized he actually thought I *was* Stalin. He screamed at night and wrote vulgarities in his own shit on the walls. And they made me sleep in a bed with him. Every night for do you know how many nights? How many nights, Nikolai, would you guess? How many nights was I gone?"

Nikolai shifted in his chair. "One hundred? Maybe you were gone one hundred nights?"

"Ah, Nikolai," said Misha. "You're starting to make me think you don't care. I thought maybe you'd been marking the days on a calendar. I thought maybe you'd been writing every day."

Nikolai grimaced.

"It was one hundred and fifty-seven nights, actually, in bed with that monster. Can you blame me if I'm as crazy as he is?" Misha slapped his hands down on the table, and against the dark wood they looked like the sun-bleached skeletons of two turtles. "You think your fucking doodles stop this? You think somebody says, 'Oh, an unconventional painting! Communism is fucked, never mind!' "

"Please, Misha, keep your voice down," said Ivan flatly. "Even here, some discretion. Please."

"Discretion? Fuck your discretion. Did you know that I spent most of my nights gagged at the beginning, before I learned not to talk? Did you know that they keep half-people in cages there? Most of the people in there really are crazy. It's not all intellectuals and dissidents. We didn't all sit around and have erudite political discussions. And these people in the cages, a lot of them would scream. This was a very harrowing sound, especially in the beginning. Then it got less harrowing, but that's probably part of the point of the whole thing. At the beginning, though, this sound was not human to me. It was very troubling, let's say, to listen to it."

Nikolai bit his lip and held his tumbler so tightly that his fingers turned nearly purple. Ivan swirled his vodka absentmindedly with his finger, drawing his hand to his mouth every so often to chew on an alcoholic fingernail.

"At first," said Misha, "I tried to explain that there was a mistake. At the very beginning, especially, when they were cutting off my buttons. I thought if I was very good and reasonable and intelligent and calm, everybody would see that a mistake had been made." He issued a great cloud of smoke that nearly obscured his face, and when you couldn't see him, it was almost possible to believe that he was some unnerving prophet come to tell the present about the future. "But this was not the case. Everything I said—everything—was treated as nonsense. Some of the nurses were kind and gave me pieces of candy, and some nurses were cruel and slapped me across the face with the hard side of their hands while I was tied down or when nobody was looking. Most were indifferent and gave me pills—these enormous brown pills that choked me on their way down and that made the room around me shimmer and disappear. But what they all had in common was that they treated me as though I were absolutely mad. And you know the funny thing, Ivan?" He leaned forward, and Aleksandr could again detect the yellow smell of fatigue, shallow breaths, and narcotics.

"No," said Ivan, resigned to answering rhetorical questions. "What was the funny thing?"

"The funny thing, Ivan, is that I finally started to wonder if I actually was mad. You'd think I'd have a pretty good handle on my own sanity, but not so. Having everybody treat you as though you're crazy is an interesting psychological experiment. Everyone should try it sometime. And wondering whether I was crazy made me crazy. I started to get obsessed with my own language, with forming words perfectly. I rehearsed what I'd say to the nurses in my head all day, writing it down, getting it right. I pored over sentence construction and grammar. I had it in my head, see, that this problem of mine—this failure to communicate—was just a sort of mechanical malfunction."

Ivan shook his head and pressed his soaking fingers against his temples. Nikolai glared at the green light above Misha's head. Aleksandr stared straight at Misha, trying to form his jumbled face into a shape he might someday remember.

"But when I tried to talk to the nurses at the end of the day," said Misha, "they blinked at me. Or they petted me cruelly, like I was a stupid dog that the whole family loves to make a joke of. I started to chew my hands. After that, I stopped trying. I stayed very quiet and still and mostly spent my days looking out the window. I made up mental games to pass the time: in my head, I'd replace all the greens in the courtyard with reds, and all the browns with blues, until I created a new design to look at. I counted the words spoken to me in a day—let it be known, friends, that it wasn't that many. When my bedmate addressed me as Stalin, I started to answer."

Ivan brought his hand to Misha's shoulder, to the place where the reef of his clavicle disappeared under his thin shirt.

"Eventually, once they're quite sure all your mental resources are spent, they'll come invite you to talk. Everything is up to you, they'll say. Do you like coffee, tea, meat? Let's go get some, shall we? We might be able to find civilian clothing in your size. That Ukrainian

you room with? You know how much he hates Russians? You have a
real shot at rehabilitation, Misha. The others, no—but you, you're special. And then they'll take you out, and maybe you'll say some things,
and maybe some of them will be about your Ukrainian roommate, and
maybe they'll be true or maybe they won't be, but it won't matter to
you anymore. You care only about this promised tea. It becomes the
highlight of your week. You wait for it like a schoolgirl waiting for her
young man. You wait for it like a dog waiting for his bell.

"And so when I was released—abruptly on a Tuesday, with no
warning, just handed the clothes I'd come in wearing and given a discharge form and no responses to my questions—I found myself clinging to the bars of my bed. It was just past lunchtime, you see, and I'd
been looking forward to my pill. So you'll have to forgive me if I'm
somewhat skeptical about your efforts here. Your discretion. All due
respect, Vanya, of course."

Aleksandr looked to see what Nikolai and Ivan would do. Nikolai gulped the last of his vodka. Ivan pressed his hands into Misha's
shoulders as though offering some kind of atheistic benediction, then
removed them.

"Well," he said. "I suppose I can see your point."

In the apartment the following week, surrounded by great stacks of
waxy carbon paper, Aleksandr told Ivan what Elizabeta had said, and
Ivan told Aleksandr to stop worrying. "Look," he said. "If they want
to get us, they'll get us."

Misha had gone to stay with his mother, who cried when she saw
him and tried to buy him all the potatoes that were left at the market.
Work on the next issue had been suspended for a few days. Nikolai and
Ivan skulked around Ivan's apartment looking shifty and depressed.
Aleksandr spent most days that week sitting in a corner of Ivan's apartment, pretending to play a game of chess against himself but really
thinking secret thoughts about Elizabeta. After a week Ivan stood up,
slapped himself lightly on the face, and said enough was enough. They
had to keep working, he said, if only because none of them had anything better to do.

Ivan placed a sheet of carbon paper in the typewriter and started to recopy the issue. The copying required attention, but almost nothing could keep Ivan from talking when he wanted to. "They've probably got bigger problems than us. More expedient examples to make," he said. The typewriter issued a shuddering whinny. "Goddammit." He tore the paper from the typewriter, tossed it in a parabolic arc toward the trash, then looked at Aleksandr, who was sitting on a pile of books and stroking Natasha with his toe. "Honestly, I don't know what I pay you for."

"You don't pay me."

"Oh. That's right. I knew there was a reason." Ivan inserted a new piece of paper, and his typing became rhythmic and impressively fast, as though he were playing a sonata on the typewriter. "Where did you hear this, anyway?"

"Elizabeta. My friend. What? She lives in my building. What?"

"*Who* is this woman?"

"In my building. Like I said."

"Something you want to tell me, Alyosha?"

"No."

Ivan's face was awash with glee, and Aleksandr knew that was a bad sign. "I trust you've been following the recent reports on sex in the Soviet Union."

Aleksandr shook his head miserably.

"You haven't? Oh, how have you missed it? It was in all the papers. The Party has found that premarital sex causes impotence, neuroticism, and frigidity. The Party has determined that the ideal length of the sex act is no longer than two minutes. I think it very wise that you consult these findings before getting to know your friend any better."

"Stop it."

"At least you're not living in an Intourist hotel where all the prostitutes are KGB."

"You need to stop it, please."

"Okay. For now. So, you heard this from your friend Elizabeta. And how did she hear it?"

Aleksandr swallowed and pulled at his thumb. "From someone she knows."

"An official?"

"I don't know." The cat issued a high-pitched protest, and Aleksandr realized he'd been stroking her too hard with his foot.

Ivan raised his eyebrows and let a small percentage of the amusement go out of his voice. "Okay," he said. "And how did she figure out you were involved?"

"Because of the chess essay. Because of my schedule."

"She must be paying very close attention to your schedule."

Aleksandr swung off the book pile he was sitting on and stood up. "I guess so."

"They know. Of course they know. But I don't flatter myself that we're worth the trouble yet."

The typewriter clicked and whirred.

"Seen Misha lately?" Aleksandr said after a moment.

"I brought him a tart yesterday. He's still furious, still crazy. He keeps raving about these big plans to do something serious, something disruptive. They took away his internal passport, you know, and gave him a wolf ticket. He'll never work. His poor mother just sits and tries to get him to stop talking. He still weighs about six kilos. I think he's developed a morphine addiction. I don't know how he manages to keep talking as much as he does."

"Aren't you worried about it?"

"I don't worry, if you've noticed. Misha's not going to do anything that gets him put back there." Ivan stood up quickly and turned on the television. It was Vremya. It was always Vremya. A sour-faced anchor issued a battery of talking points. Ivan turned down the volume and handed Aleksandr a sheaf of papers. "Here. There are five. Do Vasilevsky Island, and when you come back, I'll have five more. And Aleksandr? It probably makes sense for you to try to ask your friend Elizabeta exactly where she heard this. Just for security purposes." Ivan winked.

"Shut up," said Aleksandr, but hearing her name made him stupidly happy. He sped through Vasilevsky Island that day in an uncommonly good mood and got back to the apartment before Ivan had even finished copying the next sheaf.

And then, as suddenly as Elizabeta had started coming, she stopped. Aleksandr didn't see her in the hallways. He didn't see her in the kitchen. He lingered outside the bathroom, sure that she'd eventually turn up there, until the steward chased him away. He didn't knock on her door, though he did walk by it several times. Her slippers were always there, which meant she was always out.

It was possible that he should knock. But he wasn't sure. He waited and agonized about the waiting. He hemmed. He weighed the competing considerations. She had started the whole thing, so it was gentlemanly to let her come back on her own. Better not to push it. As the days stretched to weeks, however, and as the weeks compressed into a series of unending moments in which he was not with Elizabeta, his rationale changed. She'd come to see him the first time, after all. She was probably waiting for him to come to her. It was only diplomatic, and chivalrous, to return a visit with a visit—or, in this case, many visits with one. He'd be rude not to, and he so hated to be rude. And after further philosophical revision and fretting—and an attempted oblique consultation with Nikolai and Ivan that ended in their laughter and Aleksandr's deep embarrassment—he swallowed down his terror and approached her room.

Outside apartment nine was a man leaning against the door. His hair and eyelashes were almost ice-white; his eyes were such a beautiful blue that they seemed wasted on a man. His coloring could be Slavic, but his demeanor absolutely was not. There was too much relaxation in his pose, too much openness in the way he watched the people pass him in the halls, unafraid to meet their eyes. Clearly, he wasn't concerned he'd be noticed. Clearly, he was from the West.

"Are you waiting for Elizabeta?" said Aleksandr. He tried to speak slowly; he knew that Russian could be one interminable word if one talked too quickly.

"Yes," said the man. He was young, though his hair was cut with mild gray around the temples. Up close, the blueness of his eyes was irrepressible. Even from a single word, Aleksandr could note with a marginal thrill that the man's accent was quite poor.

"Where are you from?"

"Brussels." The man sneezed and looked wary. "Excuse me."

"Why are you here?"

"That's what everyone wants to know, isn't it? Every time I'm stalled in traffic, somebody in a black raincoat approaches me and asks why I'm here, why I'm not in a tourist zone, why I'm not with a group. You people certainly know how to make a man feel welcome."

Aleksandr took a step back. Outside of the Saigon, he hadn't heard anybody complain so loudly about anything since he'd arrived in Leningrad. It was galling to realize that it made him nervous. "Don't ask me," he said. "I just play chess here."

The Belgian nodded. "You waiting for the girl?"

"I guess so."

"Then you don't *just* play chess here, eh?" said the man. A look of self-amusement illuminated his eyes like the blue flash of a passing ambulance.

"I suppose." The man was awfully nosy and tactlessly quick to issue his own opinions. Aleksandr was used to being treated with indifference; he was used to people avoiding each other like the wrong ends of magnets. It was a frightening way to live, but at least it wasn't vulgar.

The Belgian blinked his eyes, the blueness of which was starting to feel intrusively Western: his eyes were becoming the blue of cornflowers and van Gogh paintings and United Nations helmets. "She's a nice girl," he said. "It really is too bad she's getting married."

"No. What? No."

The Belgian shrugged and put his cigarette in his mouth to show that he didn't care. His eyes were becoming the blue of oxygen deprivation. "She is. You didn't know? To some Party official, I hear, who looks like a prehistoric beast. Large man. I've seen him. You'd think he walked out of a museum for dead things." Aleksandr said nothing; the thought of saying anything about the subject—or maybe about anything else ever again—suddenly seemed monumentally taxing. The Belgian wore a bewildered expression, as though Aleksandr were just the latest of the Soviet Union's mounting mysteries. "Sad, isn't it?" he said. "I rather like her myself. But what can you do? The woman's got to look out for her own interests."

"I don't believe it," said Aleksandr, although he was already starting to believe it.

The man released a whoosh of smoke-free air from his mouth. He
rolled his eyes. He kept talking around the cigarette. "Suit yourself.
That's kind of your thing, isn't it? The Soviets?"

"What?" said Aleksandr miserably.

"Believing whatever you want to, regardless of the facts. Please
don't let me stop you. Please don't let me get in the way of this. It's
your great national tradition, I understand."

Maybe it wasn't true. Maybe the Belgian was mistaken, or maybe
he'd meant the other girl, the roommate, and had gotten them confused. Elizabeta would never marry a Party official, for one thing,
and—Aleksandr hoped savagely, then felt sorry for hoping it—a Party
official would never marry her. It just could not be a good move pro-
fessionally.

"Hey," said the Belgian. "Where'd you go?" He waved his hand
across Aleksandr's face, snapped his fingers several times in quick succession. His eyes were the blue of fingers in winter on hands that nobody held. Elizabeta and a Party official. Maybe it was a good match
after all. Maybe they'd have lots to talk about.

"You people," the Belgian was saying. "You people are a weird
bunch. Getting sentimental about your whores."

Suddenly Aleksandr was seized with an overwhelming desire to
hit this man, to pummel him with an aggression that was neither intellectual nor metaphorical. Games were pacified war, and no game was
more overtly warlike than chess. But sometimes you needed violence
to be real and losses to count. Sometimes you needed to defend something that really mattered, and not only because it symbolized something that mattered.

Also, the Belgian was smaller than Aleksandr.

Aleksandr's fist clicked against the knob of bone below the man's
eye. The Belgian looked startled, then emotionally wounded, then resigned. He gave Aleksandr an almost fraternal slap across the chest.
Aleksandr tried to yank some hair and only grazed the Belgian's head.
The Belgian tried to get a handle on Aleksandr's rib cage with one

hand while trying to tangle one of his legs around Aleksandr's. Aleksandr tried to knee the Belgian in the balls and missed, and he was glad he'd missed. It was over in less than a minute, the two of them standing feet apart, relieved that no one had seen it.

"Sorry," muttered Aleksandr.

The Belgian blinked, and his enormous light eyebrows seemed to waggle under the weight of his umbrage. He clicked his neck to one side and the other, rolled his shoulders back, inspected himself for damage. Aleksandr watched him. There was a soreness growing behind his kneecap, a stillness blooming in his heart. "Can I— Are you hurt?" said Aleksandr.

"Please. Don't flatter yourself."

"I'll go. If you could tell her I came by, maybe." But he didn't care, really, whether the Belgian did or not.

Aleksandr began to walk away. "Hey," said the Belgian, but Aleksandr didn't turn around. There was nothing to see behind him, he knew, nothing the Belgian could tell him that he wanted to know. "I wouldn't want you to have to take my word for it," the Belgian yelled, his accent flattening through his anger. Aleksandr walked faster, then started to run. The bruised soft side of his knee was pulsing and the neighbors were slamming their doors around him and the plaster molding was dropping white chips on his head and his run was opening up into a sprint. But he couldn't get away fast enough to miss hearing the Belgian shout at him that the next time he saw her, motherfucker, he should look for the ring.

8

IRINA

Moscow, 2006

Elizabeta lived a few miles north of my hostel, out in a gray neighborhood with rows of identical flats that expanded outward like the units of a self-replicating virus. The streets became narrower and more finicky the farther north we got, and after a while I relieved my indifferent taxi driver of his duties and struck out on foot. I took several wrong turns as I hunted for Elizabeta's apartment, searching through sixteen-letter street names that often differed by only one vowel. I looked down alleyways at fluttering clotheslines, schools of androgynous blond children, large dark dogs that seemed to answer to no one. Above me, apartments were stacked on and over each other like cliff dwellings.

I had just about stopped looking when I found Elizabeta's store, above which she claimed to live. It was hidden in plain sight amid houses with Russian flags snapping from the windows, pools of standing water congealing in front yards, men with cigarettes sitting wordlessly on front stoops. At the end of the street, a coterie of young men were jumping their bikes off a low concrete ledge, and their periodic shouts made the whole neighborhood seem like the innocent bystander to some sort of crime.

Elizabeta's door, once I found it, was implausibly skinny. I knocked, and in the lengthy silence that followed, I wondered whether I would have to endure the indignity of walking in sideways. Muffled sighs began to issue from behind the door. Getting up seemed to require an enormous effort from Elizabeta, and I once again felt a crashing suspicion that this meeting was, on the whole, not a good idea. I heard a fierce cough that sounded as if she was trying to expel something that her body was not willing to part with. But instead of a withered babushka, with a worried face and a mouth collapsing where teeth used to be, the woman who opened the door looked healthy enough. She was pretty in a matter-of-fact way, with bright eyes and good bone structure—she had the kind of beauty that endures reasonably well, since it's not overdoing it—and she wore makeup that was subtle but that you weren't supposed to miss. She was dressed all in black, though her expression wasn't mournful. There was something mocking right around her mouth, I noticed, a squiggly near-eruption of smiling. I recognized it because my own face does the same thing sometimes— mangles itself most unattractively when I'm most trying to look serious, if something strikes me as funny or strange or stupid.

"Ah," she said. "You are Irina. The girl who is not a journalist."

"Yes." I couldn't remember the last time somebody had called me a girl—anyone who was inclined to do so in the States was probably too afraid of getting sued. Even Lars, who you'd think would be a likely candidate, never called me a girl—convinced, as he was, of my unseemly old age and overly chaste dealings with men.

"Come in, then," she said. "If you keep standing out there looking so hopelessly American, you're liable to get sexually assaulted."

She led me through the store. It was cramped and dusty and papered almost wall-to-wall with Soviet-era propaganda; in a poster above the cash register, athletic farmers in a bright green field worked underneath a banner proclaiming YOU ARE THE MASTERS OF THE NEW LIFE! I followed Elizabeta up a claustrophobic back staircase to her apartment. Inside, the living room was clean and almost bare, with a few black-framed photographs on the walls and shelves neatly arranged with books organized according to color. The greens swept along one corner, the blues faded to blacks along another. A rickety rocking chair sat at the center of the room, moving just enough to look inhabited by a particularly undernourished ghost. A birdcage was hanging in the back corner of the room with a small jewel-colored bird looking out through its ribs.

"Are you going to want tea or something?" she said, looking me up and down with some suspicion.

I nodded. I was relieved by the extent of her English; the ability to communicate scorn should be the true test of fluency in any language.

She swung the door of the living room open into a yellow kitchen, where I could just glimpse a hissing gas stove, purple bouquets on ragged wallpaper, a few dull photographs taped to a small nonmagnetic refrigerator. I waited. The living room smelled like dust and artificial cinnamon—the kind that comes from candles, not from cooking. The little green bird ruffled its feathers huffily, and I got up to look at it. Its eye was stern and mottled like igneous rock.

"That's Fyodor," said Elizabeta, coming back into the living room with a tray.

Fyodor blinked at me. "He's very nice."

"Not really," she said. "And he sure is taking his time to die. He's outlived many of my better human companions."

She put down tea and some dusty-looking biscuits and then sat down in the creaking rocking chair. I sat on the sofa, which was threadbare and swirled with garishly ugly fabric roses. On the wall across from me was tacked a dark-toned portrait of a solemn, well-dressed woman.

"Do you have a pet?" said Elizabeta, her chair making silvery clacks against the wood floor. I knew then that I must seem more pitiful than I'd realized, to have elicited a level of small talk this tragic so early in our acquaintance. "They are quite a commitment."

"I don't really do commitments," I said, sounding childish even to myself. I took a bite of biscuit to avoid saying anything else. It exploded in my mouth like a sandstorm. I put the biscuit back down and folded my napkin over the edge of my plate.

"Sorry," she said, looking at my neglected pastry and not sounding too terribly broken up. "I am not domestic, you'll notice."

"Thank you for agreeing to meet with me," I said, sipping my tea.

Elizabeta shrugged. "Like you, I do not really have commit-ments. Just the damn bird." She dunked a cube of biscuit into her tea, then flung it at Fyodor, who gobbled it greedily. "At least he likes my cooking." The bird bobbed its head mildly, as if in half-ironic agree-ment.

"So," I said, suddenly feeling the awkward absurdity of flying across the world to sit and make small talk in a Russian living room with an old woman and her pugilistic pet bird. "You said you didn't work for Aleksandr Bezetov, exactly."

She gave me a wry look. "Not exactly, no."

"So how do you know him?"

"I don't, really. We lived in the same building, back in the day." Her voice, which had been relatively strong throughout the conversation, was starting to sound tangled by vines. "Excuse me," she said, and dis-appeared into a fit of coughing so long and intense that I looked away. Her thin shoulders shuddered brutally. Evil tearing noises issued from her chest. Her coughing became wild and inconsolable, a howl of some permanent, universal grief. When she recovered slightly, there were small clots of blood in her handkerchief.

"Are you okay?" I said, even though she was clearly not okay. I'm intimately familiar with the irrelevancies generated by extreme distress—the platitudes of consolation, the clichés of kindness. I was annoyed at myself for having nothing better to say.

"Fine," she croaked.

"Is it—are you—I mean," I said, deploying in one go my whole personal arsenal of halting idiocies. I experienced a flash of sympathy for Jonathan, for my mother, for the doctors, for everyone who had tried with me, and failed, and endured the exacting judgment of my disappointed, dying gaze.

"It's not tuberculosis," she said. There was a dewy thread of blood hanging from her mouth, but I didn't know her well enough to say so. "It's not contagious. It's emphysema. Damn cigarettes."

"Should you—should we—go to the doctor?" I said, gesturing to the blood-flecked handkerchief.

"Not yet. They don't do anything about the blood. I'll go when I can't breathe at all. It's better now." My face must have suggested some pale horror, because she said, "It's not as bad as it looks."

I've spent enough time in hospitals to know that this is generally never true, but I appreciated the sentiment.

"What were we on?" she said.

"Bezetov."

"Ah. Bezetov. Right." Her voice seemed to fully emerge from its cloud of coughing—wry, feathery, nearly unscathed. "Nice young man. As I recall. What's your interest in him?"

"Well," I said carefully. "I'm trying to get a meeting with him." It seemed inappropriate to bring up now, I thought—it was like visiting your dear old grandmother for tea only to ask her probing questions about the will.

"Trust me, friend. If it were so easy to get a meeting with Aleksandr." She stopped talking, and I tried to figure out if the midsentence halt was an issue of translation. "Why do you want this meeting, exactly?"

"My father admired him, and they'd had some kind of correspondence," I said stupidly. "Actually, my father tried to have a correspondence. Bezetov didn't write back. You did."

She raised her eyebrows. "Oh?"

I produced the letter and handed it to Elizabeta. She stared at it for a few moments.

"That's you, right?" I said. "That's your signature?"

"Yes. God, I had terrible handwriting. But I don't remember writing it. Or reading it. Sorry."

I looked down.

"What do you want him to say to you?" said Elizabeta, handing me back the letter.

"I have this—diagnosis, and I like chess," I said. Elizabeta's face registered no understanding. She blinked, rustled in her black layers, and waited for me to start making sense. "I couldn't stay home," I concluded.

"So you came to Russia to chase a dissident through the snow? You picked a weird vacation. He's surrounded by security all the time. You understand the situation, don't you?"

"Sort of," I muttered. I felt violently foolish, an idiot American tearing a destructive path through a rain forest or a Graham Greene novel.

She squinted at me. "You know he's running for president?"

"Oh yes, I know that," I said. "Of course I know that. You must be pleased for him." I'd been reading this in bits and pieces all year—usually in colorful text boxes at the bottom of the international sections of newsmagazines, headlined by self-satisfied wordplay. "State Strategy: A Chess Genius Turns His Mind to Politics," they read, or "Check Your King: Former Chess Champion Takes on Putin." It had occurred to me—somewhere between crumpling my life into plastic bags and getting my visa stamped, between leaving my lover and losing him—that this presidential campaign might create challenges for me, and that meeting a bewildered young woman, flailing in every sense of the word, might not be Aleksandr Bezetov's absolute highest priority. But I'd chosen to mostly ignore this, like many of the more inconvenient facts of my life.

"Not so completely pleased, maybe," said Elizabeta, her mouth becoming a curt little comma. "He can't win, and it makes a lot of important people want to kill him. A lot of people who know how to do it with relative discretion. Poisons, you know, or plane crashes. Putin has basically put it on the government's agenda for the year. Aleksandr never flies Aeroflot, even internally. Especially internally. Although the more famous he gets in the West, the more uncomfortable it gets for the FSB to try it. That's part of why he likes to talk to you reporters all the time."

"I'm not a reporter."

"Okay. Whatever you're calling it. But the problem is, like I said, people are always trying to kill him. Not often women, it's true, and never Americans yet, but one never does know."

"I'm not trying to kill him," I said, mildly offended.

"Even if you weren't, I can't help you. He won't remember me. I don't have his information." Her voice was starting to break apart again, like a single note opening up into a four-part chord. I thought she was about to start coughing, but she didn't.

"Oh," I said, and I felt that that perhaps could be that. This had been an elaborate scheme, psychologically costly and financially disastrous, and it was most definitely too embarrassing to go home with *that* as my excuse. People would say, "Oh, you're still alive? Weren't you supposed to die dramatically in some vast eastern expanse, and weren't you supposed to learn or find or do something first? I suppose you can have your job and boyfriend back, if you want, but I'm sure you understand that this is extremely awkward." Going back would be like going too late to a party thrown by people you hardly know, then getting stuck sitting there with them, with the lights up, drinking warm beer and talking about mutual acquaintances who already left. It would be like showing up at the chilly apartment of some half-dead Russian woman, then browbeating her for information about a forgotten friend, then choking up and staring at the ceiling for some length of time when she didn't have it.

But what was the alternative? Roam the bridges of St. Petersburg until the time seemed right to jump into the Neva? Engage in full-throttle stalking of this chessman, throw stones at his window, leave little notes in his mailbox, get myself shot by his burly unmerciful companions? All of that, too, seemed anticlimactic.

The sharp edges of my silence must have been starting to make Elizabeta uncomfortable, because she gestured at the grim-faced woman in the portrait. "You know the story of Solominiya?" she said. Solomoniya glowered disapprovingly at me from underneath heavy brows.

"No. Who was she?" Tortured to death, no doubt, for some point of principle or virginity. Female saints always got that way by choosing death over sex. Maybe I could get myself canonized, I thought. That would at least keep me busy.

"She was the wife of Vasily the Third."

"Ah, of course."

"She couldn't produce an heir—that's always the way with powerful people, isn't it? The wrong women produce the heirs, and then somebody has to get banished or killed. Anyway, Solomoniya was banished to a convent so Vasily could take another wife. But lo and behold, nine months later, she bears a son."

I raised my eyebrows, trying to look scandalized, although I am basically incapable of being scandalized. Elizabeta tossed another chunk of biscuit to the bird.

"Solomoniya fears for the life of the child and promptly declares him dead. Nobody knows what became of him. And there the matter rests until the excavations of 1934, when they dig up Solomoniya—and next to her body lies a tiny dummy baby."

"So the baby lived."

"He lived, and his line technically would have produced the rightful heir to all of Russia—not that that's much to claim, and not that any modern person believes that anybody's the rightful heir to anything."

"So why do you keep her up there?"

"She doesn't look happy to be there, does she?" said Elizabeta. Solomoniya's scorn seemed to rain down on us, her dark eyes communicating all the mute, immobile rage of people denied, confined, disappeared.

"She doesn't."

"I don't know. I suppose I've always been interested in how things could have gone differently. Moments when things might have gone one way and instead went another."

I thought of my father's letter and his concern with the moment when one realizes that though there are many ways things might be, there is only one way that they are—and that no matter what, one will have to stand it.

"Aren't all moments like that, though?" I said.

"Some more than others, I have come to believe," Elizabeta said lightly, before coughing again. When she came up for air this time, I let a respectful beat pass—a moment of mourning or solidarity—and then said, "What was Aleksandr like?"

"What was he like?"

"Well, you know. What did he do?"

"Oh, who knows? What does anybody do? He fiddled around with his game, I always supposed. He was into the samizdat thing. They published a journal that a handful of people read. Sometimes my friend and I—I lived with my girlfriend Sonya then—would sneak past his door and put our ears against it and listen. Sonya had all these theories about him; thought he was a secret sex maniac or a sort of idiot, or a serial killer, or KGB." Elizabeta turned to Fyodor and puckered her lips at him, and I could tell she was trying to keep her face from doing something involuntary and revealing. I've had too much experience with facial sleights and emotional misdirection not to notice this type of thing when I see it. It occurred to me, briefly and casually, that Elizabeta and Aleksandr had been lovers.

"And what did you think?"

"I guess I just thought he was a very nice boy. No, not nice. Sort of interesting and confusing. I liked him." Elizabeta's face turned a marginally different color, and she looked up at Solomoniya, who stared back bleakly. "But our acquaintance was short-lived."

"What did you do in those days?"

"I was a secretary," she said, and looked away, and I was struck flatly across the face with the uncomfortable reality that Elizabeta had probably worked for the Party. She was so irreverent that it hadn't yet occurred to me. But everybody, more or less, had been implicated—the smart people and the cynical ones, the listless survivors and the true believers. So she'd typed stuff for men with misguided economic notions. What did it matter? What did I understand about it? I noticed that Elizabeta still wasn't looking at me.

She took a sip of tea. "Our friendship was short-lived, and then it was too late."

"Too late?"

"I mean by then he was famous. This was a different time, remember. Being a secretary involves a great deal of massaging of the male ego, even in the offices of our great social utopia. I couldn't do it when I wasn't being paid to."

"That's a principled stance," I said. It came out worse than I'd meant.

There was a horrid pause. "You must need to get back to your hostel," Elizabeta said, standing up. I stood up, too, so as not to be left idling with an angry Russian woman dressed in black—even a weak, miserably coughing one—hovering above me. Elizabeta was small, but she was the type of person whom you didn't want looking at you in a certain way.

"I'm sorry if I upset you," I said. This was a phrase I learned from college boyfriends.

Elizabeta laughed, and this time her laugh sounded like buckling ice on an undiscovered planet. "I am not so easily upset. But listen."

She disappeared into the kitchen and then returned with a yellow index card. She handed it to me. "This is the information of a man in St. Petersburg." She'd written the name in an underconfident, overly careful Latin alphabet.

"Is this a friend of Aleksandr's?"

"This is a man who has been trying to get in touch with Aleksandr. A man in your line of work, I think. Calling, calling, calling. Maybe by now he has managed to do it."

I didn't know what she meant by my "line of work." Was he a fugitive non-tenure-track professor? A person who stumbled blindly through foreign countries and degenerative diseases as a career? I looked at the name. Nikolai Sergeyev, 132 Vasilievsky Ostrov, St. Petersburg.

"Thanks," I said. "I'm sure this will be helpful." Another person to cold-call, I thought. Fantastic. I was becoming a professional telemarketer, a sad-eyed celebrity in maudlin television ads for my own lost cause.

"You know your way back?" she said.

"I'll get a taxi."

Elizabeta looked at me evenly. "You know that some of the taxis aren't really taxis."

"What?"

"Some of them are really thieves."

"How do you know which ones are which?"

She shrugged. "You find out the hard way, I guess."

Suddenly I'd had enough of Elizabeta, with her faulty lungs and her sour-faced bird and her portrait of a woman who had somehow missed her own proper fate. I didn't know why I so often found myself in contact with people who insisted on speaking cryptically, in little proverbs and hints. Lars was like this, too, and he didn't even have the excuse of a childhood spent in a police state.

"Good luck," said Elizabeta, and I thanked her and went out into the dusky neighborhood. Oncoming car lights illuminated the trash cans. I walked in little circles for quite a while before I found a cab.

————

The next afternoon I wandered Moscow. I admired art nouveau arabesques and neoclassical sunset-colored facades on all the post-Communist buildings. I stared at the gargantuan statue of Peter the Great above the Moskva, with his grotesquely small head and creepily long fingers. I went to Gorky Park and watched parents pay a nominal fee to have little Petr or Ivanka photographed with a depressive, flea-bitten tiger. Peat-bog fires east of the city had driven up temperatures, and in the evening I sweated my way through the statue park and counted the pallid roses at the foot of Lenin. The next day I called Jonathan.

Navigating the phone card was a disaster, full of such stern admonitions from the operator that I felt pretty bad about myself before he even picked up the phone. When he did, I heard muffled subaquatic noises and felt sure for a sickening eternal moment that he had somebody over.

"Hello?" He sounded alarmed, and it occurred to me that it was four in the morning where he was.

"I'm sorry," I said. There wasn't an audible sound, but the phone line seemed to convey an attitude in its silence—derision or disbelief or an adult exhaustion with the self-absorbed hijinks of children.

"Are you coming back?" His voice was the tense crackle of a man on the edge of sleep—which, I realized, I'd never gotten familiar with.

I thought, but I didn't really have to think. "I don't know what to say."

He was silent, but it didn't feel like the kind of silence that would hang up on you. It felt like the kind of silence that would wait, breathe quietly, and hate you across the swirling dark ocean.

"Can't we be friends?" I said, then almost hit myself over the head with the enormous Brezhnev-era telephone for saying it.

"What would that even mean at this point?"

"It would mean we're okay with each other in the universe." That was what I wanted for us, I realized as soon as I said it. I could stand it, I thought, if we were still friends, on balance—on whatever invisible psychic ledger kept track of these things. I couldn't have him over there in Boston hating me or forgetting me. I couldn't have him revising who I was so that he could properly dismantle me, turn me into a pathological mistake or a lesson learned or a bullet dodged.

"This is insulting," said Jonathan. "Seriously. What do you want me to say? Never mind. I don't care what you want me to say."

"I'm sorry," I said, which is a phrase that only gets soggier if you say it over and over. We were quiet. Sometimes I wish I'd been the kind of person who could stand the ignorance, the excruciating optimism, of not finding out.

"How are things?" I said.

"Please. We are not having this conversation. You've forfeited your right to this conversation."

"Okay."

"You didn't invent this thing," he said.

"What?"

"You didn't invent it. You didn't have to do it this way. People do it differently. We could have done it differently."

I wasn't totally sure I knew what he was talking about, but I thought I probably did. And he was right. Other people do it differently, with prayer and alternative medicine and blessings counted and cataloged. My inability to do it that way stemmed from immaturity and ego and an impious reverence for functioning human brains. I wasn't exactly proud of this. But I couldn't go home to do it the other way—to lose myself from the best parts down, to be spoon-fed by a man who hadn't even seen me cry.

"I really cared about you," he said.

"Well," I said, and I knew I was going to have to hang up right away. "I guess that was your first mistake."

St. Petersburg had an entirely different feel than Moscow—it was all planned streets and arcing avenues and stylistically unified architecture. On Teatralnaya Ulitsa, the buildings appeared to dance. Long cords of icy sunlight seemed to obey intended routes, making crisp ninety-degree turns around corners. The smell, too, was different. Both cities, I noticed, smelled bad—unforgivably, devilishly, abusively bad—in places. There was a smell in one corner near my hostel in Moscow that seemed to make the air opaque; your knees wilted, your spirit flagged, when confronted with it. It seemed concocted, preordained. It didn't seem like the kind of smell that could have emerged organically without supernatural intervention. If some people look at the complexity of the universe and see proof of God, I look at the dire complexity of that smell and see the suggestion of Satan. In St. Petersburg, there was the fine-dirt smell of eggplant; below it, a casually salty marine smell, like dirty aquarium; and just below that, something meatier and wilder, the smell of iceberg and whale. There was the smell of vodka and beer caked along alleyways, after a night of thaw and half a day of indirect sunlight, and this smell came to make cold tragic fingers against my rib cage whenever I smelled it, because it meant abandoned hopes, revised game plans, the instructive clashing of desire and reality. It meant an evening of fun had come and, inevitably, gone.

I went to St. Petersburg soon after Elizabeta gave me Nikolai's information, crinkling into my bag my damp clothes and directions and taking a night train. I'd photocopied my passport twice and put one copy in my left shoe and one into a box of tampons. I'd found my own car, full of prissy antimacassars and the hearty stink of urine. Of course I'd vowed not to sleep, and of course I'd woken up halfway through the trip with a middle-aged man splayed out on the seat across the aisle from me, making half-snores and little sucking noises in his dreams. In the morning I felt awkward and too intimate, as though we were on the other end of a night of the worst kind of sexual mistakes. In St. Petersburg I'd found a hostel similar to the one in Moscow, with long drafty hallways and a vaguely hostile staff. And there I sat for a few days and waited for the nerve to look into finding Nikolai. I toured the city, admired its clean architecture and commemorative statues, spun my wheels, and spent my money. My Russian was improving marginally, though not as fast as I'd hoped. I was about ready to sit down and call this man, arrange a meeting, and subject myself to all its attendant futilities and absurdities and hazards. But as it turned out, Nikolai got to me before I got to him.

I'd taken to spending long afternoons seated in a tiny café next door to my hostel, poring over newspapers and shivering. The café was always ten degrees cooler than the outside, and the outside—even in July—could take on a dull-edged chill in the late afternoons. So I was wearing a few sweaters and a half-awake grimace when a large man plopped down across the table from me and asked me, in rough-hewn and fragmented English, if I was Irina Ellison from America.

I was startled. The man had a face that looked as if it had been scoured by steel wool; his head was the shape and size and durability of an American football helmet. I looked at his hands to see if they were holding a badge of some kind, and was relieved and then confused and then scared when I saw that they weren't. I couldn't tell if this was the kind of man it would be smart to lie to.

"Yes," I said. "That's my name. Who are you?"

"My name is Nikolai Sergeyevich," said the man. "I hear you have been looking for me." The lacy network of light scars across his face made him look almost comically sinister from afar. Up close, they appeared to be only the remnants of adult acne.

"I haven't been looking for anybody yet," I said. "I've only been thinking about it."

Nikolai rubbed his hands together. When he turned his face to the side to signal the waiter for coffee, the light made his face look like a slice of marbleized ham. He was fat, and his was the kind of fat that really asserts itself, through heavy breathing and the noisy rolling of flesh.

"You are looking for Aleksandr Bezetov, I understand," he said. "I want to help you find him."

"Why?" The waiter brought a tiny black coffee, and Nikolai grunted a thank-you.

"We were great friends back in the day," said Nikolai, taking a sip of his coffee and pulling his face into a grimace of disapproval. "We were basically children together."

"In Okha?" It didn't seem likely.

"Not children," said Nikolai. "Youth, I should say. We were young men together during Soviet days."

"Oh," I said. A string of obvious questions ran through my head: How did you know I had your information? How did you know I was looking for Aleksandr Bezetov? How did you know my name? I thought briefly of the man at my hostel's front desk and how noisy I'd been about my mission and my whereabouts. But I didn't say anything. I've always been hesitant to question absurd premises—other people's or my own. It seemed undiplomatic to ask him who the hell he was and what the hell he thought he was doing.

"You're at the embassy, then?" said Nikolai. There was a standing hostility in his voice that seemed to be occasionally eclipsed by sheer effort, as though somebody had firmly admonished him ahead of time to be nice to me.

"No," I said.

Nikolai looked confused. "Of course." His lacerated face creased with worry, as if he thought he might have offended me. "Well, I think if we pool our information, we might just have the chance to track down Aleksandr Bezetov. My old buddy."

"I don't have any information."

"Ah," said Nikolai, sinking back into his chair with a fleshy smack. "How would you characterize your role at the embassy, then?"

This was baffling.

"I'm not at the embassy," I said. "I'm just on vacation."

Nikolai looked at me—my several sweaters, the gray tea in its cup bleeding onto the newspaper. "A vacation," he said. "I see. I just want you to know you're supposed to be registered if you're working out of the embassy."

"I'm not."

"Because we couldn't help but notice that you're not registered."

"I don't know what you're talking about," which, again, was true. "Who's 'we'?" And then, finally—because I didn't like the way his face was looking at me, like the world's most reproachful piece of poultry—I asked, "Who the hell are you?"

"Look," he said, leaning close to me, and he smelled unexpectedly delicate, like expensive shampoos in lavender and men's cologne in some scent that purports to be masculine. "We don't need to decide anything today. I've already told you who I am. I am looking for my old friend."

"You really haven't told me who you are. Why are you looking for him?"

"And why are you?" he countered.

I was quiet for a moment. "Because my father knew him, almost," I said. "Because I couldn't stay home." I was aware of how I sounded—simultaneously lame and wildly suspicious, an incompetent spy with a ridiculous cover.

"Okay," said Nikolai. "Something about your father. Fine, sure." He handed me his card, which suggested he had several addresses and an implausible number of mobile telephones. "Call me anytime, if you decide we could work together."

I didn't say anything because I didn't know what to say. Nikolai heaved his mass to standing. "Well. Perhaps we'll be in touch. In the meantime," and he slammed a few rubles down on the table to cover his coffee, "remind your customer that you're supposed to be registered."

He plodded out of the café, leaving his half-drunk coffee still steaming on the table. It was only after he'd left and walked out into the misting gray afternoon that I thought to wonder how he'd known where to find me.

———

After that, it got harder to sit still. The mosquitoes in my hostel kept me up; I spent long nights hitting myself in the ears and hissing profanities, but nothing worked. Welts rose on my knees and calves and feet. I looked maimed, leprotic. I thought of all this as St. Petersburg's little way of telling me to go the fuck home, idiot. But I didn't. The bites puckered and exploded and left scars the color of dust, but still I did not go home. And by midsummer I was inured to them—along with much else.

The air grew dense with littoral winds. The white nights came, and the skies stayed pearly and cloud-streaked until dawn. It was impossible to sleep. Down on the Neva, kids sat around smoking and tossing fire, and I found myself down there with them—walking along the banks, absorbed in that dazzling azure sky, staring at the upraised bridges that looked like the forked jaws of a felled beast. The Neva, so I read, would not flood this year. It flooded with some regularity, when low-pressure regions in the North Atlantic moved onshore and created seiche waves that brought the river up too high. It had flooded catastrophically in 1824, in 1924, in 1998. I'd stare at the Neva—with its reflected floodlights and shimmering midnight sun—and try to believe that its beauty was just a cover. And I liked to imagine it for some reason: the tempestuous twisting of water into a seashell spiral, the creation of mammoth standing waves, the river rising to the bridge until it buckled and broke. There was something terrible about any disaster, of course. But maybe there was something worse about things you could see coming and could not stop: celestial flash of earthbound meteor, or terminal diagnosis in tiny font, or cyclonic lows on the Baltic Sea.

At nights in the hostel that summer, I'd lie on my bed and remember. I would think about my father, and my memories of him always unspooled backward, from most recent to most distant. First, his rasping shallow breaths right before we turned up the morphine; then the staggering ghostly men of his ward in the years of his institutionalization; then his juddering mouth and his carved-out eyes and his hands, which threaded endlessly forward as though obsessively stringing an invisible rosary. The way he'd sit at the piano and play nothing, then aimless trills, then flawed Mozart sonatas. And before that: indoor soccer when my mother wasn't home, chess games after dinner, hugging trees well after it had gone out of vogue.

At the end of his life, I remember staring into my father's eyes and trying to make them the eyes of the man who'd taught me world capitals and music. But I couldn't. My imagination failed me. The man who died as my father was not the man who lived as my father. I don't think he would disagree with me on this.

I would be thirty-one in the fall. That meant I would be entering the three-year time frame in which 70 percent of people with my CAG number start to exhibit symptoms. After onset, there can be variation in the progression of symptoms, in the length of time certain competencies are maintained, in life span. But I wasn't interested in gambling on these details. A disease that takes away your cognitive abilities also takes away your capacity to value your cognitive abilities. You can decide ahead of time that you never want to be a zombie person, that once you can't write a sentence or tell a joke you are gone, the part of you that is unique and recognizable and human is gone, and that there is no value to life as a nonperson once you've experienced life as a person. But by the time you get to that point, you don't think that way anymore, if you think at all. By the time you're there, you're interested only in being warm, in being well fed, in being pain-free. Your demands are modest.

So strategizing your own exit ahead of time is a challenge. You have to outsmart your future self; somehow ensure that the priorities of today inform the choices of tomorrow. And you have no partner to rely on in this, since nobody—nobody—will help you. Even your own mind will someday turn on you and sell you out.

So I lay on my bed, those early nights in St. Petersburg, after Nikolai first found me, and started thinking seriously about my options. I didn't know what I'd see first—a lurch or a lunge or a throbbing jerk of my head—but whenever my body started driving without my steering, I'd know. And as the days grew longer and longer—my bank account emptying like a hemorrhaging organ, the nights growing luridly bright past midnight, the drinkers outside my window shouting into the dawns the hoarse joy of being young and alive—I'd start to imagine. And then my hands shook so hard that I'd wonder if they would ever stop before starting again.

9

ALEKSANDR

Leningrad, 1982

A year passed, although Aleksandr would never be able to fully account for it. He began playing independently, he knew; he acquired a useless second, Dmitry, who'd been expelled from the academy for relentless mediocrity; he registered in some tournaments around the city, where he avoided the gaze of any academy students who were playing or, increasingly, watching. During the spring and summer, he played brilliantly, apparently, on more than one occasion—he knew because he could look the games up on microfiche and, later, on the Internet. At the Leningrad City Chess Championship, he'd done tricks nobody had seen coming, he'd outwitted people who were older and more accomplished and more applauded. But his chess games had become like the functions of his autonomic nervous system—no more joyful or willful just because they were miraculously complicated. He regarded chess as his very best party trick. Something about living around the edges of the journal had made Aleksandr lose chess. And something about losing Elizabeta had made him not care.

It was startling how completely an absent person could fill the empty spaces in your brain—how all the uncharted dark matter could illuminate to reveal nothing but the same face, the same voice, carbon-copied over and over like a piece of underground artwork. It was bewildering, the way that reality could be overtaken, wrestled down, and murdered by the sheer weight of possibility. It was nonsense, he'd be the first to admit, to pine for a year for a woman whose moment in his life had been incidental, glancing, as implausible as a meteor shower or a brain aneurysm. She had bobbed to the surface of his life, then disappeared again. She'd hovered for half an hour above his personal lake of loneliness, a sea monster in a smudged photograph, probably not even real. She'd been abovewater for minutes. She'd barely even waved.

But still: when he looked back on that year, in spite of how horribly it ended, the thing that he remembered most viscerally was the feel of a woman's phantom fingers against his neck, keeping him from turning his head to look back at her.

She'd come to him once before she moved out of the building—to say goodbye, he later understood. When she knocked, it had been several months since someone at the door had made Aleksandr hopeful. Recently, knocks had been from the man next door, who increasingly wanted Aleksandr to drink with him; once the steward came by and gave Aleksandr an improbably constructed stew, which had grown a thick epidermis by the time he thought to eat it. It had been mildly embarrassing to have his happiness overheard, but it was a misery to have his solitude so widely noted. The neighbors felt sorry for him, he realized—and as soon as he knew it, he felt even sorrier for himself and tried to avoid everyone. So when Elizabeta's knock came in early September, his first impulse was to stay very still and quiet and pretend that he had disappeared or died.

But Elizabeta was having none of it. He could hear her rustling outside the door, and he knew that he would not be able to avoid opening it. Still, he was going to make her wait. "Aleksandr," she said. "Open up."

He did not, though he did sit up in bed. Through the fortochka, thick threads of sunlight illuminated the room's slow-moving dust.

"I see your slippers," said Elizabeta. "I know you're in there. Open up. It's me."

He stood up and went to the door. He rested his hand lightly on the doorknob. He remembered the first time he'd opened the door to find her there. He felt the alarming way that life turns quickly and then quickly turns back. He opened up, and there she was. She looked the same. He probably looked ugly; he certainly felt ugly. And he didn't mind her seeing, since she had made him that way.

"It's you," he said. "So it is. And who is that, exactly?"

"Can I come in?"

"Nice of you to ask."

He stood aside so she could enter. Normally, he would have brushed aside the copies of *64* so that she might sit on the bed, but this time he didn't bother. She looked awkward, and he was glad of this. "Why are you here?" he said.

She touched her hair, then her forehead. She crossed her arms. She was holding a letter in one hand. "You heard, I guess," she said.

"I heard."

"I hope you understand why I'm doing this."

"I do not."

She squinted and turned her head to the fortochka.

"When is the blessed union taking placc?" he said.

"He's a good man." The side of her face looked incarcerated in shadow.

"Good? No, I doubt that. You can tolerate him, maybe."

"I can tolerate him."

"Terrific. We should all have a life we can tolerate."

She started fiddling in her pocket for a cigarette. "Do you have a light?"

He fished around in his pocket and leaned over to bring the flame to her lips. He took three steps back again, so she would know that this gesture had not brought them any closer.

"What's that?" he said, pointing to the letter. He hoped it was from her—full of tender and tearful explanations, proclamations, apologies. Abject pleas for forgiveness. Declarations of enduring love. He had never told her he loved her, but she wasn't stupid. Then again, maybe she was. Most of his initial assessments about her had been proved exactly wrong, so now he was withholding judgment. He hoped that she'd offer him the letter and beg him to read it so that he could have the petty pleasure of refusing.

"You got a letter," she said. "From the United States. The Leningrad City Chess Club forwarded it."

He was sorry that it wasn't a letter from her, but he still held irrational feelings about it, and he didn't want to take it. "Oh yes?" he said. "That's nice."

"I thought I'd bring it up for you."

"Nice again."

"Do you think it's a fan letter?"

"I can't imagine." She was still looking out the window, still smoking—just standing there, avoiding his gaze, waiting for what? What a sorry coda this was; he'd had enough respect for their acquaintance that he felt it deserved a cleaner end. The months of silence, in retrospect, seemed more fitting, less pitiful. It was the difference between being decapitated in an instant and being clubbed to death for hours—while pleading for your life, while trying to stand up. He was suddenly disgusted with both of them. "You should go now. I'm busy." He gestured vaguely to his bed, which he hoped suggested that he'd been busy thinking through chess problems and not busy staring at the wall.

She held up the letter. It looked like a white flag in her hand. "You're not going to read it?"

He sat on the bed. He picked up a copy of *64* and stared at it. He'd already done all the problems. "Keep it for me, why don't you?" he said, not looking at her. "I don't feel like reading any letters right now."

He thought she might say something else. He waited for her to say something else. But she didn't. She only stood there dumbly a moment longer. And then she left, closing the door behind her with a care that, he had to figure, she was faking.

———

The wedding was in October at a downtown wedding palace, and Aleksandr showed up uninvited just in time to watch Elizabeta walk down the aisle to the national anthem. For the rest of his life, Aleksandr would grimace whenever he heard the song. Other people would notice and remark on how genuinely Aleksandr must have loathed the regime. But it wasn't the regime that came to mind for him when he heard the song—not Stalin's twenty million dead or men falling down in the skull-white gulag or Misha's piss-soaked psychiatric prison. It was Elizabeta walking down the aisle toward a Party official, his face smooth and expectant in the wan, faintly buzzing light.

Aleksandr stood at the back of the palace along with a few people from the building and a few people who'd come in off the street to get warm and a few women who, from the look of them, were probably Elizabeta's colleagues. Elizabeta's hair was coiled in rings around her ears. The man was as the Belgian had described him, looming and lurching even as he stood perfectly still. Elizabeta looked strange in white, when Aleksandr had always seen her in black. She was like a domesticated flower, bred through the centuries to be the wrong color. If she saw him, she pretended not to. Sonya, her roommate, stood holding limp roses and looking bewildered. Nationalistic prayers were said, papers were stamped, bride and groom were read the conditions required for legal marriage. Aleksandr turned around and walked away while the photos were being taken.

Afterward he went to the Saigon. Through his grief, the bobbing green lights looked like the phosphorescent residue that clings to the inside of your eyelids. Nikolai and Ivan were fighting about something—in the next issue, Ivan wanted to publish a petition in defense of some hapless Lithuanian, and Nikolai vehemently opposed the idea—but Aleksandr wasn't listening. For the first time ever, he was hoping to be caught—just for the theatrics of it, for the self-martyrdom. It was a cheap longing. But there was something compelling in the image of getting himself tangled in some kind of public heroism when Elizabeta was entering into the most personal kind of villainy. Maybe it would make her see. But then—see what?

Later, he would be sorry he'd thought these things. Though he wasn't superstitious, he never forgot that he'd spent Ivan's last night at the Saigon lost in great abscesses of self-pity. He never forgot that he'd found himself ready to trade in everything for a moment of regard from a girl. And that was why in low moments, on future dark nights, he could think of Nikolai and almost forgive him.

The last evening Aleksandr spent with Ivan was snowy. It was the second week of November, and snowflakes careened madly around like drunken doves. After Elizabeta's wedding, Aleksandr had found staying in his apartment during the evenings nearly unbearable. He could stand his apartment only if he came home terribly late, terribly inebriated, or both. He'd taken to buying Volzhokoe wine out of the red vending machines, since wine from the markets was usually raw alcohol, apple juice, and petrochemicals. He'd developed an approximately four-minute tolerance for his apartment at night with the lights on—enough time to throw his chess books off the bed and onto the floor, to run down the hall and splash his face with cold water, and to wrestle himself out of most of his clothes before collapsing. Any more time made him anxious and sick and sad; the look of the candlelight on his bed made the room look darker than no light at all. So he'd taken to going over to Ivan's during the evenings to drink shot after shot of vodka and listen to jazz on Voice of America or watch terrible state television. That fall *Traders of Souls* was on Channel One, over and over and over, and sometimes they'd watch and laugh at the lurid anti-Semitism, and other times they'd just get quiet and drunk.

Ivan seemed to tolerate Aleksandr's visits with an attitude ranging from bemused indifference to near-fondness. Although Ivan lived alone, too, something about his apartment didn't seem to register or reflect loneliness. Maybe it was the cat, or the books, or the constant copying and researching and typing, or the ongoing hostile conversation with the radio, or the phenomenal number of journals that Ivan somehow acquired—*Sovest'*, the pro-Communist Leningrad newspaper; *America*, the U.S. government's propaganda organ; *Woman and Russia*, the first and, as far as Aleksandr knew, only feminist samizdat. However he did it, Ivan seemed to live in the very center of his own life—not around the margins, at an awkward distance, never quite knowing where to look.

When Aleksandr reached Ivan on the last night, he was sitting in front of his tiny television, jotting notes for the next issue while watching a miniseries. The syncopated antics of the actors were a little frantic, a little desperate. Still, Ivan slapped his bony knee and smiled and offered Aleksandr a swig of vodka. The cat vibrated as loudly as the typewriter. On the television, through the static, came broad misunderstandings and wild stereotypes and unfortunate physical mishaps. It was an almost homey feeling, like some of Aleksandr's better nights in Okha, before his father died, when he was very small. Aleksandr caught himself thinking such thoughts and straightened up, cracked his neck, and swigged his vodka. Sometimes he felt as though Ivan could hear him thinking, and he didn't want Ivan to hear him thinking that.

"Are we going to include the Lithuanian, then?" said Aleksandr.

Ivan shrugged. "We probably will. Despite the objections of our dear friend Nikolai Sergeyevich."

On the television, a grim-faced man was falling-down drunk. His frantic, coarse-faced wife made hapless efforts to conceal it as she served dinner to a well-dressed man and his wife.

"Why doesn't Nikolai want to use the Lithuanian?" asked Aleksandr.

"Kolya is a continued mystery to me." Ivan barked a brief laugh at the television. "He is a man of many strong, inarticulate opinions."

On the television, the drunk man looked queasy and doubled over in the direction of the well-dressed man's shoes. The wife screamed. Ivan laughed.

"He thinks it's too provocative," said Ivan. "Don't involve the Baltics, that's what he's always said. He thinks it's one step too far. But what does he know? He's not exactly running the show, is he? Not exactly a creative driving force, huh?" He stood up and started to pace, running his fingers along the stacks of books and papers. "He keeps the records, he incurs the risks. But he doesn't really care. Nikolai Sergeyevich is my friend, but I'll tell you this: he'd get caught up in whatever it was that surrounded him. He's a radical in search of a cause. We're only lucky it's ours."

Aleksandr thought about this. Outside, the snow was making feathery white fingers against the window. Pieces flew away into the orbit of the streetlight, spinning slowly and turning the color of embers.

"So," said Ivan after a moment. "I hear your girl got married?"

"Yes." Something about looking out the window at the snow made him not mind as much; it was like being able to control the pain of some gruesome internal injury by keeping impossibly, inhumanly still.

"Better to him than to you, though."

Aleksandr dragged his gaze away from the snow. "What do you mean?"

"With a girl like that, it's better to stay one of her regrets. Better to stay on that side of the ledger, you know? You don't want to be the man standing between her and her ghosts. You want to be one of the ghosts."

"Maybe," said Aleksandr, and he thought he could like that formulation. Right now, maybe, he was standing in the back of Elizabeta's head, etched in black and white, flickering like a hologram, muted and waving. Right now, maybe, at this very moment, they were haunting each other.

Ivan sat down, jostling the sofa and scattering his papers. "You haven't lived in a place unless you have at least one major regret there," he said. Aleksandr experienced a charge in the air, a flash of prekinetic energy, and wondered if Ivan would say something about it. The moment passed, and Ivan sat back and pounded Aleksandr on the shoulder. "So welcome to Leningrad officially, tovarish."

Aleksandr was about to sarcastically thank him when the comedy program cut out, the television hissing to a black-and-white buzz before crackling back to life. When the image rematerialized, the comic actors were gone, replaced by a somber and dark-clad newscaster who unleashed a spattering of language like rubber bullets on an unruly mob.

"Why are they doing that?" said Aleksandr.

"Shh." Ivan clicked up the volume and stood close to the television.

"What is it?" The newscaster was introducing a program about Stalin's strategic genius during World War II.

"Shh." Ivan's eyeball was almost against the screen. "Be quiet." Together they listened, but the newscaster was only expounding on the glories of the Russian nation.

"That's very strange," said Aleksandr.

"He's dead."

"What?"

"Brezhnev's dead."

"Did they say that?" Aleksandr wondered if maybe he'd missed something. He listened harder.

"No," said Ivan. "But look at how he's dressed. Look at his expression. Why are they cutting in to a comedy program with this pseudo-historical shit?"

There was a sheen of panic to the newscaster's expression, Aleksandr noticed. Something dark and knowing seemed to bob to the surface of his face from time to time before being forced down again.

"He's dead," said Ivan. "I would bet on it." He stood up and started pacing the room, swinging his head slightly, like an annoyed horse. He clasped his hands behind his back. "Well." He stopped walking, swore in victory, and started walking again. "Well. This is going to be interesting."

"Are we covering it? Before it's announced?"

"We'll start, anyway. It won't stay unannounced forever. A week, tops, I'd say. But they'll want to get succession sorted out in quiet."

Aleksandr nodded and looked out the window again. The snow was coming in quicker currents, crystalline spirals that swirled tighter and tighter until he felt almost dizzy. He wondered what would be coming next.

"The funeral is going to be something," Ivan was saying. "They'll really do it up right. It will be the greatest show they've put on for a while. The security will be very, very tight."

"So what are we going to do about it?"

Ivan looked almost dreamy. His eyes were becoming iron-colored in the low light; his expression was stricken and oracular, as though he were seeing through Aleksandr and all the way into the forbidding future.

"Alyosha," he said. "We're going to paper the city."

Walking back from Ivan's, Aleksandr did a minor dance in the street. When the news was announced, public celebration would be unthinkable. But now, before the news was out, he could whirl around in the snow without worry—he could cheer, and hoot, and throw fistfuls of snow that came back down at him in sparks and made him shiver. There was nothing to celebrate, really, he knew that. There was another Brezhnev after Brezhnev, and another Brezhnev after that. But for the moment there was no Brezhnev, and Aleksandr was one of the only ones who knew. He careened and skidded, stamped muffled boot-prints into the snow. The stars looked sharper in the wintertime. The darkness, which was so complete and came so early, made the salt stains of light in the sky more luminous.

Aleksandr considered what Ivan had said about regrets—how they tied us to a place, made us belong there. Aleksandr wondered what Ivan's one major regret was. He'd meant to ask him, but the television had cut in so quickly, and the moment had passed.

He pressed his bare hands into the snow until his forearms ached. He did flamboyant kicks in the air. Drivers of white Volgas, if any were passing, remarked without interest that there was a very drunk man on the sidewalk.

————

The knock came a few nights later. It was the middle of the night, and for a half-dreamed moment Aleksandr thought it was Elizabeta again—until he remembered that she'd moved out and that she didn't knock like that, anyway, with meaty, demanding knuckles scraping against the door. The next moment he thought he'd been evicted— maybe the steward had learned of his involvement with *A Partial History of Lost Causes* and had decided that the risks were too high, there were children in the building, idiot, didn't he know anything? She'd come to run him out of the building in the night, giving him a head start in the damp darkness, in case anybody was already after him. Maybe she'd throw his things out after him, socks and suitcase making a haphazard chessboard against the white snow.

But the knocking grew louder and more frantic and then he knew: he was fucked. It was KGB at the door, and they were coming to kill or bribe or break him, and any of the three would be easy to do.

But it wasn't. It was Nikolai, hunched in the darkness like a creature.

"Let me in," he choked. "For fuck's sake, let me in."

Aleksandr did, and Nikolai half fell into the room. He was shivering, though he was generally not the shivering type. Aleksandr backed away, and Nikolai staggered toward the bed, where he sat—crunching Aleksandr's sheets underneath him, smearing dirty snow on the bed— and spent a moment breathing loudly. Aleksandr realized how much he did not want to ask Nikolai what was wrong.

"Well," said Nikolai. "You might as well know that Ivan Dmietrivich is dead."

"What?" Aleksandr found he couldn't hear himself. "What?"

"He was hit by a bus." Nikolai was still breathing far too loudly, with great desperate wheezes that seemed to arise from some horrible oxygen deprivation—as though he'd been held underneath the Neva far too long, or been cast out of his spaceship without a helmet and had banged on the window, clutched at the door, and turned pale and stricken as his lungs collapsed, his ears rang, his body understood. "Honestly," he said. "Can't you offer a man a drink?"

"What are you talking about? A bus? What are you saying?"

"A bus. You know? The large public transportation vehicles? Are you familiar? Misha is in the hospital."

"They were both hit by a bus? The same bus?"

"They were drunk. It was late. You know how much they drink."

"This just happened?"

"Yes, it just happened." Nikolai's breathing was becoming more hysterical than seemed appropriate for his heft. "I don't usually come visit you in the middle of the night, do I? I don't usually find myself unable to sleep without a good-night from you, do I? Why would I come here now if it hadn't just happened?"

"A bus? At night?"

Nikolai glared at Aleksandr. "It was a night bus."

"What happened to the driver?"

"What?"

"Was he arrested? Where he is now? How did he manage to hit two people with his fucking bus?"

Nikolai blinked at Aleksandr. "It was late. They were very drunk, as I said. It wasn't really a discussion."

He was quiet, and then asked Aleksandr for water so wearily and pleadingly that Aleksandr found himself walking down the hall with one of his cleaner chipped cups, filling it with the water that always tasted vaguely of blood and metal and sardines, and walking back and offering it to Nikolai. They sat on Aleksandr's bed, on the sheets that would never get warm again tonight after being turned out so long in the midnight chill. Then Nikolai began to talk.

They were coming out of the Saigon, Nikolai said, when it happened. Misha had been thrown twenty feet and was deposited on a dead bush, its frozen branches breaking underneath him and splintering his face. Ivan had been killed almost instantly, his legs and most of his internal organs cut underneath the front wheels of the bus. Aleksandr's imagination hovered over the word "almost." He couldn't stand it. It made his own internal organs rebel and collapse, shrink away from the light, when he thought of it.

Misha would live. Nothing could kill Misha, Nikolai said, and attempted a laugh that sounded like a cough. Aleksandr didn't laugh. He stared at a tea stain on the floor. Some remote part of his head wondered where it had come from. Had it been there always? Had Elizabeta noticed it? Had he done it himself one of these recent nights, after he'd come back from Ivan's half drunk and half blind in the dark, too lonely to notice or care where his teacups landed when he scattered them? Next to him, Nikolai seemed to fade. He slumped down. His breathing became slow and shallow. Aleksandr thought he might be falling asleep.

He could almost see it. The two of them stepping into the street, the biting gray slush kicking up into their ankles, the bus a dull yellow ambush. There was something too terrible about dying in a busy street with snow that was unclean and overused. Ivan deserved to die in great shoals of clean white snow, drifted and ridged like salt from an evaporated sea. He deserved better than to die in the exhaust from inefficient vehicles, in an alley between stalls that sold bloodied fish and rotten potatoes during the day. But that was how it had been, Nikolai said, and Aleksandr's imagination had never been such a liability as it was the night after Ivan died: he could see him, jaw unhinged, his face a melting mask, his expression otherworldly and, for the first time in Aleksandr's imagination, afraid.

When Aleksandr woke up, Nikolai was gone. He'd left Misha's hospital room number on a slip of paper, and his socks balled up under the bed. When Aleksandr went to pick them up, he found them crusted with blood. He dropped them in revulsion. Then he threw them out the fortochka.

Walking through Leningrad, he skirted the city's center, cutting south on Ligovsky, giving wide berth to the Saigon. He knew that there was nothing there now; in the night, the upset stalls had been righted, the blood had been mopped up by industrial state mops, the bus had been towed away to some broken-down automobile ossuary on the outside of the city. But he could still imagine it every time he blinked: the screech of rusted brakes, maybe, the thick thud of a person falling too hard into snow.

It wasn't that he couldn't believe it. He could believe it, the way he could believe that there was no life after death, that the world would someday hurtle itself into the sun, that he might always live alone. It was the kind of information that, once believed, left one with almost nothing to do but lie down on the ground and believe it some more.

The hospital was a stocky flint-gray building with bars on the windows. At the reception desk sat a woman with faintly red hair and skin stretched too far over her bones, as though her skull had continued growing for several years after her face had stopped.

"Yes?" she said, not looking up.

"I'm here to visit Mikhail Andreyevich. He's here. In room 219."

"If you know where he is, then go," said the receptionist. "What are you asking me for?"

Aleksandr walked down the hallway. The walls and floor were the color of a femur. Every few doorknobs were bunched with plastic flowers in leering yellows and oranges, stiff-limbed stuffed animals, tiny Soviet flags. Aleksandr thought about the people behind the unornamented doors.

When Aleksandr entered the room, he was relieved to see that Misha seemed to be asleep. He lay with his eyes closed, his face a tessellation of gashes of varying severity. Aleksandr walked toward him and leaned over to look more closely. A particularly deep laceration threaded just underneath Misha's eye, and it was easy to tell how close he'd come to losing it. Aleksandr touched Misha's hand lightly. His skin was the consistency of mosquito paper and the color of the unwashed hospital sheets. There was something perversely comical in Misha's survival. Misha had, after all, already been halfway out the door—part skeleton, part mad, mostly ghost.

"Get better, Misha," Aleksandr said. "Good luck." He cupped Misha's forehead briefly.

Misha's eyes snapped open. Open, they occupied an unnerving amount of his face, as though he were a nocturnal creature adapted to looking only into darkness. "Who the fuck are you?" he said.

Aleksandr immediately removed his hand from Misha's head and pretended to be righting the sheets, which had curled out from their corners. Bits of foam erupted from the exposed mattress, stained with substances in dark and ominous colors. "I'm Aleksandr Kimovich," he said. "I'm a friend of Ivan's. I was a friend of Ivan's."

"Are you with Nikolai Sergeyevich?"

"Nikolai's not here right now."

"No." Misha sat up. He perched himself on his elbows. Through Misha's skin, Aleksandr could see where his elbow bone bisected. He could see his jutting breastplate creating a second collarbone across his chest. "I'm saying, are you fucking *with* Nikolai Sergeyevich?"

"We've met. At the Saigon, remember, and at Stalin's centennial." Misha only blinked, his enormous bat eyes shining and reproachful. "I don't know what you're talking about," Aleksandr said finally.

"I remember you." Misha closed his eyes. Aleksandr felt much calmer around Misha when he had his eyes closed. "You're not very memorable. But Ivan trusted you. He told me that when he came to see me a few times at my mother's. I don't know why, personally. You seem sort of slow to me."

"I'm not the one handcuffed to a bed," said Aleksandr. He stopped tugging at the sheets and let one corner come untucked. He hoped Misha would roll onto it in the night and feel the cold of the recycled mattress against his skin.

"But Ivan trusted you," said Misha. "Come here."

"Where?"

"Closer."

"I'd rather not." Misha smelled like formaldehyde and lime cleansers.

Misha's eyes fluttered open again, and Aleksandr could see the shivering capillaries in his eyeballs. He could see the faint gesture of a heartbeat in his wrist. "Aleksandr," said Misha almost imperceptibly. "It was Nikolai."

"What?" said Aleksandr, although something in the back of his head was starting to shudder and grind to life. It was a feeling he knew from chess: it came in the moment when he knew what he was going to do next, before he completely knew why.

"He was behind us. He signaled the bus." Misha's voice was almost nothing, the sound of a skull slipping into snow.

"How? How did he signal?" Aleksandr spoke without moving his lips.

Misha's eyes looked wet and unseeing, orbs of volcanic rock stuck awkwardly into his head. He stared at Aleksandr hard. Then he jerked his head.

"That," said Misha, "is how he signaled."

"If you saw him," said Aleksandr, trying to keep his voice even. "If you saw him signal, then why didn't you shout?"

"I didn't know it was a signal until afterward. He jerked his head. I saw him jerk his head."

"Okay," said Aleksandr. "Okay." He blinked and saw Ivan and Nikolai arguing over the Lithuanian. He blinked and saw Nikolai's leather jacket. He blinked and saw Nikolai the night before, his bloodied socks, his ragged breaths. He blinked and saw Nikolai's notebooks.

"Well, what am I supposed to do?" Aleksandr hissed at Misha.

Misha looked at him witheringly. "I'm sure *I* don't know. I'd think your little advice column, or whatever, is finished. You've got bigger problems now, tovarish. I'm sure the smart thing to do is to lay low and behave yourself."

"What are you going to do?"

"Me?" Misha snorted. "I'm obviously supposed to be dead. I was thinking of blowing up the Kremlin. I was thinking of assassinating Brezhnev. You hear that?" He was shouting. "I'm going to fucking kill Brezhnev. I'm going to have a day of it. I'm going to get myself killed, and I'm going to defile the corpse of Lenin first. Fuck them all! Fuck them *all*! You hear me?" Aleksandr could hear the rustling and clucking of a phalanx of nurses on the march down the hall, armed with sedatives for Misha.

"You're going to get yourself put in Matrosskaya Tishina," said Aleksandr. "You know that?"

"Don't trouble yourself," said Misha. "Try to be less stupid, okay? Just remember about Nikolai." Then he was once more shouting, thrashing the sheets, knocking over his bedside water, and hurling profanities. The dismissive red-haired nurse from the reception desk entered and stuck Misha in the neck with an epic needle. His eyes froze in place, and his withered hands dropped to the sheets.

"The pain medication has made him crazy, perhaps," said Aleksandr.

The nurse's mouth twisted, and she looked at Aleksandr a little longer than people normally did.

"Yes," she said. "Perhaps."

———

The first thing Aleksandr did was break in to Ivan's apartment. It was easy to do: he slid his internal passport between the cheap lock and the shoddy doorframe, and the door popped open. The cat was quivering and belligerent and threw herself against Aleksandr's legs with homicidal rage. He hadn't thought to bring anything for her, so he tossed out some linty bread crumbs from his pocket and hoped she wouldn't notice. He pulled the light string.

The apartment, never orderly, had exploded. The mattress had been overturned. The dresser bulged with open drawers and overflowing clothes. Papers were two inches deep on the floor, and they caught at Aleksandr's ankles as he walked through the room. The poster of Brigitte Bardot was, ludicrously, gone.

Okay, thought Aleksandr. I see.

There were some drafts for the upcoming issue underneath the couch, and he wrestled them out from puffs of dust and loose coins and a smear of something sticky and indecipherable. On the coffee table, Ivan's ancient Leica was decapitated, all its film exposed to the unforgiving light. Underneath Ivan's best shirt, Aleksandr found some photographs—a woman, a little boy, an old couple—but he didn't recognize anyone. He thought again of Ivan's regrets and wondered if any of these people counted among them. He realized that he'd never heard Ivan speak of anything besides the next or last issue, the depravity of the government, the idiocy of Aleksandr and Nikolai, the torment of Misha, or the needs of the cat. Aleksandr wheeled back through his memories of Ivan, but there was nothing else—no childhood, no loves, no personal disasters. No explanation for living alone with a cat. No moment of revelation that led him to risk his life over and over, to antagonize a system that would, realistically, remain in power forever. And that was all it had been—antagonism. They'd been an irritant, perhaps, on a good day, like a monkey pestering an elephant that can, at any time, snap the monkey underfoot and crunch its head flat. For the elephant, it's only a question of when. It's only a question of summoning the energy.

It was entirely possible that Misha was right.

There wasn't much left in Ivan's apartment to find. The KGB had taken a lot, more than they could possibly find useful. They seemed to have taken dirty socks and irrelevant receipt paper. They'd taken bits of coinage. The typewriter with the carbon paper was, of course, gone. Most notably, they had taken the books.

The cat whimpered, and Aleksandr picked her up. He could feel the whirring of her little chest and wondered what mechanism it was that kept it running.

"I guess you're mine now, huh?" said Aleksandr.

Natasha nipped him on the thumb.

———

He borrowed an ancient typewriter from one of the academic subscribers. He got more carbon paper. He spent four days typing, until his thumbs and elbows pulsed in protest. He was good at sitting still and engaging in slight repetitive motions; chess had prepared him for this, if nothing else. He stapled them all together in the oncoming white light of dawn, as his last candle was melting down into a waxy pool. He left Natasha with some desiccated mushrooms on the floor.

He took the train up to Moscow alone, standing up sideways in the hallway, since all the cars were full, and watching the engineer tap the wheels for metal fatigue before the train pulled away from the station. Aleksandr wore a coat with another coat underneath. Under the second coat, he held twenty-five copies of the final issue of *A Partial History of Lost Causes*.

The metro in Moscow was choked with security. Men sat with their hats off, looking blankly through the windows into the whirring underground darkness. Underneath the subterranean chandeliers and light-drenched alcoves, everybody was wearing black.

Two streets from Red Square, he could hear the brass horns, too jaunty and bombastic for the occasion. He knew he couldn't get close. There would be scores of gray-coated, grim-faced soldiers, red flags slung over their shoulders, their knees snapping in time together. They would be thronging toward the Kremlin, Brezhnev's coffin squatting darkly in the center. In the Kremlin there would be heads of state, Arab nationalistic leaders in keffiyehs, African dictators in traditional garb. They would all bend their heads together, assuming expressions of reflection and loss.

Outside the moving stand of soldiers, there were mourners: nearest the center were the ones who'd been recruited and paid; nearer the outside were coils of genuine grievers, and curious passersby, and people who'd brought their children to see history, and people who just didn't want to go home yet. Some of them looked positively gleeful— a small vial of something alcoholic was passed from hand to hand, and an old man spat gray expectorate on the ground every time Brezhnev's name was mentioned. One woman wept openly, her face unfolding, rubbing her brown sleeves across the delicate skin under her eyes until her cheeks became inflamed, and saying, "He was a good man. He was a good man. What will become of us now?"

When the crowds parted from time to time, Aleksandr could catch snatches of the ceremony as it progressed: the gray-and-red-clad soldiers, the brass band, the gold-limned black coffin, which, from a distance, looked like a transatlantic steamship on a pitching sea. There was something callous in its ostentation, its forbidding elegance. Something so palatial didn't seem to want to mourn as much as parade.

Aleksandr could feel the sheets pressed to his chest, absorbing the shock of his rapid heartbeats. He wasn't sure how he should proceed.

Ivan had never done something this stupid—he'd always operated with the utmost discretion, with careful and obsessively confirmed lists made of the initial recipients. He let the pamphlets thread out of their own accord after the initial copies were distributed; other people copied them in twos and fives and sevens and passed them on to trusted friends. It was a diffusion of risk that way, he'd always said. Still, risks didn't always get you killed. And precautions couldn't always keep you safe.

Aleksandr stepped back from the crowd, letting the people become a seething mass of dark-colored coats that shivered and peered as one. The wind began to pick up, its icy fingers drumming against his spine and taking liberties with his pants. Dead leaves, the color of rust and flint, whipped along the ground. In the street skittered programs commemorating Brezhnev, his gloomy face gazing sternly from underneath his single monstrous eyebrow. Delicate plumes of snow materialized from nowhere and cast themselves through the air.

Aleksandr took out the papers. He waited. He could still hear the tinny clanging of the band, the thick thudding of feet stamping in unison against the cobblestones. The wind seized upon him with the aggression of a vengeful arctic ghost, and he felt himself let the papers fly. They whirled outward in four directions, spinning through the air like weather. They were beautiful as they caught on the wind—they looked like white long-winged birds, maybe, or shivering bridal veils. He knew that soon they would come back to earth to be muddied and ripped, tramped underfoot by men in heavy boots. But maybe a few people would be curious enough to pick them up.

He turned quickly to go, his two coats billowing out behind him and his lungs overwhelmed by the influx of air. It was descending into the particular kind of cold that belongs to a Russian late afternoon: the kind of cold that threatens, that intimidates, because it is going to get so much worse. And, at some distance, leaning against a streetlamp, was Nikolai.

Bits of snow were catching on sideways drafts to make eddies in the air. They were turning Nikolai's hair white, Aleksandr would always remember, as though he were witnessing some supernatural shock. He was looking at Aleksandr. Aleksandr was almost sure of it. He stood looking until the watching people started to disperse, propelled by the harsh pings of the national anthem, and he was engulfed by the thickening snow and the gathering crowds.

Aleksandr didn't find Nikolai again. But once he went looking, he started seeing him everywhere.

10

IRINA

St. Petersburg, 2006

And then the summer was over, and I did not know where it had gone. There were listless courses around the city, respectful and silent visits to the chilly long-abandoned houses of great writers, voracious reading of the chronically postponed Russian classics. I wrote scraps of pointless poems on the backs of napkins. I developed a taste for tea. I practiced making Russian statements about what had happened in the past, about what would happen in the future, about what might happen and what should happen. I learned to properly decline my nouns. Around me, the leaves paled and fell, leaving stark black branches that forked against the snow. It grew cold, a kind of cold that made me understand that I'd never understood cold before this—certainly not in those shallow Boston winters, mitigated by the churning Atlantic, uncomfortably brusque but leaving you with just enough composure to walk upright, to look around, to admire the way the seagulls seemed to shiver and how the tufts of snow on all the trees made the city beautiful and ornate.

The cold, that winter in Russia—it was striking in its absoluteness, its bracing singularity. It was an astronomical cold, otherworldly and menacing, and it left me bent, submissive, muttering curses to I don't know who. But there was something I liked about it, too. There was some wisdom, it seemed, in coming to terms with the fact that there could be something beyond what felt like nothing. That there were realities outside of imagination.

The Neva marbleized and turned still. Through the frost, the moon grew three haloes. Attempts at communication—from my mother, from Claire—slowed and then staggered, like a relenting hemorrhage from a severed limb. They kept at it periodically—my in-box, when I bothered to check it at the Internet café, was peppered with pleas, rants, the odd attempt at normalcy, as though I could be tricked by feigned casualness into responding—though I didn't answer. It was cruel. I know I was being cruel. But I didn't have the energy not to be.

I felt myself growing passive and immobilized. The cold pinned me down; I could feel in my bones a fatigue, an oncoming frailty. I felt lucky for the chance I'd had to disappear from everyone else. I started to wonder if I hadn't disappeared from myself a little, too.

———

I began writing to Jonathan, long-winded and inarticulate letters that I knew I'd never send. I talked to him about the beginning, about how the days after seeing him were always a little like heroin withdrawal, about the shaky, wrung-out feeling of having all the serotonin in your body explode and disappear at one burst. I said that he was a wholly singular occurrence in my life. I said that I wasn't asking him to understand anything else, but I needed him to understand that. I said that he was the most implausible plot point in the fairly implausible narrative of my life. I said that we do not know ourselves, so how could we ever really know each other? I talked about biology and pair-bonding and pheromones. I talked about Rilke's idea of love as the bordering of two great solitudes. I talked about the subject-object problem. I talked about the arbitrary mythology of romance, the post-Arthurian nonsense we still cling to, nationally and culturally. I talked about divorce rates. I talked about my mother's metastatic grief. I talked about my own cellular, atavistic, visceral fear. I talked about suicide and how many Huntington's patients commit suicide—usually once they've lost some mobility but before they've lost their minds. They wrestle themselves

into their cars to breathe in carbon monoxide; they shoot themselves
in the head if they live in a state where that is easy to do. Their hands
shake, their arms jerk. Sometimes they need to ask for help in this,
their final act of independence. I told him that I had always known I
was not cut out for terminal illness. I told him that I had always known
about him, that the first time I'd seen him I'd known about him, that
this was not just the retroactive sentimentalization of an ordinary day,
that I had known. I told him that this was not possible. I told him that
he was the single most beautiful human I had ever seen. I told him that
this was due to uncontrollable evolutionarily wired neuron firings in
my brain, my still-functioning brain. I told him I was sorry for what I
was doing. I told him there was no such thing as free will. I told him I
loved him. I told him there was no such thing as love.

I wandered the city—through the epic emptiness of Palace Square,
past the filigreed willow-colored Winter Palace, to the rotunda of St.
Isaac's, spiking up through the mist. I walked to the Church of the
Savior on Spilled Blood and stared at the gorgeous schizophrenia of
its spires. I traced the canals and counted the houses, all done up in
cupcake pastels. I walked past Kazan Cathedral, turning the color of
manganese in the November light. I watched adolescent daughters
walking hand in hand with their mothers. I watched the passersby in
the metro bend down and actually give money to the beggar women.

I began to research Bezetov. As far as I could tell, his coalition, Alternative Russia, served as an umbrella organization that included several
subgroups, such as Pomerancovo and Right Russia. Pomerancovo was
apparently the more conventionally liberal of the two—pro-West, pro-
trade, pro–civil liberties, pro-democracy, anti-corruption, pro-reform.
Right Russia was a bit more complicated—they were reactionary, contrarian, uneasy with the status quo but with vague, slightly alarming
ideas about what should be happening instead. They'd harnessed resentment from all corners, played on xenophobia and nationalism, and
were as willing to exploit frustration with Central Asian workers as
they were to exploit frustration with the regime. It wasn't entirely clear
to me why Alternative Russia counted Right Russia as an ally, though
I stumbled across a YouTube video of Bezetov answering that exact

question—muttering something about the virtues of a broad tent, the power of a diverse coalition. A man named Mikhail Andreyevich Solovyov headed up Right Russia. Further research revealed that their offices were located on Konyushennaya Ulitsa, a block from the Moika, where I went every day to throw coins.

I thought about going to see him. I walked by, and I walked by again, and I approached and examined the doorbell, just to make sure they had one, I told myself. I meandered past the windows, slowed down, looked in—expecting to see what? I wondered. Aleksandr Bezetov himself, at the office for some kind of intergroup summit, staring idly out the window and just hoping to be accosted by an aimless American? I caught glimpses of dour young people and the luminous glow of computers. I didn't see Aleksandr Bezetov. Neither did I see Mikhail Andreyevich Solovyov.

One day I did it. I hadn't necessarily planned for that day to be the day; I walked by and peered, as usual, but then some sliver of self-disgust caught me, and I marched to the door. I rang the doorbell and skittered back quickly, as though my distance from the door would absolve me from any reprimands that might be forthcoming.

The door opened. A sallow man stared out at me. There was something wrong with his face, though I couldn't quite figure out what—the angles or contours seemed off somehow, by some nearly imperceptible degree.

"Hello," I said.

"Hello." The meat of his eyeballs was inflamed, blood-colored. I wondered why they let this guy answer the door.

"These are the offices of Right Russia?"

He cocked his head impatiently toward the sign.

"Is Mikhail Andreyevich Solovyov available, please?"

He stood aside and gestured for me to enter. Inside, the office was dank, piled to the rafters with papers and paraphernalia. Two interns clacked desultorily at two oversize, outdated computers. The computers wheezed and whirred alarmingly; they seemed on the verge of giving up the ghost entirely. A phone rang forlornly, but nobody answered it.

The man who'd answered the door led me into a back room. He

flicked on the light. A trash can was overturned, and the man stooped to right it. When he did, his shirt rode up to reveal a wedge of pale flesh spidered with black hair. I grimaced. He spun a chair around for me. "Sit," he said. "Please."

I sat. Closer, I could see that he had a silver sickle-shaped scar running from eye to jowl. It was an odd scar; one couldn't quite decipher what might have produced it, though I thought briefly of small-arms combat. On the wall behind him, a tattered poster proclaimed that RUSSIA IS FOR RUSSIANS!

"Is this where I'll wait for Mikhail Andreyevich Solovyov?"

"I'm Mikhail Andreyevich Solovyov," he said. "You can call me Misha."

"You are?" I said. "Oh. You are."

He stared at me, an unwavering, unnerving gaze. I shifted in my chair. I wondered again about the scar. Maybe he'd been a soldier, though this had not turned up in my Google searches.

"And this might be a good time to tell me who you are," he said.

His pants were too short. When he leaned back, I saw a slab of hairy, bright white ankle. I decided to go with the short answer first.

"I'm Irina Ellison," I said. "I'm trying to arrange a meeting with Aleksandr Bezetov. I met with an old friend of his in Moscow, and she suggested I might try to contact some of his colleagues." I would have added something about hoping I wasn't imposing, if it hadn't been so evident that I was.

"You met with—who, exactly?"

"Elizabeta Nazarovna. She was his secretary, I think."

Mikhail Andreyevich—I was having trouble thinking of him as Misha—snorted. "His secretary? Is that what the kids are calling it these days?"

I chose to ignore this. I stared at the poster above Mikhail's head. "I understand you and Aleksandr Bezetov are colleagues?"

"We are." He straightened up in his chair, and his sneer softened marginally. "We absolutely are."

"You can get me a meeting, then?"

"A meeting. Well." He coughed. "A meeting is difficult."

"Just a short one."

Mikhail Andreyevich sat back in his chair. He chewed his lip for several long moments while looking at me curiously—trying to decide, I guess, how much of his time I was worth. "Bezetov is a chickenshit," he finally declared.

I had not been expecting this. "I thought you said he was your colleague."

"That doesn't mean he's not a chickenshit. I've never met someone with a more maudlin attachment to his own life."

I blinked. "Is this why you can't get me a meeting?"

He sneered again, making his scar zigzag. "He surrounds himself with this army of handlers. He's in full-body armor every time he leaves the house."

I pictured bulletproof vests. I pictured chain mail. "Well," I said. "Doesn't he need it?"

Mikhail Andreyevich snorted again. "Yeah, well, we all need a lot of things. Only a few of us get them."

I was suddenly miserable. The conversation was twisting aggressively, wrongly; some odd torque was at work that I couldn't quite fathom. I'd assumed that Bezetov was beloved by everyone, as he'd been beloved by my father. This was the essential premise, the only one. I shifted in my seat. "So Right Russia is—not affiliated with Alternative Russia?" I said.

"Affiliated, sure. We're all very affiliated. But they don't like us. We're the embarrassing bastard stepchild. They keep their distance from us as much as possible. We're not their type. They prefer Pomerancovo. You know. Fuzzy-headed, idealistic. Western-backed. Insane."

I decided not to act surprised that he was bothering to tell me all this. "And your position is what, exactly?" I asked, though the posters had given me more than a few clues. "You have—policy differences?"

"We have aesthetic differences."

"That's kind of shallow, isn't it?" All at once I felt absolutely sure that bullshitting my way through this conversation was the correct course of action.

"Spiritual differences, then."

I scoffed, just to scoff. Mikhail Andreyevich sighed witheringly.

"We think change needs to be authentic, permanent. We think it needs to come from within. We think it needs to be populist. Bezetov is a dreadful elitist."

"Is he?" I brightened momentarily. I found I was more comfortable with elitism than abject cowardice.

"Absolutely. He doesn't even like the Russian people. You couldn't pay him to interact with them. He's up there in his castle, typing up his press releases, and he doesn't know anything about the nation he's trying to run."

"Isn't he just trying to stay alive?"

"Whatever. Any idiot can stay alive. Any fucking amoeba can stay alive. That's just evolution. It's what you do once you've managed to stay alive that counts."

I pondered this. He made it all sound so easy.

He leaned back in his chair with some decisiveness. "You know," he said, "I'm not surprised you're here."

"You're not— What?" I was surprised I was there.

"It's what I've always suspected about him. The Americans are in charge of everything. He doesn't have an original thought in his head."

"What are you talking about?"

He waved his hand at me with exasperation. "I understand, I understand. The need for discretion and all that. Of course."

"I don't have a clue what you are talking about."

"Right, right. Me, neither." He stared at me with a creepy know-ingness, then smiled a smile that was nearly kind. "You're a fan, then? That's the story?"

"Sort of."

"Well," he said grandly. "Of course. We're all terrific fans of Beze-tov's. And you want to see him, particularly, why?"

I told him, or I tried to. I was learning how to say it better. He listened. His face, if possible, seemed to turn even yellower. "Really?" he finally said.

"Really."

"*Really?*"

I glared. Mikhail Andreyevich squinted. "You sound like you're looking for a therapist."

I flinched. "No."

"A priest, then."

"Even worse."

"He has symbolic value to you."

"He has, uh, literal value to me, too."

"You think he's going to be able to tell you something you don't already know?"

"Anybody could tell me something I don't already know."

"The right something, though?"

I was exhausted. I felt a dull cinder of pain behind my eye. "I don't know. I don't know. Maybe not." I coughed feebly into my shoulder for effect.

Mikhail Andreyevich chewed some more on his lip, which looked abused, macerated. This was unbecoming. "What do you know about him?"

"He's— Well, he's the chess champion."

"Yes. Very good."

"And he's running for president." I felt like a child.

"But you know his campaign is a stunt, right? You know he knows he will not win."

This man, it was becoming obvious, was disgruntled—and so the strange, sharp-edged defensiveness that was emerging in me was, I told myself, obviously unwarranted. Bezetov's moral credentials were impeccable. I tried to sound light, unguarded, as though I were arguing a point of politics or philosophy, nothing personal, nothing brutal. How much I'd loved to argue about those things once.

"Sure, he knows he won't win," I said, "but that's what's impressive about it. That's what's brave about it. That's the point."

"Is it? I don't know about that."

"What is the point, then?"

"The question isn't whether you like your revolutions fast or slow—it's whether you like them temporary or permanent. Bezetov absorbs the attention, the money, the support from more pragmatic people—people who might have an actual shot at election and who could reform moderately from within. Bezetov gets the limelight because of his fucking chess career, and everyone thinks, Oh, how spectacular! How dazzling! Chess strategy at the state level, and all that makes for a compelling narrative. I will never understand that man's public relations situation. It's extraordinary. No matter what he does, he gives the entire Western world a boner. But what's the best thing for Russia, really? Is it losing their chances again on some aging chess star's vanity project? Or is it electing some serious people who will pull and tug and compromise their way to a more humane life? What's the brave thing, really?"

My defensiveness was collapsing into something else, something miserable and small. Aleksandr Bezetov was a man whom my father had deemed important. I didn't want to hear him slandered. My quest was absurd at its absolute best, this I knew. It was misdirected, it was odd—even if Aleksandr were a hero, even if he were a saint. I found I desperately did not want to hear about it if there was more to him than that: if his colleagues had complaints, or if they'd found him wanting in one way or another. His job was to deliver me the wisdom of a life-time. If he couldn't do that, I had no reason to be here. And I had no reason to be anywhere else. I was quiet, eyeing Mikhail Andreyevich's posters.

"But, I mean—I'm looking at your posters and, forgive me, but I read your Wikipedia page, and—"

"And?"

"And you're not exactly a moderate yourself, right?"

He laughed. "I'm not anything anymore."

"What does that even mean?"

"I don't really believe anything. I'm just trying to make the conversation more interesting."

"Is that a worthy goal? Making the conversation more interesting?" I didn't disagree. I was interrogating him reflexively because I'd decided not to like him.

"When you've had seventy years of no conversation, yes, I think it's a very worthy goal."

We were silent. I was cold, and I rubbed my hands together to kick up the circulation.

"You know about the film he's making?" said Mikhail Andreyevich after a moment.

"Of course." Then, "Remind me."

"He's trying to establish a link between the apartment bombings and the regime."

That sounded familiar. I remembered something about the commencement of the second Chechen war: a series of odd coincidences that looked, on the surface, somewhat sinister. Still, my impression up to that point had been that this was the kind of paranoid silliness that led my shriller liberal comrades in Cambridge to make dark intimations about George W. Bush and September 11.

"The thought was that it was a political move?" I said.

"To usher Putin into power. He came in on a hard-line security platform."

"Do you think it's true?"

"I'm not sure it's true. I certainly hope it's true. That might be egregious enough to make all the difference."

"Make the conversation more interesting, you mean."

"Right."

He cupped his chin in his hand—it was an oddly dainty, feminine gesture, and maybe it made him feel confiding. "To be honest with you," he said, "I'm pretty impressed with the film idea."

"You are?"

"Yes. And I'm not impressed by everything Bezetov does."

"I've gathered."

"But this, I think, will raise some interesting questions."

"What's your involvement with the film?"

He coughed. "That's, ah. At this point. Somewhat unclear."

I sat back. "You're not invited to be a part of it?"

"It's not a question of invitation, you know? It's a large organization with a lot of auxiliary elements, a lot of different functions, a lot of different roles. It's a bureaucracy, really."

"I see."

"So maybe Right Russia isn't involved, you know, directly, but we're involved in the movement, you know, so in a broader sense, we're involved in the making of the film?"

"Like in the same way that everybody's involved with everything?"

"Don't be difficult. Don't be dense."

"Would you like to be more involved in the film than you are?"

He smiled tightly. "Like I said, we'd all like things we don't get."

It was interesting to have stumbled into the knowledge of a rift within the camp, first thing—like walking into a field and stepping directly into a sinkhole. Of course I should have imagined pettiness and infighting, resentments and reactionaries. Of course I should have imagined schismatic nuances. I didn't know what I had imagined, really, and the more I realized that, the more I realized that I hadn't thought to spend a lot of time imagining anything at all.

So I leaned forward. I knew—I must have known—that this would annoy the man.

"Tell me what Aleksandr was like in the eighties," I said. "He ran a samizdat journal, right?"

Mikhail snorted again. I was beginning to wonder if that was a trademark. " 'Ran' is perhaps a strong word. He was involved. I'll grant him that. He was involved."

"He delivered it himself? Door-to-door?" This was well known—even in the limited research I'd done, it had come up. "That must have been dangerous."

"Dangerous. Yes. Assuredly. The man might have been the target of an assassination attempt or something."

There was a twist to his words, but I said, "Exactly."

I could immediately tell I'd driven him to the edge of apoplexy. He slowed his breathing, I could see him counting to decet in his head. He leaned back. "Let me ask you a question. This is a good opportunity for me. To learn about how Bezetov is broadly perceived."

"You mean elsewhere?"

"I mean elsewhere," he said severely.

"I don't know." I tried to think. I tried to parse what my father thought of Bezetov, and what I thought of Bezetov, and what CNN thought of Bezetov, and what the world generally thought of Bezetov. "I guess it's thought that he did a lot for the dissident movement—"

"A lot how?"

"Well. Just his involvement with this paper."

"Which was what, exactly?"

I felt I had already addressed this, so I ignored the question. "And in spite of the costs—"

"Costs? What were these costs?"

"To his career," I finished lamely.

"Well," said Mikhail after a moment. "It didn't seem to hold him back much in the end, did it?"

"No. I guess not."

He probed his lower lip with his tongue. "So he's seen as a hero, you're saying?"

"Vaguely." I squirmed. "To the extent that he's seen at all."

Mikhail leaned back. "I guess that's not surprising."

"If it makes you feel any better, I don't think the West is paying that much attention. You know, generally."

"I see."

"Where were you during that time?"

"I was in a psychiatric prison. For disseminating statements not officially recognized as truth."

"Oh." I was beginning to understand.

Andreyev stood up abruptly, nearly upsetting the trash can again. "I don't think I can help you any further," he said, going to the computer. He typed exclusively with his forefingers. "This is the contact information for his spokesman, the media relations guy. He deals with inquiries formally." He copied down a name—Viktor Davidenko—and a mobile number and handed it to me.

I stared at the name. "Don't you have anything else? I mean, this is the person everyone goes through, right?"

"And you're not everyone?"

"No, I just thought—" I stopped. I stood up. I didn't know what I'd thought.

"Listen. You can do this one of two ways. You can call him, arrange a meeting, see if he'll talk to you, which he most likely will not. Or." He eyed me. "You could put on some eye makeup and comb your hair and swing by the Pravda Bar around five-thirty any afternoon and see if he'll talk to you *then*. He's always there. I'd suggest the latter option. If you can remember to comb your hair. But it's up to you."

Mikhail Andreyevich was marching me to the door, past the interns, who looked up, alarmed, and then returned to their clacking. The door opened onto ludicrous cold, the falling of an implausibly early dusk. Mikhail peered at me. "And if you do manage to reach Bezetov," he said, "tell him to call me, okay? I have some things I need to discuss with him."

————

I walked down Nevsky Prospekt, away from the river. The encounter with Mikhail Andreyevich had left me feeling sour, uncertain. And then, strangely, angry—I was full of the narcissism of needing the world to bend to you, and the petty outrage you feel when it does not. I felt a frantic energy, the odd sense that I could run all night or put my hand through glass or strip down naked in the cold and survive. I knew that whether Aleksandr was who I thought he was, or who my father thought he was, was not the question. He needed to be good for Russia, for the people to whom he belonged, and not on behalf of a senile music professor now six months dead. It was a gross sense of entitlement—and yes, of course, a grossly American kind of entitlement—to feel otherwise, to try to lay claim to this person somehow.

And yet. When I thought of my life, it seemed contoured primarily by the vast number of things I had wanted and not gotten. My demands had been relatively modest; I had not wanted an extraordinary life. I'd wanted an ordinary life with an ordinary life span and ordinary consolations and an ordinary love that would, inevitably, degrade in ordinary time. These were not outrageous requests. Perhaps I'd thought that my one outrageous request—to meet this man, to absorb his wisdom, to go to my grave with one interesting stolen secret— would be granted in lieu of all the others. Though it's true that when I caught myself thinking this, I realized I was essentially supplicating an entity that kept track of such things—requests granted, requests denied—and that this was a kind of stealth religious belief. So I told myself to quit it.

Still, one had to wonder. I'd doubted my mission; I'd questioned my motives, and reconsidered my hopes, and examined my unexamined privilege until my eyes glazed over. But I hadn't entertained the idea that perhaps Bezetov was an unworthy target of all this angst, all these hopes. I was an unworthy supplicant, perhaps, silly, misguided, arrogant, undeserving. But Bezetov was assuredly unassailable. If he could not offer wisdom, there simply was no wisdom to be found.

Humiliatingly, I found myself walking toward Kazan Cathedral, though not for any reason beyond the aesthetic (the Implicit Attitude Test had revealed me to be consistent in my indifference to all major world religions). I walked inside. The crown of the cathedral was nearly as grand as St. Peter's. Crenellated light streamed through the cupola. A black and white cat lolled, insensate, on a box in a corner. In another corner, richly colored saints gazed out from gilded frames, trapped forever in two dimensions.

Typically, blasphemously, I thought of Jonathan. It's not the great tragedy of life to wind up without another human being. Half of marriages end in divorce—what a boring, obsessively repeated statistic this is—and I don't flatter myself that we would have been any different. Dodging that particular bullet leaves me with something to feel good about, anyway: one major life failure avoided, if nothing else. One can become so sentimental about a person's absence, but it's impossible to be consistently sentimental in his presence—when you're confronted with the quotidian selfishness and silence that, I'm given to understand, comprise most of a life. But we were just so new. We were at that ruthless, lovely edge, all the indignities as yet unimagined and unseen. We didn't know yet what would have ever made us stop loving each other.

At first I'd tried to see the devastation of leaving him as possibly salutary; I'd hoped the pressure of it would make me stronger, better, like a diamond compressed from coal, a pearl emerged from the constant nick of sand on sand. But in the end—especially now, especially after talking to Mikhail Andreyevich—I found it exhausting.

I sat in the church for a while. I stared at the candles in their red glowing holders, burning on behalf of hopes or prayers or lost causes. And I remembered walking along a different river—carved up by a different kind of tenderness, a different kind of terror.

11

ALEKSANDR

St. Petersburg, 1982–1986

When Aleksandr finally made it back to St. Petersburg from Moscow, there was a man waiting for him in front of his building. Aleksandr had spent a paranoid, insomniac night on the train, Nikolai's face leering into his dreams every time he dozed, and he froze when he saw the figure standing underneath an emaciated tree branch, a few meters from the building's collapsing doorstep. But it was not Nikolai. It was Petr Pavlovich Nikitin, hunching into the wind.

Petr Pavlovich stared at Aleksandr. He tossed his cigarette on the ground and watched it hiss and curl against the snow. But he did not come over. Aleksandr understood that Petr Pavlovich was waiting for Aleksandr to come to him.

Aleksandr considered turning around. He considered getting back on the train and going—to where? To what? Back to Moscow to hide? Back to the Saigon to drink?

And then he didn't. He walked toward Pavlovich, terror snarling in his teeth. "What do you want?" said Aleksandr.

"Take a guess."

Aleksandr looked up. In his fortochka, he could see the distorted silhouette of a man—arm and back and misshapen head—engaged in a methodical activity that looked a lot like searching. Aleksandr could only imagine the steward twisting her hands and biting her lip and trying to remember anything, anything, that she could say against him. He'd kept odd hours, she might say. He'd run with a strange crowd. He'd been fucking a prostitute and hadn't even been discreet. Aleksandr knew the steward would be sorry she hadn't thrown him out earlier.

"That was a nice little performance in Moscow there," said Petr Pavlovich. In the austere light, he was sallow-cheeked, vaguely jaundiced; his nose ran unbecomingly. Overall, he did not look like a man with the power to ruin a life.

Aleksandr craned his neck and looked around.

"What, expecting someone else?" said Petr Pavlovich.

"Where's Nikolai?"

"How should I know? I'm not his nanny." Pavlovich sniffed vigorously. "I was sorry to hear about your friends."

"I'm sure."

"It was regrettable. Young men. Most regrettable."

"Regrettable by whom? To whom? I mean, who regrets it?"

Pavlovich pinched himself on the nose and looked at Aleksandr magnanimously. Bits of snow blew onto his eyebrows; they looked like the furry legs of an albino tarantula. "It is to be regretted, surely," he said. "By anybody."

At this, Aleksandr turned from Petr Pavlovich and began marching through the snow toward the building. The ice made an empty sound under his feet.

"I wouldn't go back up there if I were you."

Aleksandr turned. "No?"

"They're not quite through."

Aleksandr thought of them rifling through pants and chess sets, books and letters (of these there were few): the paltry accretions of a lonely life. He wondered what else they might sense, standing there, looking for samizdat; he wondered if they might grimly assess and photograph and stow the accumulated mass of solitude and longing and explosive frustration that had been his one true possession in this life.

"There's nothing up there."

"No? Maybe not." A thick gurgling issued from the back of Petr Pavlovich's throat. "Excuse me. Nasal polyps. A great hassle."

The gurgling made Aleksandr bold. "How long has Nikolai been with you?"

"Don't be crass. You're never going to have the career you deserve if you keep talking like that."

"How long had you been planning to kill Ivan?"

"That was an accident."

"Right."

"It was an accident. And that's not my purview, anyway. I hope you understand that. I stick to sport and propaganda, strictly."

Aleksandr said nothing and stared numbly at the expanse of the yard—the gunmetal flank of the building, the frozen and brittle clothing on the line. Above them, the light was bleeding out of the sky.

"I have to admit," said Petr Pavlovich, "I'm impressed by your willingness to live in this shithole. We all are. I didn't think it was a palace you had here, but when you were so adamant about staying, I imagined something a little more tolerable."

Aleksandr studied his window. He could still see the men, backlit by the marginal light of the failing lightbulbs. He could not tell what they were doing.

"But this." Petr Pavlovich waved at the building. "This is horrendous. You must have been really serious about your little project in order to live in a place like this. Who knows what kind of people you probably lived with? Whores at the very least, I should imagine." Aleksandr realized with a sock to the solar plexus that Elizabeta, too, had been in his file. "You must have really believed in this nonsense."

"I did."

Petr Pavlovich looked at Aleksandr with an expression that bordered on tenderness, and that, Aleksandr thought, was not going to be tolerable. Petr Pavlovich sniffed triumphantly. "Well, I'm sure you've changed many minds."

The men came down then, two of them: one with the musculature of a wolverine, the other with a face that looked boiled for hygiene purposes. Neither of them looked at Aleksandr. They carried their meager harvest from his room, and Aleksandr recognized some of his things—a shirt, a passel of letters, a book, a dirty sheet. He winced. He should have changed that sheet. Then again, he hadn't been expecting company.

Petr Pavlovich turned to Aleksandr and began speaking briskly. "So. You have a city tournament coming up in Moscow, am I right?"

"Yes."

"I imagine you would still like to go."

"Yes."

"Of course you would. Smart boy. You're a chess prodigy, after all. You're not a political genius. I think we can agree on this much. The Kremlin is very generous, and very impressed with your chess ability, and willing—despite it all—to overlook your past indiscretions, assuming we can reach an understanding here. It is possible that we can forge some relationship."

Petr Pavlovich looked at Aleksandr with the paternalistic searching expression of a doctor who is hopeful, in a vague way, that you'll decide to take some unpleasant but lifesaving medicine.

"These city tournaments you're doing, they're small potatoes, don't you agree? For a mind like yours? You should be playing at the national level. You should be playing, quite frankly, abroad. You want to continue to play for the Soviet Union. We want you to continue to play for the Soviet Union."

It occurred to Aleksandr that Pavlovich was talking about supply and demand.

"But it's all up to you. If you can improve your attitude. If you can amend your ideology."

And maybe Aleksandr would. Maybe he would. The person he loved most in the world had seen fit to marry a Party official; the person he admired most for opposition was dead; the only other two people he'd thought he could trust were treacherous and insane, respectively. Models for alternative options were diminishing. Who could judge him for this? Who was left to judge him for this?

"Otherwise?" said Aleksandr. It's possible he knew even then that he was being theatrical.

"Otherwise, you're done playing. For one thing. Maybe you'll be done with other things, too. Who can say? But the chess, we know for sure, you're done. There's been tolerance here. There's been patience. We don't need to talk about otherwise, I don't think. I think we know what you're going to do."

Maybe Petr Pavlovich was right. Maybe Aleksandr would go up to his room in a moment and sit on his bed and stare at the liver-colored spots on the floor and consider it. He'd tried to live honorably for a few years in Leningrad. By anyone's standards, he had failed. Out the window, the snow would ignite in the streetlights. On the bed, the KGB officers would have left his chess set. They'd have known that he was going to take it with him; they'd have known that it was all he was going to take with him; they'd have known where he was going. On his way out, he'd walk past apartment number seven, but he'd make a point not to look at it.

"You can go up now," said Petr Pavlovich brightly. "You'll want to be packing, I'd imagine."

———

The new apartment had flawless indoor plumbing, a brocaded mirror, and two different bedrooms ("for guests," Petr Pavlovich had said as he gestured majestically). There was a living room with a fireplace and built-in bookshelves filled with unreadable, politically acceptable books. The refrigerator was stocked with fresh meat and imported wine. A bowl on the counter overflowed with an entire jungle of fresh produce, including a banana the shape and color of a crescent moon. Aleksandr had never eaten a banana, though he'd had an orange once, as a child in Okha, when a freight train carrying fruit to the Party elite had overturned. Outside his window that spring bloomed bell-shaped fritillarias and the exploding radiant hearts of euphorbia.

He'd never known how dirty he'd always been until he finally stood for thirty minutes in a scalding shower with limitless soap. He thought of the grains of dirt, abrasive against his skin, that had always populated his bed in the kommunalka, and he recognized guiltily that they had fallen off his person. He drank Armenian cognac. He smoked Cuban cigars even without an occasion. Losing Elizabeta and Ivan had made him vengeful, and he knew it. He felt he deserved whatever he could find. He flopped around in his new sheets, some different genus entirely from the kind he'd had before. He never knew that bedding could be so silken and unobtrusive. The rosettes of eczema that had bloomed along his ass for his entire life finally cleared up.

He signed on to the CPSU. He joined the Komsomol officially, finally. On his new internal passport, his smile was like a sneer. In his new living room, he did a joyless cartwheel just because he had the space.

He was assigned a new trainer, a man who inexplicably wore what Aleksandr took to be a woman's scarf around his neck at all times—except during tournaments, for which occasions he unveiled a meaty, tendony neck. He was an unimaginative chess mind, and his tendons contorted acrobatically whenever Aleksandr made a move that he didn't like or didn't understand. And ubiquitously, intrusively, there was Petr Pavlovich, who stationed himself at the very center of Aleksandr's life, who followed Aleksandr nervously to hotels and restaurants, and shot him warning glances if he got too mouthy, which he rarely did anymore.

And in a few weeks, Aleksandr found he'd begun a new life. He found it was not too late.

He grew fatter—slowly but with the steady inevitability of aging. He'd look in the brocaded mirror and swear he could see the setting of light wrinkles, insistent as an oncoming season, though others said that was not the case. If Elizabeta had previously hijacked his entire consciousness for nefarious purposes, now she crouched darkly in the epicenter of his brain like a many-stemmed tumor. He tried hard not to summon thoughts of her. He tried hard to be thinking about other things all the time—chess mostly, but also the most efficient rationalization for his current behavior and the best way to organize the refrigerator (having his own refrigerator was an endless source of joy). He set aside large swaths of time to think about Sakhalin—he'd remember the glinting stands of white birches; the occasional visits to Yuzno-Sakalinsk, which smelled of mud and conscripted workers;

the glowering Korean ships that docked in the harbor at night and sold stealth coal for the thermal power plants. He ate enormous salads drowning in real mayonnaise (before, it had only ever been vinegar and furniture polish). He tried to do push-ups. He tried to become vain about clothing. He tried to be very absorbed in the particular details of his particular life, as inoculation against excessive absorption in the details of someone else's.

Every day, every day, he had long one-sided conversations with Ivan in his head. He tried to explain that this was all that was left for him now. He tried to explain that it was the only pragmatic course of action—and they'd been pragmatists always, hadn't they? It was pure ideology that got you fucked. He tried to explain that he was sorry. Sometimes he got defensive and explained, slowly and sarcastically, that if Ivan was such a terrific judge of people and of reality, he wouldn't be the one who was dead. Then he explained that the thing about life was that you had to decide how you were going to survive it. The dead could afford to be morally self-righteous. Everyone else just had to manage.

Aleksandr explained and explained, but Ivan never seemed to be listening. He certainly never answered.

———

Aleksandr began winning. He developed a taste for everything he was exposed to. He met Rusayev, who'd been world champion for a decade (though only by default-winning, after all of Fischer's histrionics), and Petr Pavlovich prattled on about what an *honor* it was for him to meet such a great chess mind while Aleksandr picked sluggishly at his smoked mackerel. Rusayev was older and bewhiskered, and he forgot Aleksandr's name within minutes of their introduction. Aleksandr kept winning. He was given a more generous stipend. Memories of Elizabeta could still make him flinch from embarrassment, but no longer from pain. When he spoke on the phone to his mother, whom he had not seen in three years, he lowered his voice if there was another person in the room. He kept winning. When he met Rusayev again, he was remembered.

He attended cocktail parties, he attended dinners, he attended functions, always alongside Petr Pavlovich, who beamed at him with the proprietary smugness of a parent or a sports coach. Aleksandr was becoming a drinker, increasingly, and he liked to gaze through a veil of indifference and bleariness and monosyllabism as Pavlovich clapped him manfully on the shoulder. "I think you've made a terrifically wise choice," said Petr Pavlovich at the celebration for Aleksandr's USSR semifinals win in 1982. "I always knew you could be rehabilitated. I always knew it." At the New Year's party in 1983, he said, "You know, we're modernizing. We're all modernizing. The Party is modernizing. It's not all ideological purity, this and that. Stalin went too far, we can all agree." He was waving a tiny cracker, a dark jewel of caviar at its center. "We're a practical people, and this is a practical philosophy." At a May Day celebration that spring, he lurched toward Aleksandr—his body melonny from sweat, his breath spicy from the tomato juice he'd been drinking—and said, "It's about justice, am I right? It's about a modicum of social equity." He sniffed and blinked rapidly; his face was seized with the pleading expression of an ineffectual teacher begging a charismatic student not to lead a mutiny. "We don't all need to be radicals. We just need to be in general agreement here, am I right? The philosophy can evolve. We can evolve. But the basic premise is unassailable. And I'm so glad you've come to see reason."

Had Aleksandr come to see reason? Aleksandr had not. But he'd come to see the merits of a materialistic life, perhaps; he'd come to count the relative blessings of safety, and satiety, and solitude. He could believe he was not cut out for defiance; he could believe he never had been. He could believe in the gruesomeness of his mistake. Ivan was dead, and that was proof enough of the lethality of innocence. What had he known about it all? He should stick to chess, to knocking wood figurines around on a board. The stakes in international chess were high enough, and nobody died, most years.

He went to Interzonal. He went to the Candidates' Tournament. He won, he won, he kept winning, and he enjoyed the attendant celebration—the chattering flash of cameras, the interviews that appeared in small boxes in the newspaper. It's possible he even enjoyed the cloistered, petty pleasure of doing exactly the thing he was most expected to do. He was a reminder that chess was the Soviet Union's game, even if geopolitics was not, and any dregs of national feeling he had could be animated, marginally, occasionally, by this thought. He always read his interviews, and they were always remote, always ridiculous, always vastly more self-congratulatory than he ever remembered feeling. Life was tolerable. He never thought about Elizabeta. He kept his mouth shut, for the most part. If he occasionally drank a bit too much at parties and made snarky remarks about the FIDE or the Party, few people seemed to notice or care. Officials were typically civil. If they knew his past—and they must have known—he couldn't see it in their obsequious smiles, in their yellowed gazes. If they knew—and they must have known—they had decided, kindly, to forget.

He was doing the only thing he'd ever been good at, and he was doing it as well as could be expected. He was alone—alone, always, and never more alone than when he sat three feet away from another man and played—but he'd achieved equilibrium in his aloneness; he lived at the center of his solitude and hardly scraped against its edges anymore. By 1983 he was scheduled to go to Pasadena, California, to defeat the Americans in the world champion semifinals. There would be a fifty-thousand-dollar prize. He never thought about Elizabeta. At night he dreamed of palm trees and hard currencies.

There were women at the parties sometimes, though Aleksandr rarely spoke to them. The Party wives were mostly older, matronly, forbidding, wearing high-necked secretary blouses and giving off the faint scent of dogma and aerosols. Most of the other women were there for the officials—they were women in Elizabeta's profession, or something like it, their clothes immaculate, their faces overdone, wearing tight-fitting stretch dresses and laughing unlikely first-soprano laughs. They were off-limits, it was understood, and Aleksandr never went near them unless he had to pass by to get a refill. One night, however, he found himself talking to a woman whose origins were unclear to him—she was too young to be a token female Party member, but not attractive enough to be one of the escorts. Her face was flushed and her lips were too full, one degree beyond erotic and veering toward grotesque. She was drinking red wine, and it made her lips currant-colored and lurid.

"You're Aleksandr Bezetov?" she said. "The chess prodigy?"

"A prodigy?" Aleksandr was already quite drunk by that point, feeling a buoyancy slicked with careening despair, counting the coastal tides inside his head. "Aren't I getting a little too old to be a prodigy?"

"How old are you?"

"Twenty-two."

"That's not so old."

"And how old are you?"

She turned her face to the side. There was something irritated about her eyes that made her look constantly overwrought. Her skin was bad, though her hair was terrific. Aleksandr was getting to be a discerning critic of women. "A gentleman never asks," she said.

"And who said I was a gentleman?" Her plate was overflowing with rhombuses of continental cheese. He leaned in and stole a cracker. "You're older than I am, probably. Twenty-four, twenty-five. You're probably too old to find a man here, if you're looking. How did I know that? you ask. Am I a prodigy? No, I'm not a prodigy. And not a hero, either, no matter how much you might insist."

"I'm not insisting." She hadn't been smiling, so she could not now let a smile meaningfully fade.

"I mean, someone has to defend chess from the international mafia." He hiccupped.

"Oh? And who is doing that?"

He pointed to his head and nodded gravely. "I am. Through independent thought, you know? And my subversive style of play? I might be a credible threat to Rusayev one day, you might have heard."

"I might have."

"Rusayev is a dinosaur. An apparatchik dinosaur. Have you ever been to California?"

"Of course not."

"I'm going, you know. In three weeks. To Pasadena. What do you think the women are like in Pasadena, California?" He didn't recognize his own voice. He could barely hear it.

"I'm sure I can't imagine."

"Do you want to hear a joke?"

"Not really."

He raised his glass. "Adam and Eve must have lived in the Soviet Union, because they were naked, had one apple between them, and thought they were living in paradise!"

A hand grabbed him by the lapel; from its preternatural smoothness, Aleksandr knew it to be Petr Pavlovich's. Another hand reached in to grab his drink away. "I'm sorry," said Petr Pavlovich. "But Mr. Bezetov is needed elsewhere. Excuse us."

———

One week before Aleksandr was to go to Pasadena, Nikolai appeared at a party. Aleksandr had known this would happen eventually, but he was surprised at the surreal serenity that he felt when it finally did. Nikolai emerged from behind one of the faux potted plants that comprised the bulk of the decor at these events. Aleksandr had imagined a clean, surgical terror splitting a seam down his chest; instead, he appraised Nikolai dully, with the benumbed feeling of watching one of his own recurring nightmares. Like Aleksandr, Nikolai was fatter—he looked as if he'd been spooned into his shirt—but his face was less ugly. Or maybe it was only that he seemed to have grown into his ugliness.

"Hello, Aleksandr," said Nikolai. "Fantastic showing in Kaliningrad."

Aleksandr looked at his plate of cornichons and herring. So many times he'd imagined asking Nikolai if he'd been running Ivan all along. And he imagined Nikolai saying, "Running him all along? I hardly had to try." The more he thought about it, the more Aleksandr knew that the real insult of Nikolai's betrayal was how little he'd tried to hide it, how little he knew he'd have to. He'd taken notes right in front of them, for fuck's sake—he hadn't even had to pay attention—and Aleksandr had thought, really, what? That Nikolai was so devoted, so committed to the cause and the written word, that he was constantly recording new influxes of inspiration? He hadn't thought that; he'd always thought Nikolai was a bit of a philistine as well as a bit of an asshole. But he'd been so blinded by his trust in Ivan—who would always be a twenty-one-year-old kid now, smart and well-intentioned and right about a lot of things but wrong about the one thing that mattered most—that he hadn't tried to reconcile his vision of Nikolai with Ivan's. Ivan knew more about it, that's all; Ivan was the mastermind, the visionary, the great brain. And now Ivan was dead and would never be able to revise his opinion—on Nikolai or on anything else. Aleksandr had accepted his own strengths and weaknesses, and he believed now in the practicality of doing one's best at whatever it was one did best and leaving it at that, so he could recognize ungrudgingly that Nikolai was the only one of the three of them with any degree of competence whatsoever. And competence was the new prevailing value of Aleksandr's life. Nikolai had outmaneuvered them, that was all; he'd won, and he'd deserved to win, and Aleksandr refused to be a bad sport about it all, personally.

"Just warming up for Pasadena," said Aleksandr. He watched Nikolai masticate a tiny pickle for longer than seemed strictly required.

"Oh, you still think you'll be playing there?" Nikolai said mildly. He swirled his pancake around in its sour cream.

Aleksandr bit down on nothing. "Yes," he said. "I expect so."

"Hmm."

"What?"

"That's not what I heard."

Still, there it was: hatred, cramping in his mandible, amplified by the knowledge that it was wholly unwarranted. He didn't deserve to hate Nikolai anymore. He'd forfeited the moral ground from which hatred was possible. They were colleagues, essentially. Confederates. Comrades. The differences between them were quantitative, not qualitative. If Nikolai was a few degrees more implicated than Aleksandr was, give it a year or two. And here was his comrade, Nikolai, giving him a piece of horrible but relevant information.

"What are you talking about?" said Aleksandr.

"There are political considerations, I hear." Nikolai cringed as though sorry to be the one to say so, though Aleksandr was quite sure he was not sorry.

"What kind of political considerations?" said Aleksandr. He didn't want to ask. If he had anything left in this life besides chess, he wouldn't have asked. But then, if he'd had anything besides chess, he wouldn't be here at all—he wouldn't have been so predictably bought, and he wouldn't have been so easily maintained, and he wouldn't be standing here, across from Nikolai Sergeyevich, while his cornichons grew flaccid on his plate.

Nikolai raised his eyebrows and smiled obnoxiously. "I'd ask Petr Pavlovich about it, if I were you."

Aleksandr zigzagged across the room. Petr Pavlovich was in a corner, telling a boring anecdote to a small coven of bored listeners. Aleksandr pulled urgently at Petr Pavlovich's elbow until he raised one finger at his listeners and smiled indulgently at Aleksandr as though he were a loved but manic child. They retreated to a corner, where Aleksandr immediately began hissing.

"I'm not playing in Pasadena? I'm really not playing in Pasadena?"

Pavlovich bobbed his head and spoke without moving his lips. "Hush. You're making a scene."

"How was this decided?"

"It's, ah. A relatively recent development."

"*Why* was it decided?"

"Please keep your voice down. *I* don't mind, you know. I don't mind if you go. But it's not about my preferences."

"You're going to forfeit a player? For the first time ever? I don't see how this is in the interests of Soviet chess."

"Again, it's not *me* forfeiting a player. It's not *me* doing anything."

"FIDE, then."

"Stop doing that with your jaw. You could show a little appreciation. It's strictly about your safety."

"It's not."

"Fine, it's about the Olympics, then. They boycotted Moscow. We can't send you."

"You'd send Rusayev."

Pavlovich rolled his eyes. "Enough."

"You would."

"Enough. Rusayev's different. You're young. You can afford to wait three years."

At this, Aleksandr dropped his plate. Sopping fragments of smoked fish and pickled vegetables dislodged themselves and went sliding surprising distances across the marble floor.

"You're all so enthralled with Rusayev," said Aleksandr. "You know he's only world champion technically. He inherited the title by default from Fischer. But you all worship him. You bend over backward to preserve his title."

"Arrogance doesn't suit you," said Petr Pavlovich, bending down to clean up the food with his handkerchief. "Neither does alcohol."

"Can't I afford to be arrogant?"

"You could be doing better."

Aleksandr scoffed. "My rating has overtaken Rusayev's this year."

Petr Pavlovich stood up. "You could be doing better in other ways."

Aleksandr looked down into his vodka. His ears buzzed. He thought of his sneering comments about Oleg Chazov, the FIDE president, uttered within earshot of a FIDE official. He thought about rolling his eyes at a slide show about the superiority of the Russian athlete. He thought about telling that stupid joke to that bulbous-lipped, unimpressed woman, and how it wasn't even a good joke, and how she hadn't even laughed.

"If you want to play Rusayev for world champion in the fall, you've got to start behaving yourself better. It's not too late for you, Aleksandr. I advocate for you every day, I do. Every single day."

In his vodka, Aleksandr could see part of the reflection of his own globular, inelegant nose. He didn't like to think of Petr Pavlovich defending him to the Party—in that wheedling voice, that apologetic tone, asking for more time, more leniency. Aleksandr realized that he'd become a petty, irrelevant dictator himself. There were probably entire armies of thinkers and strategists who sat around figuring out how to get him to do exactly what they wanted. And they were probably always successful.

"Do you know that? You know that, don't you?" said Petr Pavlovich. He sounded hurt. Aleksandr refused to respond to hypothetical questions. "You're not going to Pasadena," said Petr Pavlovich. "I'm sorry. You can still play Rusayev for world champion in the fall. But you need to help me out here."

Aleksandr did not look at Petr Pavlovich; he knew there would be that distorted, forgiving tenderness in his face, and he did not want to see it.

"You need to behave yourself," said Petr Pavlovich. "Please stop doing that with your face. Let's get you another plate."

———

And, through the blowsy spring and into the horrid summer, Aleksandr behaved himself. He listened politely. He feigned attention whenever it was required, he kept quiet whenever it was possible. He made no demands. He asked no follow-up questions. At parties, he stood quietly by picture windows and shoveled great masses of gourmet food into his mouth, and when anyone from the Party tried to talk to him, he pretended to always be chewing.

The World Championship match began in September. Moscow's buildings groped the sky with a modern, monolithic insatiability; the kommunalki were epic, blanched white, cluttered in rows like crooked teeth in the maw of an animal. Leningrad was forced by sheer architecture to acknowledge its past, its old defeats and triumphs, its roots in rationality and Euclidean geometry. In Leningrad—in the long avenues, in the arcing canals—one could find the past's hope for the future. In Moscow, the future had been captured, torn down, and bent to the will of the present. Enormous signs defaced the sides of buildings: HELP THE MOTHERLAND—BUILD COMMUNISM, THE IDEAS OF LENIN LIVE AND CONQUER. Marching down Gorky Ulitsa, Aleksandr saw how the street might evoke a jaunty sense of usefulness, if he were someone who was inclined to think that way.

On the day of the first match, an escort met Aleksandr and his second, Dmitry, who had been appointed by the Party. The escort walked them through the Hall of Columns, with its ornate light fixtures and richly patterned wallpaper, and waited while Aleksandr stopped by the gorgeous, gilded bathroom to vomit. Outside, Aleksandr could hear the rustling of five hundred journalists from twenty-seven countries. He wished nobody had quoted this statistic at him. He flushed the toilet and splashed his face. The escort banged on the door.

After climbing the steps to the main stage and tripping lightly, Aleksandr found himself sitting across from Rusayev. Rusayev was a solid man in any context, and he looked even heartier and more hostile on the other side of a chessboard. The crowd shifted and settled; they were expecting to be disappointed. Rusayev had won the USSR Chess Championship four years straight, and it was almost offensive, the crowd thought, to pair him against this obscenely young man—who was so dark-browed, so awkward and faltering in his movements. Aleksandr was a man who seemed to apologize for his own existence in every step he took. They were not a good match, the crowd thought, and the game would be an easy win. The crowd hated easy wins.

Aleksandr wanted to touch the board before they began, to gather himself into the game, but it was not allowed. The timer was set. Rusayev mustered a look approaching respect. Aleksandr had been assigned white by the tournament directors, and as he introduced his knight's pawn, he let everything—the audience, the great hall, his own mind—disappear into the clean chromatics of the board. They began.

———

As chess journalists and students, social historians of Russia, and masters of trivia often remarked, it was Rusayev's match almost from beginning to end. Aleksandr opened with too much sloppy aggression (the impetuousness of youth, it was whispered). He lost one game for every two draws, until he lost two games in a row. This had never happened to him, but there it was (proof that the young upstart was at least half as stupid as he looked, it was said). When the secretaries brought the transcribed score sheets back to the press room, the reporters from *Sovietsky Sport* stamped their feet in annoyance and pouted that the whole thing had been an unmitigated embarrassment. Nobody had been routed this squarely since Fischer's leveling of Taimonov on his way to Spassky (and such mismatches in ability were, frankly, tedious, it was muttered). Even the board boys looked indifferent.

Then there were seventeen draws in a row. Most of the press left. The tournament was moved out of the magnificent Hall of Columns and into the fraying Hotel Sport. Aleksandr's jaw clicked whenever he ate. He woke up at night to horrible leg cramps that sent him jumping up and down, half asleep, to the continued disapproval of Dmitry. He wandered Moscow during the days, staring at the gorgeous Oktyabrskaya Hotel across from the French embassy, counting the metallic muscles on the statue of Iron Dzerzhinsky outside KGB headquarters. In Red Square, he stared mournfully at the lovely lights of the State Department Store and then shuffled through a forty-minute line to admire waxen Lenin in his tomb.

Aleksandr had never felt farther from Okha than he did in the days wandering Moscow. He could feel the vastness of Russia prickling at the back of his neck. In the white dawn, he squinted out his hotel windows at the horizon and felt sure he could see the eastern plains tapering into nothing, could see the identical villages and hamlets that pocked the landscape like craters on the moon until they became fewer and fewer and finally disappeared into the stoic, flinty face of the continental shelf. He was at the edge of the world, and the terrible enormity of outer space was bearing down on him. It gave him vertigo—like walking too close to the edge of a steep drop, or looking up at the sky and pretending that you are not looking up at all but down, down into an endless sea of illuminated sea creatures, their star-bright organs burning out of an unfathomable abyss.

He dreamed of playing Rusayev so often that he sometimes confused mistakes he'd actually made with mistakes he'd invented in his sleep. Winter came. Two months into the match, Rusayev won again.

And then, finally, just when almost everyone else had stopped paying attention, Aleksandr won a game. Fourteen more draws followed. And when the audience—and cerebral individuals the world over—cracked their necks and rubbed their eyes and turned back to the tournament, they found different men at play.

Aleksandr's incipient defeat had made him more stubborn-looking. When he looked at himself in the mirror, he saw that he'd adopted the half-awake gaze of a nocturnal animal. He burrowed himself further and further into the game, and everything else took on a filmy, aquatic feel. The incidentals of his life—the transport to and from the building, his state-provided meals, the cold nights in the hotel with Dmitry—came to seem utterly artificial, shadows cast by the Platonic reality of the game. Outside the tournament, he grew inarticulate, withdrawn, bleary-eyed. He gave deeply unsatisfying answers to journalists who wanted to know about his strategy. He had no insights to share, no history he felt warranted reporting, although he sometimes told them small anecdotes about his sisters on the island. More than one TASS profile remarked that in spite of being a brilliant chess mind and all, Aleksandr seemed more than a little dumb.

Inside, though, he stayed vigorous, alert to Rusayev's every twitch and eyelid flutter. He saw columns and rows of the board in every street; he started categorizing his own movements in algebraic notation. D3, he moved straight ahead to the lunch buffet of pork and borscht and Pepsi-Cola, timid and humble as a pawn. Qe7, he sailed stately, imperious, across the stage to his chair, his eyes locked on his target, his gaze lethal with power and surety. Nc4, he twisted—rearing, equine—out of the path of a passing government vehicle in the street.

Rusayev was not doing as well. He'd lost five kilos over the course of the tournament; he wheezed into his handkerchief and ate almost nothing at meals. His skin had taken on a sagging, redundant quality; he looked increasingly like an old elephant on a ritualized journey to death. There were moments while making a move when he lurched alarmingly far forward, and the already still audience grew stiller as they waited, waited, for him to collapse. Although he never did, there were some who commented that peasants—in other, wilder, less modern times than these—would be inclined to attribute his transformation to sorcery, and to regard Aleksandr with more than a little dark suspicion. This was the future, however, and nobody thought those things anymore.

The newspapers began to mutter about Aleksandr, since they loved a good mutter. Aleksandr was the youngest man to compete at this level since Mikhail Tal, they muttered. He's almost as young as that autistic American teenager, they muttered. He will not win, of course he will not win, it's a travesty to suggest that he might. But still, it was muttered, he might. He might.

Then Aleksandr won the forty-seventh game. Then he won the forty-eighth. Rusayev was two games ahead, but the momentum of the tournament had shifted. Aleksandr sat up straighter. He slept better at night. Rusayev coughed into the sleeve of his shirt and glowered at Aleksandr with watery, red-rimmed eyes. Early on the morning of the forty-ninth game, Aleksandr received a phone call.

It was five in the morning, and Dmitry answered the phone. He listened for a moment and then handed it to Aleksandr. "It's Petr Pavlovich," he said.

"Of course it is," said Aleksandr, taking it. It was warm for February, which meant it was very cold, and Aleksandr didn't turn on a light or get out of bed. Outside, he could hear melting snow sluicing through the gutters. "What?" he said into the receiver.

Petr Pavlovich sniffed. "Not very friendly in the mornings, are you?"

"What do you want?"

"Need some more sleep, do you?"

"What is it?"

"Don't worry, you can go back to bed. They've suspended the tournament."

"What?" He sat up, feeling the oddly humid frigidity of the hotel air clamp down on his shoulders and torso. It was its own fucking ecosystem, this hotel room.

"FIDE has decided to suspend the tournament. For now. Until the irregularities can be resolved."

"Irregularities? What irregularities?"

Dmitry turned on the light and stared, his eyes crusty with sleep, his expression abjectly interested.

Petr Pavlovich sneezed. "Just certain aberrations."

"What are you talking about?"

"Don't agitate yourself."

"You mean that I'm winning now?"

"I certainly do not mean that. And you're not exactly winning."

"I was never supposed to beat Rusayev, was I?"

"Oh, God, you're tiresome."

"Why now, then?"

"Have you taken a look at Rusayev? The man's ill."

"He's not ill," said Aleksandr. He kicked at the edge of Dmitry's bed, sending Dmitry scuttling toward the wall. "He's just old. He's just decrepit. He's just exhausted because he's starting to lose, and losing is exhausting. I should know. I've been losing for five months. You didn't seem too concerned about that."

"You're being childish."

"You're being corrupt. I've given him forty-eight free chess lessons."

"This has been going on for half a year. It's an embarrassment."

"An embarrassment to whom?"

"To everyone. Not least of all yourself. We had higher hopes for you, Aleksandr."

"No, you didn't. Obviously, you didn't."

"There's a press conference tomorrow," said Petr Pavlovich. "There will be an announcement that the match will end without decision. It's become a test of physical endurance."

"It hasn't."

"There will be a press conference tomorrow. You'll attend."

Across the room, Dmitry was pulling up the curtains, revealing a sour, underwhelming dawn.

"I won't," said Aleksandr.

At this, Pavlovich laughed. "Aleksandr, you forget that I know you. I know you better than anyone does, probably, at this point." He sneezed again. "You will attend. You will. Of course you will."

———

The day of the press conference, Aleksandr woke up early. Across the room, Dmitry was still sleeping, mouth half open, hands curled into fists like a newborn, and Aleksandr found himself staring, wondering what the rest of Dmitry's life had been like. It made him squirm to think that Dmitry had made similar compromises, endured similar challenges, only to sit next to Aleksandr at a table and worry over his stress levels. At least Aleksandr had sold his own soul, assuming he had one, for something a bit more glamorous.

Dmitry opened his eyes and sat bolt upright. "What are you doing?"

Aleksandr took a step back. "We need to get ready."

Then again, here they were: stuck in the same hotel room, breathing the same stale air, watching the same dull programming night after night, chewing over the same chess moves—and at least, at the end of it all, Dmitry had a fiancée, another life, to return to.

Dmitry blinked.

"The press conference," said Aleksandr.

"You need me there?"

Aleksandr didn't like admitting that he needed Dmitry anywhere, and he wasn't about to say so out loud now.

"It's protocol," said Aleksandr. Dmitry had a worshipful regard for protocol.

Twelve minutes later, they were hurrying down slushy streets. Dmitry's nose ran chronically, and today was no exception: he tilted his head back and feigned interest in the sky; he surreptitiously found excuses to run his sleeve along his face. Aleksandr did not know why the nasal challenges of everyone around him should be such a large part of his own emotional life.

At the press conference, Aleksandr stood awkwardly onstage next to Oleg Chazov, the FIDE president. On the other side of Chazov stood Rusayev. The journalists looked exhausted, vitamin D–deficient, bored beyond belief. When the cameras flashed, the light made their lanyards glitter. In the audience, Petr Pavlovich stared at Aleksandr with bittersweet fondness, like a mother proud of the military boy she was about to send to his death.

Chazov droned into a microphone about the interminable match. He gestured to Rusayev, who smiled weakly, with the shining eyes of a religious supplicant, and licked his lips. He looked prophetic, other-worldly. Aleksandr tried not to scowl.

"As you all know, this match has been going on for months and months," said Chazov. "The players have pushed themselves to the point of exhaustion and beyond."

Aleksandr opened his eyes wide. He tried to look not exhausted, not weak. He tried to communicate to the crowd that he was young, that he was alive, that he was smart—most important, that he was winning, or that he might be, if they would just let him keep playing.

"Our players have played honorably. Aleksandr Bezetov here, de-spite some faltering beginnings"—and here the crowd laughed lightly, knowingly, and Aleksandr stopped trying not to scowl—"has proved a—well, an astonishingly enduring opponent. And Igor Rusayev is, of course, our cherished current champion. He has played some of his best games during this match, and watching him play has been a privilege and an honor for us all."

Rusayev bowed humbly. This felt false to Aleksandr—only the victorious were allowed to look so self-abnegating. Wasn't there any shame (just a little, just a little) in having earned the title so sloppily once, then defecting from his chance at properly defending it? Aleksandr had been doing him a favor by playing this match; he'd been giving Rusayev an opportunity to retroactively justify his whole ludicrous career, and that wasn't something he could do on his own.

"But now," said Chazov grandly, "we must conclude this exercise. It has become absurd."

Rusayev smiled bravely.

"It has become a test of physical will, more than mental agility. It is no longer a fair arena in which to judge these men's chess capacities."

Maybe it was the reference to "fairness"—abstract nouns, of late, had a tendency to make Aleksandr feel savage. Or maybe it was the way Rusayev just stood there, looking sallow, overly polite.

"Excuse me," said Aleksandr. "I'm just— Excuse me." The journalists swiveled to look at Aleksandr, as if remembering for the first time that he was there. They raised their cameras, they raised their notepads.

"What?" Chazov looked horrified.

"Well," said Aleksandr. "We both wish to keep playing, if I'm not mistaken?"

"What are you saying?" Above Chazov, Lenin and Gorbachev gazed evenly out of framed portraits. Gorbachev's birthmark was the color of raw meat and the shape of the kingdom of Thailand.

"Well," said Aleksandr. His voice was coming out strangely—too solicitous, half an octave higher than was typical. "It's not clear to me why the FIDE should intervene and disrupt play when both players are willing to continue."

The journalists began to scribble. Pavlovich shook his head furiously. A camera flashed in Aleksandr's face. It was too late to retreat.

Aleksandr cleared his throat, trying to maneuver his voice back to its normal pitch. "We all know he didn't win his title honorably. Perhaps he'd like to honorably defend it?"

"Enough," said Chazov severely.

"I'm just wondering," said Aleksandr. He looked at the video cameras. He remembered something about following the one with the light. Pavlovich was glaring in disbelief. "I'm just wondering if there's something a little corrupt about this. Maybe we should ask Rusayev directly what he'd prefer."

Chazov was gesturing to the journalists to turn off their cameras. He mimed cutting his own neck; he mimed unplugging technology from walls. He edged his way in front of Aleksandr and the microphone. "We're having some confusion here," he said. Petr Pavlovich held his head in his hands, and Aleksandr hoped momentarily that no trouble would befall him because of this outburst. "Everyone break for lunch," said Chazov hurriedly. "We'll be back with updated information shortly."

———

Petr Pavlovich called the next morning. Out the window, car horns bleated; a mossy smell kicked up from somewhere. Aleksandr could barely remember what it was like to live in the world.

"Well, Aleksandr," said Petr Pavlovich. "I don't know what to tell you."

"Isn't it your job to know exactly what to tell me?"

Aleksandr could hear Petr Pavlovich lighting a cigarette. He breathed noisily into the phone.

"In their magnanimousness, they have seen fit to allow you to continue to play."

"Because it was on television."

"You must never, never do anything like that again. I know you don't really understand what my job is. I know you think I'm out to get you. But I am telling you as a colleague—I won't say friend—but as a colleague who respects your game. You must never, never do that again."

"On television?"

"Anywhere. Anywhere at all. It's completely unacceptable."

"I don't see why they care so much about who wins. They get their fifty percent of the winnings either way."

"You have been so much more trouble than you're worth."

"But I am going to be world champion, aren't I?"

"You're not fit to be world champion. You're not fit to represent Soviet chess."

"But I *am* going to be world champion, aren't I?"

"Don't you understand anything?"

"Aren't I?"

"Don't you understand *anything*? Someone has to be."

Aleksandr mulled this for a moment. "And you guys really want it to be that obsolete clown?"

There was a sniff, and Aleksandr tried to assess its emotional content. Over the years, Aleksandr had come to know the vast variety of Petr Pavlovich's sniffs and snuffles; he could diagnose and interpret them; he knew them the way a mother knows the subtleties of her newborn's various cries. Petr Pavlovich had a sniff when he was irritated and a sniff when he was disappointed—he even, bizarrely, had a phlegmy, chuckling sniff when he was satisfied. He also had a sniff that meant he was feeling passive-aggressive. This was the one he employed most often, and it was the one he issued now.

"Are you going to be fired?" said Aleksandr.

"Not by you, friend. That's not your prerogative."

"By the Party."

"Every time you have a temper tantrum, you know, they give me a raise. They see how hard my job is, and tovarish, that's a good thing."

His words fired like pistons. Aleksandr flinched.

"Every time you come across as an ungrateful, temperamental child, they understand better what a delight—a *pure* delight—it is for me to wrangle you. So please, if that's your concern, have at it."

Silence. Aleksandr waited for Pavlovich to sniff again, but he did not.

"What you've never seemed to understand is that I'm genuinely concerned about your career. I see a talent like yours, and I want to protect it. I want to help it. I want to be instrumental in its navigation of the system. I want to mitigate its exposure to certain corroding effects."

Out the window, Aleksandr watched a car splash mud on the side of a building.

"But it's not you I care about, tovarish. It's only your brain. Let's get that straight."

Aleksandr, who'd long thought that he and his brain were one and the same, did not know why he found this insulting. "Yes," he said. "I don't think I was confused on that point."

"So you can go back to playing," said Petr Pavlovich. "That's the upshot. I hope you're happy. I hope you're overjoyed."

"Thrilled."

"Good. I'd hope so. Your happiness is just such a radiant thing, you know? It lifts us up and makes us better people. It's truly a joy to witness. It's an inspiration to all generations."

"All right. Enough."

"The match will resume on Tuesday."

"Noted."

"You're welcome in advance," said Petr Pavlovich, sniffing sadly. "I'm sure there's a thank-you card already in the mail."

———

The match resumed, and Aleksandr found himself gripped by caustic paranoia. He began to regard Dmitry with grave suspicion. He watched as Dmitry chewed his lips unconsciously or shaved his stupid face (needlessly, always needlessly) or talked inanities into the telephone—to his tedious girlfriend, allegedly, though Aleksandr no longer felt sure that was the case. There were a few openings in which Rusayev responded a little too quickly, a little too cleanly, and Aleksandr began to wonder whether Dmitry had been bribed to pass on his opening moves to Rusayev. As soon as Aleksandr wondered, he was convinced. The theory moved in his head like a mechanical apparatus. The gears shifted; the pulleys pulled.

When Aleksandr went to the Party doctor—to be weighed and assessed and prodded like a piece of prize cattle—he was asked about his stress level, his nightmares, his anxieties, his fears. Aleksandr sat on the edge of his seat and refused to answer. These questions were too pointed; Aleksandr wouldn't be surprised if this guy, too, was in on it. No matter: he wasn't a chess prodigy for nothing. Aleksandr swung his knees and spoke brightly about the satisfactions of the game: the consolations to be found in triumph, the wisdom to be found in loss. The doctor's mouth went flat as a blade. He made a note on his paper.

In the end, the match took fifty-three games—an unending, unthinkable number. The journalists were alternately awed and gleeful and bored and disbelieving. When the final moves were made—when Aleksandr sacrificed his queen to the ready arms of Rusayev's waiting bishop—the audience leaned forward, intent, breathless. The cameras snapped like offended turtles. Aleksandr cracked his knuckles and shuffled his fingers. He realigned his shoulders. He was the first to see when Rusayev's gaze started to swim—not with tears but with the blurry confusion of a child who has been asked to explain how he solved a copied math problem. The audience didn't see, though, so they hunched forward and held still and wondered collectively at the nature of what they were witnessing—insane, suicidal, miraculous? Out into the universe, the taut figures of Aleksandr and Rusayev were cast on beams of light that dodged checkpoints and disregarded diplomatic protocol. Bits of dust fell from the ceiling and caught the limited glow of the lamps, making the room frosted and dreamlike. Aleksandr drummed his fingers, which he knew was cruel and theatrical. Rusayev's face hemorrhaged momentary disbelief before easing into the nearly grateful expression of someone whose bitter disappointment is outmatched in the end by his profound fatigue. He had seen. He took his next turn with a resigned graciousness. The rest was ritual, the stately etiquette followed by a retreating army. Rusayev smiled slightly and swallowed. Aleksandr blinked and saw his future flash before his eyes. His hands shook, his head emptied, a cable ran arctic-cold from his throat to his stomach, and he was surprised even then by how the best moment of his professional life could feel so much like absolute terror.

And then it was over. Rusayev's king was idling on the tile, and Rusayev was signing the score sheet, and Aleksandr's ears were failing him. A man was loping up the stage with a cavernous smile, an outstretched hand, and a trophy.

Afterward, Aleksandr sat at the hotel bar while Dmitry went to pack. On state television, an ugly news reporter was talking about Aleksandr's win. His youth was much remarked upon, as though the best thing that could be said of him was that he'd had the courtesy not to be around for very long.

———

The next morning Aleksandr woke, as he often did, to a ringing phone. "Get it, Dmitry," Aleksandr groaned, until he remembered Dmitry was gone; he'd left the night before, pink-eared and elated to be finally done with his job and returning to his silly fiancée—Galina, was that her name? Aleksandr realized he'd never asked. He stood up. On the floor, Dmitry had left some scattered belongings, the accrued bits and pieces of his half a year as a glorified refugee butler. There were pens and coat hangers and mysterious scraps of paper—receipts of purchase that Aleksandr did not recall being present for, though they'd been side by side the whole time. Who was Dmitry? Where was he now? Why wasn't he answering the phone?

For a short, buoyant moment, Aleksandr thought of who might be calling to congratulate him—his mother, most plausibly, though she usually waited for him to call her these days. It was unlikely to be anyone from the chess academy; their undisguised resentment had bothered him back when he felt he deserved better. Now it seemed appropriate. He did not wonder whether it might be Elizabeta, because he never thought of her anymore.

The phone kept ringing. He knew—and really, he'd always known—that there was only one person it could possibly be.

Petr Pavlovich sniffed happily into the phone. "Congratulations, friend," he said.

"No thanks to you."

"Quite a lot of thanks to me, if you think about it."

"I don't."

"How does it feel?"

Aleksandr went to the window and looked out at the graying morning. The day already looked like a dirge. There was a horrible taste in the back of his throat. "Like nothing. It feels like nothing."

"Oh, come. Don't be bitter."

"It feels the same."

"It surely does not."

Petr Pavlovich was right. It did not feel the same. Now that he'd gotten what he wanted, he had justified his entire life—every isolated and selfish and odd childhood habit, his lack of friends, his lack of romance. His decision to stop the journal, his decision to hang around these people for the past four years and eat every imported delicacy they fed him. It had all paid off; it had all been warranted. He'd chased his own ego across an enormous country, and here, in Moscow, in Hotel Sport, he'd finally caught it. He was the best chess player in the world for now—though every moment he crept closer to the day when this would no longer be the case, and who was to say (even now, even right this second) that there wasn't somebody out in the vast world who could beat him? Some wild-eyed prophetic prodigy in a cave somewhere, perhaps, or some nobler version of himself in some alternate universe who hadn't had the stomach to make the compromises he'd made. The victory, such as it was, was bitter—that was to be expected. How odd that it also felt elusive. He watched the second hand flinch its way across the face of the clock, and in each moment, he wondered. Was he world champion now, really? Was he world champion *now*? You couldn't ever be sure. Funny that he'd never thought of that when he was deciding whether to cash in the entire rest of his life for a chance at this. He'd never be able to be sure of his success. Even if he were world champion, truly, the man who would someday beat him (and of course it would be a man) had already been born, no doubt—he was already making puzzles in the sand, or tearing chess games out of the newspaper, or staring silently at the wall for hours on end. He was already lonely. He was already worrying his parents. They were already seeing in him the radiant seeds of greatness or lunacy or both; they saw their child driving a wedge into the world and opening up a new rift where he would someday sit, anointed, applauded, when Aleksandr was old and forgotten.

"Are you there?" said Petr Pavlovich.

"I don't know."

"Don't be philosophical."

Outside, the leaves on the trees turned pale side up. They looked as if they were admitting defeat.

"This is what you've been working for your whole life. You should be doing cartwheels in the streets. What has everything been for if not for this?"

Aleksandr did not believe that Petr Pavlovich meant this kindly. Still, there was nobody else to whom he could say this—this or anything.

"I don't know," he said. The window was cool against his forehead; it communicated a calming, pragmatic presence somehow. Aleksandr thought briefly of his mother. "I don't know what it was for."

Petr Pavlovich was silent. "Are you dressed? You need to come out for pictures."

"What pictures?"

"With your trophy, of course." Petr Pavlovich sniffed cruelly. "A family portrait."

12

IRINA

St. Petersburg, 2006

And so, entirely out of ideas, I put on my only revealing shirt and went to the Pravda bar. Inside, the place had an atmosphere of unrelenting grime; the air felt opaque with grit and an obdurate unwholesomeness that was, in a strange way, refreshing. I squirmed on a barstool, drinking white wine and mouthing my way through *Kommersant* and eyeing possible candidates for Viktor Davidenko as they entered. It felt decadent, profligate, pathological to be drinking before nightfall. I fluttered my fingers against the bar. This was what I'd come for, no? To sit in bars and await the arrival of strange men? It wasn't what I'd come for, exactly.

After a few false alarms, the man who had to be Viktor Davidenko entered the bar. He was tallish, six-two or something, the kind of height that could seem epic or almost normal depending on one's biases. He had a beard, but I somehow didn't begrudge him that. I wondered if someone looking for me would have trouble figuring out who I was. Or was I the only possible candidate for myself in the entire bar? I didn't like to think that; I liked to think that I could be anyone. But then I looked around—at the butcher lesbians, at the femmes fatales with their immense scaffoldings of eye makeup, hanging all over everywhere—and I had to level with myself. I was the only nervous-looking, polite-looking person in the whole establishment, and if anybody had been looking for me, he would have found me immediately.

I walked over to Viktor Davidenko's table. I crossed my arms, then uncrossed them. Then I said hello.

"Yes?" His voice was a bit gravelly, a bit sullen—exactly the sort of voice you'd imagine. He had a heavy brow and, underneath it, fairly astonishing blue eyes. His hair was curly and, you could tell, barely subdued.

I introduced myself. He looked me up and down, as Misha had promised he would.

"You're a journalist?" He'd switched to English. His accent—you could tell from even one word—was a complicated affair, incorporating multiple experiences and existences and institutions of higher learning.

"No."

"Are you a blogger?"

"No."

"Are you on social media?"

"Not really, no."

He sighed. It was a profoundly aggrieved, hectored, performative sigh, and it made me immediately like him.

"Can I have a few minutes of your time anyway?" I was beginning to panic mildly. This was my first interaction with an ambassador of Bezetov's actual team, and I feared I was wildly failing to say the thing I needed to say.

"I suppose."

"When? Should I come to your office?"

"Office. Ah. No. How about right now?"

This seemed somehow slightly less than professional, though it's true that my reasons for being here couldn't be construed as entirely— or even marginally—professional. But in recent months I'd taken to regarding my quest for Aleksandr Bezetov as something like my job—I avoided it like a job, at any rate, and I approached it with stress and sporadic diligence and no small amount of resentment.

"Well," I said. "Okay."

He took my hand, and for a brief, absurd moment, I thought he might kiss it.

"Viktor Davidenko," he said, dropping it. "Please sit down."

I did. There was a courtliness to all of this that felt a little silly but also highly self-aware. I sat up straighter, so as to be ready for whatever pageantry was forthcoming. Viktor ordered three shots of vodka, which I found impressive and terrifying until he passed one over to me. I took a sip and coughed.

"Where did you learn English?" I said.

"Oxford, most recently."

"What were you doing before that?"

"I was importing Japanese video recorders."

"Really?"

"Really."

"And now you're the media relations person?"

"I am that person. And you?" He looked amused.

"Where did I learn English?"

"What do you do?"

"Nothing."

"Of course. Would that be a diplomatic sort of nothing? A commercial sort of nothing?" His quasi-British accent made him sound like he was always on the brink of apology. His expression made him look like a person who had never apologized in his entire life.

"I don't know what you're talking about," I said.

"Academic? Sheer awkwardness?"

"I really don't."

"Ah. Very good."

I knew I was being assessed by some convoluted system of social metrics that I didn't yet understand. I took another sip of my vodka and let the alcohol mince my mouth.

"So, what, then? What do you want?" He held his second shot, tracing the nimbus of moisture it had left on the table. "You want me to get a chessboard signed for you or something?"

I turned my face to the side. Something about this man made me not want to tell him everything all at once. "My father was a fan of Bezetov's," I said. "I just want to meet him."

"Your father was a fan?"

I nodded. I knew how this sounded; I knew what particularly obnoxious fragilities in my psyche this guy was already starting to see, to think he saw. I wanted this part of the conversation to end as quickly as possible.

"Bezetov has a lot of fans," said Viktor.

"Right."

"Presumably, a lot of people have fathers who were fans."

"I am sure."

"And they don't all come here looking for him."

"Assuredly not."

He leaned back in his chair and took a gulp, followed immediately by a fiercer gulp, of his drink. "This is kind of a sentimental project, isn't it?"

I winced. I hate being accused of sentimentality. But I knew there was no way to assert that you weren't sentimental; any attempt to do so was automatically suspect. "I guess so. I guess you could say that." I took a moment to take another sip, flamboyantly. "He's very busy, I'd imagine."

"Well, not that busy."

"Oh?" I waited for clarification long enough to understand that none was forthcoming. "How long have you been working for him?"

"Two years."

"And how did you get hired?"

"I went to a rally."

"And did what?"

"I approached him. I gave him my résumé."

"I see. You showed up, you're saying?"

"I mean I have a terrific résumé."

"I don't at all doubt it. Is that how he hires all the staff?"

"What staff?"

"Who works there?"

"There's me. There's Nina, Bezetov's wife. A pure joy. There's

Vlad, the security guard, two-thirds retarded. There's Boris, my assistant. He wouldn't tell you he's my assistant, but I assure you, he is."

"What would he tell me he is?"

"He'd likely claim to be a peer of some kind. There's not a whole lot of logic to the decisions Bezetov makes about people. If you met his wife, you'd see. Don't mention I said that."

"Of course not."

With a flick of his finger, Viktor ordered us another round. He sat back and looked at me for a long moment. "So that's it? Your father was a fan and you want to meet him?"

"Yes." I didn't know why I was lying to him. It could only bolster my case to tell him the truth—maybe Bezetov had some kind of Make-A-Wish Foundation for terminally ill American adults. But Viktor Davidenko was attractive, I guess, and there was an unusual clarity to his gaze, and I did not want to see what his face would do if we had to have that particular conversation. "Yes," I said again. "I suppose that's it."

He looked skeptical. "We are inscrutable even to ourselves, I suppose."

"More often than not, I find."

"But really? That's it? You're not here to interview him or something? Tell him how to do things differently? Offer your expert policy opinions?" All this was delivered rapid-fire, without discernible irony.

"What? I— What? No. No."

"Oh." He picked up the menu and began to study it. I waited for him to say something else and noticed, in a detached way, the wave of anxiety that was cresting in my sternum. It's an interesting thing, to watch the discrete components of a face resolve into beauty. If there was something unusual about this man's face, it was that its overall sternness was cut by the sweetness of his eyes. I badly wanted to steer us back into the realm of answerable questions. I said the only thing I had to say.

"I just met with Mikhail Andreyevich Solovyov."

He put the menu down and eyed me with an expression that could only be described as world-weary. "Misha. I see. And how was that?"

"He's got a vendetta, it would seem."

Viktor widened his eyes into an expression of mock hurt. "Does he?"

"I got the sense that there were, you know, factions within the camp."

"Factions? Dear heavens. Tell me more about that."

"He seems aggrieved."

"He was run over by a bus. That'll make anyone bitter, I'd imagine."

"I didn't know that. But I mean, that wasn't Bezetov's fault, right?"

"Fault is such a fuzzy concept, don't you think?"

"Not really," I said. Viktor Davidenko shrugged and went back to staring at the menu. I forced my voice into a lower register than it normally wanted to go. "What's the relationship between Right Russia and Alternative Russia, exactly?"

He made a face. "Muted indifference. No, that's not right. Grudging tolerance."

"On the part of Alternative Russia, you mean?"

"Obviously."

"Right Russia is a public relations liability?"

"In some quarters, yes, in other quarters, no."

"Like anything, I suppose. So why does Aleksandr tolerate Misha's faction? Does Misha have something on Aleksandr?"

"Some kind of blackmail, you mean?"

"Does Aleksandr owe him a favor or something? Or does Misha know something about him?"

Viktor eyed me wryly. "Like a mistress, you're saying?"

"Oh, I wouldn't suggest that—"

"The thought never crossed my mind," he said. "But no. I do not think Bezetov's secrets are of the sexual variety. He'd probably be a much better boss if they were."

"So why associate with Right Russia at all?"

"I can't talk to you about that," said Viktor cheerfully. "But this is what I'd suggest. He has a rally next week. On Saturday. At Gostiny Dvor."

"Right." I'd seen the posters around the city on those aimless and glassy-eyed afternoons of wandering, in between reading and sleeping. The Assembly of the Dissatisfied, it was called. There were tiny flags and icons symbolizing various causes, some of which I was familiar with—there were environmentalists, human rights people, free-market people, controlled-economy people, and many more that I didn't recognize—and I thought it was interesting that one march could incorporate such a wide variety of wingnuts. In the center of the poster was a picture of Aleksandr Bezetov: he peered out at me distastefully, as though he already knew that I was going to try to bother him. Above him, in surreal colors, was a distorted and x-ed out picture of Putin. His puckered, vaguely serpentine face registered a look of continual disapproval over the proceedings.

"You should come," said Viktor. "Wear that shirt again."

It occurred to me dimly that I was being flirted with. I am genuinely bad at discerning this. "Do I talk to you again?"

"Me? No, certainly not. You never talk to me again. You'd never outsmart me, but Aleksandr is, shall we say, cautious. This conversation didn't happen. I'm not supposed to meet with people like you."

"Women?"

"Funny."

"Americans?"

"Getting warmer."

"Who do I talk to at the rally?" It occurred to me that Viktor might not have believed a single thing I'd said to him, and then I thought to wonder for the first time whether I should believe anything he'd said, in a definitive way.

Viktor leaned toward me. "You'll see Nina. The wife. She has red hair. You can't miss her."

"Okay."

"Ask her for a meeting."

"You're the media relations guy and you're telling me to accost his wife at a rally?" I had wanted to avoid doing exactly that.

"It makes her feel important to arrange things," said Viktor. "She'll give you a meeting."

"What's she like?"

He looked up. "Why? You after her job?"

My mouth fell open. I closed it. "No. No. Of course not, no."

"It wouldn't be professional for me to comment on my boss's wife."

"No. Of course not. I'm sorry I asked."

"But I've staked my career on pushing professional boundaries. So I'll say she's—she's not making him happy."

I rolled my eyes. I was bored of talking about this already. Might she be castrating? Might be she be emasculating? Might she be shrill? I was sick of hearing about the failings of wives, ever, and was suddenly filled with gladness that I would never be one.

"What?" said Viktor.

"Oh, I don't know. Making someone happy is such a tall order these days."

"You think so?" He was looking at me, I noticed, in the way I remember men looking at me, back when men looked at me. There was a brief, comical period in college when I was widely deemed mysterious. All people meant by this was that my listening face was not terribly animated. I could see Viktor Davidenko gearing up to think me some kind of puzzle, and this never works—not because people solve you, particularly, but because they learn there's nothing much to solve. Seeing yourself through somebody else's eyes is like taking a guest through your long-unvisited apartment. The bits of your personality that you've come to take for granted are like the souvenirs of a life you are already bored of remembering. This old thing?, you want to say, pointing to your personal trivia or your political beliefs or your body. Got it in Barcelona for four euros. It's not real. This joke? I make it all the time. You'll get sick of it. I am sick of it. But the new person doesn't know that yet, and you are not actually about to tell him.

"And you?" I said.

"And me, what?"

I realized I didn't know what I was asking. "You're motivated by—what? You believe in Bezetov?" I tossed this off flippantly, though I desperately wanted to hear that the answer was yes.

"Yes." He leaned forward. "I do."

"Why?"

"Why? The lady wants to know why. It will matter, is the bottom line. I do believe it will matter. You look at the '91 coup, the way that the demonstrators then could not be dispersed by force because there were simply so many of them. It is an enormous country. He will not win. Of course he will not win. But I do think it will matter."

Here, in this statement, I found my vague attraction made specific: he was a person who believed, ultimately, that Aleksandr could be important. I'd been drawn to Viktor already, maybe, but that attraction was narrowed down to that most concrete and self-serving thing: the shared affinity of vision.

"You have someone at home?" he said.

"I did."

"You left him?"

"I did."

"For this?"

I slid my tongue along my lower teeth, feeling the unevenness that had resurged in recent years. All that orthodontia, such an investment, for what? Though I knew this was a rabbit hole that did not warrant pursuing. When you thought about it, everything—all of life—could seem a series of wasted preparations. Why did you exercise, and why did you consume the appropriate staggering amount of vegetables per day? And why were you vain about your body or your brain or whatever it was you were vain about? And why did you sob for a week and refuse food and lie the wrong way in the bed and watch the necrotic light creep over the horizon only because a boy who never loved you still did not? Such anguish, such narcissism, such ahistoricism. All the grand projects were, after all, not so grand. Little petty fits, all of them, piecemeal staving off of the inevitable, scraps and dregs of self-distraction, all of it existing only to mitigate the fact, the central fact, the unbelievable irreducible fact, of our transience.

"I suppose so," I said slowly.

"That must not have made him happy."

I shrugged in a sudden, flinching fashion. I was mirroring the way he had shrugged a moment ago. "Probably not."

"Has it made you happy?"

"Not yet. I am cautiously optimistic."

"That is probably too optimistic."

There was some slyness happening on his face, like a pentimento, an echo of a previous intention. There'd been a tension in the conversation all along, running some syncopated counterpoint to the surface. We were more adversarial than was merited, that's what it was.

He raised a finger for the check and paid the bill before I'd even begun fumbling through my wallet. There was the sense of attraction gearing up, swinging in a new, unexpected direction, as it could. I thought briefly of that parade of men in college: insubstantial, finally; it was hard to clearly remember a face or a personality, though it was easy enough to remember the disappointments, misunderstandings, abuses. I wondered what attenuated mini-romances of 2006 were even like—people must wonder whether they're being dumped for not having a sufficiently robust Internet presence, or whatever. The Internet: a whole new arena in which to fail to significantly exist. As soon as I realized I was thinking about that, I knew I was drunk.

Outside, there was too much clarity to the buildings, as though they'd been freshly etched; the stars were a degree brighter than seemed totally plausible; I felt, generally, like a recent recipient of corrective lenses. This—all of this, I knew—was silly. One thing I did not like about drunkenness was that it unlocked all of one's self-pity at once—in my case, self-pity was vast and gnawing and insatiable; it required constant combat to subdue. When I was drunk, my defenses were down, and I could easily spend an hour staring in the mirror, thinking that I was too pretty to die.

"Well," I said, suddenly clunky, suddenly professional. "Thank you for your time."

I offered my hand and knew immediately that this was the wrong thing to do.

"You are quite welcome," he said, taking my hand and shaking it rather more elaborately than was required. "I will see you at the rally, then."

"Yes," I said, drawing myself up into dignity, attempting to make a coherent exit. "I will see you at the rally."

———

I walked back slowly, in ever widening circles. The Neva looked colder than usual, shivering with leaves and bric-a-brac. I stopped to stare at it, trying to get my head to clear. Looking at the water, for some reason—or no reason—disinterred an image of my father. Perhaps it was a memory of a memory, or perhaps a memory of a photo. At any rate, I gazed into the water and I could nearly see him, facing some eastern window, his shadow severe in the low-hanging light. I could almost see his stooped back, the slumped angle of the shoulders. I could almost see in it some preemptive defeat. By the point the picture was taken, or the memory was formed, he knew. He knew, he must have known. And yet how impossible to parse the moment when the proper exit is before you. How impossible to know whether you're getting out at the right time. A game of strategy, that, that no one could win. Maybe he thought about it, and maybe he miscalculated, and maybe then it was too late. Or maybe he thought about it and rejected it, nobly, with clean sagacity, accepted the indignity of insanity and death as part of life, consciously, bravely. Or maybe, maybe, he was just too terrified. At any rate, who am I to judge?

I watched the women hurry home along the river: they were uniformly thin, wearing cheap fabrics in bold patterns. Under their coats, I knew, tiny crosses swung against jutting clavicles.

But it's easy to judge, we're born to judge; we live for it, really. It's the way we decide that we are the self we are instead of all the other selves we might have been. And I judged enthusiastically, mirthfully, even him, the man whose disaster was the perfect template for my own—maybe I judged him especially. I thought when I was young that I would have the certainty to do it, that prevailing ethics and aesthetics would win the day, and that as long as suicide could be chosen rationally, thoughtfully, then the catastrophe was only the universal one, nothing more or less—as long as agency could be maintained, as long as the conscience could have the last word, then there was nothing more for a human being to ask from a lifetime. I judged him for not doing it. I resented him for not doing it once he'd disappeared entirely and no longer had to deal with it, and I saw it as a failure of sympathetic imagination on his part, a failure of honor—not the only failure, most likely, nor possibly the biggest one, but the one we'd had to live with longest and thus the one we would always remember. The failure was the legacy. The failure was the only thing left.

Along the Neva, I watched an older woman push her mentally disabled daughter in a wheelchair. The daughter was wearing eyeliner, and I thought of the care that had gone into making that a reality—the mother licking the pencil, bending her thumb against her daughter's eyelashes.

If I'd defined my father's failure in such stark terms—his unwillingness to part with the last feeble snatches of his existence, his greedy and small clinging to what little was left—if those were the terms by which I defined failure, I knew I had a hazier vision of what I meant by success. In part, I was trying to avoid causing my mother the exact brand of anguish that my father had caused us—the particular pain of wishing rabidly for the death of a person you once desperately loved. Though if I was honest with myself, I knew that I was doing something not dissimilar, not demonstrably better, by running away. Did I really think they'd forgotten me? Was my self-esteem actually so low? It was not. Jonathan would get over it one day—he'd find new love, he'd find new memories, those memories would pile on top of the memories of me, pushing me ever further to the bottom of his consciousness, time would elapse, great swaths of time, such time!, and the time he'd spent with me would become ever briefer, comparably, until one day it might feel incidental, anecdotal. But I knew that day had not yet come, and in the meantime, I'd done nothing less than traumatize him. And my mother. I did not think so little of her that I felt my departure was, fundamentally, any kind of favor. I didn't believe that she'd be able to relax now, soak up the Arizona heat and the love of an inane man, enjoy life. I hoped there'd be some of that, but I could not pretend that all the great difficulties were truly over. To do so would be to invoke depths of grotesque faux self martyrdom that not even I possessed. No, there was no way to romanticize it: this trip was essentially a temper tantrum. But then maybe insanity invites insanity; illogic invites illogic. There was simply no good answer. There was no right way to go, only countless wrong ways, each as unique as a snowflake.

I did not know what the humane thing was, but I knew I was not doing it.

I turned away from the Neva and started walking toward the bridge. The air was unbendingly cold, the city entombed in a darkness that was beginning to feel permanent.

I learned something once, I think, from my father's illness. Mostly,

I did not learn; mostly, I resented and resisted and made it elaborately clear how little fun I was having personally, to anyone who was paying attention, which nobody was. But once, maybe, my jaw aching with the tedium of it, in one of those awful, mostly unremembered years, there was a small revelation of a kind. Once, maybe, I looked into his stricken, blanking face and I knew something that I couldn't stop knowing.

Behind me, the Neva was growing dim. The horizon was relinquishing its last monofilament of light.

Personality is continuity. Personality is the myth of continuity. And the person is lost when nothing can be old to him, when nothing can be familiar, when all parallels, all symbols, all analogs, are gone; when the world is perpetually stunning; when we are newborns again, at last.

PART TWO

PART TWO

13

ALEKSANDR

St. Petersburg, 1986–2006

The eighties melted into the nineties, and Aleksandr lost weight again. His currency among women strengthened, and there was something of a nationalistic uprising in his personal life. All of a sudden they were everywhere—thin-browed, thin-faced, pale, and long-limbed, pressing their warm asses against his thighs all through those long winters. They found his jokes hilarious, and his prominent nose distinguished, and his chess talk *fascinating*. When he started going on CNN, when he started being invited to speak at the elite American universities, it was an inundation: he nearly began to resent them for their beauty, for their unapologetic availability. He took to sleeping with women whose last names he did not know; then he took to sleeping with women whose first names he did not know. He didn't ask, and he tried not to remember if they told him. Sex became tedious for a while; sometimes he longed for a woman to reject him just for a surprise.

He thought of how Elizabeta had left him back when he was deserving of love and it would not have been wasted on him. And now he was ruined for it, he knew, and did not warrant it.

In the other Leningrad—the one Aleksandr no longer lived in—
the lines for toilet paper stretched around corners. On television, that
smiling, simian American president kept making his demands. When
the satellite countries broke away—with relative ease, as if the Soviet Union were a rotted thing that was more than ready to abandon
its auxiliary elements—he sat up straight and allowed himself thirty
seconds of optimism. He was an early supporter of Gorbachev; he
waited in the cold until his ears were red, and he cried when he cast
his vote for Yeltsin. The Museum of the History of Atheism and Religion turned back into Kazan Cathedral. The Communist Party was
banned; the ruble became a convertible currency; confiscatory privati-
zation overtook state-run concerns; inflation shot to 20 percent. The
shelves at the markets filled back up, but no one could buy. Once prices
tripled, people began to turn out their dogs, which roamed the streets
like beggars, mangy and chagrined. The population was decreasing by
six hundred thousand people a year. Shock therapy was hard on the
common people, certainly, but it was the birth pangs of capitalism, the
plinth upon which the towering new Russia would be built. And in
the free-market economy, Aleksandr wrote a book on business and
chess that made five million dollars. He intended to sink gratefully into
the luxuriant wealth of the brand-new post-Communist oligarchy—
hot tub, women, the kind of travel that comes with steaming face
towels when you cross the international dateline.

He went to clubs. He never danced, he only watched. He encountered blondes. He encountered brunettes. He encountered Central
Asians who turned out to have no pubic hair whatsoever. And one
night when he was out late, five years after he'd become world champion, maybe, he encountered a redhead who was smiling a secret smile
to herself.

"Hello," he said. "What do you know that I don't know?"

She shrugged, and at the time he believed that this meant there was
something. Later, he knew that he should have taken her at face value.

"You're the chess champion."

"Yes."

"But you already knew that."

He ducked his head. "I suppose."

She was drinking champagne. He wondered if she was celebrating something. She cocked her head to one side; her red hair was ineffably gorgeous in the light. No, he decided, she was not celebrating anything. She didn't need to.

"And who are you?"

"Nina," she said, extending a hand. Her wrist was impossibly delicate and feminine, tremendously well-made. She looked like a human to whom some attention had been given, whereas Aleksandr often remarked that God had made him (Aleksandr) in the dark, one hand tied behind His back, possibly drunk. Aleksandr didn't really believe in God, of course, but he liked the joke, and told it often. He thought of telling it now but looked at the wrist again and decided against it.

She smiled at him then. "It was bold the way you made them resume play during the World Championships."

"Bold?"

It had been a long time—too long—since someone had thought he was brave. No: maybe nobody ever had. Elizabeta might have once, for the paper, but that was ages ago, in another lifetime. Was this assessment from Nina undeserved? Maybe. The risk he'd taken with the FIDE had been more calculating, more clinically self-interested; after all, he wasn't standing up to them because they were morally bankrupt—he was standing up to them because they'd wanted to screw him over, and he'd lost too much already to let them screw him over at that late date. So she admired him for an impulse that was as petty and shallow and reflexive as slapping someone's hand away when he's digging in your pocket.

"Yes," she said. She clasped his hand. "It was courageous. Not everyone would have done such a thing."

"Well," said Aleksandr. He felt the thrum of social tables turning; he knew that he could take his time answering and that she would wait for him. "It was self-interested, you know."

She laughed a little. He could smell the champagne she was drinking, vaguely vinegary; cheap, he thought. He wanted to buy her something better. "Rationally self-interested," she said. Later, he'd look back and realize how, at the beginning, Nina would often say a catchphrase or a snippet of some academic or intellectual jargon, sometimes out of context and often obliquely; this kind of talk seemed to suggest deep understanding, vast knowledge. It soon proved that she'd internalized a certain number of terms that, when deployed alongside a knowing expression, could make men believe she had a brain, if they were already inclined to hope so.

"Yes," he said. "Rationally self-interested. Don't tell my handlers."

"I wouldn't dream of it. That Rusayev. Tell me. Is he really as ugly up close as he looks on television?"

They laughed. He told her anecdotes, partially embellished, about Rusayev's hygiene and habits and quirks and demands. He performed an extended impression of Rusayev's tendency to learn forward and taunt you with the mad hope that he might be ready to make his move, then lean back again, then forward, then back, until you were beset with nervous exhaustion. He also tended to leave his finger on his piece for a comically long time, rolling his wrist, leaving one hand, then two fingers, then one finger, retreating more slowly than the Americans from Vietnam, he said, and Nina laughed. It was a lovely laugh— bell-like and clear. It wasn't necessarily a laugh that seemed to reflect actual amusement, but that didn't matter to Aleksandr just then.

At some point in the evening, he started looking at her harder. He realized she was someone whom he would need to remember meeting, and so he tried to make a mental note of what she was wearing, and how she looked, and what she'd first said to him. If this went somewhere, he'd want to remember those things.

At the end of the evening, he walked her to her door and gazed at her fondly but did not, for the moment, kiss her. He could have, he knew, he could have done anything he wanted; he did not fear rejection. But he wanted to be able to tell her later about how he'd wanted to kiss her and had been too shy. He wanted that to be part of the story they would tell each other.

The next night he did kiss her, and he took her home. And after that, they were a couple.

He took her to private clubs with private leashed-off balconies, with gleaming vats of vodka and fresh juices already waiting for them. He took her dancing. Her took her to the ballet. She wasn't an intellectual, but neither was she a philistine—she loved visual art, she loved singing. She didn't know art history or music history, but it didn't keep her from responding to art and music; she wasn't a theorist, and how refreshing that was. For her, he suffered through opera—twice—and it was worth it, almost, to see Nina rapt: the beautiful blankness on her stricken face.

She became interested in biorhythms, in energy fields. She liked to watch Kashpirovsky's mass-healing séances on TV. She did not care for politics. She found public displays embarrassing. They watched the coup together on television, agog, but she did not want to go outside once it was all over and Yeltsin had saved the country. He tried dragging her down to Moscow for the Yuri Shevchuk concert, when 120,000 people swayed in Palace Square, but she rolled her eyes. She'd sooner cry in public, she said, than get sentimental about a pop singer in public. And that ended the conversation, since Aleksandr had never—not once—seen Nina cry, though he'd suspected her of secretive offstage crying once or twice over the months.

It didn't matter. It did not matter. Here was a woman who could love him for what he was, not what he had tried—ineptly!—and failed—miserably!—at being. If this woman wanted competence, he had that to spare. If she wanted ruthlessness, he was learning. Better to be loved—or whatever—for our own actual sorry selves and not for some distorted version of who we might have been. It was that discrepancy that led to disappointment, among other things.

And then there was this: he was thirty-two. It didn't have to be Nina in particular, but for decency's sake, it had to be someone. He was still decent when it came to family: he'd rescued his mother and two of his sisters from their backward hovel in Okha (the third had married a semi-toothless sturgeon fisherman and had refused to come).

Nina and Aleksandr might have been mismatched, but their dual mismatch provided a kind of symmetry: she was so much more beautiful than he, he was so much more talented and accomplished than she, and was this not the trade-off made by most powerful men? It was a tenuous understanding, an uneasy policy of mutually assured destruction—either of them could wound the other with all the ways in which he or she was not what was wanted once. If he'd wanted to hurt her, he could have pointed out that there were countless gorgeous

women in the world, and there was only one chess champion (currently: him). He could have pointed out that beauty was fleeting. But
she could have pointed out that everything was fleeting—chess compe-
tency was only slightly more enduring than beauty; both, it turned out,
were games that favored the young. Anyway, what was power on the
chessboard vs. power in the bedroom? Chess was a metaphor for war,
but sex wasn't a metaphor for anything. So whose power was more real
in the end?

They fell into a routine in which she was playfully critical of him,
and he was eye-glazingly tolerant of her, and this seemed to flatten
the unevenness of their relationship's landscape. Aleksandr might be a
chess champion, but he was also just a man and was thus deserving of
the ambient scorn of beautiful, exacting women. He did not disagree;
in fact, he felt he deserved more scorn than even Nina would be able to
provide him, though for reasons he never discussed with her.

He bought them a gorgeous apartment overlooking Nevsky Prospekt (expensive). He bought them a high-maintenance little dog with
a lazy eye (also expensive). After an appropriate interval, Nina and
Aleksandr were married.

A decade passed in slow motion, then faster and faster. When Aleksandr looked back, it returned in snatches, on repeat, hiccuping and
distorted sometimes, like a scratched record. There were some good
times, of this he was sure—some nice nights with Nina, especially at
the beginning, though in memory it became difficult to ascertain how
many of the nights were actually nice. Was it one night or two or a half
dozen or a dozen? Or was it typical, was it usual, for them to slow-
dance in front of that enormous picture window, with St. Petersburg
cracked open before them, backlit by the moon, shining with all the
grandeur of ancient Rome? What you imagine is what you remember,
and what you remember is what you're left with. So why not decide
to imagine it a little differently? It is possible that it wasn't all a horrendous mistake from the outset. It is possible that they were happier
than he sometimes suspected.

But when he tried to remember the good, most of what emerged
was the mundane: there's Nina in 1993, combing her hair in front of

the mirror; there she is again in 1997, maybe, her hair slightly longer, her frown slightly deeper. He remembered her evolving sleepwear, the cyclical courses of her shoes—seasonal, astronomical, in their regularity. He remembered the things they acquired: the sound system that seemed to seethe in the dark, with an array of dials and knobs and buttons that looked to Aleksandr like the operational apparatus of a spaceship; the computers that began as looming presences, half the size of Aleksandr, and slowly shrank down to sleek nefarious objects, bafflingly unobtrusive. He remembered also the parade of Nina's friends, wearing bright colors, talking conspiratorially. They came for lunch, they came for dinner, they came—eternally—for drinks. They were a rotating cast: he could never get their names straight and was always mixing one up with the other, and always being scolded, and always making a point to remember, and always, always, immediately forgetting again. The women often mocked one another for failings that Aleksandr couldn't see or understand—anyone who missed the evening was considered fair game. No matter how thoroughly a particular woman had been eviscerated by the others in her absence, the next time she appeared, she would be greeted with the same breathless concern, the same false smiles, the same astonished arching of eyebrows at the same grim litanies of the outrageousness of children, the callousness of men. Then there was the same hearty agreement, the same clinking of glasses.

Aleksandr remembered also the halfhearted attempts at a baby. Over the years, Nina was on and then ambivalently off three different kinds of chemical birth control; in 1994 she went off again—this time earnestly, meaningfully—and they waited. Nothing happened. They waited longer. Still nothing happened. Aleksandr remembered the growing realization that it was taking longer than it should, then much longer than it should, and then the further realization—never articulated but shared, he was sure—that they were not as disappointed as they probably should have been. He watched Nina purse her lips at another negative test—the eleventh or twelfth—and he knew that she was nonplussed, slightly, but not distraught. The two of them with a baby: what the hell would they do with it? Nina was good at taking care of things—the stereo system, for example, and her ever growing collection of fussy silken clothing—but things were still and quiet and could be fairly easily kept clean. A pregnancy, a birth, a wailing baby with an always open maw—the whole thing sounded as embarrassing as it would be exhausting. After a year or two, the birth control pills reappeared in the cabinet, and Aleksandr never complained.

They did not fight. They never fought. They went days without speaking sometimes, but even that wasn't really a fight—he'd sometimes just forget to talk to her. Their sex life began to die quietly, uncomplainingly, with all the meek gravity of a religious martyr: first sex became conventional, then infrequent, then brittle and harassed and, he thought resentfully, resentful. And then it became a fluke, a comet glimpsed blearily through a thicket of stars—it happened sometimes when she'd been drinking, or he'd been cajoling, or they'd been laughing (rarely, rarely). Sometimes he'd engage in self-conscious rituals designed to bring them back to whatever they'd once been, but that was when he most realized that he wasn't sure what that was. Still, he tried: he'd put awful early-nineties love songs on the stereo system, the kind that they'd heard in their nights out on the town, back in the early days. It was meant to be ironic, but like all irony, it was also slightly sentimental—and since Nina was possessed of neither irony nor sentimentality, she pursed her lips and stared at Aleksandr and failed to smile.

In lieu of sex, Aleksandr began watching TV. He watched Yeltsin hiccup his way through a presidency, red-faced and drunk and increasingly incompetent: it was hard to believe that he was the man who'd shouted down a coup, who'd kept Russia from teetering into a total police state. The nation's life expectancy for males was down to fifty-eight, mostly due to alcoholism and suicide. Half of the economy was run by organized crime. At night Aleksandr would pace the floors and think about his country, which seemed to have outlived its own relevance. In this, he felt that they had something in common.

Aleksandr still followed chess; at night, while Nina was sleeping, he'd sneak onto the ever smaller computers and ruthlessly beat the best insomniac chess minds of the world. Excitement ruffled through online forums as they recognized him from a defense or an opening, and he felt an echoing twist when he remembered how he'd once been at the promising opening gambit of his own career, and his own life. Now he'd fulfilled everyone's highest hopes, and there was nothing left for him to do but haunt the communities of online enthusiasts. His chess successes seemed like the litany of accomplishments of some Soviet leader that he'd been made to learn about in school.

He rarely played in real life. Petr Pavlovich arranged a lackluster match in 1995 at the World Trade Center in New York. Aleksandr played an Indian champion and beat him handily. The win felt cheap, hollow, the afterthought of victory. Outside, the lemon-colored light sculpted the sky. The Twin Towers loomed with a fatal clarity through the crystalline windows.

After that, Aleksandr didn't hear much from Petr Pavlovich. He had other people to manage, though fewer. The FIDE was less ensnared to the bureaucracy—no longer throttled by the corruption— and anyway, there was less at stake, less to prove, less hope that the Cold War could be won through cultural triumph, through withering superiority at the finest game in the world. It was a game of missiles in the end, and diplomacy, and national pride, yes, but mostly, it was a game about who had consistent access to toilet paper and cheap protein, and at this game, Russia had decidedly lost. They didn't need a chess champion to be the standard-bearer; Aleksandr could no longer embarrass them the way he once could. They were already embarrassing themselves enough.

Occasionally, Nina and Aleksandr threw parties and Petr Pavlovich came, invariably resentful, usually alone. He stood in corners and grabbed at every single passing appetizer. Aleksandr's feelings about Petr Pavlovich shifted depending on how he was feeling about his entire life that day. Sometimes he saw Petr Pavlovich as the necessary intermediary that had enabled Aleksandr's own survival—their relationship was parasitic or symbiotic at best, and Aleksandr knew that he should feel grateful. Other days Aleksandr looked around his life— his huge apartment, his vacant heart, his shining trophy, dusted every other day by the maids—and he wondered if there was a more authentic life, a more authentic shadow self, that might have been possible. Though it was true that when he tried to envision such a life he came up blank—what else might he have done? Maybe they would have let him give chess lessons for a time, though likely not in Leningrad. He might have gone back to Okha to teach whatever promising talent the town was yielding these days; and he might have had some status as the boy who had gone off and done well, though the child who returns can never have quite the same currency as the child who stays away. His family would have been proud of him, no question, though there probably would have been some sense that he'd given away too much, and for what? For some vague principle that was as inarticulate as it was remote. Life was full of untenables, of insurmountables, of absurdities; the question wasn't whether you could hammer your life into some kind of purity (you couldn't) but whether you could live around the roadblocks and whether you could run with the premises (your government system, your current coordinates in place and time, your mortality) and make something of yourself anyhow. Aleksandr had done that for a while, and wasn't that adulthood, and wasn't that life? Wasn't retreating from it retreating from reality? You could passively resist, sure; you could protest, of course. But wasn't it a little like refusing to get out of bed in the morning, since you knew one day you were going to die?

But still and all, of course, of course, they would have been glad to have him back.

———

Petr Pavlovich called Aleksandr in January 1997. Aleksandr saw his name pop up on the caller ID—a new acquisition of Nina's, which she used to avoid answering the calls of those lady friends of hers who'd fallen into disfavor that week. Aleksandr cringed and considered ignoring it, but he was ultimately defeated by curiosity. It had been many months since he'd spoken to Petr Pavlovich for any length of time. He wondered if the nasal polyps had ever gotten take care of.

"Hi there, Petr Pavlovich," said Aleksandr, and enjoyed the momentary disoriented silence that followed.

"Caller ID," said Petr Pavlovich finally.

"Right."

"Very up-to-date of you."

"It's all the wife."

"How *is* the wife?

"A joy, as always."

Aleksandr tried to remember if Petr Pavlovich had married. There'd been a woman at a party some years ago, of this he was sure—he remembered that she was delicate and chain-smoking and smiling and seemed to make Pavlovich very happy. Aleksandr wasn't sure whether that had been a wife or a mistress or a girlfriend or a friend whom Petr Pavlovich was trying and failing to woo. He'd guess the latter.

"Are you married, Petr Pavlovich?"

"I was. Thanks for asking. She died three years ago. Esophageal cancer. Quick."

Aleksandr cringed. "I'm sorry."

"I'm sure the card's in the mail."

Aleksandr coughed his voice into something gentler and more supplicating. "Did you have children?"

"Why, we didn't, Aleksandr Kimovich. This outpouring of interested generosity on your part is unprecedented. I hope you're not on antidepressants. They'll mess with your game."

"I'm not on antidepressants."

"That's a relief to hear."

Petr Pavlovich sniffed, and Aleksandr feared mightily—and momentarily—that he was crying.

"And you, Aleksandr? Any plans for children? You and that beautiful wife of yours, what's her name?"

"Nina."

"Nina. Of course. And so?"

"Ah, no." Aleksandr shifted the phone to the other ear. "No immediate plans."

"I see. You're much too busy, I'd imagine."

"What are you calling about?"

"Well." Aleksandr could hear Petr Pavlovich gearing up to make his pitch, stripping his voice of its endemic weary sarcasm. "I know you're very into technology. Very up on the latest developments. The caller ID and so on."

"Mmm," said Aleksandr. He eyed the stereo system nervously.

"As you're probably aware, IBM has been building a program that plays chess."

"I know," said Aleksadr eagerly. This he actually did know.

"Big Blue, Deep Blue Sea, something like that. It's very good now. Been in testing for years. It beats everyone who plays it. They program all possible responses to all possible moves into its—whatever—its brain, I guess, and then they program it to know which ones are most likely to be successful in every possible scenario. It's what your brain must do, essentially. You're programmed for exactly the same kind of responses."

"Yeah, but I have to think about them."

"This thing thinks, right? It just thinks faster. It's what—algorithms, right? I don't know, it's not my area. Anyway, they want you to play it."

"Should I?"

"Of course. Can't you beat it?"

"I don't know."

"It's a pile of tubes. You're the greatest living chess player in the world. I'm sure these kids at MIT who made it are smart, but it's going to be a game of Tetris for you, right?"

"Probably. How should I know?"

There was a pause. "When you were a younger man, you know, I don't think you would have hesitated."

Aleksandr went to the picture window. Outside, the St. Petersburg sky was ensconced in folds of blues and grays, masking all the new construction projects, the new billboards, the new fruits of what was fast becoming a new kleptocracy. It was the future. They wanted him to play a computer. Aleksandr would not have hesitated when he was a younger man, but he was no longer a younger man.

"It'll be a disaster if I lose," he said.

"It'll be publicity if you lose. But you won't lose."

"I don't know."

"Aleksandr," said Petr Pavlovich merrily. Aleksandr could almost hear him smiling. "You forget you're the world champion. Have a little confidence."

Aleksandr would remember the game much as he'd remember the entire decade, when he remembered it at all, which was rarely. It came back distorted, in fragments—the puckered cheeks of the man who stood in for the computer, inflating and deflating with distraught little breaths; the silence of the crowd—still, then suspenseful, then stunned. Afterward, there was the astonished grimace of Petr Pavlovich—he'd often been surprised by Aleksandr, but never this way. Then there was the gleeful chattering of the MIT people, the Internet enthusiasts, the tech reporters—the triumphalism, everybody buzzing happily about this brand-new kind of apocalypse. Aleksandr knew—even as he was playing, even as he was losing, even as he was taking the limousine back to his apartment—that he'd have to approach this evening in the same way that he'd approached his marriage. He would try not to think about it. He would try not to remember its details, its sequences, its accumulated humiliations.

Nina had been following online, and when he got home, he caught her, feet curled up under her, silk nightgown shimmering in the moonlight (Nina owned so much silk that he wondered whether she had an entire silkworm army somewhere in the closet)—and he knew that she'd been poring over the results, the analysis, the obsessive online speculation. She might not understand the details, but the tone—the headline, the upshot—was inevitably clear.

"I'm sorry, Aleksandr." She closed the computer quickly.

"Yes." He beelined for the cabinet and poured whiskey into a water glass.

"I really am."

Aleksandr considered ice, then rejected it. "I really am, too."

"Do you want to tell me about it?"

He did not want to tell her about it. He did not want to tell anyone about it. He did not even want to tell himself about it in his own head. The people who had watched had understood. What was there to say about it? Nobody would ever beat that thing. Nobody would ever again do sums on an abacus. And could he be sorry? What kind of person could be sorry to watch history march forward, and progress be attained, and problems be solved? Yes, yes, there was some romance lost when they mapped the entire globe, but still. You couldn't root against it; that was like wishing that all the tiny villages of the world would keep their untranslatable, useless languages and their horrific hygiene practices just so we could all go and look and think that they were authentic and quaint. Aleksandr had an ego but not that kind of ego. He would not demand that the world know less so that he could know the most.

"You look awful," said Nina.

He poured another whiskey. "I'm fine."

"You look like you're about to kill yourself."

"Well, I'm not."

"Or me."

"Never fear."

Nina went to the couch and produced a nail file from somewhere on her person. Aleksandr poured a third glass. On the couch, Nina commenced vigorous filing, and he watched her for a few moments. He never understood how she managed not to start filing her actual fingers. Aleksandr sat down at the computer.

Nina looked up. "You don't need to look at that stuff about the game."

"I wasn't going to."

"You really don't."

"I really wasn't.

"There's some stuff on there you don't want to see."

"Christ, Nina," Aleksandr roared. "I know."

She looked at him, eyes brimming with emotion. He wasn't sure he'd ever seen Nina look sorry for him. He knew he did not like it.

"Really, Alyosha," she said. "It's only a game."

———

There was a détente then—there must have been. Some benumbed years, an admission of estrangement that resulted, oddly, in more kindness. Once he stopped trying to make Nina his wife, he could better appreciate her as a friend of a sort; a person to enjoy spending money on and with. There are as many ways for a marriage to work as there are ways for a marriage to fail, and theirs, he thinks now, was working. He knows because he is sure—absolutely sure—that on the day of the bombing, he was gazing at Nina with fondness.

It was the tail end of August 1999, and they were spending the weekend in Moscow with some friends of Nina's. He'd been waiting

for Nina to finish trying on shoes at a store in Manezh. He was standing outside the shop and watching her through the window—he could
see the slight sour curve of her frown as she pressed her porcelain heel
into some punishing scrap of footwear—and he knows that things
must have been going better for them because he remembers admiring
her, thinking how beautiful she was, how proud he was to have an exacting wife who knew what she wanted in a shoe. Striated light came
sieving through the big picture windows. Nearby, a little girl shrieked
on a small plastic indoor ride—it was a blue bewhiskered walrus that
moved slowly up and down—and Aleksandr felt that the world was
well. They were headed out that night to a sushi dinner, followed by
an evening at a club, and Aleksandr was already looking forward to
his sashimi and his buzz. Inside the store, the light caught Nina's red
hair, and it glinted nearly gold. "Mama, Mama, Mama, it's a walrus!"
said the little girl on the ride.

And then somehow half the building was gone. The light was nuclear, the roar cyclonic—and all of it, all of it, seemed to come several
moments after Aleksandr had shattered his clavicle on the ground.
Nina staggered out of the store, still wearing her unpurchased shoe.
Next to him, the little girl from the ride was missing most of her hand.
Her mouth was open in what must have been a howl, and Aleksandr
had crept halfway to her, his chest a crucible of pain, before he realized
that he could not hear.

His hearing was restored within the day, and the little girl lived, and
only one person died that day. They went back to St. Petersburg, and
Aleksandr turned on the television to watch what would happen next.

Buynaksk was hit a week later, then Moscow once more, and Volgodonsk—malls, highways, apartment buildings. At the apartments,
the timers went off at night to maximize civilian casualties. The
government announced the Volgodonsk bombing two days before
it happened, which Aleksandr found personally insulting: a government conspiracy, if indeed this was, should at least be executed with
more care. "Are you watching this, Nina?" Aleksandr yelled from the
couch, and winced. It still hurt to breathe. "Are you paying attention
to this at all?"

"What is it, Aleksandr? Do you need more codeine?"

From the couch, Aleksandr's collarbone healed, but he kept sitting, and he kept watching. He watched the blaming of the Chechens; he watched the commencement of the second Chechen war. He watched the pro-war party sail to the Duma, and Putin—Yeltsin's invertebrate-smug prime minister, that mere lieutenant-colonel in the KGB—sail to the presidency. He watched the suspension of regional elections.

"Aleksandr." Nina coughed. "Don't you think you might like to get out for some exercise?"

Aleksandr hated Putin with a hatred that felt personal. When he remembered the others—Brezhnev and the decrepit, staggering parade of geriatrics thereafter—he didn't remember a feeling so urgent as his hatred for Putin. Putin's first act in office was to restore the Soviet national anthem. When Aleksandr heard the song again, after a nine-year gap, he saw Elizabeta walking down the aisle, applauded by bureaucrats, and he almost threw up.

"Aleksandr," said Nina. "Do you think you're taking all this a little too seriously?"

After the bombing—after seeing the little girl's blue penguin shirt streaked with arterial blood, and after crawling to her across a ruined marble floor—he felt less tolerant of his own life. Nina cajoled him into returning to his old ways, but they didn't take. The caviar stuck in his throat. The nights out seemed empty. He found himself thinking more and more about Ivan and how Ivan would have lived, if he'd lived. Ivan wouldn't have spent a decade in strenuous appeasement of the regime. Ivan wouldn't have spent the budding years of democracy slowly poaching in hot tubs, one indifferent young woman on each arm. Every morning Aleksandr arose and looked at himself in the mirror and tried to remember who he'd been when he'd been brave.

His friends—his rich friends, who still enjoyed their caviar—told him that if he was so bothered by it all, he should throw his weight behind the fledgling pro-reform movement. He was a national hero, after all, an icon of chess, which was purer than religion and more elegant than sport. He had money. If he had ideas, he might make himself a figure. Did he have ideas?

He did have ideas, though they were vague—he was pro-business, anti-corruption, pro-transparency, pro–civil liberties. He was a capitalist. He was a realist. But at first he wanted to support an umbrella net-work of oppositional groups—believing that a robust opposition was the initial and most necessary step—and he started by contacting any-one who was willing to be publicly defiant, including earnest reform-ers, conspiracy theorists, quacks, and leftist loonies. At early meetings, he'd regularly see pictures of Trotsky fluttering alongside posters quot-ing Milton Friedman. They called it Alternative Russia.

"I don't like them smoking in the house," said Nina.

At first, all they did was talk. They agreed that the post-Commu-nist kleptocracy was only marginally better, in some ways, than the tee-tering incompetence of late-stage Communism—and in other ways, it was perhaps worse. They agreed that the regime's indifference was so callous that it could hardly be called indifference at all. As time passed, Putin gave them more to talk about. After the bombings came the sail-ors abandoned on the *Kursk,* a nuclear submarine that sank quietly in the Barents Sea during Putin's first summer in office. Later, it was clear from the notes they wrote on their bodies that some of them had lived for days, while the Kremlin insisted that they were already dead, while the offers of help from the Brits and the Norwegians were ignored, while Putin continued his vacation on the beach.

Then there were the theatergoers in the fall of 2002, dead in a horrifi-cally botched hostage rescue attempt. They'd crawled out gagging from state-issued morphine and died in the snow when the Kremlin didn't think to call any ambulances. Aleksandr talked about this in Alternative Russia meetings. He also talked about it quite a bit outside them.

"Stop talking about this stuff all the time," said Nina. "You're being morbid."

"I'm not morbid. Life is morbid. Reality is morbid. Our govern-mental system is morbid."

"If I hear you refer to our 'governmental system' one more time, I'm going to die of boredom."

"Please don't let me stop you."

In 2004 came the school siege at Beslan: the children held hostage for days, then killed when the government stormed the school with tanks and thermobaric weapons. A year later, the parents of the dead children went to Moscow to demand their own arrest—they'd voted for Putin, they said, and thus were culpable for the murders of their children.

Though Aleksandr was keen at calculation—at weighing the consequences of rational self-interest—he could never quite understand any of it. What was in it for the state to watch hundreds vomit and die in the elegant Moscow streets, to let sailors write goodbyes on their bodies and choke to death on their own carbon dioxide? There was ineptitude, yes, but it was hard to believe that was all: it was a murderous apathy that amounted to sadism. It reminded Aleksandr of how, when the infant mortality rate had grown troubling under Communism, the Party had decided to simply subsidize more births.

Nina came and sat next to Aleksandr on the bed. "It's sad, Aleksandr. Of course it's sad. But it's really none of our business."

Then came the string of assassinations. There was Anna Politkovskaya from *Novaya Gazeta,* who'd survived poisoning and Chechnya only to be shot down in the stairwell of her own apartment building.

There was the ex-KGB man in London who'd been poisoned with radioactive sushi by men who had disappeared back into the teeming English mists; a man who'd turned colors people should never turn, who'd lain on his deathbed and pointed an accusatory finger back at the East.

There was a journalist for a Russian business magazine who'd been reporting on Putin's attempts to illegally sell arms to Syria and Iran by routing them through Belarus. He'd had a son about to enter college and a daughter about to deliver his first grandchild. He'd gone out one day to buy oranges, come home, and thrown himself out his window, according to the official report.

"Are you seeing this, Nina? Are you reading this stuff?"

Nina rolled her eyes and flopped over in bed. But Aleksandr was thinking.

"Stop," she said. "I can hear you thinking."

Over the years, Aleksandr had come to view Putin as erratic and somewhat unpredictable. He wasn't puritanical; he did not strike out every chord of dissent. He was tolerant, almost magnanimous, when it came to the papers. The token one, *Novaya Gazeta,* was especially mouthy—even after Anna Politkovskaya's death—though Aleksandr fully believed that Putin allowed it in order to earn himself a faint glaze of democratic credibility. He liked being able to bring the paper to Brussels and say: See? See what I let them write about me? But Putin did crack down on what counted, and what counted was television. Aleksandr had once spoken at a conference alongside a deeply unpopular economist, and when he watched it on television, the unfortunate man had been digitally removed from existence—there'd been his hands, his ghostly shadow, but his head, his inconvenient words, were gone. And it hadn't all been puerile hijinks. One time Aleksandr awoke to a peal of shattering glass and the sound of a sickening thud against the floor. Upon investigation, he found a plastic bag containing the oozing conch of a human ear.

After that, Nina told him to shut down Alternative Russia. Or at least, for the love of God, to move the headquarters out of the apartment.

"I know you're doing this because of your involvement with the Party back in the day," she said. She cupped his face in her hands and leaned toward him. He could see the flickering pulse in her neck. "And I want you to know you don't have anything to feel guilty for."

"Don't I?"

"It was the times. It was the times. That's all over now."

"Is it?"

"You've made a nice life for us, Aleksandr."

"Nice for whom?"

She leaned back. "Oh, please. Nice for both of us. You don't like the apartment? You don't like your gadgets?"

"They're your gadgets."

"You are a wealthy man. You are wealthy and you are influential and you are sought after."

"By the FSB, maybe."

"And if you're not happy with your life, you have the means to go ahead and change it." He could feel her radiating misery.

"That's exactly what I'm proposing."

"Are you having a midlife crisis?"

"Stop psychoanalyzing."

"Is all this because you lost to the computer?"

At this he'd punched the wall, though not hard enough to do damage to either the wall or his hand.

Nina didn't flinch. "If you break your hand, you know, the media is going to notice."

"Shut up."

"I'm not the only one who psychoanalyzes."

"Shut the fuck up, please." Nina didn't stop filing her nails. He looked at her, and he marveled at the cognitive dissonance of knowing someone as intimately as he knew Nina—of knowing how her toes looked when her toenails grew too long (though, in fairness, Nina almost never let this happen), and how her coughs echoed in the shower when she was sick, and how her face looked when she was pale and haggard from sleeping—and really, really, not knowing her at all. He thought of times at parties or dinners or out in the world somewhere, moments when he'd glimpse her out of the corner of his eye, caught in light or shadow, and think what a mystery she was—this person who lived in the core of that coiled three pounds of neurons, whatever it was, whoever she was, inscrutable, unreachable, no less mysterious just because Aleksandr didn't believe in the extraphysical.

"Clearly, something is bothering you lately."

"Ninotchka," he said. "You are criminally insane, criminally indifferent, if you are not bothered."

"I don't like Ninotchka, you know. It's patronizing."

One thing about Nina: she could still surprise him. Then again, he could still surprise himself, even after all the years of knowing himself (and maybe no one else; maybe no one else, ever).

Three weeks later, he announced his intention to seek the presidency of the Russian Federation.

14

IRINA

St. Petersburg, December 2006

On Saturday I took the metro downtown. A terse, tinny voice coming out of the loudspeakers admonished everyone to stay away from Gostiny Dvor, so I knew I was going in the right direction. Aboveground, I encountered a surprising mass: thousands, I think, maybe ten thousand, standing in the square underneath pale yellow buildings that looked like frosted cakes. Red flags snapped against the mass of brown coats, all dense and woolly and dark, like an army of seething otters. A smattering of different flags with their stark Cyrillic—there were ultranationalists, it seemed, radical lefties, Trotskyites. There were the true Communists, sick with their nostalgia. Somebody handed me a flag, and I waggled it mildly. Somewhere behind me, I overheard a low smattering of American English, but when I turned to look—my eyes overflowing, no doubt, with idiot eagerness at finding a fellow traveler—it stopped, and its origins remained mysterious. I looked around but did not see Viktor anywhere.

On a box, in the center of the crowd, was Aleksandr Bezetov. I'd seen pictures of him, and he looked much the same. So I don't know why I was surprised. Maybe a part of me imagined he'd have some sort of an aura—the otherworldly signifier of a person with an inexplicable connection to the future or the dead. Instead, he looked even more ordinary than average; he was shorter than I thought he'd be—I thought of his overreliance on head shots—and his nose was an unbecoming red. His breath came in frost-colored puffs as he spoke.

"My friends," he said. The teeming crowd ruffled in appreciation at the thrill of such familiar address. "We have no chance of winning." Miraculously, the crowd cheered.

I squinted through the wintry mist, the heaving people, the multicolored flags popping like firing guns. I compared this man to the man I'd watched with my father all those years ago. This Bezetov was sturdy around the middle and durable, whereas he'd been thin in that match, cracking his knobby knuckles. But there were the same hooded eyelids, the fleshy nose that was the shape of a rejected potato. The mouth, which looked too lazy and inarticulate for the rigors of the game.

"There is nothing to be gained by pretending we have a chance of winning," he said. "To do so would be a lie. We are not running to win." The crowd cheered more loudly—the red-cheeked, pale-browed young women with those tremendously angled bone structures, the fuzzy-faced men who must have been aging, relatively minor dissidents. On the horizon were reams of police, stern and barrel-chested and not meant to be missed, even though Bezetov surely had a permit for this event.

"We are running to lose," said Bezetov. "And in the losing, we are running to be noticed. We are running to be blocked. We are running to be opposed." The crowd was growing louder; Bezetov's voice was growing hoarser.

"We are running to be suppressed," he shouted. "We are running to be systematically ignored, legally erased. We are running to be assassinated." The crowd erupted again. "We are running so that when we are . . . suppressed, ignored, killed, the world will take notice. We are running so that there might be a record. We are running so that there might be a memory."

The crowd shouted and waved their flags. A woman behind me issued a coloratura shriek that made me wince. The crowd had a surface-level patina of triumph, but there was a suggestion of sub-merged mania, too, as though they were just about to produce pitch-forks and storm the Bastille. Next to me, a child jumped up and down in one spot. A man careened a woman around, both of them shouting nonsense. A young man stood alone, shivering and smiling so hard that I thought he would break into pieces and go skittering across the square. I pulled out a notebook and pretended to be absorbed in it. I was registering for the first time that I was deeply uncomfortable with outpourings of genuine political emotion.

At the edge of the crowd, near the podium, stood a woman who was watching Aleksandr and looking bored. She was thin and light and her efficacious manner gave her the air of a business envelope. She looked too indifferent to be in charge but too efficient not to be involved. She had red hair. She was Nina. I crept in her direction—getting one toe smashed by a surprisingly heavy child, getting one breast groped by an old man who looked at the sky when I turned around. When I reached the woman, she looked at everything around me—the shearing sun, the hard-packed snow, the clumps of young men hooting and hurling chips of ice—before I could get her attention.

"Excuse me," I said, waving my hand.

"Yes?" she said. She looked surprised, as though she actually hadn't seen me standing there.

"My name is Irina Ellison," I said. "I was wondering if I could get a meeting with Mr. Bezetov."

She looked me up and down with unapologetic frankness, as if she were assessing me for physical fitness and finding me wanting. "And who are you, Irina Ellison?"

"Nobody," I said eagerly. Nina's gaze grew cloudy. "I'm an Ameri-can lecturer," I amended. "At a university."

She remained silent. Tiny furrows appeared next to her mouth. She looked as if she was sucking very hard on something bitter. "Is that all?"

"That's all." I didn't know exactly what she meant, but I knew that—absolutely—was all. "Can I get a meeting, do you think?"

"Probably not. He's very busy."

Nina was turning away from me, her attention drawn by the

backfiring of a motorcycle in the square. I should have proposed some research, I realized, some feigned academic pretext for this pursuit. Maybe there would have been some tolerance for that.

"Please," I said. "My father and Mr. Bezetov were correspondents."

"Then have your father arrange a meeting."

"He's dead now," I said. "My father." In English, I always say "passed away," as a courtesy to whomever I'm talking with. It's not because I believe that "passed away" is the right term—away to where? one wonders, passed to what? It's because "dead" feels too confrontational, too vulgar. But in Russian I didn't know any other word.

Nina cocked her head toward me, but I couldn't tell where she was looking. "I'm sorry," she said. If the edge in her voice was relenting, I couldn't hear it. "But Aleksandr has corresponded with a lot of different people."

She looked behind her at an enormous man with sunglasses who was standing a few feet away. He gave a slight nod. I had the feeling that I was on the verge of being escorted away.

"If you could just ask him," I said. "I came a long way."

She inclined her head once more, and abruptly I could see myself in her vision: red-nosed, with messy hair and a bewildered aspect, speaking the kind of American-accented Russian that is alternately viewed as comic, tragic, or an automatic indicator of stupidity.

"Who's your customer?" she said finally.

"My customer?" This had been Nikolai's question, too, and I wondered if some translational mismatch kept producing this problem.

The woman pressed her lips together as though dealing with the faked idiocy of an unwilling student. "Whom do you work for?"

"Nobody anymore."

"Anymore?"

"I had a job at a university," I said, although for a moment I couldn't remember if that was true. "This was a while ago now."

"I see," she said, looking at me with an expression of incomprehension. "So you're a tourist, then?"

"Sort of," I said. "Yes."

She stared at me hard, then shrugged. "Perhaps it is possible," she said. "He has Wednesday off. He might have fifteen minutes for you. You will not be alone, of course."

"Of course," I said, although I couldn't quite sort out in that moment what this meant.

"Come to this address Wednesday morning, and we will see. Okay? You'll have to wait. I'm not promising anything." She slipped me a business card, from which I promptly sustained a paper cut.

"Okay," I said. "I can wait." These days, that was my expert activity, my major accomplishment. I was a champion, grade-A, world-class waiter, unchallenged, unrivaled. I was confident in my waiting abilities.

"Fine." She sniffed. "You are an odd young woman."

Something about this—the pronouncement of judgment issued by a quasi-hostile European—made me miss Lars so much that I almost started to cry. I rarely cry—finding it an activity I can consider and then reject engaging in, typically for lack of energy—but there are occasional seizures of emotion that grab me at strange moments: in parking lots, in supermarkets, elicited by old couples picking out fruit or little children grabbing at a mother's dress. The woman looked alarmed.

"I know," I said. "Thank you for your help."

She sniffed and turned away, for which I was grateful, because the vista before me—the roiling crowds with their tiny flags and their indecipherable shouts and their enormous gall—was starting to smear, and I didn't want anybody watching me as I tried to make my way through.

———

I took the long way home—across the embankment, past the cannon at the Peter and Paul Fortress, the sphinx's humped crown a misshapen shadow in the distance, before heading across Dvortsovvy Proezd to my island. My mind streaked with war and revolution. I thought of the assault on Nicholas II—the murderous clawing at the palace doors, the shots sailing through the sternums of the men, the women crumpling and crying in their taffeta. I thought of Stalin's purges—the shivering red-faced intellectuals, the ones who wept, the ones who spat at their captors. I thought of the lines of Jews waiting for their exit visas in the eighties, turning around to look at the bleak landscape that once was their home; I thought of Yeltsin on a tank, screaming down a military coup; I thought of the school siege, the terrorism, the brinkmanship, the bluffs, of the last decade. And then I thought of Aleksandr's rally, the way a thousand heads turned if he pointed and another thousand shouted if he spoke.

I went home, nodded to the icy-eyed night manager, and sat on my bed. I watched the chilly stars grow sharper as darkness fell. Over the weeks, I'd started to feel a certain sense of belonging in my room: my beach towel, decorated with fish whose lurid blues had faded into gray, had taken up a permanent residence in the communal bathroom; my salt-stained boots sat in the hallway outside my room like the relics from an atrocity. I'd stared so hard at the floor that I'd started to make an absurdist geography from the stains: near the bedside table was an Indian subcontinent; near the window was an entire Africa, complete with satellite Madagascar.

I thought of my father's map, with its jaundiced Soviet Union; I thought of how I was now in its vast midst. It was as though I had climbed up on my father's desk, kicking away his papers and disturbing his souvenirs, and crawled into the map. It was as though I'd been sucked through the television to the other side: a place where time held the world in unending potential energy, and the static broke the air into pieces, and everything was the color of a chessboard.

———

Aleksandr's apartment was sunny and enormous, decorated with the slightly oblique tastefulness of a modern-art museum. There was a black and white sofa in the parlor, and the complicated chords of a sonata for piano—dissonant, in a minor key—floated faintly from somewhere above my head. Sharply dressed women and slightly frumpier men walked in and out of the main apartment with great purpose. When the door swung open, I could see a flat-screen TV turned on mute to a government news channel. I could hear the shriek of an espresso machine.

I was patted down by a brawny security guard who lingered indecorously on my inseam. Then, as Nina had promised, there was a wait.

Every time the door opened, I looked up expectantly and confronted suspicious looks from whoever was leaving—a goatish woman in thick glasses, a very young man with a clipboard, a few meaty gents with earpieces and grim expressions. Viktor did not appear. Nobody called for me. Nobody spoke to me. It reminded me of my doctors' visits back in college, when I'd been given pamphlets on vitamins and management and "living with" Huntington's and had waited for eons, epochs, watching the occasional nurse shoot me a sympathetic wince.

Finally, Nina emerged. I was half sleeping by that point, my head bobbing me savagely awake every thirty seconds. My hair, always unfortunate, had been done no favors by the time spent waiting. Nina frowned at me. Today she was wearing a beige blouse with an intricately scalloped neck and had her mouth done in orangey lipstick. She was paler than I remembered, and her hair was pulled back in an unforgiving bun. Her cheekbones jutted from her face like installation art.

"You're still here?" she said.

"Apparently."

"Very well, then. Come in."

She led me into a high-ceilinged hallway. The walls were white, decorated with tiny prints of Moscow and St. Petersburg done in reds and blues. Above me, the Neva snarled in inky cobalt; St. Basil's reared, strangely menacing, above a sanguine horizon.

"Nice apartment," I said. I could feel her roll her eyes, even though she had her back to me.

"Mr. Bezetov has about fifteen minutes for you," said Nina. "I told him I had a strange American waiting for him, and he seemed interested. I trust you'll be able to explain yourself more thoroughly. He is very busy."

"I understand," I said, and then the hallway opened up into a room. It was epic and echoing; lacy cords of sunlight struck down from a snowy skylight in one corner, and a baby-grand piano squatted in another. In the center of a room, at a black desk, Aleksandr Bezetov sat typing furiously on a laptop.

"Aleksandr," said Nina. "Your visitor."

"One moment," Aleksandr said in Russian. Nina was already

gone. He was dressed more casually than he'd been at the protest and was wearing wire-rimmed glasses that looked Western and a tad self-conscious. His face—which, on the stump, had been energized, animated, his thick eyebrows casting as though looking for political contraband—held a vaguely bored expression. His tongue probed thoughtfully at his lower lip. His sleeves were rolled up.

After a moment, he looked up at me. He raised one eyebrow. I took this as my cue.

"Hello," I said in Russian, and Aleksandr made a face.

"Please," he said in English. "I've been speaking Russian long enough that this hurts me."

His English was flat and professional and very clear. It reminded me somehow of stones skipping on a river.

"So," he said. "You probably wonder why I agreed to meet with you."

"I suppose," I said, although I hadn't. I'd hoped he would meet with me; I appreciated that he'd decided to. But I hadn't thought it could be anything more than a kindly indulgence, because today he had the time for it.

"Well," he said. "I know you probably don't realize this, but you've been causing trouble for me. You can sit, you know." He gestured to the spindly chair across from his. He resumed his typing as I unwound my scarf and took a seat.

"I have?" I said.

He stopped typing. "Yes."

I said nothing, waiting for clarification. I didn't know how I'd managed to create trouble for Aleksandr Bezetov without even managing to create any trouble for myself.

"Have you possibly been approached by a Nikolai Sergeyevich?"

There was a dull ding in the back of my head. "Yes."

"And perhaps he's tried to convince you that the two of you have some interest in common? Perhaps he's tried to suggest that he's a friend of mine?"

The ding was resolving into a dissipated vibrato. I was already starting to feel like an idiot. "It's been confusing," I said.

"I don't doubt it."

This wasn't how I'd imagined our meeting going. I wasn't sure what I'd expected, but I suppose I thought Aleksandr would be kindly and gentle and maybe a tad professorial; that he'd patiently answer my questions and then inquire politely about my own interests and then blandly dismiss me with the most generic of best wishes for the future. In my most involved fantasies, he'd be able to answer some questions close to my still-functioning mind and heart—he'd be able to reveal some deep wisdom about proceeding with grace toward doom, and that wisdom might somehow illuminate my future or my past. Either way, I hadn't expected to be cross-examined.

"I'm sorry," I said. "All I did was approach an old friend of yours to see if I might get your contact information. I didn't realize that would be troublesome."

Aleksandr issued a weary sigh, as though he'd been asked to coach a high school chess club. "No, of course you didn't. I'll be quite clear. The Russian government suspects I am a pawn of American intelligence. They've always thought that. Now you're here, looking for me, making a spectacle of yourself, and you attracted their attention. They think you're running me, or trying to, or something. Do you understand?"

His breath was becoming thick with the strain of remaining civil. Sarcasm buckled to the surface of his voice, like the eruption of some long-suppressed subterranean substance. "As it is, in case you're wondering, I am not run by your CIA. But if I were, they'd be a lot subtler about it than you are being."

"So who is Nikolai?"

"He's a well-regarded bureaucrat in our very legitimate government."

"Oh." I was getting it. "Okay."

There was a pause in which Aleksandr resumed typing, and I wondered if our conversation had somehow come to a cryptic end. I tried to remember what I had been doing when Nikolai appeared at the café those weeks ago. Had I been doing something suspicious, something that denoted sinister and illegal activities? I didn't see how I'd managed it without noticing. I could barely remember any moments of import in the last few weeks—and those that shuffled to the surface, when I groped for them, were small and personal and oddly sentimental: watching a snow flurry blur out the stars through my hostel window, buying pastries from a woman who always gave me an extra bialy "for my children," walking around the Neva until my skin was raw and my eyes were leaking and my head was filled with a symphony of Russian poetry.

"I don't understand this," I said. "I don't see how I got anybody's attention. I don't do anything. All I do is sit around in cafés and read."

"Yes," he said. "They don't quite know what to make of you. But they think you're a representative of the American government, if an unwitting one."

"An unwitting one?" I was insulted now.

Aleksandr eyed me, and I could see him registering my half-open coat, my ill-fitting sweater, the gauzy bits of hair that flew away from my head as if they were fleeing political persecution.

"Yes," he said.

I fingered the seam of my coat and looked down. I felt very tired. There'd been a bone-deep fatigue of late, coming in dark waves that made my eyes feel as if they were orbiting my skull. I didn't know how to interpret it or how hard I should try to. It wasn't a physical harbinger of onset—I'd read enough accounts to know—but it seemed a psychological readying, and I was mostly grateful for it.

"All of this," he said, "creates some further difficulties for me. And for you, I might add. More for you, I would suppose. I have many bigger difficulties already."

"So do I," I said, still looking down.

Aleksandr sniffed. "I'm sure you didn't have any intention of causing trouble."

"I had no idea."

"I wholeheartedly believe you did not." He stared at me. He seemed to be keeping his eyes self-consciously wide and still, which was as good as rolling them. "If not for trouble," he said, "why are you here?"

A good question, this.

"Do you remember," I said carefully, "a letter from an American academic in the early eighties?"

He sat back in his chair. "I've received a lot of letters in my life."

"I'm sure," I said quickly. "I understand that. But it was a pretty odd letter."

"Odd how?"

"It wasn't about chess, exactly. The letter was asking you how you proceed when you know you're losing."

"When I'm losing?"

"Yes."

"Am I known primarily for losing?"

I hadn't expected him to be arrogant. It shouldn't have been surprising—he was the best chess player of all time. The best hamster trainer of all time probably has an ego, too. But a part of me had been hoping that, upon my request, he would sit up straighter, reach into his coat pocket, and produce a typed manifesto. Here, he might say. I've been waiting for you. There is so much here that you need to know.

"No," I said. "Of course not. It's just that he knew that in your long career, there had certainly been . . . moments when you knew you must lose. And he wanted to know how you kept playing."

"I can't imagine I responded to such a letter," he said. "If I got it."

"You didn't," I said. "That's why I'm here."

He looked at me for a long moment. Then he took off his glasses and pinched the skin between his eyes. "When did he die, your father?"

I looked at him.

"You wouldn't be here if he weren't dead, right?" It was a challenging thing to say, I suppose, but he managed to say it kindly.

"He died in February," I said. "But he'd been sick for a very long time."

Bezetov nodded. He put his glasses back on. I tried to make myself say something politely admiring about the modern art on the walls, but my gaze faltered on the dark-coated men hulking in the doorway. "I notice you have a lot of security," I said.

"I do," he said, waving his arm at them. "They cost me tens of thousands of dollars, and they will probably fail me in the end anyway. I can minimize my risk, but it's an ultimate futility. It's only a question of time."

"I know something about that," I said. The radiator started to kick up, making spitting sounds and giving the room an overcooked smell.

Aleksandr looked out that great picture window, even though there wasn't much to see: in the late-afternoon dark, there was only the reflection of the gilded orbs of his lamps, the sharp glint of light on his computer, the frightful paleness of my own face.

"You mentioned you saw an old friend of mine," said Aleksandr. "And which friend was that?"

"Elizabeta Nazarovna. Do you remember her? She lived in your building. She said you might not remember."

He said nothing and kept looking out the window. I thought I noticed a minor tightening in his neck muscles. Out the window, a cascading wash of headlights filtered through the gloom.

"I remember something about her, I think." He let the sentence sit, lightly buffered by silence. "And how is she doing now?"

I thought of the murderousness of her coughing, the way her hunched shoulders shook like trees in a cyclone. I thought, too, of the way her voice glinted; how listening to it was like looking down a hall of mirrors.

"She does not seem well."

"I see." He waited. I could feel him hoping for me to offer more, but I didn't know what was expected. "She is alone?"

I thought of the clasp of her hand in mine, the nudity of her thin fingers. I thought of the size of the apartment, how the birdcage seemed to dominate the decor. I realized that there was no bedroom—just the cramped living room, the toy-sized kitchen. She must be sleeping on the couch.

"It seems so." Then I understood, from the way Aleksandr clenched his jaw and the way he erased his eyes and the way his words seemed to shiver on a tightrope, that he had loved her. And I was struck by the unforgivable stupidity of refusing love. And I was further struck by the violence of my own mistake, and I felt lucky for the limited time I would have to live with it.

"You should see her," I said. Then I felt presumptuous. "Maybe. If you want to."

"Maybe. I'm very busy these days."

"That I see," I said. I realized that there was an approach I had not tried. "Maybe I could be of help to you?"

He stood, and I was struck again by the reality of his shortness. His authority came from his thick eyebrows and vigorous jaw, the muscled compactness of his shoulders, the tired intelligence of his eyes. He didn't look like a man who'd spent a lifetime flitting toys across a board.

"You want a job," he said brusquely.

I coughed. "Not a job. I just want to be of use."

There was an impatient silence. I stood up, too, because it seemed the thing to do. He looked at me. "You are an academic at home, yes?" he said finally.

"Formerly."

"You can write in English, yes?"

"Yes."

"You will not be speaking any more with our friend Nikolai?"

"No."

"Very well," he said. "You can help us with the American press. You can send them e-mails. Okay? You can type things up. Okay? Not sexy, not glamorous."

"I don't need sexy."

"Good, then," he said. "Since they already think you're causing trouble, you might as well, right? You can come in on Monday. How long will you be expecting to stay in the country?"

I thought about how to answer. "I don't know yet," I said. "But probably not that long."

"All right," he said, orienting me toward the door. "We'll use you while we can." He opened the door for me, and I was confronted again with the smell of gourmet coffee and a beach of white carpeting stretching door-to-door. I held out my hand to Aleksandr. He took it.

"Thank you," I said.

"You're welcome. And Irina?" He was ushering me out. "When you know you're losing, I am told it is sensible to resign."

———

The next week dissolved in much the same way as the others had: in a dreamy, almost drunken suspended animation, impinged upon by the faintest fragments of memory and hallucination. Often I felt clinically numb, and I watched myself with the third-person detachment of a person on heavy painkillers. Occasionally, I felt strangely exhilarated, my head filling with snatches of speech and irrelevant images. Out of nowhere, I remembered the cartoon skunk on the cover of a coloring book from the late seventies; one day at an apple orchard with a boy I loved in middle school; the yellow dog across the street from my childhood day care that had one day mysteriously disappeared. And I marveled over the mind's ability to record so much information that it would never, ever need.

I wrote more to Jonathan, more unsendable, unreadable, unforgivable letters. I told him I knew these past months were months I'd lost with him. I told him I knew I'd missed dinners and walks and sex and laughter and showers and earnest, whispered discussions and the kind of fights you pick because you think it's sexy when the other person is a little bit mad at you. But then I told him about the other thing I was missing, the other thing I was making him miss. The first jerk of an elbow or a hand. The spiraling loss of competencies. My brain's grim retreat across a sealed border. I told him about his mounting resentment, and the way he'd feel guilty for it, and the way it would consume him. It would consume him, I told him, whether he ever believed me about this or not. The living always resent the claims of the dead, especially when the dead are still living. I told him I spoke with authority. I told him I knew I'd made the right decision, even if I would have to know it for the both of us.

Through my window in the mornings came pink light: if I woke up at a certain time, the whole room would be infused with the pink of the Sistine Chapel, the pink of a face brought back from the dead. I'd sit and wait to hear the plucking of harps, the stirring choir, and when I heard nothing, I would roll over and try again to sleep. I was always struck by how unafraid I was of sleep, even though it was the closest approximation.

Strange things were starting to happen with time. The moments started to bunch and buckle; whole hours could disappear into staring fits from which I'd emerge lost and unstrung. Then there would be an agonizing eon distilled into the stirring of a coffee, the turning of a page.

Nights became restless and feverish. I'd skim the edge of sleep, hearing the echoes of sarcastic laughter and the clicking of keys. On the wall, shadows made filaments and lace. I'd wake up muttering, recovering from dreams that followed me around in the day. In them there were more mute memories: my mother and father leaning against a tree, surrounded by leaves, slow-falling and yellow. There were chessboards from Boston, melting into the chessboards of my childhood. I remembered the triumph of my father's ever conquering queen. I remembered the crack of the skull of my father's king against the board.

Then, too, I remembered the crack of my father's arm against the stove, his head against the bathroom tile.

———

When I went back to Aleksandr's apartment the following week, Viktor was there. He eyes flitted to me momentarily. Then he went back to shaking his head savagely at what a shorter man was writing in a notebook. "Nashi will kill that," said Viktor. "They'll surround us. You need a better layout."

"Hush," said the other.

"Look what they did at G8. You're wasting your fancy pen."

"Please hush."

Viktor glanced at me, then nodded to the sitting man. "Assistant," he mouthed.

I immediately retreated to the foyer and busied myself by looking at the prints. Though I'd been told to come by, I was aware of how lost I looked. I had a flash of myself at fourteen, my first day of ninth grade, wandering the halls in a hopeless quest for the geometry classroom. On the wall, I squinted into an amber-colored Nevsky Prospekt and tried to look engrossed.

A moment later, something changed in the air. Aleksandr was behind me. "You like those?" he said.

"I do," I said, turning around.

"They were done by a friend of ours. A very rich man. He was in oil. He did printmaking to civilize himself."

"Is he here?" I said.

"He's in a penal colony in Siberia for eight years," said Aleksandr. "He was funding us. But Putin has a sharp sense of how to prioritize. He's not interested in stopping everybody. Only everybody who he thinks might actually count. This friend of mine, the printmaker, he was very, very rich. He had billions. Do you know how rich you have to be to put a billionaire in jail?"

"Pretty rich," I said.

"Yes," said Aleksandr. "Pretty rich. Nobody ever talks about how indecently *rich* Putin is, but I like to bring it up a lot. Do you how many billionaires we have in Russia?"

"How many?"

"Sixty-one. Sixty-one billionaires, and Putin could put every last one of them in jail if they threatened his business interests. That's what people don't understand about him. He's not an ideologue. He's just pragmatic. He's just greedy. He could be liberal or conservative—he doesn't care. He supports Syria and Iran because tension brings up oil prices. And you let him get away with it."

"Me?"

"The West. You're easily impressed by staged democracy. We have something here we call an election, after all. But that doesn't mean we're not a police state. And there's money here now. So the West lets our oligarchs export their questionable assets, and they grant Putin democratic credentials in order to do it. If the U.S. was serious about restraining Putin, they'd start denying visas. The oligarchy can't afford a new Cold War."

I looked at him. "What would you do about it as president?"

He waved his hand. "It's not a campaign the way you're thinking of it—like, oh, I'd support this and that legislation. I'm not winning. I want to coordinate a broad platform, not promote my own ambitions."

"That's a little vague, isn't it?"

He raised his eyebrows at me, and I knew then, if I hadn't before, that the way to get him to like me was to push back at him. "Since you asked, then. Extreme caution must be used when assessing the components of the existing mechanism that may still be used in establishing the new state. Otherwise, chaos would ensue."

I took a breath and plunged forward. "Existing mechanism? That all sounds very prudent."

"It is prudent."

"Do your supporters know it's prudent? Do they know it's extremely cautious? They don't seem like the most cautious of people, from an observer's perspective."

He looked at me, and I thought he might call security to frog-march me out the door. I would have, if I'd had a security apparatus at my disposal. But he didn't. He smiled as if he'd discovered a chess opponent who was somewhat better than expected, though still fairly terrible.

"We must have a return to gubernatorial elections. We must draft a new constitution, since the current one is baldly authoritarian."

"Isn't single-handedly scrapping the constitution a tiny bit authoritarian?"

His eyes flared slightly. He was amused. "It will arise from a national consensus."

"What percentage of Russians consider themselves fans of Stalin?" I said. "Is it forty-five percent?"

He smirked. "It's fifty-five percent, actually. So you can see what I'm up against."

"Yes," I said. I leaned in toward the prints again. One, in rich greens, was of a little café at the end of a long street.

"That's the Saigon," said Aleksandr. "We used to hang around there. Maybe you've seen it? It's a hotel now. I think its rooms go for something like six thousand rubles a night. So. You're ready to start?"

"Yes."

"You can copyedit these," he said, handing me a stack of papers. "They've already been translated, but we need a native speaker to catch the subtler problems."

I scanned the top page. *Aleksandr Bezetov, in assistance of the Democratic Union, will spend public debate at the St.-Petersburg university, addressing to a question of to what degree the state should soften oil monopolies in modern economy.*

"Okay," I said. "I can fix this."

"I used to do that kind of thing," he said. "Mindless errands. My job was to run around the city and shove illegal newspapers into people's hands."

"Did you ever get caught?"

"We were always caught. We were caught before we even really knew what we were doing. But we thought we were being clever."

"Were you being clever?"

"Not very," he said. "I was a notable figure then. Less so than now, perhaps, but even so. I was on some list before I even knew my way around the city. They had us the whole way through. So this time"—he straightened up—"I know that much. I know that I am already caught. I am not hiding. Also, I am not flattering myself. No matter how you look at it, it's a futile endeavor."

"Why do it, then?"

"Nothing much else to do. Chess tires me now."

"Do you still play?"

"Not so much. I needed a new hobby." He put his hands in his pockets and frowned, as though an unhappy possibility had just occurred to him. "Do *you* play?"

"I used to sometimes. I played with my father when I was small." I looked down. "And I had a friend I played with sometimes in Boston. I was never very good. I could never think more than a move ahead."

"Count yourself lucky. Thinking more than a move ahead never got me anywhere in life. Only in chess. And even then it was sometimes a burden. I saw fifteen moves ahead once, in Norway, but there was a much easier path to victory, and I missed it. Looking into the future too hard, I've found, can be paralyzing."

"I've found that, too."

Aleksandr looked at me suspiciously. "Anyway," he said, clapping me on the back. "I'll let you get to work."

I took the reams of paper—the press releases, the drafted e-mails, the artlessly phrased leaflets—and sat in a corner. Around me there was arguing and joking and the sound of words clacking fiercely onto pages. I started to skim the first e-mail, catching the first misspelling and the first inelegant turn of phrase. I felt more awake than usual. There was something satisfying about doing a small, good thing after all these weeks of living in a morass of uselessness. I thought about what Aleksandr had said about chess, about the paralyzing effects of imagination. I knew that to be true. Any time I let my mind wander more than three steps into the future, it reached the limits of comprehension and fell off the edge. But for now there were concrete concerns—small, surmountable problems: typos, grammatical irregularities. I could live with these. I bent my head over the pages, and I started to work.

15

ALEKSANDR

St. Petersburg, December 2006

Aleksandr stood on top of a box in Gostiny Dvor and shouted into the crowd. It was a sizable turnout—maybe not the biggest group he'd seen since he began, but near it. He'd have to ask Nina about the head count. Today they were a bit more frenetic than usual: boys kicked bits of hail like footballs; the crowd clunked their feet against the unyielding snow like a group of ungulates getting ready to stampede. He should be thankful for the energy, he knew. But the wind angled itself through his clothes—it always managed to do this; no matter how many layers he wore, it laced its fingers together and then ran them up and down his pant leg and collar provocatively—and he was again struck by the thought that he was beginning (already!) to be tired of this. The crowds, the slogans, the shouting at the sky, as though it would count for something in the end. He was committed to it, he was, he was, and he would keep at it until they caught up with him somewhere—sneaked polonium into his imported sushi, dismantled the engine of his airplane, shot him dead in the stairwell of his own apartment building as they had done to Anna Politkovskaya in October. But there were times—like now, and now wasn't a good time for it—when it all felt preordained. They weren't the first crowd to clot and yell, to issue demands.

He took a gulp of icy air. "We are running to lose," he shouted. This line always got the biggest shouts, which had to make him wonder. "And in the losing, we are running to be noticed. We are running to be blocked. We are running to be opposed. We are running to be assassinated." He cast his eyes around the crowd. This line was his dare—or maybe his invitation—to the universe. It was coming, he knew it was coming, so it might as well look artfully stage-managed. But the flags fluttered in unison, and the crowd cheered. Today was not the day.

He looked at his notes. He tried to make his speeches different every time he delivered them—on this day, did you know, Pushkin completed *Eugene Onegin,* and Poland declared independence from Russia for the first time?—so that people could listen to him now and again and still expect to hear something new. He tracked his eyes back up to the crowd; he arranged his face into an expression of surprised interest so that he could convincingly sell the fun of knowing that today was the anniversary of the day that Khrushchev sent a dog to die in outer space. And as he did, he caught sight of a young woman standing kitty-corner from his box and taking notes. He delivered his line and looked back. He always noticed when people took notes at his rallies—it was a habit, he was sure, from Nikolai—although Nina often reminded him that note-taking wasn't necessarily a bad thing: it could be a citizen journalist, or a European blogger, or the real Western press. "What's wrong with you?" she'd say, tossing her long leg over his in their giant black and white bed. "Don't you want people to be paying attention to you?" And he'd say he did, he did, although he knew that at least some of the people who were paying attention were doing so for very bad reasons. "You worry too much," Nina would say, making her face into a monstrous mock pout (apparently what he looked like to her when he was worried, which he always was). And because it was insulting to try to make a woman worry for you when she was naturally disinclined to do so, he usually just shrugged and rolled over and fell asleep facing the wall.

But this woman—what was it about her that didn't seem journalistic? She seemed so unassuming, so unsure of herself, that one wondered whether it might not be a pretense. She looked like she could be Russian—she had brown hair and a grim expression and skin the color of table salt—but he knew immediately that she was not. Something in her stance was half off; she stood too far apart from everybody else to seem comfortable but too close to seem actively hostile. She was not pretty—she was too monochromatic, too self-conscious, he thought, in the way she moved and glanced—but her eyes held a wry intelligence that made him look at her twice. She was approaching Nina. Nina would dismiss her quickly, he knew; Nina's greatest strength in life was a capacity to dismiss, and Aleksandr relied on her to be rude on his behalf. Somebody needed to be, and Aleksandr was a little too polite even after all the decades and all the women. It was good for Nina to have something to do besides click around the apartment on high heels and dye her hair red and keep her body in such a state of hygienic star-vation that Aleksandr sometimes wondered how she could have been a product of natural selection. Nina was talking, he saw, to the woman with the notepad.

He could see Nina shaking her head and turning around to look at Vlad—the head bodyguard, the best because he was the biggest—then turning back to the woman. There was a current of desperation in the woman's eyes, he could see, not abject pathos, exactly, but the quiet suggestion that here was a person who had not gotten something that she'd wanted very much. Aleksandr pulled on his gloves. He found himself hoping that Nina could give her whatever she was asking for.

———

After the rally, in bed, Aleksandr ran his cold feet up and down Nina's leg.

"Stop that," she said. "You are a cruel man."

"Did you think the rally went well?"

"As well as always," said Nina, which was no answer at all. Aleksandr wished he could care a little less about what Nina thought of him; they were married, and he was rich, and she was beautiful, and that should be enough, but he often found himself restlessly worrying at the gaps between them, sticking his fingers into the fissures and pry-ing them farther apart. Tonight he managed to say nothing.

"I wish you would cut that line about assassination," said Nina.

"I thought you said I worry too much."

"You do worry too much. That line is you worrying in front of the whole crowd. It's not manly."

"Do you want to see me do something manly?"

"I'd rather not tonight." She kissed him dryly on the cheek and rolled over. "Sorry, grib." He had never liked that she called him "mushroom"—first because he worried that he looked a little like a mushroom (dark, lumpy-faced, on the stout side now) and then because he worried that he behaved like a mushroom (brooding furtively in the dark when nobody was looking). But Nina always said that was nonsense—that she loved mushrooms and she loved him—and she kept calling him "mushroom" and he stopped asking her not to.

"Who was that woman with you at the rally?" said Aleksandr.

"I don't know, exactly. A very odd American."

Aleksandr turned over and propped his head with his hand. "A fan?"

"I guess so," said Nina, wrinkling her nose. Here, too: she might show the faintest tremor of jealousy at the idea of a young American woman traveling internationally to get to meet him; she might reflect *fleetingly* on the fact that there were many, many women who would pay for that opportunity, who would be grateful to talk to him, who would not roll over in bed if they were next to him.

"Was she chess or political?" said Aleksandr.

"I couldn't tell." Nina's voice was becoming creaky and reluctant, dislodging into sleep. "I scheduled you a meeting for Wednesday. Bring Vlad."

"I always bring Vlad," said Aleksandr. An American visitor was odd. His chess fans were usually Russian and almost exclusively male. Yet he'd have known her if she was a delegate from an NGO; she would have had a more professional approach and outfit and wouldn't have scared his nice wife by shivering at her pitifully in the snow.

"She's an American professor," said Nina.

"Oh yes?" Aleksandr sat up. Something was snarling in the back of his head—some meaning taking shape, like tea leaves settling into symbol.

"What's wrong?" said Nina, although he could hear in her voice the profound indifference of fatigue.

"I'll be back in a minute."

"What's wrong?"

"I'll be back."

He went to his study, flipped on the light, and started riffling through his notes. There had been something about an American professor at his security meeting the week before. Some years ago, Aleksandr had paid to turn a low-level FSB man—Grigorii, a baby-faced clown from Nizhny who'd sat shaking in his boots the first time and tried to demand a higher sum—who had been photocopying Aleksandr's file ever since. For the most part, the endeavor had proved a stupendous waste of money. But at the most recent meeting, Grigorii had said something strange—it was obvious from the get-go that he'd had something beyond his usual predictable babble, because he'd looked a little more smug and obnoxious than usual—and he'd stuck out his feet and leaned back in his chair.

"They think you have a new boss," he'd said, and smirked.

Aleksandr had kicked the leg of the table. "I don't have a fucking boss," he said. Vlad glared him into silence. Aleksandr had never gotten used to listening to lies about himself, and he usually insisted on correcting them, even though neither Vlad nor the turncoat seemed to care in the end what was true and what was not, as long as they were paid.

"They think the embassy has a new officer, a sort of awkward young woman, and that she's on your case."

"Please," Aleksandr had said. "It's embarrassing to even listen to this."

The little shit had smiled, had scratched his beardless chin. "I'm just telling you what's in your file."

Where were his notes from that meeting? Aleksandr flipped through his papers—the facts for the speech, some statistics on the depopulation of Siberia, a few fragments on the film project—and then found the notes. The officer in question was supposedly an "awkward female American academic." How many of them could there be, running around the same city? It was probably the same woman.

She wasn't really CIA, he knew that much. Over the years, they'd approached him occasionally, and done him favors from time to time, and accepted some from him, but they understood, fundamentally, that he'd have no credibility with anyone if he let them own him. He wasn't pressing their agenda, anyway. He wasn't pressing anyone's. As much as they liked him on CNN—because he was sarcastic and skeptical and liked to talk about civil liberties—he was a radical fiscal conservative. He wanted a flat tax. He wanted extreme deregulation. They wouldn't like him at the American universities if he talked about that stuff, though mostly he was on about press freedom and democracy—and so they clamored for his autograph, these kids at Princeton with their Che Guevara T-shirts.

But the rumors mattered. They mattered because when he traveled the countryside, when he listened to the concerns of the people in Yekaterinburg and Nizhny Novgorod and Irkutsk, he needed them to trust him. The people wanted to talk to him and were inclined to like him; he had a common face and an uncommon energy, and he seemed to remind mothers of their most capable son. They liked to complain to him, and they liked how he eviscerated Putin—with an impression accomplished by sucking his cheeks into vicious little concavities and making his eyes go flat and dead—but they stopped trusting him when they heard rumors. *I heard he works for the Americans. I heard he's an agent of the American CIA.* He couldn't afford it—it was too damaging, it tore too savagely through the carefully wound threads of trust he'd established across this enormous, lonely country—and he had to make this woman, whoever she was, stop whatever she was doing.

He considered going back to bed—to hold the angular slashes of Nina's shoulders, to run his fingers against the rocky cordon of her spine—but he decided against it. He was too awake. He flipped back to his notes on the bombing film. The first page of his notes was a photograph: a black-and-white snapshot of the first apartment-building bombing, its top twisted off, its living rooms and sofa beds and kitchen counters reduced to a collapsed pile of gray cinders. In the corner of the photograph, a small boy ran wide-mouthed across a smoldering alley.

The boy reminded him always of the girl—his girl, his handless girl and her soundless scream. And when he thought of her, he thought of the apartment buildings exploding in stars of fibrous orange, giving off little atomic clouds that made the city barely habitable. Then came the fear: the frantic desperation of a siege, the people stockpiling, placing bets, holding out. Then came the talk: terrorism, it was called; Chechens, no doubt, it was decided; all a part of this global Islamic jihad that had taken a swipe at America's embassies a year earlier, although America, it was agreed, had at least halfway had it coming. Then there was Putin, fucking Putin, skipping to his victory: smug, assured, issuing commandments and condemnations. The people were glad to have someone in charge. It was only because they were so afraid—chafing against the iron grip of terror, choking on the metallic stink of death (though Misha, who'd thought he was dying more times than was typical, said that the smell of death was actually something closer to sassafras).

Aleksandr knew that fear. He'd known it back when he was a sniveling chess idiot, smiling big dumb smiles over chattering teeth at his chess chaperones and begging the God he didn't believe in to make him less like Ivan (less brave, that is, and thus less dead). He knew that fear now, now that he was an adult and making an adult's painful choices and taking an adult's painful risks. It was a powerful thing.

Putin knew that, too, of course. Aleksandr often wondered if there was something of that primordial death fear in Putin—behind his flat affect, his reptilian sneer. The man must lie in his silken sheets, knowing that he'd lied and wronged and suppressed and assassinated his way across the biggest country in the entire world, and that country was at his back as he fell asleep facing the sunset—and he must wake up sometimes gagging on the smell of sassafras.

At the end of the day, though, it had worked. Putin had won the country. Self-satisfied, smiling that sour subsmile, walking away with the nation's trust and democratic mandate. One had to wonder. These terrorists, these bombings. These Chechens, who had come all this way to do it. Nice of them to do such a great favor for Putin right before the election. One just had to wonder.

So Aleksandr was going to make a film that would voice some public findings, some public wonderings. His first idea had been to publish an article about it, but Boris and Viktor—his post-adolescent but obnoxiously intelligent advisers—had looked bored when he discussed it. Their eyes had glazed over. They'd recently been watching a documentary about the origins of 9/11, they said. In it, a schlubby American filmmaker made wounded faces as he interviewed politicians and men on the street. He was polite. He asked literal-minded questions. He somehow made the other people look stupid.

"We should do something like that," Viktor had said. "Something accessible."

"You know that guy's a socialist, right?" Aleksandr had said.

"He makes effective films."

"He makes montages. He puts clips of horrifying historical events against pop songs. They're music videos."

"People watch these films. These films change public opinion," said Boris.

"I didn't see this film sinking Bush's second term."

Boris had looked at him and said the one thing that could have persuaded Aleksandr: "When have we talked seriously about sinking Putin? Or whoever he appoints next? I'm saying that this film will make them *uncomfortable*."

They'd been at work on the film for a few months, and Aleksandr had to think that if anything would get him killed, this would be it. But he did not expect the film to have a magic effect. He did not expect it would appear and suddenly usher in decentralization, the end of censorship, the dismantling of the current regime, free and fair elections. All he could hope was that a few people would see it on YouTube, and that, as Viktor said, it would make the administration uncomfortable. All would be different if there was free television. One month of free television and there would be a coup d'état.

Aleksandr went back to bed. Nina was asleep, her red hair a spray against the Egyptian-cotton pillow, her arms locked at her sides as if holding a yoga position. It was amazing how silently she slept, with such ferocity of purpose. The woman did nothing with nonsense. But that was why he'd married her, after all. He'd had enough of silly girls, young women who fell over themselves and spilled their drinks on their expensive blouses and laughed too loudly at the wrong part of a story. Nina was trivial, perhaps, but she was unapologetic about it, and poised, and pragmatic, and she did nothing to flatter him. At his age, at his income bracket, there was nothing better for a man.

It was true that he still sometimes thought of Elizabeta—not often, not obsessively, but more frequently than he thought of any other woman besides Nina. It was embarrassing to admit it, even to himself, in his own head, and remembering her was like simultaneously remembering all the worst shames of his life: the day he lost to a computer program; the fact that he'd once slept on a dirt floor and broken the necks of chickens with his bare hands; his personal conduct for the entirety of the 1980s. Why—as he lay next to a beautiful woman in classy, suggestive pajamas—did his thoughts turn to a nonromance three decades old? But they did sometimes, not often, not often, and he'd be back in the old kommunalka, watching her bang her hand against the steward's door, listening to her shout some spirited entreaty, messy hair flying everywhere.

Such thoughts were a waste of energy, and Aleksandr knew he needed to save his energy for more complicated difficulties, more interesting problems. He clasped his hand around Nina's torso and held her until she shoved him off in her sleep.

———

The day of the meeting with the American woman, Aleksandr entered his office to find Boris playing video games. Boris often played video games during working hours; it was, he said, when he did his best thinking. ("What thinking is that?" Viktor would often say.) Next to him, Viktor was scribbling notes on a napkin.

"What is this drivel you're writing?" said Boris, not looking at Viktor. On the screen, what looked to Aleksandr like a soft-featured gnome bopped across a chartreuse landscape.

"Just thanking your mother for last night," said Viktor.

"I'm relieved to hear that your impotence problem has been resolved."

Aleksandr had found them at a protest eighteen months earlier, and he'd made them run errands until he knew they were serious. Viktor had a heavy brow and blue eyes; Boris was shorter and had a crooked nose that Aleksandr thought odd but that the women seemed to find heartbreakingly attractive. They were arrogant and brilliant and in constant competition; Aleksandr often remarked loudly that if they were his sons—if he'd had sons—he would have volunteered them for the land forces of the Russian Federation as soon as they turned eighteen. As it was, they were not his sons, thank God, and he let them bully and cajole each other as much as they wanted, as long as it kept them sharp.

"Who bought you that pen, goluboi?" said Boris. "I've never seen such an affectation."

"You're just jealous of my literacy."

Nina had thought he was crazy for taking in Viktor and Boris so readily. He often talked about how they'd kicked the energy of the outfit up a notch, and how he'd often thought that even if they were FSB, it might have been a fair trade. Aleksandr understood better—now that he was older than Ivan would ever be—how desperate Ivan must have been for a confidant in Nikolai, how greedy he'd been for reassurance. Aleksandr made Viktor and Boris work together because he knew they would fight; after having watched Nikolai's slavish devotion to Ivan, Aleksandr believed in the importance of a certain standing hostility between co-workers. They were also young— too young to carry the weight of having behaved wrongly during Soviet times—and they annoyed everyone else with their entitled idealism, their freedom from a history of crushing moral calculations. But then, as Aleksandr often remarked, Alternative Russia needed a few people who hadn't been ethically compromised. Among them were those who'd publicly sold out and those who quietly pretended they never had (himself among them); there were those who'd once believed and had officially come around; there were those who would always, always do whatever was most pragmatic, and who (today) found something practical in a contrarian stance. Then there were the types like Misha—Misha, who had gone ultranationalist in his old age, and who did nothing to discourage Right Russia's more racist, xenophobic, and anti-Semitic edges, and who occasionally showed up at Aleksandr's rallies to shout disruptive things and wave implausible signs.

"You seem to be taking your time there. Are you struggling with the spelling?" said Boris. The video game issued cheerful synthesizer sounds.

"Real men, you will find, can last longer than thirty seconds at their activities."

Viktor kicked Boris's chair leg and went back to drafting the itinerary for Moscow, where the two would be heading in a week. They'd already been to Volgodonsk and Buynaksk, and in Moscow they'd be interviewing an ex-soldier who was making money in ways that Aleksandr had agreed not to scrutinize on camera. The interviews were to compose the final and most important third of the film—following an analysis of Putin's political gain from the attacks and a delineation of the discrepancies in the press reports—and Aleksandr badly envied their going. Aleksandr couldn't go anywhere anymore.

Viktor and Boris went off to draft questions and follow-up questions, and the afternoon was swept quickly away. Vlad came in with a toothless death threat; one of the assistants came in with a speaking invitation at Yale University. At four o'clock sharp, just as Aleksandr was starting to lose energy, he was brought a perfect, tiny espresso that gave him the will to go on. Then the door opened and in walked Nina, a few steps ahead of the strange, startled-looking American. "Your visitor," she said, and clicked out of the room.

"One moment," said Aleksandr.

The American took off her hat, which made her hair stand straight up. "*Zdryastvuytye*," she said poorly, which made Aleksandr wince.

"Please," said Aleksandr. "I've been speaking Russian long enough that this hurts me."

Later, he wouldn't be sure what had made him hire her, exactly. It wasn't pity, although he couldn't help but feel an inexplicable lurch of empathy for her; it wasn't that she was smart (although she was) or that she was beautiful (because she wasn't). It was, he finally decided, the way she'd asked about Elizabeta, and the way she seemed to stumble her way into understanding something profound about him while he sat there and watched. He rationalized that it was a good quality in an employee: an ability to infer, to piece together a narrative, to take imaginative leaps into the psychology of others. And he had no doubt that she could competently fix the press releases (although Viktor, who'd studied at Oxford, could do just as well). But really, deep down, he hadn't hired her for her fluent English. He hadn't hired her to type or proofread or copyedit. He'd hired her to sit around and keep him company in his only undiscovered secret.

———

In the evening—once the army of typers and talkers had left, and Aleksandr had eaten his dinner of vegetables and high-end fish, and the sky out the living-room window had turned the color of a mostly healed bruise—Nina clacked against the oak floors and started up some tea. Aleksandr often came across Nina's array of multicolored teas in the cupboards—strange tinctures beyond the realm of his understanding, usually involving obscure Latin American tubers—and they were the only evidence in the kitchen, he often thought, that Nina was a carbon-based life-form, requiring consumption for survival.

She waved a malodorous tea bag at his face. "Do you want some of this?" she said, although he had never once accepted her offer.

"No, thank you," said Aleksandr. "What's this one do?"

"It's for digestion."

"What do you have to digest? You don't eat."

"I eat plenty," said Nina tiredly. "How was your meeting with the strange American?"

"It was fine."

"Oh?"

"I hired her."

"You what?"

"I hired her," he said. "I'm going to coopt her, you know? It makes sense."

Nina's water started to boil, and she poured it over her tea leaves. A bitter smell flushed up, acrid and assaulting, and Aleksandr stepped away. "You're going to pay her?" said Nina.

"She says she doesn't need money. I'll give her something nominally."

"That's very odd." Nina took a sip of her tea. "What if she's spying on you?"

Aleksandr had considered this. But after thirty years of paranoia—of seeing spies in corners, and ghosts in shadows, and murder in public transportation, and conspiracy in terrorism—he felt sure that she was not.

"What if *you're* spying on me?" he said, and tugged at Nina's hair.

"Grib, stop," she said. "I just blow-dried it."

———

That night—again, and he hoped it didn't suggest a trend—Aleksandr couldn't sleep. In bed, with Nina silent beside him, he tried to keep his legs from thrashing. He took deep breaths, but they caught somewhere behind his uvula, stirring little tides of anxiety, eddying over deep pools of energy. He wanted to go to Moscow. He wanted to run a marathon. He wanted, he realized, to get out of the apartment.

For a time, even in recent years, Aleksandr still occasionally went walking. But like American heads of state who insist on taking exercise outside, he was always trailed by a small army of his black-suited security staff. It was tiresome for him, and boring for them, and nothing in the way of freedom or reflection could be achieved. So in the last few years he'd mostly stopped. His universe had become this apartment—tastefully decorated (that was all Nina) and carefully managed, his toast and tea ready for him at five-fifteen in the morning, his afternoon espresso steaming hot at four, his laptop blinking an aquatic blue in the dark, whirling him into contact with the universe. Living in this apartment was like living in a museum, he sometimes thought, everything so immaculately clean, the objects chosen and placed with the care of a curator. Each room had a different unobtrusively pleasant smell—lemon in the kitchen, lavender in the bedroom, some sort of oceanic wind that made him sneeze in the bathroom. He walked the apartment end to end some nights, and when he put his foot down in that forgiving white carpeting, he could smell the rawness of Sakhalin dirt. In his sublime, epic, multilayered bed, he could feel the lethal cold of his room in the kommunalka.

No wonder, then, that he sometimes woke up choking on something that felt like fear. Sometimes he couldn't quite stand it—the subtle ostentation, the supernatural calm, the fucking *order* of it all, like a planned economy.

He sat up. He got out of bed and put on his coat over his pajamas, and he put on his running shoes—bought as a Christmas present by Nina, who had grinned and pinched at his hefty trunk—and he punched in the security code at the doorway, blinking a subterranean green, and he found himself outside on the sidewalk. He tried to remember the last time he'd been out alone. There were some early acts of rashness, before the ear came through the window, and there had been a few moments of defiance since then. He'd sneaked out early one forgotten anniversary, when he knew there was no time to order something, and he'd been proud of his romanticism—risking life and limb to get his wife a diamond bracelet. Had she worn it? He couldn't remember.

The cool of the morning air, the squeak of the snow under his shoes—they were quickly soaked, and a gangrenous ache started climbing up his calves—reminded him of those painfully cold mornings back in the early eighties when he'd run about the city before dawn started melting across the sky, free in his shrinking anonymity. He could envy this strange American woman, almost, and whatever wound had made her leave her country alone and come here to work for him for free. Whatever it was, whatever it had broken in her, it had also broken the mechanism that was small, that huddled, that took tiny steps and looked behind shoulders.

In the distance, Aleksandr could almost see the inky spines of the modern office buildings, the peeling gilt of the moldering palaces, the slate-colored twist of the Neva. No one knew he was out, and under his heavy hat he might walk around unrecognized for hours. He'd spent years risking everything for the major freedoms—the right of the people to vote, to buy and sell, to cruelly caricature their leaders. But there was the small thing, too, of walking unsupervised through the snowy streets. Aleksandr headed down Nevsky Prospekt. The bakeries were just starting to open, and light came bleeding through the windows of Kazan Cathedral. Aleksandr turned down Naberezhnaya reki Moiki. In the dour crepuscular light, the Moika looked like aluminum. Soon Nina would be waking up and climbing on the treadmill, and maybe she'd wonder where he was, and maybe soon she'd start to worry. Maybe she'd leave two messages on his cell phone, curt and exasperated, and maybe the third would open up into something long and pleading and tender. Maybe she'd call Vlad, and maybe he'd take a car out and track Aleksandr's muddy sneaker-prints across the city. But for now Aleksandr was safe from all of that. For now he was out in the world: alone, the wind carving up his lungs, his city a little closer with every step.

16

IRINA

St. Petersburg, 2006

Aleksandr was brilliant, of course. Anybody could see that, and everybody did. But he wasn't quite as I'd imagined him, or maybe it's more accurate to say he wasn't quite as I imagine my father had imagined him. When the maid set down his afternoon espresso, Aleksandr never thanked her—he rarely even looked up. When his colleagues disappointed him, he snapped at them; when he heard something he deemed stupid, he raised an eyebrow with such withering contempt that all talk in the room ground to a halt. The apartment was absurd: it was as decadent as Versailles, with an endless supply of dumb little contraptions intended to make life easier than it should be—an appliance that simultaneously toasted your English muffin and fried your eggs, bottles of perfume with wood stems for all-day fresh fragrance. And the marriage was exactly as Viktor had described it. It was the kind of marriage that embarrasses everybody by its transparency—all of its petty dynamics and long-standing resentments were obvious in the way that Nina handed Aleksandr his espresso and the way his eyes followed her out of a room. Aleksandr's colleagues respected him—and more than a few of them were in awe of him—but Nina's departures were always followed by a tense, soggy moment when everybody looked down at their papers and tried not to show their pity. I didn't spend a lot of time speculating about it. Marriages fall apart so often, and in so many different, excruciating ways, that trying to sort out the particularities of anybody's is like trying to unspool the proximate cause of death of a person with no immune system. Though at times there was an edge of fatigue in Aleksandr's eyes, or an ironic twist to his words, that made me think of Elizabeta and the way he'd looked when he heard her name.

But then it's possible I was just projecting. Everybody likes a story about love long gone. When I thought of Jonathan—if I thought of Jonathan—he came back in flashes, on mute, through static. Our time together had taken on the surreal dimensions of a dream or a childhood.

I took to keeping longer and longer hours at Aleksandr's, since there was nothing impelling me toward anything else. I got the sense that Viktor and Boris were similarly situated—they were the kind of young people who probably slept on half-deflated mattresses, who kept their books in a pile and their appliances unassembled. They seemed to be living the refugee life of students who haven't yet learned that they're supposed to find meaning in things, not just ideas.

But even though I started spending long days in Aleksandr's apartment—twelve, fourteen, sixteen hours, stumbling ever later out into the bitter dark, ringing the door and being buzzed into the hostel, receiving looks from the man at the front desk that ranged from disapproval to indifference to knowing amusement—Aleksandr and I spoke no further about my father. Sometimes he'd walk toward me with a look of determination, and I'd be almost sure that he'd found something—my father's original letter, perhaps, or some conclusive answer to my father's questions, or some magic strength to live and to die. But he didn't. He handed me no answers. What he handed me instead were press releases, drafted e-mails, rally posters. Gruesome numbers about the bombings: the 300 dead, the 108 buildings destroyed, the hundreds of Chechens detained, the seventeen who were ultimately found guilty. They were the kind of facts that make one self-conscious about the search for illumination. Which was a good thing, since none was forthcoming. Weeks passed, in fact, before Aleksandr and I had another proper conversation.

It was late, and I was about to reluctantly leave for the day. I'd been retranslating an editorial for a British newspaper, and I waved it at Aleksandr. "There's that," I said. He was sitting at his laptop. On the picture window behind him, I could see the reflection of a game of on-line chess. On the table sat an actual set—expensive, probably, ancient-looking and beautiful. I wondered about that. I had never seen him play.

"Thank you," he said, waving me away.

I couldn't look away from the set. "Are you playing?" I said.

"Chess."

"Yes, I see that."

He dragged a bishop into the center of the screen, then made the corresponding move on the set. "You played at home, right?" he said. His voice was hoarse, as though he'd recently talked quite a lot or hadn't spoken in several days. It would have to be the first, I decided.

"Not too much. With one of the chessmen in Harvard Square. And with my father, some, as I said." I waited for him to comment. He did not.

"You know the Fool's Mate?"

"No."

"It's the shortest possible route to checkmate. It's this." He reset the game on his chessboard. "Two staggered pawns and a bishop in the right place. That's it."

"Does that ever happen in real life?"

"No, never. It's just theoretical, really. It's a scrupulously theoretical game." He sounded, I thought, slightly bitter.

I stared at his set. The manes of the knights twisted out behind them as if moved by some mythical battlefield wind; the kings were bent, gnarled, stately. They were magnificent, more like statues on a medieval bridge than what I had to remind myself they were—essentially toys. The look of the kings made me bold.

"How did you learn to play?" I asked.

Aleksandr scratched his nose. "I saw a problem in the newspaper and I solved it."

"Yes, but how did you learn?"

"That's how I learned. I was four." With his thumb, he tapped over the fool's king. It landed on the board with a click. "Then my mother found me a trainer. Then I enrolled in a correspondence course. Then I came here. The end."

"Oh," I said, and I didn't know what else to say.

"Did you know that in Saudi Arabia they play without bishops or queens?"

"I guess that sort of makes sense."

"It really is a subversive, militantly feminist game, when you think about it."

"Who was your last match?"

He looked at me, as if trying to ascertain whether I was being cruel. "A computer," he said. "Didn't you know?"

"Oh." I lowered my eyes. I remembered this now, vaguely—the amused headlines, the newspapers tripping blithely sardonic over the revelation that man had invented his own match. The best chess mind in the world was defeated by a machine; what, then, was the use of chess minds, or minds in general? I was almost glad that my father hadn't kept his own mind long enough to see it. "I remember something about that, I think," I said.

"You probably do. *Newsweek* called it 'The Brain's Last Stand.' " He laughed ruefully. Then he started to tell me about it.

The thing about the loss, he said, was this. If there had ever been a point to chess—and Aleksandr would be the first to admit that there might not be any point to chess—it was conclusively defeated by the revelation that all chess problems of the world could be unscrambled unconsciously by robot neurons firing into the void. Great chess was no longer the elegant accomplishment of the human mind; the true accomplishment was the ability to create something bigger and better than oneself and to then stand back, amazed. Humans should retire or else find more modest modes of occupation. Everybody knew this. Even the jokes afterward—at the bars, on the news, on the Internet—reflected this knowledge. "In a related story," one of the talk-show hosts had said, "the New York Mets were beaten by a microwave oven."

The worst part was the speed with which the program played—Aleksandr's moves were instantaneously matched and outsmarted by the computer, without the hemming and sweating and doubting that made any brilliant human move feel as though it could have been otherwise. The computer moved with a clinical ruthlessness, and it made Aleksandr understand with a sickening certainty that there was nothing he could think of that the computer hadn't thought of first. It worked with the efficiency of a guillotine.

The man who played for the computer was soft-looking, chubby-cheeked, his hands like chicken cutlets, his leporidian face innocent and wide. He made a little gesture with each move, a nearly imperceptible half-shrug (Aleksandr was never sure whether or not the cameras had recorded it) as if trying to disown it—not me, he seemed to say, not me who's doing this to you, who's humiliating you, who's unraveling the human brain. I'm just the conduit here, the messenger, the mechanism. I am, humbly, just the pawn.

In the end, it took a paltry nineteen moves—the shortest loss of Aleksandr's career. He'd opened with the Caro-Kann Defense—not his usual against human opponents, but for a little while, things were under control: he met the computer's advancing duo of pawns with his own staggered pair, and a brief frenzy of exchange commenced. Next came the ritualistic introduction of the knights. He'd broken his own rule—don't move the same piece twice in the opening—but the beginning was conventional and promising enough. The computer advanced its knight farther, and Aleksandr introduced the second of his. The three knights assembled in a crooked-elbow single file. The computer advanced its bishop. Aleksandr advanced his pawn to e6, bringing it to the flank of his farthermost knight. The computer roused its second knight in response. Then Aleksandr flicked his pawn forward to h6, and as soon as he lifted his finger, he knew. The avid watchers knew. He'd moved it too early in the sequence—he should have introduced his bishop, then awaited the grand entrance of the computer's queen, and only then brought his pawn to h6 to menace the computer's closest knight. That knight would have retreated to the center of the board only to be followed by Aleksandr's. The h6 move in response to the knight was a mistake. It was a mistake, but it wasn't a mistake of strategy—it wasn't a misjudgment, an incorrect forecast into the future. It was a mistake of memory, of basic competence—like losing your car keys, like dropping a dish.

The computer's knight took another pawn, at e6, and crouched breathing down the neck of Aleksandr's king. Should he have taken the knight immediately? Maybe. Later, many, many people—mostly anonymous, mostly on the Internet, mostly people who'd had a decade in their pajamas to think about it—would say that he should have gone straight in then. But he hadn't. He'd wanted to give his king another square to maneuver. He'd allowed the common knight sacrifice, which was not a reflection of the computer's fantastic strategy, in particular; that sacrifice was a dull, almost juvenile move, well known to theory. He'd used it himself against Rusayev in one of their fifty-three games—back when he'd been the new astonishment, the brilliance at which everyone had marveled.

At this point, the newspapers said later, there'd been a look of "terror" on Aleksandr's face that obtained for the rest of the game.

So he'd lost the ability to castle, which the computer then did—quietly, brutally, without comment, the soft man's brow remaining smooth and dry.

Aleksandr took the knight, as he had to, and the bishop sailed into the space that his pawn had prematurely abandoned and put him in check. He jockeyed his king to the right; he had nowhere else to go. It was only the tenth move of the game.

The computer's second bishop crept halfway down the board and sat there waiting. Aleksandr halfheartedly menaced it with his knight, and it temporarily retreated by one square.

There was another exchange of pawns, this one dirtier and more desperate. Aleksandr's neck was soaking wet, and he instinctively looked around the room for an exit. Across the table, the fat man looked calm, his cheeks alternately swollen and slack with the movement of his self-satisfied breaths. This man—who was he? Had he helped to build the computer? Had he studied chess theory and computer code for years, learning how to translate the one into the other, hoping to create an entity that could extrapolate and infer? Probably not. Probably he was a nothing, a person who knew how to push a button or two. Aleksandr thought bitterly that he wasn't only a traitor to chess, as some of the Internet critics had said. He was a traitor to people.

Aleksandr had closed his eyes and sacrificed his queen to take a bishop and a rook. He took the fat man's bishop greedily, as a kind of petty, interim revenge. This was a frantic move: he could feel himself falling down a well; he could hear the scrape of fingernails against concrete. Everybody could. The fat man coughed. The crowd murmured, looked away.

And then he'd resigned. He might not have been smart enough to beat a computer, but he was smart enough to know when he was beaten by a computer. He wasn't going to submit to a humiliating inevitability; he wasn't going to let himself be chased into ever more hopeless cover as the entire world watched. He stood up. He walked out. He did not shake the fat man's hand.

Afterward, people kept asking him about the pawn—the h6 move, a beat too early. He'd had to tell them he didn't know, he didn't know; it was a mistake, and he didn't know where it had come from or why. On the Internet, conspiracy theorists wondered whether he'd thrown the match intentionally, so that he might one day demand a rematch, so that he might one day win more money. But that wasn't true. Maybe it wasn't true, either, that a computer couldn't be beaten. Maybe it wasn't true that a computer's brilliance exceeded all human imagining. Maybe it was just that Aleksandr was forty. Maybe it was just that Aleksandr was tired.

Now the computer sat in the Smithsonian in Washington, D.C., and every day it played reenactments of that final game for public viewing, automatically and on repeat.

Aleksandr told me this, and we were silent. It was the kind of confession that makes you so uncomfortable that the only possible response is to offer one of your own.

"Well," I said. "I have a disease that's going to make me lose my mind."

Aleksandr raised his eyebrows. "What?" Behind his voice, there was a faint hint of laughter. People's response to outlandish information is often to laugh.

"It's called Huntington's," I said. "It's what my father died of. They can test you for it. It's motor functioning, first, actually, then cognitive functioning. Cortex on down."

Aleksandr looked away, which is what everybody does. Then he looked back, and I watched him trying to harness the proper reserves of compassion and pragmatism and empathetic imagination so that he could formulate the right response. Announcements like the one I'd just made have a tendency to fluster and upset people, and their shock and bewilderment often become the central facts of the discussion. I've had a long time to think about Huntington's, and they haven't. But it's true that I sometimes resent the way other people's responses so often own these conversations, and I appreciated Aleksandr's efforts to avoid making that the case.

"This will happen to you—soon?" he said. I could hear him keeping his voice careful and clear.

"This year. Or maybe next."

"God." He looked down. He took off his glasses and squeezed the skin above his nose, a gesture I'd seen him do often enough, and for mundane enough reasons, that I did not believe it to be affected. "God. Irina. I'm so sorry."

It had always been a difficult thing to say to someone. I always felt guilty for ruining the other person's day, and the other person invariably felt guilty if their day hadn't been sufficiently ruined. I will admit it sometimes felt strange to me to make the confession to someone and later catch them laughing, or flirting, or eating a sandwich, instead of tearing at the injustice of it all or sitting quietly at the center of a grand and monstrous grief. The disaster of my life might be only the worst thing another person heard that afternoon; they might have forgotten by dinnertime; they might have been more heartbroken by watching certain movies. I'm always confronted, quite horrifically, with my exact net worth in the eyes of the other person—whether they cry, or have to sit down, or pull their mouth into the expression of a frown even though their eyes are somewhere else.

"Christ," said Aleksandr. "Are you afraid?"

I wasn't sure anyone had ever asked me. People had called me brave, had assumed that there was a courage being exhibited when I smiled at things and showed up to work and brushed my teeth. I wasn't sure that there was. I went to work for the same reason that a person with a gun to his head walks upright: there was absolutely no other option. I could have lain down and died, I suppose. But that was precisely what I was trying to avoid.

"Yes," I said. "I am terrified."

He nodded as though he knew that was the right answer. He picked up his fallen king and rolled it between his forefinger and his thumb. "This is what made you come here."

It wasn't a question, but I said, "Yes."

"This is why you're looking for all these answers about losing games and certain defeat."

"Right."

He put the king facedown on the table. "Let me show you something."

He got up and reached for a large cigar box on the shelf above the desk. He sat down again with the box between us. He opened it, and out popped papers. There must have been hundreds—some were yellow and weathered, others were crisp and white, others were the kind of heavy cream-colored papers that one might reserve for the most important of business transactions. Some of the papers had handwriting—chicken scratchings in faded pencil; bold inky strokes that blurred into smears; the labyrinthine swirling of cursive Cyrillic, almost indecipherable for a person used to reading print—and others were typewritten. A few, ominously, were done with text cut out from magazines.

"What is all this?"

"Death threats," he said. "All for me."

"Oh." I looked at him. I understood that he wasn't trying to make me feel better—or worse, for that matter—but that he was only sharing with me a common reality. It was the taciturn exchange of reminiscences by veterans of some unwinnable war. It was the acknowledgment of the truest and most terrible thing about us—not the only thing but the thing that everybody else tried to ignore. "May I?" I asked.

"Please," he said. "Go ahead." I started to paw through them. *I will hunt you down in the night and cut off your balls,* read one. *You are a traitor to your people and to your country,* read another. Some were subtle—hinting at people and places Aleksandr should probably think to avoid—and others were explicit, explaining in lurid detail exactly how Aleksandr should be killed. Some looked amateurish and unhinged, and I imagined unstable people with matted beards writing by candlelight. Others looked professional and purposeful, and it was easy to envision a different kind of person: a person in a black suit, a person with the money and means to turn threats into reality. A person who wrote what he meant.

"Amazing," I said, because really, it was. And then I said, "Are you afraid?"

He nodded too quickly, and I wondered if, like me, he'd been waiting for somebody to ask.

"I am," he said. "I really, really am." He folded the notes back up and stuffed them into the box with a care that bordered on tenderness. "But there's fear and then there's fear, right?"

"What do you mean?"

"Well, we're both afraid. But your fear is liberating. Mine is confining. Yours brought you here. Mine keeps me in this apartment."

"It's a nice apartment."

He squinted at me. "Yes. A very nice apartment."

"You go to your rallies. You go out. You take great risks."

"I don't fly. I don't eat out. I talk to the Western press constantly, and why do you think that is? Not to give Larry King a good program, I promise. It's because if I'm famous enough in the West, there will be annoying questions should anything happen to me."

"That's smart. That's only smart."

"And you?"

"And me what?"

"Whom do we tell if anything happens to you? Did you have anyone back home?"

I looked at him. I realized what he was asking. "Would I have left if I did?"

"Yes," he said, and nodded slowly. "I am starting to think you would."

That night it rained an unseasonable rain: mild and muddy, great sheets of water tearing from the sky. I took off my hat and then I took off my coat, and then, when I was halfway down the street of my hostel, I took off my shoes. Maybe I would get hepatitis. Maybe I would get pneumonia. For a moment I saw it as Aleksandr saw it: I saw the beauty, the nutty singular luck, of being alone and unaccounted for and barefoot, somewhere out in the enormous world. It was a blessing, perhaps, of a sort. It was like the free fall of the man with a broken parachute: we can't know what he sees on the way down, when the sun angles in a certain way over the rolling landscape, and he reaches out to scrape the clouds. We can't know what he learns in that otherworldly weightlessness.

But then I was in my bed, and I'd frozen myself thoroughly, and my situation seemed less romantic and more pitiful. I turned my face to the wall and folded all of my limbs into my body and tried to sleep. It was almost Christmas, I realized. Somewhere in the month behind me, I had turned thirty-one.

———

After that, Aleksandr and I were friends of a sort. Or maybe it's more accurate to say that there was a charge between us—an energy that was neither romantic nor sexual but was somehow more urgent than bland affection. We knew where the other person was standing in a room. We watched to see how the other person was taking certain information, certain jokes. We trusted each other all of a sudden, with our death threats and our diagnoses.

Of course, really, it was nothing more than this: both of us were marked for dead in different ways. And both of us had such big egos that it had never occurred to us, really, that anyone else had to die. And meeting somebody else who did was, in some ways, a revelation.

Whether this new understanding between us led to my having a greater role in the making of the film, I don't know, though I would suspect so. My one and only credential was native English, though it was true that Aleksandr had adopted advisers based on less. Boris and Viktor, it seemed, had been plucked from a crowd of similar young men only because of some hardscrabble energy that Aleksandr thought he detected in them. For a man with so many people trying to kill him,

Aleksandr was erratic in choosing his confidants—and I wondered about that, too. I wondered if that wasn't his way of tempting fate or trying to deny it. It seemed, though, that he had not made any missteps yet.

The film Alternative Russia was producing was to be an investigation of the spate of bombings that had struck a few Russian cities in the fall of 1999. I remembered these events only vaguely from reality. They'd happened while I was writing my dissertation, and I had the faintest impression of having watched some of the coverage while pulling all-nighters. In America, they were the kind of news story that was covered only on specialty channels or in the pages of foreign affairs magazines. There was some vague tsking from newscasters with shiny hair. They stumbled over the cities' names and arranged their faces into expressions that registered the public's ambient, confused disapproval of bombing, generally, before moving on to stories about dead white children and dogs saving other dogs.

Viktor and Boris, whom I was beginning to think of as Aleksandr's henchmen, were editing the footage for production. I was helping to fix the syntactical mistakes of the voice-over script. For days on end, we engaged in grueling, repetitive viewing of a string of gruesome images: the jagged maw of a building, smoldering red and black; a rivulet of tattered people, all looking assaulted and surprised; the steaming ruins of a highway. The film made the case that the bombings had been ordered—or at least tacitly endorsed—by Putin, in order to scare everybody into voting for him and acquiescing to his incursion into Chechnya. The film's argument hinged primarily on two facts. First, the government had issued a statement expressing its extreme and bitter regret at the attacks in Buynaksk, two days before Buynaksk was attacked. Second, it was initially reported by the government that an explosive called hexogen, or RDX, was used in the bombings. Hexogen, according to the Russian government, was produced only at one heavily guarded military facility in Perm—an unlikely target for crazed Chechens, as Boris pointed out. After the media made note of the incredible hexogen coincidence, the government retracted its initial account.

Those first few weeks at Aleksandr's, I began to feel more alive.

I'd wake up in the mornings, the room smelling thickly of frost, and it was such an unexpected relief each day to know where I was going. I'd gear up in three coats and long underwear; I'd pack up my day's worth of text and proofs and press releases. I'd scrabble over snow, lightly beveled by nocturnal wind. In the underpass outside the Vladimirsky Island metro stop, I'd trip over the vendors stacking their tables with DVDs and porn and souvenir thimbles. Waiting for the metro, I'd watch the damp-looking dogs and their owners, eyes blanked by ketamine. Sometimes it would still be dark out when I reached the outside of Aleksandr's apartment building, and sometimes I'd wait, staring at the sky, admiring the clean brutality of the stars. Sometimes I thought about Jonathan. Sometimes I thought about my father. Sometimes I thought about Aleksandr's death threats and the ways in which he was living the answer to my father's questions. Most often I thought about myself: how grateful I was to have a few moments longer of wakefulness, and a task that merited those moments.

A few days before Boris and Viktor were to travel to Moscow, the apartment held a meeting to discuss the latest political outrages. One of Aleksandr's rivals, an oppositional candidate who espoused a slightly more nationalistic brand of contrarianism than Aleksandr favored, had lately disappeared. His staff had not known where he was. His wife had not known where he was. He'd emerged after a week, wearing enormous black sunglasses and hanging on the arms of his bodyguards, and had immediately held a defensive press conference: "What?" he'd said. "Can't a man get away for a week? Doesn't a man deserve a little vacation, a little privacy?" His wife promptly left him. The rumor was he'd been taken to Kiev by the FSB, given psychotropic drugs until he spilled any bits of dirt or strategy, then brought back in an anonymous black car, retching, lolling his head, without any memory of what had happened. Then there was the human rights lawyer who, just that week, had been gunned down in the middle of a Moscow street. He'd been trying to prosecute the alleged rape of a Chechen woman by a Russian soldier. He died in the street in broad daylight, and afterward nobody had seen anything. Then there was the story of one of the country's richest oligarchs—a man who'd gotten rich on oil but who'd fallen into the government's disfavor when he'd gotten a bit too mouthy about rampant national corruption. He was said to be next in line for arrest, and as a response, he'd bought Nicholas II's entire collection of Fabergé eggs on the international market so that they could once more belong to Russia. "For my homeland," he'd said mistily into the camera.

"Things are going well in this country," said Boris. There was a silence. I drew a border around my notes.

"So," said Aleksandr. "You boys are excited about Moscow, I trust? You'll be taking the car."

"Right," said Viktor.

"And the credit card."

"Obviously."

"And staying at the Moskovsko, of course. Stay away from the Gostinitsa Rossiya; they'll try to poison you with breakfast."

"Yes," said Viktor, "of course."

An amused expression was unfolding across Aleksandr's face, as though he'd played a hilarious trick on all of us that we were about to discover. He nodded at me. "And Irina will, of course, be going with you."

"What?" I said.

"What?" Boris said. He uncapped his pen, and for a moment I was afraid he was going to stab somebody with it.

"You'll take her with you."

Viktor smirked and Boris gaped.

"Really?" said Viktor. "Does she speak Russian?"

"Does she speak at all?"

"Nyet," I said, to be funny.

"She can take notes for you."

"We can take notes for ourselves," said Viktor. "We are functionally literate now, have you noticed?"

"You two are clunky, and you're twelve," said Aleksandr. "It's good to have an innocuous-looking woman with you—excuse me, Irina. It will make people comfortable. The soldier will talk to you more."

"No," said Boris. "I don't think so, no."

Aleksandr looked at me when he answered. "Yes," he said firmly.

"Yes." There was a string of tension between Aleksandr and the two boys. Viktor's neck tensed. Boris opened and released a fist. They were, it seemed, on the brink of mutiny.

But then Nina appeared in the doorway, head cocked to one side, red hair pulled back into a forbidding bun. "My mushroom," she said. "The vegetables are ready."

And with that Aleksandr was gone, and Viktor and Boris were abandoned—their mouths open, their eyes rolling back in their heads as far as they would go.

———

For the trip, Aleksandr loaned us a sleek black limousine the size of a boat. The seats were in a circle, so Viktor and Boris and I were forced to look at one another—or out the windows—the whole way. I opted mostly for the windows. We were meeting the soldier at a club, and Aleksandr had asked Nina to loan me a suitable garment for the excursion. What she'd given me was gauzy and orange and far too small; it stretched unbecomingly whenever I reached out my arms, so I kept them firmly at my sides. It was also too light for the weather, and I skimmed my thighs against the leather seats to keep them warm. Inside the car were bottles of high-end water, extracted from mysterious Siberian springs, and green bulbs of champagne. I felt alternately as though I were on my way to a wedding or a funeral. Viktor and Boris started to tell jokes somewhere around Novgorod Oblast.

"So Stalin comes to Putin in a dream," said Viktor. "He says, 'Putin, in order to maintain your power, you must do two things: paint the Kremlin green and kill all of your political enemies.' Putin looks at him and says, 'Why green?' "

"I've heard that one," said Boris.

"You've heard them all, I suppose," said Viktor.

"I think your mother told it to me in bed."

The interviews that Viktor and Boris had collected so far had been wispy, insubstantial things—compelling for their human interest, but far from ironclad in their evidence. The interviewees told stories that had the haunting familiarity of myths, but in the end there was nothing terribly solid to be gained from them. We watched the interviews in the limousine's DVD player as we drove. The first interview was

with a skittish female university student who wore harsh glasses over
her delicate features and kept pulling her skirt down over her knees.
She had heard two men talking under her window on the night before
the first bombing—a low, flat voice insisting that it be placed *here,* not
there. There had been a sound of scraping, and at first she'd taken it for
an animal of some kind, but then there was more talk, the congested
sound of a heavy man breathing, the retch of a curse.

Was that all? Boris asked from behind the camera. You could hear
the disappointment in his voice.

The young woman blinked and adjusted her glasses. Yes, she said.
That was all.

In the explosion, she'd lost her mother and her little brother, and it
wasn't for a few weeks—until the ringing in her ears had dulled and
the meat-colored burns on her thighs had started to heal—that she'd
remembered the men and remembered that their accent had not been
Chechen.

The next interview was with an enormously fat woman whose el-
dest son had overheard something at a bar on the night before the attack. "Going to be a big day tomorrow?" someone had said, and then
somebody else had laughed a little too cruelly. The woman's son had
told her this while he was in bed, trying to recover from the crushing of
his spinal column, which he never did. He'd been a gymnast. When he
learned he'd be paraplegic for life, he'd wrestled himself into a homemade noose, in a final feat of athleticism, and hanged himself.

She stared down the camera as she talked about it. The camera
zoomed in on her. Tears sprouted in the edges of her eyes, but they
didn't spill over onto her cheeks. It was an affecting moment, emotionally. But her story didn't mean much once you'd thought about it for
thirty seconds.

The final interview was with an older man who was spritely, almost elfin. When the camera zoomed in on him, he resembled nothing
more than a half-starved arctic fox. He talked about something he'd
seen during the attacks: in the melee, amid the running and screaming
and the tearing off of smoldering clothes, he'd seen a man standing
against a tree. He'd thought the man was in some kind of shock, and

he'd started over to assist. But when he got closer, he'd seen that the man was smoking a cigarette and that his lips were twisted into an expression that could be interpreted as a smile. Our older man had turned away and gone to help a woman who lay flattened underneath a piece of cement window ledge.

Later, he told the camera, he'd thought about the man standing under the tree. He'd been there during the explosion, though it took the journalists thirty minutes to arrive, and it took the police nearly an hour. He'd worn a dark coat, and the most striking thing about him was his indifference.

The image of the man dissolved into blue, and Viktor turned off the DVD player. "It's not very convincing, is it?" he said.

"It's moving," I said. "It's heartrending, that's for sure."

"That's not worth much. We don't need to rend any more hearts."

"It's convincing if you're looking to be convinced."

"That's the mark of a weak argument."

We passed villages with damp-looking wooden houses, and I could almost feel the chill dripping from their ceilings, the drafts coming through the blocky walls. There were a few snatches of the romantic East, what you'd imagine if you were the kind to imagine this sort of thing: the spires of Orthodox churches spiking out of wintry mists, a sense of foreignness that stemmed not only from a dislocation of place but also, somehow, of time. There was a feeling of traveling not back or away but out—out on some kind of a Z axis, into a fairy-tale time that never, in fact, was real. My face must have reflected a certain dreaminess, because I caught Boris looking at me with an expression I recognized as contempt. "You think this is kind of romantic, don't you?"

"What?"

"You do. I can tell. You think you are having a little adventure. Well, let me tell you something. This isn't romantic, okay? And it's not an adventure. This is severed heads in alleyways. I don't know why you're here, but this isn't study abroad, okay?"

I nodded. I was surprised and a little numb—it was like the moment after a burn or a wounding, before your body has registered its pain. Maybe I would be a help, maybe I would not be, and I could understand why my presence was resented. But I knew I was not on study abroad. This trip, whatever it was for, was not for the photographs or the postcards. It was not for anecdotes to tell on first dates, for souvenirs to show at dinner parties a decade in the future, for wisdom to tell to adult children going off on their own adventures. It wasn't a matrix or a road map or a source of knowledge that would ever inform my future, as I didn't seem likely to have one.

But there was no way to say any of this, and no reason that it would be convincing. It might be emotionally affecting, but that's not the mark of a good argument—on this we can all agree. So I said nothing, and pursed my lips, and turned away to look out the window.

————

And then we were smashing into the splendor of downtown Moscow at night. All around us there were beautiful women wearing almost nothing but lurid makeup and waiting in long lines outside of pulsing clubs. They looked absolutely terrifying, as well as freezing cold. I stared. The women tossed their hair. Their silver heels cast a spiky sort of light out into the street. Enormous IKEA billboards dominated the skyline. We passed the Pushkin Theater, glowing like an illuminated eggshell in the streetlights. We rolled by the Nord-Ost on Melnikov Street, and I thought of the siege there back in 2002: Spetsnaz blasting poison at the terrorists and hostages alike and everybody dying horribly in the snow. Then we were whirling past more clubs, more restaurants, more dripping, filigreed opulence. We passed the glittering Vagankovsky Cemetery, populated by victims of the eighteenth-century plague. We passed the gilded cupola of St. Isaac's and the wide grinning arc of Kazan Cathedral. We passed a brightly lit café called Gifts of the Sea.

"For homosexuals," said Viktor, leaning in close to me. "Boris, do you need to make a stop?"

The driver dropped us off in front of a club called Absinthe. In the upper windows, I could just make out a stack of pink cubes, a faint dusting of purple light. At the door, a gorgeous woman was turned away; in a rage, she threw her purse into a snowbank.

"How are we going to get Irina through face control?"

I stuck out my tongue.

"Nice," said Boris. "That will definitely improve your odds."

"Good thing we're bribing our way in," said Viktor. He pointed to the top windows. "They watch them from up there."

"Who?"

"The rich men. They get private booths up there with one-way mirrors, and they watch the women dance. If they see one they like, they invite her up for a drink."

We assembled in a line behind red velvet ropes. I stamped my heels against the snow and clamped my hands against each other, trying to keep myself warm. I was thinking that the inadequacy of women's formal wear in the face of extreme weather was probably a patriarchal conspiracy.

"It is not really an invitation, I shouldn't think," said Viktor, rubbing his nose. His time at Oxford had left his English peppered with uniquely British affectations—arabesques on his speech that seemed funny when paired with his accent. "Our blatnoy is up there, I'd bet."

"Why would he want to meet here?" I said through clenched teeth.

"I think it's where he spends most of his evenings. We wouldn't want to disrupt his schedule."

We watched more. In that top corner, something was skewing the light coming through; a phosphorescent-green entity floated out to the window and then flicked away.

"Do they have— Is that an aquarium in there?" I asked.

"I shouldn't be surprised," said Viktor. "I wouldn't be surprised if they had a three-ring circus in there."

"They only serve sushi up there," said Boris. "It's why the world's oceans are running out of fish."

"Have you been to a club like that before?"

They laughed. "No," they said. "But tonight's the night."

"And we're going to make a habit of it someday," said Viktor.

"What day is that?"

"When we're rich," said Viktor. "We're men, so we don't have to be pretty. Only rich."

"Oh, yes?" I said. "And when are you planning on being rich?"

"In the new world order, I suppose," said Boris.

"I thought we were already in that," I said, because I was freezing, which was making me feel difficult.

"When Bezetov's president, he'll make us his most trusted advisers," said Boris.

"Ha. When Bezetov's president, he'll probably start by cutting the salary for federal employees," said Viktor.

I looked at them. "Do you guys really believe that?" I said.

They looked at me. "Which part?" said Viktor.

"You actually believe that Aleksandr will be president one day?"

"Sure," said Boris. "Not this year, sure, we know that. But one day. Look at the Ukraine, you know? It'll happen here eventually. And when it does, he's the obvious choice, right?"

Viktor nodded. "He's been the voice of reason, always. He's Vaclav Havel. Except he'll be the chessmaster president instead of the poet president. Uniquely Russian thing."

"And he's young still," said Boris. "Youngish. He's got a long career ahead of him if he can be careful enough. It's a long life."

I looked at them again. Listening to Aleksandr's speech—as he extolled the virtues of futility, the courage of working against the current—one could believe that nobody thought he would ever succeed. One could believe that failure was, in a way, the point.

"Yes," I said. "I suppose that for some people, it is."

"What?" said Viktor. "You've got your money on someone else? You throwing your hat in the ring? Who else could it be?"

I squinted at him, and when I did, I could see snatches of a future—Aleksandr at the Kremlin, throwing open the windows, firing the security apparatus while the people cheered in the streets—that would happen, if it happened, without me there to watch it. "I don't know," I finally said. "I guess I really don't know."

At the door, Viktor slipped the bouncer a wad of cash. We'd called ahead about this. The bouncer eyed my diaphanous costume bemusedly but took the money. He ushered us through the door. Inside, the music was loud enough to make small reverberations in my sternum. The aquarium, it turned out, was built in to the wall and part of the ceiling. It cast a wash of watery light over the dance floor, and when the fish flicked close to the pane, the light mottled with the psychedelic colors of tropical marine life. The bouncer gestured at a staircase that coiled around the back of the club. "He's up there," he said, pointing up the stairs. "He's always up there."

The air was overrun with the competing claims of outlandish body sprays; I thought of ads featuring alpine vistas and wild rivers. The club's floor was covered in a film of some unidentifiable substance that was the color of mercury and the consistency of silt. At the bar, Technicolor cocktails emerged from behind a smoke machine. The whole place had the feeling of modernity gone amok, as though it were the most elite club in outer space, although along the edges, it was a little more baroque: the sweep of the staircase, the heavy velvet tapestries along the back walls, made me feel that I might look up into the rafters and see horrified operagoers gazing at all the nudity through their lorgnettes. In the center of the room, women danced around in enormous translucent cubes. "SexyBack" was playing. The girls crept up to the sides of the cubes and licked the glass. They were wearing silver pasties and shimmery body paint and nothing, discernibly, else. Boris stared, but Viktor pulled him along.

"Another day," said Viktor.

"In the new world order?" I said.

Our soldier, Valentin Gogunov, was sitting upstairs in a VIP lounge. As Viktor had predicted, he was watching the girls from behind a mirror while drinking an iridescent cocktail. When we closed the doors behind us, the room was corked with silence. We waited. We could feel the throttle of the song under our feet, but we couldn't hear anything anymore. Gogunov ignored us for several long moments with one finger in his mouth, until, presumably, Justin Timberlake's distorted hiccupping was over and the girls had stopped dancing. Then he spoke. "Hello," he said to us, not looking at us. "You are Bezetov's posse." A woman in a shred of pink fabric was dancing near a sullen security detail. "If you could go get us some drinks," Gogunov said to the woman. She pouted momentarily and went.

"The posse," said Viktor. "Yes, I suppose so."

"Sort of a ragtag assortment, aren't you?" said Gogunov, turning in his chair to face us. There was something rehearsed in his manner, and

I found myself liking him for that. Here was a drug runner who really thought about the impression he was making, and you don't see that every day. "You look like graduate students," he said. At this, Viktor cringed.

"You like any of the girls out there?" Gogunov said to him. "We could have them sent up."

"Not just yet," said Viktor. "We'd like to do the filming first."

Gogunov eyed me. "What's the story with the American?"

I wasn't sure how he'd been able to tell that I was American before I even spoke.

Viktor looked at me. "What's the story, American?"

"Mr. Bezetov hired me," I said. "I'm fixing the syntax on the English subtitles."

Gogunov regarded me, then turned to Viktor. "Is he fucking her? He could do better."

"All right," said Viktor. "Enough. She's our colleague."

"Your colleague? Oh, great," said Gogunov. "What, you're going to make her chairman of the Central Bank? Whatever, I don't care. You can keep the American. I'm sure it's all part of Bezetov's master scheme for world domination. Or capitalist utopia. Whatever it is this week. Hey, you have that way of obscuring the face in the film, right?"

"Right."

"And a way to distort the voice? My voice is very distinct. I want that thing that makes the voice low and terrifying."

"Yes," said Boris. "Fine."

"I don't give a shit about your documentary," said Gogunov. "Just so you know."

"Fine," said Viktor wearily. "We are not asking you to give a shit. We are not paying you to give a shit."

"You can put it underneath my name. Not my real name, of course. 'Former Soldier: Does Not Give a Shit.' You can write that."

"Anything for you, soldier," said Boris.

"I don't think your Bezetov's going to get anywhere with this," he said. "I want it on the record. I want it noted that I'm not stupid. If Bezetov's trying to commit suicide, he could do it a lot more cheaply than this. He wouldn't need all the fancy equipment. He wouldn't need to buy the rights to American pop songs. There will be pop songs, right?"

"If this is suicidal, it's very nice of you to join us," said Boris.

"Oh, I'm not joining you, friends," said Gogunov. "My people know all the tricks. Anyway, why bother a small businessman?"

"Why bother a small businessman if you haven't already, you mean."

Gogunov made a face. "I just want to get my revenge on the fucking Russian ground forces. Worst years of my life. Half those people were common criminals before they signed their contracts, you know? Hard to have a civilized conversation with anybody. I'm a man of letters. And then you don't know what fun is until you've had dysentery in Siberia. Ever had shit freeze to your ass? It happens. Now, how much are you paying me?"

"What are you telling us?"

"Depends on what you're paying me."

"You seem like you do fairly well already," said Boris. "For a small businessman."

Gogunov frowned. "Entrepreneurs are the backbone of society."

"I only hope you can manage the tax burden," I said.

"Just barely," said Gogunov. "But I suppose it's my civic duty."

"Well," said Viktor. "Consider this your civic duty, too."

"For love of the motherland?"

"Whatever."

"You can turn the camera on," said Gogunov cheerfully. "Though it's probably worth reminding you that my security apparatus is just as extensive as your Bezetov's and probably somewhat less scrupulous. And they're very, very defensive of my character."

"Yes," said Boris through gritted teeth. "We understand."

"I can't predict how they will react to any number of slights, such as a failure to obscure my face or voice, or failure to compensate me properly, or failure to be protective of my privacy."

"Yes," said Viktor. "We got it." He set up the camera, and Gogunov settled back in his chair.

"How do I look?" he said.

"You should be in the pictures," I said.

"Wrong answer," said Gogunov.

"It doesn't matter how you look," said Viktor. "You're going to look like a shadow."

"Right answer," said Gogunov. He leaned forward. "You understand I'm not fucking with you fellows, right? I'm addressing you, too, gorgeous. You have children, girlfriends, lesbian loves? Little expensive pets?"

"No," said Boris. "But we're awfully fond of ourselves."

"Good," said Gogunov. "That's as it should be. I'm not doing this for democracy. So don't think I won't have you all killed if you screw me over."

"We won't screw you over," said Viktor. "And we don't care why you're doing it."

"I'm ready now," said Gogunov.

Viktor assembled the camera, which issued a clinical red light. Gogunov looked down at his nails, then up at the camera. Suddenly, he seemed slightly bashful—he was self-conscious about arranging his face, even though he seemed to believe it wouldn't matter. "Can I start?"

"Whenever the muse moves you," said Viktor.

Gogunov waited a couple of moments more, and then he started. "I was a guard at the military facility," he said. "I wasn't supposed to be on duty that night."

"And what night was this?" said Viktor.

"This was the night of September 3, 1999." Something about talking on camera—even though it wouldn't be his voice or his face doing the talking—had made Gogunov polite, almost deferential. It occurred to me that this man—this drug runner, this soldier—was mildly afraid of public speaking.

"The night before the first of the bombings," said Viktor.

"Right."

"The one at the mall."

"Right," said Gogunov. "I'd switched schedules with one of the other guards, who was sick that night. He was always getting sick— maybe he was faking, I don't know—but it worked out for me either way. We had a deal. I wasn't in charge of the RDX silo, but I had a good view of it. Most nights we'd spend half the shift drinking cognac and bullshitting each other. But that night I'd opted out of all that and gone to stand by the door. I was stone-cold sober, and I know what I saw."

"What made you go stand by the door?"

Gogunov winced. "I was texting my wife, to be perfectly honest, and I didn't want the guys to see. I'd just gotten texting on my phone, and she was always making me text her. That should have been a clue. We were married seven years, and the texting should have been the *first* clue. Don't put that in, okay? You'll edit that out, right?"

"Yes," said Viktor tiredly. "Probably."

"Anyway. This was maybe quarter to three in the morning. A convoy of trucks wheeled up, and the door was opened for them."

"What did you think of it at the time?"

"It's the military's facility. It exists for their use. It's not uncommon for orders to be placed for these materials—although less so then, before the second war, and rarely, it's true, in the middle of the night."

"And?"

"And it wasn't recorded in the logs, which is, as you can imagine, a pretty serious, pretty unusual oversight."

"And so?"

"And so I don't know what the fate of that RDX was. All I know is that it sailed out of the facility at three in the morning, and it went to military men. There was no break-in. There were no Chechens."

We let the camera see it. We let whoever would one day see the film hear it. Gogunov leaned forward.

"There was something else," he said. "One of my coworkers brought me tea around three-fifteen, which was about the middle of my shift. He handed it to me, and I took a sip and spat it out. It tasted horrible—beyond rancid, not like something organic that had rotted but like something you were never supposed to consume in the first place. I almost vomited onto the concrete right there. 'What the hell is this?' I asked him. 'It's tea,' he said. 'What did you put in it?' I asked him. 'It tastes like poison.' And it did. 'What,' he said, 'is the milk off? It's just tea, milk, and sugar.' 'What sugar?' I asked, because we were out of sugar in the back office. 'I took some from the truck,' he said. 'From the bags of sugar. Just a tiny bit.' '*What* bags?' I said. I went out to look. Sure enough, on the trucks, on these bags, was printed the word 'sugar.' The next day, the mall in Moscow exploded."

He took a sip of his drink. He was slowing down. He was starting to enjoy the camera.

"I don't know what happened to that RDX. I don't know for sure. But I do know that the military facility at Perm does not, and has never, spent its resources on the armed defense of sugar."

He looked into the camera. "That's it," he said. "You can turn it off."

Viktor turned it off. "That's helpful," he said. "That's really helpful." He started to fold up the camera's arthropod limbs.

Gogunov leaned forward again. "That's not all," he said. "I lied a second ago when I said that that was all."

"Yes?"

Gogunov took a sip of his drink and smiled. "The real question is who supervised this transfer? Who let go of the RDX, and where did they think it was going? Why did they think they were mislabeling the truck? I was just a common soldier. And you know, they don't buy us flak jackets, so I'm inclined to be bitter. My perspective is maybe not worth as much as somebody out at Perm. Somebody who is in charge, who might know the answers to these questions. You get a real answer from any of them, and then you've got military involvement. Not just tacit endorsement or blundering incompetence. But military involvement—government involvement. As much as I hate the Russian army—and I fucking *loathe* the Russian army—even I don't think they engage in these kinds of tricks for fun. And as much as I think you people are ridiculous—and words can't do justice to how ridiculous I think you are—even I can't resist a good conspiracy theory. That's just human nature. They've done studies on this."

"Okay, okay," said Viktor. "You have a name for us?"

"There is a man out there," he said. "The lieutenant running Perm. Andrei Simonov. I am sure he knows. But I have no idea how you'll get him to talk to you. I don't think you can buy him. I don't think you can blackmail him. But then you people are charmers. Especially that one." He pointed at me. "She's a dream."

"Enough," said Viktor.

"You know," said Gogunov. "I am not a fan of your Bezetov, particularly. I don't like his face."

"You've mentioned," I said.

"He'd probably do better with this country than Putin, but that's not much of a compliment. And I don't think he's going to win this election. But there's this. Even if the town madman kills the dragon, the people will cheer. They will celebrate him. They will make him their king." He winked at me. "It's an aphorism. It's a metaphor. Putin is the dragon, in this case, and Bezetov—"

"I get it."

"Think about it."

"I will," I said.

"I bet you will. You must have gotten here by thinking, yes? Since it wasn't by sitting around looking pretty, that's for sure."

"Enough," said Viktor, and I looked at him.

"You are free to stay," Gogunov said. "But I'm going to order up a lap dance now."

"We'll go," said Boris, and we did—retreating down the stairs, underneath the cerulean light of the aquarium, past the box of emaciated women miming fellatio. Silver pixels caught in my coat, and I held on to Viktor's shoulder to keep from drowning.

Outside, the car was waiting for us. Viktor packed the equipment into the back. We drove away from the club. I turned and looked out the window again as we whirred through the city. As Gogunov had instructed, I thought about what he had said. And all around us, lights wavered like undiscovered civilizations across an ocean, and music pounded out into the street, and drunk girls collapsed silently into the snow.

17

ALEKSANDR
___

St. Petersburg, 2007

For New Year's, Nina insisted on a party. She wanted it catered, though Aleksandr had said that the risk was too high; instead, she'd bought everything separately and spent the afternoon watching the servants assemble great plates of appetizers—herring soaking in cream, boiled beef tongue, salmon caviar, salads drowning in mayonnaise, pickled cucumbers to go with the vodka. Vlad stood at the door wearing a suit, pretending to welcome the guests and eyeing them up and down—for forbidden faces, for pocket bulges, for eyelid twitches. He had a list, and he checked their names and IDs against it, and when he'd found the guest's name—and only then—did he smile and nod at one of the servants to offer a plate of hors d'oeuvres.

Nina stood nodding magnanimously at anyone who entered. She took jackets, then covertly handed them to one of her women attendants. Aleksandr stood off to the side— out of the line of vision of the doorway, out of the line of fire of the doorway—and greeted his guests. Mostly, they were friends and friends of friends and close colleagues, though there were a few other, more distant people, too. Aleksandr ducked into a linen closet and pretended to look for napkins when he saw Misha enter. In recent years, Aleksandr had tried to avoid being in the same room alone with Misha. Over the months, Right Russia had only grown shriller; Misha tolerated ever meaner elements in its ambit, and Aleksandr tried to keep his dealings with them to a minimum. Aleksandr had even asked Vlad to keep the wingnuts away from him so that he wouldn't have to talk to them socially, though Vlad had said that was really not his job.

At any rate, Aleksandr had to admit that Nina had done well with the party. The lights were low, the tables were decorated with vases of some sort of pale winter flower, and tiny tea candles lined the window-sills. Outside, St. Petersburg was twinkling and delirious, done up in its New Year's finery, illuminated by the adamantine windows of fif-teen thousand fraying mansions. In the corner, Irina stood drinking a glass of white wine and talking to Viktor and Boris, who seemed to be tolerating her presence better since their return from Moscow with the interview. At eleven-thirty, the staff came around with chilled bottles of champagne. Aleksandr rarely drank, and when he did, he almost always drank alone. Alcohol was too easy a target; it was hard to taste something acrid in it, and the early effects of a poisoning could be too easily confused with intoxication. But it was New Year's, and Aleksandr was feeling a tad reckless—it wasn't a feeling of celebra-tion, exactly, it was the kind of subdued, bittersweet tenderness that takes you into rooms to look out over your gorgeous nocturnal city, alone. So he took a glass of the champagne and went into the study. Through the window, he could see the glowing onion domes, the an-gular business offices, the indigo fold of the sky, the splashes of neon light from the clubs. From the living room came the trill of a woman's laughter; the gruff arpeggio of a man telling a story. Aleksandr liked having these sounds in his apartment, but he also liked walking away from them and into an empty room.

Irina and the boys had come back from Moscow earlier in the week, and he'd listened and felt childishly jealous when they talked about riding through the streets, watching the women, gazing at the capi-talistic vigor of the Arbat, even if they couldn't shop there. They'd en-countered some difficulties—hotels that knew who they were wouldn't accommodate them; restaurants that knew who they were wouldn't serve them—but they were protected by a veil of some anonymity, and they were stopped only when rumors went running out ahead of them. They could still go to museums mostly unmolested; they could watch the great Muscovite nightlife from a car in the street.

Aleksandr shivered. Out the window, the preemptive fireworks flashed icy silver against blue sky; the starlight skimmed across the river, making it glitter like the eyes of animals in the dark woods.

Sometimes, though he wasn't proud to admit it, he had to wonder how it would end for him. He hoped—when he hoped for anything—that it would be a shooting or a quick shove out a high window. He mightily feared a poisoning, although a high-end poison—polonium, for example, something that would be impossible to trace back concretely, something that would be impossible to treat (unlike thallium, which was cheaper but could be combated with a dose of Prussian Blue)—was expensive: two or three million dollars in cash for enough to kill a man. So he had economics on his side, at any rate.

Aleksandr was approaching the nation's average life expectancy for a male, anyway, and sometimes he wondered if it weren't a little presumptuous, a little elitist, to wish for more time. When he'd traveled across the country, he'd seen entire villages—the detritus of state-sponsored farm cooperatives—that were composed almost entirely of drunks, dying, disabled, the young people all gone to the cities, the barns left unpainted, the vegetables rotting in rows, the old people treating their heart attacks with swigs of fetid homemade hooch. Who was Aleksandr to live when other people lived like this?

When a finger grazed the side of Aleksandr's shoulder, he just about leaped through the window.

"Don't be so jumpy," a voice said.

Aleksandr turned around. Misha's head was cocked to one side, his shirttails falling out of the back of his suit. He was holding a tumbler of vodka between his fingers, and he was letting it tilt so far to the side that Aleksandr was sure it was going to fall from his hand and stain the carpet.

"Misha. How are you?" Aleksandr offered his hand, although he didn't like touching Misha. The years had not been kind to him—

there was still that persistent sickliness, the sense that the contours of his face refracted the light unnaturally, in defiance of physics.

"How am I?" Misha sneered. He did not take Aleksandr's hand.

"Yes, Mikhail. It's a polite question. It's what polite people ask each other." Aleksandr wasn't sure how Misha had gotten invited. Nina must have been looking at an old list.

"Well, if that's what the polite people are saying. Thank you for teaching the peasant your ways."

Aleksandr stared at Misha. He'd had to train himself to look at Misha when was first back from the psikhushka—he'd had to force himself to hold Misha's gaze and talk straight to his face. Misha had seemed so horrifying then; he'd been a monstrous anti-prophet, and his message was as terrifying as his face. Now he struck Aleksandr as merely reduced. He was no uglier or more paranoid than most people. "What do you want today?" said Aleksandr.

"Why do you assume I want something? Why can't I just be saying hello to my old friend?"

"We were never friends."

"I can't argue with that, I suppose." Misha ran his hand along Aleksandr's desk. Trapeziums of artificial light sifted through the picture window and went wheeling across the carpet. In the distance, Aleksandr could hear the blare of premature noisemakers. "I do want something, come to think of it, Aleksandr. Now that you mention it."

"Yes?"

"You're doing a movie, I understand."

"This is not a secret."

"I want Right Russia included."

"Included?" Aleksandr laughed a strategic, mirthless laugh. He wondered if anybody ever laughed like this involuntarily.

"Affiliated. I want us affiliated. I think this film sounds like a good idea."

"I sure appreciate that, Misha."

"So?"

"Do I have to point out that you've done nothing for us?"

"Not for lack of trying. You don't ask us to participate in your rallies, your little conferences. I know you're embarrassed of us." He produced a cigarette from somewhere in his pants pocket and started to light it.

"Could you put that out?"

"You don't smoke now?"

Aleksandr squirmed. "Nina doesn't like it."

"To think! The messiah of the Slavs doesn't smoke because his scary wife tells him not to!"

"Honestly, Misha."

Misha squinted at Aleksandr, then took a puff. "In all these years," he said. "In all your panels, your assemblies, your full-page ads, you've offered us nothing. It's time for some cooperation."

"Cooperation? Misha, don't be nonsensical. I need to have some credibility. Right Russia is—you're not credible, let's say. Let's just leave it at that."

"And you are?"

Aleksandr looked back out the window. All across the city, people were popping open bottles, edging closer to the person they wanted most to kiss at midnight. And here he was, standing with a jaundiced belligerent, slack-jawed and accusatory. Aleksandr closed his eyes. "Misha," he said, gearing up to sound ludicrous. "It's not you, you know, I don't think this about you. But some of your guys are a little unhinged. 'Russia is for Russians' and all that?"

"It's just a slogan."

"It's just a slogan? A quarter of the population thinks it's fascist."

Misha took another breath of cigarette, and Aleksandr could hear the halting effort of his lungs. "You want to make policies based on the polls? You know what kind of a country we'd have then?"

"It's a criminally xenophobic philosophy. People get killed for it."

"You're accusing us of murder now?"

"Don't be hysterical. I'm accusing you of stupidity. And bad marketing. I don't want it near my film."

Misha sucked at his cigarette contemplatively and arranged his face into an expression of overdone admiration. He looked down at the carpet. He gazed out the window. He offered a low whoosh of appreciation. "You have a lovely apartment. Have I told you that?"

Aleksandr said nothing. There was no right answer.

"Quite different from that old place you were in, right? Funny, isn't it, Aleksandr? How far you've come?"

Aleksandr took a gulp of his champagne.

"Where is it you're from again? Where your sister still is? Irkutsk, is it?"

"Okha. Sakhalin."

"Right. That's right. Sakhalin." Misha was silent for a moment, tracing the tip of his shoe along the floor. Corpuscles of dirt fell off, and he ground them into the carpet. "I think," he said finally, "that you owe me this much."

"Owe you? Owe you what? Owe you how?"

Misha raised his eyebrows. "You will remember, I'm sure, that I know about what happened to Ivan."

Aleksandr stared. "Know what about what happened to Ivan?"

"I'm surprised you've forgotten. I know that you let him die."

Aleksandr thought of Ivan—his painful thinness, the way he bent against the snow when he walked, the way he believed in his own limitless capacity to outrun and outwit. Aleksandr could look back and see that Ivan had been fragile, although at the time he'd seemed invincible. He was the person who'd seemed able to see the symbols and know what they stood for; he'd seemed to have the capacity to intuit the reality that ran underneath the fictions like subterranean reservoirs beneath a city. But if Ivan had been fragile, Aleksandr had been barely standing upright—he could look back and see how naive, how outrageously vulnerable, he had been. He hadn't let Ivan die. He'd spent half his life thinking about it, and he was sure. You could let something happen only if you knew it was coming; you could let something happen only if you had any idea how to stop it.

"I didn't," said Aleksandr.

"But you did. You must have. They came after him and not you? They left you alone all those years for no reason? It's not like Nikolai didn't know where you lived, even before you became their precious national chess baby and went to live in the woods. No, I don't think so. I think you must have done them a favor. I think you must have made them a compromise. Even before you made all those other com-

promises. It took me a long time to figure this out, but now I have."
Misha smiled a weirdly good-natured smile. "And so now I think you
owe me."

Aleksandr took a breath. "I don't know, Misha," he said. "I do not
know. I've thought about it a lot. I don't know why they went for Ivan
and not me. Probably because I wasn't important enough to bother
with. I was only distribution. They probably tried, and missed, and
figured that the point had been sufficiently made."

Misha looked at him strangely. "No. I am sure they did not try and
miss."

"Or maybe I was too important," said Aleksandr. He was starting
to hear the pleading tone in his voice. "Maybe my relative fame af-
forded me some protection. And my game made me a credit to Russia.
Everyone said so. Maybe they didn't want to lose me because of that.
Maybe they knew even then they were going to sponsor me. And yes,
you're right, maybe they knew even then that I'd let them. There was
no explicit compromise, Misha. There wasn't. But maybe they thought
my death would be noticed."

"Noticed? Aleksandr, since when do they care what people notice?
Maybe now this is your protection—your fame, such as it is. Maybe
now they don't want to try anything too obvious, anything that will
cause a stir at Western universities. But then? No, friend. I don't think
that was it, either."

Aleksandr thought back to the night when Nikolai came barging
into his apartment, his eyes carved out and terrified, his hands shaking
as if recoiling from the blowback of a gunshot. Aleksandr should have
known then. Of course he should have known.

"I don't know," said Aleksandr. "I don't know. I don't know. It
probably should have been me."

"There we can agree, then."

They were quiet for a moment. On his darker nights, it was true,
Aleksandr had trouble believing that there was anything he'd done—
anything—that Ivan wouldn't have done, and done better, if he'd
lived. No matter how famous or powerful or applauded he was, no
matter how much the Western press fawned over him, no matter how

ugly and crazed Misha got, and no matter how stigmatized his group became, there would always be the fact that Misha knew something that nobody else did. He knew that when they'd come for Ivan, they'd come for the better man.

"In any case," said Aleksandr, "this doesn't change that you can't be affiliated with the film. I'm sorry, Misha."

"Yes," said Misha. He grinned boyishly. "Yes, I imagine you will be."

Misha left, and when he opened the door, Aleksandr could hear the tidal rise and fall of voices in flirtation, in playful argument. He caught a glimpse of Nina, skeins of her red hair tumbling down her back. Her arm was on the arm of a rebel economist, her head tilted backward in amusement. Misha closed the door behind him.

In the dark, Aleksandr went back to the window and rested his forehead against the cool of the frosted glass. Through the door, he could hear the counting down, the shouts, the pop and fizz of champagne opened and poured. He raised his glass and toasted 2007.

———

At the end of January, Aleksandr was invited to a book-and-chessboard signing at a university library. "A little small, don't you think?" Aleksandr had said when he looked at a description of the venue. Nina had raised her eyebrows at him and asked if he wanted to squander an opportunity to lecture to a group of sympathetic young people because the venue was too small. Then she'd rolled her eyes and tapped her fingers on the table, slowly, and he could almost hear her wondering who he thought he was these days, although he had no idea when *she'd* become the defender of the masses. So he'd gone, and stood at the podium, and watched as security checked IDs at the door and patted everyone down for weaponry. Vlad and the rest of the security stood near the exits, sturdy and still as Greek columns. Once a sluggish line of students had shuffled in—and once Aleksandr felt sure that even though the hall was only half full, no one else was coming—he pulled on his glasses and took out his notes and started to speak.

From the podium, he could see the neon flashing of text messages. In the back, two shaggy-haired men swapped a crossword; in the front, a young man and a young woman whispered madly, audibly.

Aleksandr tried anyway. He wanted to impress upon them the virtues of democracy, the dangers of apathy. "In this nation," he said, "the profits are privatized, the losses are nationalized."

Across the room, he could see eyes glass over; he could hear knuckles crack. One man in the front row looked up with shining and irrepressible eyes. He leaned forward. He appeared to be taking notes. Aleksandr decided to direct the rest of his speech to this young man.

"Putin," boomed Aleksandr, "is motivated by nothing as pure as a wrongheaded philosophy. He's motivated by money, by self-protection, by indifference—which can be quite as dangerous as ideology."

Across the audience went muffled yawns. In the front row, the young man's eyes shone. Aleksandr looked down at his notes. Usually, he paused for cheering; now the whole speech was going more quickly than it should, more quickly than had been advertised.

"He is the most humorless leader we've had in quite some time," continued Aleksandr. "You will remember that *Kukly,* our former beloved puppet-comedy television program, was allowed to skewer even Brezhnev. But when they came out with a Putin puppet, they were promptly canceled. When our freedom to mock has been curtailed to such a degree, how can we pretend that we've made real progress since Communist times?"

In the back row, a woman spat out her gum, rolled it up in a tissue, and put it in her purse.

"But if Putin is a tyrant, we are perhaps complicit in his tyranny. Fifty-eight percent of the population, when polled, said that if they made a decent salary, they would immediately emigrate. This alarming statistic no doubt contributes to the sense of apathy among our nation's young people when confronted with abuse after abuse. "

The audience looked down; they looked away. The young man grinned with fervor, with seriousness of purpose.

"And so," Aleksandr concluded, "we have become a nation of people who are happy to sit on our backsides in our warm kitchens. We will be happy to do so until they take our kitchens away. Thank you."

The audience applauded in staccato hiccups. In the back row, somebody sneezed.

Afterward, a desultory line of students waited for Aleksandr to sign their books or their chessboards. A long-haired woman asked for Aleksandr's autograph "for her friend"; a stout young man asked for one "for his teacher." Finally, the young man from the front row approached, clutching a chessboard under his elbow and looking nervous.

"Hello," he said gravely.

"Young man," said Aleksandr. "It's good to see you. I think you were the only person awake out there."

The young man smiled. "Mr. Bezetov," he said. "You are my favorite chess player of all time. Would you do me the honor of signing my board?"

"Of course."

Aleksandr smiled, reached for his pen, and felt a blunt wedge slam against the side of his head. A wash of red came over his eyes; there was a moment of numbness and then pain with a surprising edge. Aleksandr clutched his head and turned back to the young man just in time to see him holding the unsigned chessboard and gearing up for another swing.

"I admired you when you were a chess player," he snarled. "Now you're just a dirty politician."

A woman shouted, and Vlad lunged at the young man, scissoring him into submission. The young man was shaking with rage, still clutching the chessboard in one trembling hand, the bony finger of the other pointing at Aleksandr.

"You are a traitor to Russia and a traitor to chess," he said, and Aleksandr would always remember it was the second insult that counted, a little.

"Shush," bellowed Vlad.

"You are!" screamed the man. There was a webbing of saliva between his top and bottom lip; his eyes—which a moment ago had seemed promisingly idealistic, bursting with a longing for democracy and a free press and governmental transparency—now seemed mildly insane.

"Shut up," said Vlad, elbowing the man in the gut.

"It's okay," said Aleksandr. "Let him shout." Because, really, that was the whole point.

And so the man shouted hoarse admonitions as Vlad marched him out of the auditorium. And when he was out and the door was shut, all the remaining students took out their phones and started to text.

Later that night, Nina held a compress to Aleksandr's head and made him a bowl of ice cream, even though she usually didn't like him eating sweets.

"My mushroom," she said. "You're so brave."

And he almost had to feel that it had been worth it for this moment, for the sympathy in Nina's voice, for the feel of her cool fingers against his neck.

"Look," Aleksandr said a few weeks later. "We need something different."

Irina, Viktor, and Boris were sitting around the table. Boris was holding a remote control and flipping compulsively between Rossiya, NTV, and Channel One. Irina was staring vacantly, spinning a kopeck around and around. Lately, she'd seemed to fade some, her skin paling almost to translucence, her eyes hardening into a grim dullness that reminded him of sepia photos of Siberian mothers in shawls, surrounded by their half-dozen living children. Aleksandr didn't know if this was a function of poor health, or loneliness, or the interminable stretch of a Russian winter—the unendurable combination of cold and dark and the omnipresent abuse of salt and sand.

"Just because you get hit on the head with a chessboard once," said Viktor.

"It's not about the chessboard," said Aleksandr. "Boris, can you turn off the TV? Irina, can you stop spinning that?" She looked at him balefully and stopped. Recently, Aleksandr had become increasingly uncomfortable in Irina's presence, and not only because her color and demeanor seemed to suggest the proximity of death, which he was already exhausted by thinking about. More so, he was uncomfortable with the extent to which he'd failed to answer her questions. He had looked through letters, diaries, notes from that time, and Irina's father did not appear—he was a specter, haunting the pages of *A Partial History of Lost Causes* (now as frail as dried leaves) and Aleksandr's silly, flummoxed poems about Elizabeta (as trite now as they had ever been).

Aleksandr painfully wanted to give Irina something of her father—some omen, some benediction. But what could you say when you had nothing to say? The man had written a letter to him, apparently. This Irina had already known.

Then there was the broader question—the question of what one does, of how one plays, when one is facing certain doom. Irina might not have known, when she first came to St. Petersburg, how explicitly the totality of Aleksandr's current existence would be an answer to that question. But it was not a satisfying answer, and Aleksandr could feel Irina's disappointment, and it hurt him. What do you do in the face of certain doom? You try to make a little movie, you try to take sensible precautions, you try to enjoy your espresso and your frigid wife and your breakfast. Is this inspiration? Is it noble? You brush your goddamn teeth. This, he suspected, Irina also already knew.

Viktor smirked and cracked his knuckles. "It's a little bit about the chessboard, I think, sir."

Aleksandr felt the knob on his head. It was taking a surprisingly long time to disappear; when he thrashed his head against his pillow on these recent sleepless nights, it throbbed so much that he swore until Nina looked at him reproachfully and took her blanket into the living room.

"Maybe," he said. "Maybe it's partly about the chessboard. But it's indicative of a larger problem, yes?"

"You've been happy with the rallies, haven't you? The turnout has been good, hasn't it?" said Boris. "This was really just this one incident."

"Yes, yes, the rallies," said Aleksandr. He scratched his head again. It was true that the chessboard signing had been an anomaly, an aberration due to incompetent promoting. Typically, the turnout at the rallies was hearty but not astonishing; he knew that people would show up to see him, but interest had in no way reached a critical tipping point, the juncture from which everything would flow easily and exponentially forward. Still, they came. They came right after Putin had accused Aleksandr personally of being a puppet of the United States; they came and stood outside with placards reading WE ARE THE WEST'S FIFTH COLUMN. They came, often in the cold, which impressed Aleksandr, especially when he thought of the bitter implausibility of his first winter in St. Petersburg, before he'd been able to buy protection from the cold at almost all times. The presence of such cold was like the absence of oxygen—it quickly became the only relevant fact about reality—and Aleksandr knew that the people who came out and endured it were serious people. But still, he thought.

"The rallies are fine," he said. "But I'm thinking it's time to try something new. An infusion of new energy, right? At least give our supporters something new to support. At least give Putin something new to condemn."

Boris clicked his pen open and shut his eyes.

"We want people to watch this film," said Aleksandr. "I know everybody's working hard on it, but nobody's seeing us working, you know? So we need to keep generating interest in the movement in the meantime. We need to be engaging in guerrilla marketing."

"Well," said Boris. His voice sounded indulgent, like he was placating a child or a paranoiac. "There are always hunger strikes. If you can't speak, you can go on a hunger strike to show that you've been silenced."

"Khordokovsky did one in prison," said Viktor. "He refused even water."

"We could do that," said Boris. "People pay attention to those."

"A bit unoriginal, don't you think?" said Aleksandr.

"You just like your dinner too much," said Boris.

"Maybe Nina could go on a hunger strike on our behalf," said Viktor. "I'm pretty sure she's already got one under way."

"Enough," said Aleksandr, and Viktor stopped smiling. "Any other ideas?"

There was a pause. The clicking of Boris's pen sounded like an insect placing its pincers delicately together. In the corner, Irina shook herself. "Well," she said.

"Yes?" said Aleksandr. He was surprised she was talking. Her desolation hovered around her like an electron cloud.

"It's going to sound silly."

"I don't doubt it at all," said Boris.

"Try us," said Aleksandr.

"Lately, I've been thinking about a funeral."

For a moment Aleksandr did not know what she meant; and then, for another horrible moment he thought he did. "A funeral?" he said carefully.

"Yes," she said. "A Funeral for Democracy."

Aleksandr exhaled and realized he'd been holding his breath.

"A Funeral for Democracy?" said Viktor. "A bit bleak, isn't it?"

Aleksandr leaned forward. "What do you mean, a Funeral for Democracy?"

"Well," said Irina. "You could get a life-sized dummy representing democracy. You could have it lying there, dead—I don't know, maybe under placards complaining about various things. And then you could march it through the street on the way to burial."

"A little melodramatic, yes?" Boris sniffed. "A little bit obvious, don't you think? A little bit much?"

"It was just a thought."

"Interesting," said Aleksandr. "I think it could be interesting." Off-hand, he sort of liked it. It was outlandish, yes, but he had nothing against outlandish. It was confrontational and bizarre. He thought young people would respond to it.

"It just strikes me as somewhat hysterical," said Boris. "That's all. But maybe that's what we're doing now? Hysterical?"

"I think what I like about it is that it would make for a good visual," said Aleksandr. "One snapshot of that is pretty powerful, don't you suppose? As opposed to the rallies, where someone would have to sift through a transcript, which would never be printed anyway, in order to get the main point."

Viktor dragged a fingernail against the dry skin on his hand. Boris chewed on his lower lip.

"Right, my men? You can tune out a person talking—you're all doing that right now. And you can refuse to read something that's put before you. But if your eye happens to land on a photograph, you can't decline to understand it. It's imported directly into your head, whether you like it or not."

"Yes, but don't you think it's a little theatrical for us? A little histrionic?" said Boris. "I wouldn't want our supporters to get the idea that we're into stunts now."

"Maybe a stunt is what is needed now. Maybe some political theater is in order. I, for one, have been getting bored of our usual tricks. Irina, I'd like you to write up a plan of action."

"Me?" said Irina. Viktor and Boris exchanged dark, inscrutable looks, but Aleksandr didn't care. Every time Irina had something useful to do, she seemed to brighten; her depression, as far as he could tell, seemed to be a pragmatic kind. This might be good for her—not that he knew what was or wasn't good for a person in her position, whatever that was, exactly.

"You," said Aleksandr. "Get out of here."

––––––––

That evening Aleksandr paced in his study and thought about the future. Against the sky, a tiny airplane flashed its cosmic green lights. He thought about what would happen when the film came out. When it came out, he figured, he'd be able to get the formal nomination from Alternative Russia. And that would make the Kremlin afraid of him, and he'd still be afraid of them, and they would hold each other in some nervous mutual regard. Like a two-way Zugzwang, in chess, when it was disadvantageous for either player to make a move.

Except that wasn't quite right. Playing Putin was more like playing that awful computer—there was nothing you could think of that he hadn't thought of first. The election was already decided, Putin's successor already picked and groomed; the only questions were which of his lackeys it would be and when the decision would become publicly known. No Russian theaters would show the film, and Aleksandr had no delusions about getting it on television. But he did have some modest hopes for the Internet, for YouTube, for pirated DVDs, for word of mouth. For people passing contraband hand to hand in the streets. It had worked for him, almost, once before.

The airplane made its way to the center of the city's sky. There was something lonely about the scene: the plane's cold flashing colors, the snarl of buildings below, and all that tremendous sky in between.

That was it, he thought: there would be a week, maybe ten days, when it would look like he had a chance. He wouldn't, of course he wouldn't, but maybe—for a week, for ten days—he'd trick enough people into thinking he would. Maybe they would get angry at long last, and maybe they would start causing some real trouble.

But maybe, he thought, not. Maybe the week would come and go, and the movie would be seen and dismissed, and his nomination would be ignored, and the handpicked successor to Putin—the man who would babysit the post for four or eight years before Putin came back for another round—would calmly, confidently sail to victory.

Out the window, the office lights were blinking like beacons, and the Neva was turning silver in the winter dusk. The small airplane was slipping out of Aleksandr's line of vision—out of the edges of the city, out of the cast of the lights—and off into a different, deeper dark.

18

IRINA

St. Petersburg, March 2007

Viktor and I began promotion for the Funeral for Democracy a full two months before it was scheduled. We used the Internet—Vkontakte, mostly—and that generated some interest among students. We made a video that went marginally viral. The essential part, though, was the posters. We thought it would be funny to make posters with sort of haphazard pictograms of dead democracy—democracy with a knife in its back, a bullet in its brain, X's for eyes. We printed them out and passed them around cafés, student centers, dormitories. The posters were ironic-looking, and they actually generated a certain degree of cachet for Aleksandr. Soon enough, students started to tear them down for their dorm rooms, so that I had to run out to the same places I'd already been and issue replacements.

The Funeral for Democracy was the first element of the three-part plan that Aleksandr outlined for the summer. After the Funeral, Viktor and Boris and I would go to Perm to try to talk to the lieutenant whom Valentin Gogunov had spoken of. If the lieutenant admitted military cooperation in the thievery at Perm, the case prosecuting the government for their involvement would be closed. The film would have made its point. And then—as a response to that anger, riding on a swelling wave of intense populist feeling—Aleksandr would win the formal nomination from Alternative Russia. There was no talk of winning the actual presidency.

What after that? What would we do once Aleksandr had the nomination? Once he'd positioned himself as an alternative candidate in a country with no real elections? Once he'd put himself firmly in the crosshairs of an enemy who had a monopoly on the ammunition?

We simply didn't know. Which is another way of saying we thought we did know and were too polite to talk about it.

———

At the hostel, I remained an odd, slightly inconvenient reality of the building, like the drain that never drained properly and the coffee cups in the cupboard that always looked dirty. I don't know what the managers made of me. They'd never had a guest stay longer; I'm sure they expected that I would never leave. In the time I'd been at the hostel, I'd watched hundreds of young people come and go. I'd watched people flirt and fight and get to know each other in a dozen different languages; they debated literature, and showed off about philosophy, and offered searing opinions about the political development of each other's home countries. There was a Belorussian stripper ("I'm in club work," she said. "You understand?"). There was an engaged couple who broke up loudly outside the hostel in the middle of a horrifically cold February night. There was an older Japanese woman who shared no language with anyone, and wore the same outfit every day, and slept curled around her backpack every night. There was a young woman who lost a baby she didn't even know she was carrying. There was a tiny twenty-three-year-old, eyelinered, multilingual, forever awaiting her visa to go study at the Sorbonne. There was a pair of slick-haired Italian men who stared at me ceaselessly—keeping them from ever seeing my breasts was ultimately a losing battle. There was a young man who rocked himself against a wall and stole sugar packets from the communal tea-and-coffee station near the door. He'd been traveling, he claimed, for fourteen months.

Then they all left, and then new ones came. Once I overheard one of them asking the night manager about me. "The woman," he said. "The older woman who's been here the whole time. Who is she?"

I think he said "older woman." He might have said "old woman." And who could blame him? Who could say that I had not earned the title?

"Oh, her," said the night manager. "We don't know. She lives here."

It was startling to hear, in a way, although of course I did live there—as much as I could be said to live anywhere, anymore.

————

At first, walking home from Aleksandr's late at night had bothered me—rare was the night when I didn't encounter a leering drunk or an aggressive panhandler or a person in clear need of hospitalization for one reason or another. I was a target for all kinds of harassment— I was visibly female, visibly foreign (especially at the beginning), and I walked around unaccompanied at all hours of the day and night. But at some point in the winter, the walk stopped alarming me. Maybe it was that something about me subtly changed—maybe something in my bearing started looking more comfortable, more aggressive, less afraid. Maybe it was that the cold made me believe, on any given night, that I was more at risk from the weather than from anything else. Or maybe it was that I started to feel—more acutely than I had felt before—that it didn't matter what happened to me, and this indifference offered a quasi-ironic protection against any real trouble. Whatever the reason, on all my walks, on all the nights, nobody ever truly scared me until Nikolai found me again.

It was early evening in late March, the time of year when you feel absurdly grateful that the sky has started staying pallid into the late afternoon. It's a time of counting the smallest of blessings, which is never something I've excelled at. But that day I was, perhaps, trying— I'd left Aleksandr's apartment early and taken a long, lingering walk along the river, finally finding myself down by the Hermitage and, hours later, watching the night raising of the bridge. It wasn't until late that I hopped on the metro, sailed underneath the Neva back to Vasilevsky Island, and picked my chilled way back to my neighborhood.

When a man emerged from the shadowy side of one of the buildings on my street, I was almost too tired to jump.

"Irina?"

I felt a twist against my wrist, like the slithering of a dessicated eel. In my throat, an entire life cycle of a scream ran its course.

"Who is it?" I hissed.

He moved, and the synthetic light from the nonstop market caught a snatch of red-raw skin. I remembered.

"Young lady," said Nikolai. "I believe we have met before."

"I know you," I said. I remembered him from the day at the café last fall, before I had properly met Aleksandr. It occurred to me, horribly, that he couldn't have followed me all the way home—through the labyrinthine metro, along the three million art pieces of the Hermitage—without being noticed. It was worse than that. He had waited for me here.

"That's a bit presumptuous," he said. I stared at him and tried to figure out what was going on with his face. It looked like the epidermis had been pulled off, carefully, precisely, perhaps as part of some medical experiment.

"You're working for Aleksandr Bezetov now," he said.

"I'm not answering that."

"I'm not asking."

I looked away. A hunched old woman passed by us, muttering to herself. I tried to lock eyes with her, but she didn't look up.

"Look," said Nikolai. "I don't know what you're doing. Maybe the Americans have taken to spying on Bezetov, and if that's the case, then by all means, carry on."

I said nothing.

"But lately, I've been suspecting otherwise. We've been suspecting otherwise. We think you're just sort of—an independent agent, might be the charitable way to put it? Or a loose cannon? It seems as though you really are just here on your own, for your own inscrutable reasons, as implausible as that still sounds. As such, we have to wonder if we might persuade you to reconsider your approach."

I said nothing. I couldn't believe that people talked like this, and

I didn't have any response—nobly indignant or otherwise—that wouldn't sound canned.

"Not talking? All right," said Nikolai. "You can buy most people, but I suppose it is true that you can't buy everyone."

I tried to move past him then, but he boxed me out with his sizable chest.

"Not yet," he said. "We're not done talking."

That was when I got scared. It occurred to me that if Nikolai thought that what he wanted—whatever he wanted—wasn't going to be gained through talking, he might try changing his tactics.

"You must think Aleksandr very brave, yes?" said Nikolai. "Living life in the rifle's gaze? And all for his political ideals. Very poetic, yes? Very courageous? You admire him. And why he grants you this access, I don't know. Maybe he's fucking you, though I don't know why he would. But for whatever reason, here you are. You respect this man. You find his moral judgment impeccable. You'd make sacrifices for him. Undoubtedly, you already have."

I looked down. It wasn't true, exactly. I hadn't made sacrifices, at least not any that I hadn't already been looking to make.

"There's a lot you don't know about Aleksandr. For example, his best friend from the seventies got himself hit by a bus. Did you know that? His best friend and colleague, the man who protected him, guided him through everything in his first days here. The man who got him interested in politics originally. The man who ran that journal originally. You knew that, right? You knew that Aleksandr was just a chess prodigy, right? He barely knew his left from right. He didn't know what to do. All he did was shuffle these pieces around on a board and pine after this whore he knew from his building. It was pathetic by anyone's standards. And then his best friend, Ivan, was killed by a night bus. Horrific accident. He was crossing the street carelessly, no doubt; terribly drunk, I shouldn't wonder. The man was an incorrigible drunk."

I stared at Nikolai.

"He never told you that, did he?" said Nikolai.

"What is your point."

"Didn't you ever find it odd that Aleksandr hasn't had a similar accident yet? He's been careless in his own way, nobody would argue."

"You mean, do I wonder why you haven't killed him yet? I imagine it's not for lack of trying."

Nikolai tsked and drew his cheeks together in a way that seemed oddly mannered and affected. "Please," he said. "There's no reason to be vulgar."

I closed my eyes. I waited for him to go, but he did not. He leaned in closer to me. He stank of undercooked meat, of cheap alcohol, of the threat of violence. I thought I might faint from sheer character weakness.

"Look," he said. "I'll be honest with you. This is the truth, Irina: your friend Bezetov wants to have his little rallies, his little public fits or whatever, that is fine. That is okay with us. That is, frankly, good for us. He wants to sit up there in his barricaded castle, stroking his own ego? Okay. Your funeral thing that's coming up? With the quirky little posters? Very cute. Fine, wonderful."

He clenched and relaxed his fingers like an animal exercising a protractible claw. "But this film. It's a bit much, don't you think?"

"Much?" I was becoming—retroactively, impotently—terrified. My knees began to actually shake. My spine was wracked with a great seizure of fear.

"It's pushing it. There has been tolerance." He pulled me close to him, and his face caught the light again. I could see where he'd sliced himself shaving. I could see hairs between his eyebrows, looking like the legs of massacred beetles. "There has been tremendous tolerance and patience on the part of the Kremlin. The Kremlin has been magnanimous, has looked the other way and endured the slanders and silliness. But know this, Irina, and tell your boss: this generosity is not infinite. The film is much too much. And your Aleksandr may be famous. He may be well regarded. But even famous people can become careless in the roads. Even the famous can have accidents."

I tried to back away, and this time he let me.

"I think you do understand. But Aleksandr seems to have forgotten. Remind him, wouldn't you?"

I took a step, and then another, and then my knees bent, and I was running.

"You will," called Nikolai. "I know your type. You will."

———

The next day I was out before sunrise, making my way through the streets as the bakeries were turning on their lights. In the station, drunks sat shivering in the alcoves until police came and prodded them away. On the metro, dead-eyed young people were returning from long nights out, their pupils the size of thumbs.

I got to Aleksandr's as the sky was turning a mottled gray. I waited outside the apartment until I saw the light go on, and then I waited fifteen minutes more. Vlad buzzed me in, and I knocked on Aleksandr's door, and I heard a voice, and I went in.

Nina was holding a shoe in her hand, her jaw set in a furious determination. Maybe it was the way the light was catching her, but her red hair and the fury of her energy and the heaving of her chest conspired to make her unbeautiful. Anger, I've been told, can make some lovely women even lovelier, but with Nina, this was not the case. Rage deformed her face and made it somehow hers and yet not hers—there was the same elegant arrangement of the same objectively fine features, but now it all somehow amounted to ugliness. It was like stepping back from a painting and letting the clots of color take a horrible new meaning.

"You," Nina said, "are a pitiful man." She sounded like she meant it.

Aleksandr was sitting with his head down, his shoulders hunched over. I instinctively covered my eyes with my hands. I tried to back away, and in so doing, I knocked over an antique wooden bowl depicting an Orthodox cathedral.

Nina looked at me. Her faced changed almost imperceptibly—there was a brief bleed of contempt, followed by a speedy recovery. And on Aleksandr's face: sheer humiliation. I should know what it looks like. Then Nina gave me a brief nod and quietly dematerialized in the doorway.

"Well," said Aleksandr too carefully. "Good morning."

"I'm sorry. I knocked. I thought I heard someone answer."

He waved his hand at me as though batting away the implied question. "It's okay. It happens."

"You're not happy," I brilliantly observed.

I found myself thinking of Jonathan then. I thought again that there was some value in never seeing the bad things—the small, ugly facts you come to know about a person no matter how hard you try not to. The petty compromises, the self-promotions, the self-protections. The tiny tics of ego or of callousness. The eventual—inevitable—failure of comprehension.

"Happy? Oh, is that supposed to be the idea?" It was an oddly personal thing to hear, like listening to someone talk in his sleep. He tapped his pen against his papers and spun around joylessly in his chair. "Should we use this unexpected time to talk about Perm?"

"Aleksandr, I—"

"The guard will meet you at a café. You won't go near the actual facility. As you know, I will not be going with you."

"Aleksandr."

"I'll just be here, enjoying the joy of my domicile. Basking in the glow of my wedded bliss."

"Please."

"Please," he repeated, waving his hand at me. "Please. We don't need to discuss this. It's a rather banal problem, wouldn't you say?"

"Yes."

"There are more important things to talk about."

"Yes," I said emphatically.

Aleksandr raised his eyebrows at me.

"Nikolai stopped me on the street again. He told me to tell you." I thought again of Nikolai's face and how close to me it had been. "He smelled terrible," I said.

Aleksandr took off his glasses. He squeezed the flesh above the bridge of his nose. He looked a little more beleaguered, a little more embattled, a little more tired than I normally thought of him.

"He was threatening me, or you, or something?"

"How does he always know where I am?"

Aleksandr squinted at me. "You have been at the same hostel for a year. You're not exactly making it hard for him." He pressed on his forehead with his index finger until a small weal appeared. "What does he say?"

"The film is going too far, he says." Suddenly, I realized how terrified I was for Aleksandr. This was striking, because I couldn't remember the last time I'd been terrified for a person who was not myself.

"I've gone too far before," he said tiredly. "I've always been too far."

It was true, I knew. He went too far, and he lived with what it meant. Not in the same way I did—his threats were external, and they would take his mind and his body at the same time. But in more ways than one, we were alike. Death stalked us; every day we caught glimpses of it out of the corner of our eyes, a grinning hyena through a thicket. We never knew when it was coming, and on good days, we could convince ourselves that it wasn't coming at all. Aleksandr could talk himself into believing that no one would ever follow him home; that the things in the corners would stay shadows, and the loud noises would always be motorcycles backfiring, and the head injuries would remain minimal and vaguely comic. And I could believe that the tests were, perhaps, mistaken; that the cataracts on some printed-out sheet ten years ago had nothing to do with my actual mind, my actual memories; that the prophesy was misinterpreted or perhaps reversible. I could believe that if I had to be the type of person who was prone to statistical anomaly, then I could perhaps become the kind of person who could access statistical impossibility. I could cut out articles about the only known survivor of full-blown rabies (medically induced coma, steroids); I could cut out articles about the resurrection of the clinically dead. I didn't believe in miracles, per se. But somehow, believing in your continued existence doesn't feel like the miracle. It's the alternative that defies logic, that beggars belief.

"They're going to kill you," I said.

"He wouldn't say that."

"He talked about 'accidents' with a rather unnerving emphasis."

Aleksandr was nodding vacantly, as though I'd been going on about some petty grievance for hours already. He looked out the window. "You know, you'd think my wife would worry about me," he said.

"She doesn't?"

"It's a funny thing, you know. She doesn't. She really, really doesn't."

"Maybe she can't stand to think about it. Maybe she has faith that you'll be okay." I knew how shallow a thought this was. I'd encountered it myself—from friends of friends and aged aunts who clasped my hand in theirs and said, Irina, you'll be okay, I know it, I just know it. What this means is: I haven't properly thought about it—I haven't subjected it to any kind of clean, brutal scrutiny—because it is unpleasant, and at the end of the day, I do not really care that much.

"Faith doesn't enter into it with Nina. Neither does denial. She knows what we pay in insurance premiums. At any rate, I don't expect that this business with Nikolai is anything more to be worried about than the kind of thing I've had to contend with already."

"But that's it," I said. "He's saying it is. He's saying they've been letting you off the hook on purpose. He's saying they're going to stop doing that."

"Is that so?" He raised his eyebrows mildly. "Think of that. Just think of all the freedom I might have had if I'd known. All the restaurant food I might have eaten. All the domestic holidays I might have taken. I've never seen Lake Baikal, you know."

"You're not taking this seriously."

"I'm taking it seriously. I'm taking it tremendously seriously. What else do you want me to do? How else do you want me to hide? Where else do you want me to *not* go? Am I going to Perm myself to do my own interviews? No. I'm sending a bunch of interns for me. I sit here on my laptop all day long. I leave the house to appear with an army of handlers wherever I go, and even then I get beaned with chessboards. I am taking it seriously. If I were taking it any more seriously, I'd lie down and die right this second just to get it over with."

We were quiet. I looked at the table, where Nina's delicate shoe was still crouched. It looked like it might, at any moment, get up and curtsy and take a twirl around the room.

"I'm sorry," I croaked. "I just want you to be careful." I did. I wanted him to be careful—Aleksandr, who could dodge his own fate through proper strategy, precaution, prediction. Aleksandr, who would have to live around his fear—deny it, repress it, outsmart it—for as long as he managed to live.

"I am careful," he said. "I am. I am. I promise I am. Now. Can we talk about Perm?"

When I got back to the hostel that evening, the night manager spoke to me for the first time in recent memory.

"Miss," he said, waving an envelope in front of my nose. "You appear to have a letter."

"A letter?" This was new. Nobody from my past life had tried this. They'd tried e-mail before I canceled my account. I didn't know how somebody would start to find me, at least not from afar, without showing up.

"So it would seem." He sniffed and handed me the letter. I could feel something heavy and finger-shaped at the bottom of the envelope. Cursive Cyrillic in faint blue writing threaded across the top like varicose veins. Something about the writing made my heart fall and then flip before I could orient myself—it was like the nameless scent of your nursery school, the heart-destroying melody of your childhood music box.

The letter was from Lars.

I tore along the top of the envelope, and I pulled out the knobby thing from the bottom. It was a king. I squeezed it while I read the letter.

Dear Irina,

I hope this letter finds you well; indeed, I hope that this letter finds you at all. When I drove through Soviet Russia in the eighties, I remember the mail system as being quite incompetent. And, at any rate, I do not know if this letter is correctly addressed—I've been making inquiries to various hostels, and this one seems to house a woman of your advanced age and unremarkable description. I hope that you find the experience of staying in hostels in Leningrad more comfortable than I did when I was there! I had some, shall we say, interesting times there back in the day. Propriety prevents me from explaining further.

Harvard Square is just the same as always, and I am still at my chessboards. I have no shortage of opponents, as the undergraduates with the harsh glasses and the tight T-shirts have taken to playing me on the weekends. They are better players than you, most certainly, but I do not find them as amusing, and they are not so entertained by my stories as you were. Being men, they are more worldly and sophisticated and thus less easily impressed. But being college students, they seem to regard playing me as a sort of . . . ironic pastime. I rather preferred your earnest if inexplicable interest, even though you never did get any better.

I think you should know that your friend Jonathan has missed you very much. He came to see me quite a bit right after you left, and he asked me many times how he might go about finding you. I struggled with whether to tell him. But it seemed to me that it was your right to run away if you wanted to. I hope you were not waiting all this time to be found.

At any rate, I find it odd to be writing to a person who may or may not be reading, who may or may not be anywhere. It is a bit like talking to yourself, or talking to the dead, and I believe I have done enough of both in this life. So I will start to end.

I know that the thing that you were running away from will be catching you someday soon, if it hasn't already. I would remind you that you have more words than you need—you always did—so you shouldn't feel so sorry about losing some.

Your friend,

Lars Bergquist

P.S. I have enclosed my king. You would never have caught him by conventional measures, but now I would like him to have you. I would not like to think of him as having surrendered, however. Perhaps he is just taking a bit of a rest.

I stared at the letter until the paper turned into a smear and a full orchestra started in my head. Somewhere off in the distance behind me, I had the sense of leaves whirling, of the wind picking up, of a tornado contracting into a terrible spring.

I had not remembered that I was remembered still. I had not remembered that I *would* be remembered still—in fragments, half wrongly, half mockingly, yes. But remembered nonetheless.

"Young lady," said the man at the desk. "I'll ask you not to cry in the lobby."

The Funeral for Democracy came in late May. The weather was finally relenting; there was a dangerous humidity to the air, and the clouds crouched low and heavy against the skyline. They looked like the sickening crests of lethal waves—the storming of some freak mid-Atlantic disaster, a cosmic cyclone observed only by the starfish and the cowering sharks. The air had a syrupy heaviness that was undercut by a dull edge of cold. It was the same suffocating chill that I'd noticed the first day I landed in Moscow, in some faraway lifetime. I had been here nearly a year.

Viktor stood on an egg crate with a pair of sunglasses and a bullhorn. I stood off to the side, selling posters at 150 rubles apiece. On the other side of the street, police paced like caged animals, tapping their batons against the ground. The permit for the protest had arrived only that morning. They might have been waiting for a pretext to make an arrest, or maybe they'd had orders to allow the protest to continue for some predesignated amount of time—just enough to make Putin look indulgent, liberal, all-merciful. I looked at them hard but didn't see Nikolai.

The crowd was pleasingly huge. Some people were waving flags, and others were jumping up and down, and the multidimensional movement of their summer garb looked liked the parading flags of friendly nations at a sporting event. Some were wearing black; a few had taken the theme quite literally and were wearing shrouds and pretending to weep. Some threw flowers. Some held pictures—of Anna Politkovskaya, of Sakharov, of Aleksandr himself—and marched, solemn and stricken. Others were viewing the Funeral as a slightly more festive affair: taking nips of liquor, concealed in pockets and boots; twirling about in capes; shouting the slogans of loopier, goofier, more marginal causes than ours. Aleksandr stood at a podium, flanked by security guards. In the crowd were sharpshooters he'd hired for the occasion. I fixed my gaze at the clouds, their cumulus haunches stacked against the horizon like game on a wall.

Aleksandr waved at the crowd. The crowd cheered itself hoarse.

And then I waved back without meaning to. What I mean is, I

didn't know I was going to wave before it happened. My arm went without my permission.

It was not dramatic. It felt the way it feels when your eyelid twitches uncontrollably, except with more heft. It took energy, after all, to heave the bone and muscle and meat of an adult human arm; it took aggression to harness the normal mechanics—the tremendous, delicate, intricate art of movement—and appropriate them for some other, darker purpose. And for a moment there was a smile on my face, for a moment I was amused by its strangeness. And then a spine of ice grew up into my heart, and lay down roots, and I was afraid.

Because there it was. That was it.

But as soon as I was sure, I wasn't. I'd looked for this so hard, for so many years, that it was possible I was hallucinating it. Around me, the scene—the shouters, the marchers, the discreet domestic intelligence officers, Aleksandr—bled into a smear. The roar dulled into ambient noise, like the sound of the blood in your head or the unnoticed electric vibrato of the universe. I watched my hand. I stared at it. I dared it to move. It was still.

Maybe not, I thought. Maybe, really, not.

I dropped the posters I was holding. I threw my hat off, idiotically. I ran through the streets, and the Neva spun below me, and I dodged old women who swore at me—and suddenly, my short, unimpressive life came back to me in snatches of motion, as though I'd spent the whole time running: there I was running across the Charles River on nights after my diagnosis; then running through the snow with my silly friends in high school; then running after my father through the rust-colored leaves of some unremembered fall. I flew across the city, and I felt that if I was moving this quickly, this competently, then I must have been wrong about the tremor. I sprinted, and I swore, and I felt that if I'd been right—if I had in fact seen and felt it—then I had undoubtedly managed to leave it behind, back in the square, in a seething mass of people who would certainly trample it to death.

I banged into the hostel, and I ran up to my room, and I lay down on my bed. The sloppy thudding of my heart in my chest was some sort of reassurance. I stared at the ceiling, and I stared at the wall, and

I stared at the seven geometric stain-continents that lived on my floor. I thought about Africa—the real Africa, not the one on my floor— and I thought of how I'd have liked to go there to see the pyramids, to see the Sphinx, to see the things that do not belong to me but that I've always (secretly, impiously) thought belong to everyone. I thought frantically that maybe I would still go one day; maybe my life would continue in its current vein (nomadic, improbable, interesting) until the day when I sat down to write my memoirs. The fact that I'd been sentenced to death long ago would be dismissed with a laugh as another unlikely youthful event. Maybe, maybe. My heart was starting to slow down, the blood making ever calmer eddies in my head.

Then it happened again. My hand gave a twitch—small, modest, but completely involuntary. I watched in revulsion as it moved against my will; watching it was like watching the posthumous twitching of a headless chicken. It was my hand, and yet it was clearly not: it had disowned me, it seemed, it had mutinied against me. It had come to kill me in the tower.

I threw my fist against the wall and let the pulp of my hand compress against the pain of my hand, which folded into the pain everywhere else.

Out the window, a little boy was spinning a pinwheel, and I remembered the scene from the T window on the day of my diagnosis: how there was a dullness to the colors, a new tedium to the scene, but at the same time a new singularity—it was as though a gray film had been lacquered over a painting that you were told was the most beautiful in the world, and it really was a pity you couldn't see it properly.

For years—for years—I'd thought seriously about what would be the way to go, when I'd go. My current option, I'd always known, was no option. Not at home, where my incremental passing would have been chronicled and mourned—not least of all by me. Not here, anonymous and alone, in a country that would relegate me to a state-run, piss-soaked institution, to babble and die alone in my own head.

So I'd thought about it. I'd thought about the clean certainty of gunshot; I'd shuddered at the notion of the choked, panicked minutes of a hanging. There was drowning, but drowning is no option if you know what drowned bodies wind up looking like. I'd been drawn to the half-assed feminine forms—pills or some such. That was the kind of suicide attempt that leaves you time for an Abraham-and-Isaac type of intervention, in case the gods could be persuaded that they had punished you enough, that your suffering was sufficient, that you believed. But then there was this: as soon as the decision seemed imminent, I tried to figure out how it was not. Immediately, I began a terrible barter. My whole life had been hinging on the pretext that the decision was already made: as soon as I saw anything—anything—that was it. I would have to act. Although there would be a grace period of good cognition between the initial symptom and the commencement of mental unraveling—and the grace period wasn't negligible, either: my father's mind was functional, more or less, for several years after his first symptoms appeared—I would never be able to count on it. There was too much chance for my will to be corroded by weakness of mind, too much likelihood that I would cower behind my oncoming oblivion and turn away from the only obvious escape.

I understood this progression in an academic sense. I'd studied the science and read the articles; I'd internalized the grammar and the vocabulary of the illness. And I'd known it, too, in a nonacademic way. I'd seen my father's arms whir like windmills, I'd seen the terror and the fury in his eyes, I'd seen the way he choked on water and words.

But there are things you know objectively to be true and things you feel subjectively to be true; the things you understand somewhere in your head and the things you understand viscerally, intuitively, behind your heart. You can know that space might be unending, and you can understand that time is contingent, and you can write out the size of an atom in scientific notation. But when you try to access any kind of experience of this, you fail. You have reached the limit of your own comprehension, and you sit uncomfortably with the reality that there are truths that lie quite beyond your ability to fully believe them to be such.

There were some days in bed then. I don't know how I spent them.

I do know how I spent them. In the window: a wedge of white, enfeebled light. On the floor: shadows, stalking their way across the room from morning until night. I came to think of the shadows and the light as caught in a kind of battle, a game of strategy. But the shadows always won, and it became tiresome to watch.

I think the manager started bringing me bread and tea after the first few days. And once I think Viktor was in the lobby—probably at Aleksandr's bidding—inquiring after my health.

It wasn't a physical fever, but it was like that: my head floating several feet above my body, my absorbed fascination with the cracks in the ceiling and the aging patches of dirt on the floor. There was the way that dreams impinged on reality, until I stopped keeping track of what was what.

And every once in a while—not often but with increasing regularity—a spasm in my arm, in my leg. My fingers fluttering against the sheets. My legs kicking, kicking, savagely, at nothing.

———

It was a week, maybe, although it's hard to know for sure. Then I got up, and climbed into the shower, and ate four sandwiches in a row from the nonstop market.

I thought of why I had come to St. Petersburg. I thought of my father's questions—of my questions—about how one proceeds in the face of catastrophe, how one gracefully executes the closing moves of a doomed game. I thought about Aleksandr's death threats, and Nikolai's wintry breath on my face, and the movie that would get made one way or another. Aleksandr's life was a kind of answer to the questions, a kind of model for how to proceed. I knew that mine would have to be as well.

I decided I could still go to Perm. It was my responsibility. It was also my deadline. What could I say for my short life if I was honest with myself? I'd taught a few students the correct use of semicolons. I'd made a few people I loved tremendously unhappy. If I went to Perm, and if we found something important, then at least there would be that. There would be an excuse for this trip. There would be an excuse for this lifetime. There would be a story worthy of a fine eulogy, if anybody was inclined to deliver one.

Long ago there were times—in dreams, in feverish nightmares, in fantasies (fearful and fretful, vengeful, petty, suicidally depressed, curious, guardedly optimistic)—when I wondered whether there might not be some relief when it happened. I had thought about it every day, every single day, for ten years. I had woken up forgetting, in the early days, and then having to remember. I had cried. I had cut off relationships. I had jumped at my own shadow. I had run away. At the end, I had wondered, might it not at last be freeing? Might it not at long last bring me a kind of peace?

It was not, and it did not. It was horrible. It was unimaginably horrible. It was as unimaginably horrible as unimagined beauty is beautiful. It was a reinvention, an inversion, a revelation.

I went back to Aleksandr's, and I remembered how to type, and speak normally, and get up in the mornings, and do what I was asked. But it was a different world, that day and every day after—garbled, mistranslated, wrong. The world became so different that I almost didn't recognize it anymore. We had no common ground, it seemed, and we sat for long hours in silence. Eventually, I gave up trying to engage it. And I remarked to myself, as I walked away from it, that it seemed to be fast becoming a stranger.

19

ALEKSANDR

St. Petersburg, June 2007

The summer floated lightly down onto St. Petersburg, as if trying to enter a room unnoticed. Green ash and Siberian birch blossomed along the streets; the canals shivered in ever lighter winds. Against the horizon, the clouds clumped and cleaved and drew apart in a lazy miosis. Aleksandr watched out the window.

Sometimes he could assess the weather from the way that Nina smelled when she came in from a day of shopping with her friends, jangling bags in tow—he could smell the sun and mild air and longer days all tangled up in her hair, even though she wiggled away quickly whenever he went to her. Sometimes near the door Aleksandr would find vaguely sun-smelling leaves or sticks or flower petals, the remnants of a life lived out in the world, and sometimes he'd take a petal between his thumb and his forefinger to feel its oil, to let its edges bruise. And sometimes Aleksandr would sit up nights and crank open the window and take deep breaths of the air that came in gusts alternately lovely and rank. There were the smells of hydrangea and bittersweet nightshade and lily of the valley, and the smells of all the things that had fallen into the snow and frozen through the winter and then thawed out into black, stringy fossils, unrecognizable as their former selves: lost shoes and bras and love letters, outraged newspapers with stern fonts, bright pink gossip magazines.

He remembered delivering the pamphlets back when the city was still Leningrad, back when he was allowed out. Under the rule of a rotten regime, he'd managed a sort of ill-advised freedom. Then, at least, he could pad outside in the early mornings or the frosted nights. He could stand in the brittle light of the fingernail-shaped moon; he could wander past the enormous monuments that stood epic and monstrous, straining against the current of history. Then he'd had allies and the exuberance of youth. And a woman to love from afar, which had at least given him something to think about during his long walks around the city. Elizabeta had dislodged something in him that he could spend a lifetime trying to reclaim; and there had been a bittersweet joy, too, in that particular lost cause.

He shook himself and cracked his neck. It was embarrassing enough to love the same woman for so long. It was worse to look back on Communism with misplaced nostalgia. He found that sentiment often in the angry letters he received from older cranks, for whom Brezhnev and Andropov and Chernenko were the backdrop of first loves and marriages and infant children. The letter writers remembered that time as tinged with a sweetness, an innocence, an optimism that—while misguided, perhaps—was preferable to its alternative. Aleksandr would write back, *Dear sir, Dear madam. Thank you for your letter. I understand your feelings. But I believe it is not the regime that you miss; it is your own youth.*

He could stand to take his own advice.

He slapped himself on the cheek lightly. He was making a list of safe lodging places and eateries for Irina, Viktor, and Boris's trip to Perm. He assumed Irina was still going, though she'd recently disappeared for a week, and he'd never gotten a straight answer about why. He'd sent Viktor out to her hostel on Vasilevsky, and Viktor had reported back that it was a silly place, a home for wayward Westerners who wanted to suffer shallowly and temporarily in order to have stories to tell. It was no place for a person to live, as Irina seemed to be doing. But the bottom line—as Viktor pointed out—was that they

weren't paying Irina and couldn't make any claims about employ-
ing her, and so it wasn't any of their business. Maybe she'd gone back
home. Maybe she'd moved on. And Aleksandr was struck by the realization that he didn't know where Irina might go—where "back" was,
what "on" meant.

Eventually, she'd returned, looking pale and panicky and casting
fatal looks at everybody who asked where she'd been. Aleksandr had
been chasing her around the apartment for a week, trying to get a moment alone to ask how she was, but she'd avoided him assiduously.
He'd mentioned it to Nina once, and she'd said, "That girl? She's still
around? Did you ever start to pay her?"

"No."

"Then you can't very well demand that she show up here, can you?
That's capitalism, grib. That's kind of the whole idea."

"It's not that. I'm worried about her."

Nina had looked at him disinterestedly and asked him point-blank
if he was in love with the American. Aleksandr had told her no, truth-
fully, and turned over to look at his own wall, disappointed by Nina's
failure of imagination.

Now he bit his lip and bent over his notes for Perm. He had no
idea how they were going to get the lieutenant there to talk. Follow-
up communications with Valentin Gogunov had revealed a wealth
of information that might be used as blackmail, but Aleksandr was
squeamish about such a tactic, and Gogunov had intimated that it
wasn't going to work anyway. The current plan was that they'd pose
as film students, but he hated sending them off with so little to go on.
He'd written them a list of possible questions and angles and ideas,
but it was difficult not knowing the inflections and the wordings, having no way to coach them into asking spur-of-the-moment follow-up
questions or detecting bullshit. Sending them was like sending a probe
to Mars—he thought of its insect legs folding up into a squat, its mo-
torized head casting this way and that. You could program it to do
what you wanted, but it was no replacement for going there yourself
and flinging your fingers into the red sand.

"Grib." Nina was standing in the doorway. She was wearing a silky
nightgown, backlit by the moon, casting a sort of shaky, wan light all

around her. She cocked her head to one side. "What are you doing?" She sounded like she actually wanted to know.

He spun around in his chair and took off his glasses. "Working on getting the kids ready for Perm."

"Oh." Her mouth disappeared somehow. She came to stand behind Aleksandr and rubbed her hands against the grain of his polo shirt. He sucked his stomach in before she could catch it. "Is that going to take all night?" she said.

"What? Why? What did you have in mind?"

Nina tossed her hair over a slim shoulder and arranged her face into what she must have thought was impishness. "I'm bored," she said. "Let's go out."

"Out?"

"You and me? Just this once. We'll take the car. We'll drive somewhere. We won't tell security."

"I can't."

"Aleksandr."

"I can't." He rubbed his eyes ferociously. "You know I can't. I'm surprised you'd even ask. If I can't go to Perm, why would I blow everything to go out dancing?"

Nina looked down, her expression flatlining.

"I'm sorry," he said. "It's not that I don't want to go out with you. It's just that it's not practical. I know you understand that." He tried to take her hands, but she kept them balled up into unyielding buds. For a long moment, she said nothing.

"Ninotchka," he said. "Please."

"You think you're going to win this thing?" she said hoarsely.

"Win it?" He stopped trying to get at her hands. "No, Nina. No, of course not."

"Of course not?" She raised her face to look at him. Through her skin, he could see her veins, blue and vaguely upraised and pulsing with whatever emotions ran to that faraway, inscrutable heart. It must be strange to walk around with vulnerability like that plastered all over your face.

"What," he said slowly. "Didn't you know that?"

"I didn't know you were so sure."

"I should have thought to mention it."

She looked down again. There was a faint kinetic charge in the air that he recalled from his chess days—from those moments when he knew somewhere deep in his pulpy cerebrum what was going to happen next, even if he couldn't have said how.

"You think this is a joke," she said. "But when I met you, you were a very different man. You used to enjoy life. You used to take some pleasure in people, and in going places, and in having fun. But it's not like that anymore. We can't go anywhere, and we can't do anything, and if I want to have a party, I can't have it catered and we need to pat down all the guests before they can enter our apartment. It's no way to live, grib."

He looked longingly at his notes. It would be another late night at this point. "I'm sorry, Nina." And he was. He was so sorry. But he'd been apologizing with every gesture, with every advance and retreat, for the better part of a decade. Were there more creative ways to grovel, more imaginative modes of self-flagellation? Possibly, but his energies had to go elsewhere. Nina would have to be content with her current collection of prosaic revenges.

"We do all this and it's for nothing?" she said. "You say glibly, 'No, of course I won't win'? That's hard for me, grib."

"I understand." There was sense to this, he thought. He could squint and tilt his head and see it the way she did. But as soon as he acutely felt her problem, he could immediately see the solution. He screwed his eyes tighter, making effulgent whorls across his eyelids. Leave, then, he thought. I dare you. He stayed still. He listened. Leave, he willed her. Leave. Eventually, she did—but she only went so far as the bedroom, where he could hear the whinny of the closet door closing, the submerged whisking of nightgown against sheet. There was a silence. And then came muffled crying so earnest that it sounded, to Aleksandr, like the sobbing of a stranger.

———

Aleksandr stayed in the study, barely asleep for the first half of the night, barely awake for the second. When the dawn insinuated itself over the horizon, red as a festering wound, Aleksandr gave up and tried to work. Irina and Boris came in quietly at nine and took their papers into separate corners. At ten, Viktor walked in, his jaw stiff and his movements brittle. He was holding a copy of *Novaya Gazeta*. "Boss," he said. "Did you see this?"

He handed the paper to Aleksandr. He'd brought copies for Irina and Boris, too. They opened their papers to the letters-to-the-editor section. In large font, the headline read, ALEKSANDR BEZETOV: THE RIGHT OPPOSITION CANDIDATE FOR RUSSIA? As Aleksandr read, he felt the arteries rioting and tangling in the back of his head. He recognized this as the physiology of rage.

Sir,

Many supporters of reform look to Aleksandr Bezetov as an important opposition figure; indeed, many hope that one day he will be our nation's second democratically elected president. I have known Bezetov for many years, and I feel it's time I publicly expressed my deep reservations about his fitness for this role.

What sacrifices has Bezetov really made for our country? What has he risked and lost? Has he truly earned his status as the opposition's cherished figurehead? Certainly, Russia needs change. Certainly, Russia needs different leadership. But I hate to see so many people staking their hope for this country in someone so corrupt, so lazy—and, though it's not popular to say so, so scared.

It's widely known that Bezetov is making a film about the Moscow apartment bombings, and that is a laudable project, indeed. But who has been conducting the actual interviews? Who has been doing the actual work? Not Bezetov—he sends his gang of 20-year-olds everywhere to do his research for him. Bezetov doesn't like to be out in the world with the people because, ultimately, he is afraid of the people. It's exactly this arrogant coldness that makes Bezetov unworthy of the reform movement's regard.

It is possible that Bezetov may yet be able to redeem himself. Insiders know that he has been planning an expedition to a certain military facility, and that—once again—he's been planning to send his interns. If Bezetov hopes to win credibility among the citizens of his future democracy, he'll realize that he needs to go there himself. Russia doesn't need another powerful billionaire who doesn't care

about the people. Russia needs a man who will make real choices—
and take real risks—on their behalf.

Sincerely,

Mikhail Solovyov

Aleksandr read, and his shoulders felt rigid, as though his shirt
had been pinned to a wall. He retreated to the couch, moving aside a
pair of gardening shears to sit. In some part of his head, he wondered
why Nina had gardening shears—they didn't have a garden, after all,
they didn't have a front yard, and even if they did, they wouldn't have
had the leisurely security to work in it. She kept sprigs of basil along
the windowsill sometimes, and maybe she'd hoped that by now they'd
be summering in a beautiful, enormous dacha somewhere outside the
city, with a litter of tiny children playing outside in the dirt. "Well," he
said. "That's pretty bad."

"Pretty bad? We're dead," said Boris.

"Not quite yet," said Viktor.

"You know this just made our lives infinitely harder, right?" said
Boris. "You know it made our chances of getting killed incalculably
higher, right? If they think you're actually traveling with us, we're
screwed. And that's what Misha made them think—that you're going
to Perm. That you'll have to go now, in order to save your candidacy."

"I do," said Aleksandr. "I do have to go now."

"You can't," said Irina.

"I have to."

"Are you trying to be funny?" said Boris.

"What's funny about it? It's my movement, right? It's my idea,
right? It's my fucking *candidacy,* right?"

"You can't. You won't."

"The idiot has a point, right?" said Aleksandr. "You're all thinking
it. You're too afraid to mention it, but you're all thinking it. What has
he risked for this? you wonder. What grants him his authority when
he's too afraid to eat a sausage on the street, or fly an airplane to his
home village, or walk around at night without his fucking security
guard trailing him everywhere? This man is some sort of hero? No,
you think. This man is a coward, a pampered coward, and he sends

out young people to do the dangerous things for him, and then he leans back and enjoys the applause."

There was a pause, and what he'd said swirled around the silence in ever wider loops, until it filled up the whole room with its spiraling echo.

"No," said Irina finally. "We don't think that. You've had hundreds of death threats. You've had body parts come through your window. They would kill you the second they had you alone in a hallway."

"Did you read this?" said Aleksandr. "Did you read it?" He was aware that he was pacing and possibly shouting. "This is going to be the line of defense. This is going to be the mantra. I have to go. He's left me no choice."

Boris was shaking his head furiously. "No, no, no," he said. "I don't think so, no. I'm done with this. I quit. I'm not going. You can't ask me to do such a thing after this. After the way this set us up."

"Put it in perspective," said Viktor. "It's a calculated risk, like all of them."

"Bullshit," said Boris. "You think they don't read *Novaya Gazeta*? You think they won't catch this? Please."

"Calm down," said Viktor.

"Jesus," said Boris. "What the hell did you do to that guy to make him write something like that?"

Aleksandr winced. "I wouldn't let him be affiliated with the film."

"You wouldn't let him be affiliated with the film." Boris kicked the couch. "Because, what, he's a little too right of center for you? A little too nationalistic? They're not the fucking National Bolsheviks. You could have cut him a deal. If you were any kind of politician, you would have."

"Boris," said Viktor. "Stop it."

"Stop it?" said Boris. "Oh, I'm stopping. I'm also not going. I could die for something, maybe, someday, but not for this kind of stupidity."

"He's right," said Aleksandr. "He shouldn't go. None of you should go, actually. You are all young. None of you should be incurring an old man's risks. Exposing yourselves to an old man's enemies. I'll go. You can all take paid vacations."

"It's done, then," said Boris, standing up. "I'm done." He walked out of the room. After a moment, Viktor followed him, casting a bleak glance back at Aleksandr and Irina.

Aleksandr put his head on his desk. He could feel Irina staring at him, her eyes boring twin craters into his back, and he didn't like it. Ever since she'd returned from her unannounced vacation, she'd had a stricken, mournful, darkly knowing look that Aleksandr found unnerving but didn't know how to address. You couldn't ask a person to make her face stop doing something that seemed involuntary. There were other things, too—her face blanching at odd intervals, as though she were going through a process of remembering and forgetting and then inevitably re-remembering something terrible. She was shakier than she'd been. Her motor skills—never stellar—were worse, and she'd taken to standing far away from things that were fragile or expensive. She was also, for the first time since Aleksandr had known her, too thin. She'd always been shaped like a bean, but now her skeletal system seemed to be issuing a protest and taking its leave through her skin. Her clavicle jutted like a continental shelf.

"Stop," he said. "Please stop looking at me like that."

"What is this?" she said. "What are you doing?"

"Nothing," he said. "I just think that jaundiced schizophrenic has a point, much as it pains me to say so. I have to go to Perm. I've got no credibility otherwise."

"This country can't afford to lose you."

"How do I know that? What do I have to show for all this nonsense? All I see are unreliable poll numbers, poorly conducted surveys."

"You see the crowds. You see how they turn out for you. I don't need to remind you. You know this. You are being intentionally difficult."

"I'm not going to win." He could hear himself being wretched—he could hear in his own voice the stomping about of a howling, unappeased toddler—but he couldn't help it.

"You're not going to win this year. You know that," said Irina. "Maybe you won't win any year. You know what Anna Politkovskaya said about you? You're not Thomas Paine, you're John the Baptist? You're right, it might not be you. But whoever it is will owe it to you. You've made the thought conceivable. You make it more conceivable every day. And in order to keep doing that, you need to be alive."

He said nothing. Alive, what was that? He'd never be alive again—feeling the exhilarating gusts of wind slamming into his lungs, reveling in the wild anonymity of being young and alone in an enormous city. It could end one of two ways, he guessed: he could wind up watching the country from the reinforced windows of the Kremlin, or he could wind up dead. He had a hazy image of himself trapped in some ornate grave, grumpily listening to the ongoing march of the city around and above him. They'd have his tomb secluded somewhere to protect it from vandalism. Nina would come once a month to sit in the rain and look at her nails.

But no, not really. Really, he'd wind up here, just here—growing older, watching out the window. People might forget that he was alive, when they thought of him at all. And there would probably come a day—when more relevant targets presented themselves, and vines grew over the memory of his campaign, and he became an old man on whom nobody would want to waste a bullet or a scheme—when it would be safe for him to go out again. Unfortunately, he would never know which day that was.

"You can't afford to be like this," said Irina. "Stop it right now."

He stared out the window, where an understated sun was looming politely. He stared at the table, at the sheaf of papers before him. He stared at Irina's hands, ten inches from his face. They were durable, inelegant hands; unmanicured, but with fingers that looked like they'd been raised fluttering along a piano or a typewriter. He was staring at the hands, he would always remember, because he couldn't stand to look at Irina's face. And then suddenly, one of the hands jumped—"jumped" was the only word for it, because it was obvious that it had not been moved. The hand took to the air and fell again, limply, heavily, like a frog casting itself into a pond. Irina turned the color of an onion and put her hands underneath the desk as if to hide them. Aleksandr stared at her.

"What was that?" he said, even though he knew, and the question was horrible to ask and more horrible to hear answered.

"It's nothing," she said in a voice that did not sound like her own.

He supposed he had known it already, but seeing it was surprising and gruesome and oddly more painful than he had thought it might be. He'd thought that the inevitability of the event had inoculated him, somehow, against its potency. But then again, his whole life had been about trying—and failing—to come to grips with the inevitable. He shouldn't be surprised that the inevitable was often the worst thing; worse, even, for the fact that it had been etched so long ago, that it was an ending that had predated its own characters.

"Irina," he said. He tried to take her hand, but she wouldn't let him. He could almost see the fluttering of her ravaged fist-sized heart. He could hear the raggedy slicing of her breath. "I saw it. I saw that. You didn't mean to do that."

She looked down. She looked out the window. Her breathing sounded like the beating of wings. Her face looked waxy and slightly unreal, as if she were an amateur artist's rendering of a human being. The whole thing felt too terrible, too intimate, to see—this poor young woman's unraveling. It was a kind of honor, a kind of liability.

"That's it, isn't it?" he said.

"It is," she said. "That's it. That is, I'm afraid, it."

He shook his head instinctively, although he knew that in doing so, he looked like he was mourning something small and silly, something that might be best termed a "shame." What was the appropriate gesture? What was the appropriate response? He adjusted his glasses in a way that he hoped made him look competent, professorial. "What does this mean, exactly?"

She looked at him grimly and didn't answer. He sat up straighter in his chair. Somewhere, way back in the hidden chambers of his face—behind his cheekbones and eye sockets, in that central core from which he'd always felt that he was watching the events of his own life—he could feel the oncoming menace of tears. He coughed.

"Well," he said brusquely. "You can't stay here, obviously. The state hospitals are horrific. We'd pay for a private one, but even so, you'd be better off in America. We'll get you a plane ticket home."

"I'm not going home."

"Irina, you must. You have to." He was relieved to be having this conversation—it was so enormously preferable to be debating something about which he might have a concrete opinion, to be issuing some kind of commandment with some kind of confidence. It gave him a matrix of a response. He was overjoyed that Irina didn't want to go home, because now he could focus on the project of convincing her to go.

"No," she said. "I can't. You don't understand."

Although she was right—he did not understand—he found himself pressing on blindly.

"But don't you have people somewhere?" he said. He knew she did, and he knew that this tack was futile. He knew that bringing it up was indulging in the kind of careless cruelty that people employ when they are so outmatched by their circumstances that they would rather say something terrible than say nothing at all.

"No," she said. "Well, yes, I do, but I don't want to go to them. That's the whole thing. That's been the point the whole time."

He'd known she'd come here to get away—he'd known that this experience was meant partly to discharge the frustrated energy of a truncated lifetime. In addition to all the lofty questions about grace and catastrophe, there'd been also, he suspected, the small thing of having an adventure—an adventure that might marginally distinguish this particular short life from all the others out there that were substantially like it. But he'd also thought—when he thought of it, which was as rarely as compassion allowed—that it had been, on some level, a bluff. That when this disease caught up with her—whirring over the North Pole, hopscotching the Aleutian Islands, taking a rumbling old train through the Caucasus, or flying first-class over all the twinkling continental first-world capitals—that when it caught her, she would let it take her home. To do otherwise was insanity. And he couldn't help but think that it was a kind of selfishness: why should he have to witness a tragedy he never summoned? Why should he be responsible for its care and management?

"Irina," he said fretfully. "Please be reasonable."

She said nothing. She stood up and walked to the window: outside, a wind was riffling through the treetops. Aleksandr could hear the wheeze of their bending.

"Why did you trust me?" she said, facing the window.

"Trust you?"

"At the beginning. When I showed up here. Didn't you think I could have been a double agent or something? Didn't you think I could have been spying on you?"

"Not for the Americans, probably. If they have a question for me, all they have to do is ask."

She turned around. "No, for Putin. Or for, I don't know, anyone. Or I could have been a random assassin, or a crazy person, or, I don't know, a stalker with a ton of pictures of you printed out from the Internet."

"I wouldn't flatter myself."

"I just mean you're so careful. You're so cautious. You won't eat pastries from the street vendors. You won't even go out at all."

He sat back in his chair. "I go out sometimes."

"You know what I mean. You're careful. That's—that's the right thing. You should be careful. So why did you let me into your work here? How did you know I wasn't out to get you somehow?"

"I don't know." He twirled his fingers against his temples. "Maybe I hoped you were."

"What can that possibly mean?"

"I don't know," he said. "Maybe it would have been a relief."

Irina smiled strangely. "You think that, but you're wrong. It wouldn't have been."

He pulled her to him then. He felt the fragility of her bony back, and he thought of the daughter she'd once been to a father, and he thought of the daughter he might have had if life had gone otherwise. He found that he believed her, even though he didn't think he could say it. So he decided not to say anything at all.

———

That night Aleksandr lay in bed, thinking about Irina and listening to Nina's shallow breathing. Somehow, Nina never seemed fully unconscious—her breath always sounded slightly wakeful, as if she were feigning sleep or playing dead. She was sleeping on top of the sheet, and he could see the severe concavity of her pelvis, the unforgiving cut of her rib cage. One denuded leg was flung over the other; they looked like a pair of pirouetting bones. In the moonlight, Nina was almost translucent—she reminded him, appallingly, of a deep-sea creature, transformed by dark and pressure and evolution into a skeletal, bioluminescent alien.

"Nina," he said. "The American girl is dying."

That wasn't his only problem. Misha's outburst in *Novaya Gazeta* had been deeply problematic; he'd checkmated Aleksandr, it seemed, and now all moves were suicide— though it was true that one of the suicides was probably literal and one was probably political. Misha's move had quite been clever, although Aleksandr had always known that he was a clever man. He knew, too, why Misha's antics had cut him so deeply. When he saw Misha, he heard the hissing accusation that the better man had died back in the seventies, and that this was Russia's loss. The dead or dying were always so much more virtuous than the living—even if, in life, they had been petty or callous or small-minded or vain, even if they'd been rash, even if they'd been terrified. Misha seemed to think, and Aleksandr could certainly believe, that it would be a different story if Ivan had lived. Ivan would have been out in the streets, out motivating the troops, with or without a security apparatus. Ivan would have gone to Perm. Ivan might have won by now. In the end, what could Aleksandr show for the campaign? What had it accomplished? He'd filled up a few squares for a few afternoons. He'd given a terminal case some inexplicable satisfaction. And he'd offered a few hours of entertaining programming for internationally inclined television viewers who regarded the whole thing as diverting as a game of chess. He'd be lucky if Putin had suffered an anxious night or a bout of indigestion over it all.

He would go to Perm. He'd get on the first flight tomorrow. He had to. That was all there was to it.

"Nina," he whispered, "I'm going away tomorrow." She didn't answer. Maybe she really was asleep. Or maybe she just wasn't listening anymore.

———

He woke up to thuds from the spare bedroom. When he walked in, Nina was organizing her clothes—there was a polychrome sartorial fan across the bedspread, shiny shirts and skirts with ruffles and mysterious items for which Aleksandr had no name; a spray of tops of every possible color gradation; dresses of intricately complicated and impossibly hideous prints. She did this sometimes: spent hours folding and assessing, holding the pieces up close for inspection, frowning at them as though the clothes—like everything else—were not quite as nice as she remembered them.

"You're up," said Nina. "Would you mind grabbing me that suitcase?"

"What are you doing?" He hoisted the suitcase from the back of the closet. "I need this for Perm, you know."

"They left without you," she said. "Viktor and the American. I understand they changed their flight. They went in the night. One of them left a note about it. I don't know."

"What?"

She shrugged. "It sounds like you left them no choice."

"What?" He could feel a panicked, disgusted feeling growing behind his heart—the dawning understanding of a terrible mistake, the sickening sense of having slept through a lifetime.

Nina started throwing her clothes in the suitcase. "They didn't want you going, of course. They wanted to protect you, of course. That's what this whole operation hinges on, right? That's kind of the entire point of the whole game?" She drew her knuckles savagely across her eyes, which were inflamed with salt and resentment. "It was sort of a forced move, I suppose, in your former terminology."

"I have to get there."

"You have to get there? Your wife is leaving you, have you noticed? That's what all this means." She pointed to the bags. They crouched along the doorway, looking like the alligators they once had been. "Typically, when you see this, you're supposed to try to stop me."

Nina was backlit by the sun coming in through the shafts in the doorway. Her red hair had never been lovelier, and he could remember the way she'd looked to him when he'd first met her—unbearably beautiful, unbearably delicate, the kind of woman you could spend a lifetime trying to satisfy and understand. He wondered why that had once seemed like an appealing project. Maybe it was a holdover need from Elizabeta. To have loved with such ardor at such a distance, to have the air charged always with a blue static electricity, to know the silhouette of the space between two people as the most palpable shape of one's life—after that, the idea of engagement, however small and petty, however quotidian and demanding, had seemed like the only answer.

"Typically," said Nina. "This is where you should plead with me and ask me if there's anything, anything, you could do to get me to stay."

"Nina," he said. "Can we talk about this later?"

Or maybe that wasn't it. Maybe it was that the lifelong endeavor of reform in Russia was something so abstract and impossible to achieve that the smaller thing—of making a difficult woman happy—had seemed like an attainable goal. Except it hadn't been. Democracy would sweep the streets, a free press would open up into a chorus of snarky disapproval, a transparent and functional rule of law would bind the government, before Nina was made happy. It simply wasn't something that Aleksandr would see in this lifetime.

"I'm going to the airport, Nina," he said.

"Fine," she said. "By the time you get back, I'll be gone."

"I know."

He went to her then, and grazed his fingers along her cheek, and for the first time in a long while, she let him. He had to admire her for this, in a way. He'd been unhappy, but Nina was the sole constant in this isolated life. She could leave, but it wouldn't make him independent; she could leave, and it wouldn't let him find someone new; she could leave, and it wouldn't mean he could do what he wanted. His one personal happiness came from the tepid satisfactions—such as they were—of a well-organized domestic life; he'd told himself that the greater, more important consolation was still ahead. For her part, he knew she was unhappy, but he had thought she liked the apartment too much to ever leave it. It made him like her a little better—marginally, retroactively—to know that this was not the case.

"It's no way to live," she said, "and there's no end in sight. The end for me is as a widow. That's the only way this thing ends for me."

He saw it then, and in the way of all things that are finally made clear, he could not believe he had ever missed it. He saw how she had longed for it, in her way: the house empty of its strangers and chatter and incessant typing; the city glittering through the windows, all of its potential available for purchase via money or beauty. "Is that why you were never afraid for me?" he said.

"Maybe it is. Maybe if we're really honest, it is."

"Well," said Aleksandr carefully. "That explains a lot."

She was crying then, silently, her hands wound into furious fists, her hair streaming down her back. "It's just that I thought that you were someone else. I thought all this"—and here she flapped her arm helplessly at the vista of the apartment, the stacks of papers crowding out the fine Oriental carpeting; the antique typewriters and laptops and cords and cable connections spilling out from under the teak tables and snaking their way around the French windows—"it's just that I thought all this would be something else."

"I know," said Aleksandr. "I'm sure at some point I did, too."

He took her to him, and through her thin cashmere, he could feel the pitiless landscape of her scapula. He couldn't remember the last time he'd held her without the characteristic stiffening of the spine. Without feeling as if he were crossing some kind of armed border.

"I'm sorry," she said. "But I don't care about it the way you do. I can't care about it the way you do. I think democracy will be the death of this country, if you want to know the truth. If you'd ever asked me about it, you'd know that by now."

He nodded his head against her hair and smelled the foreign, expensive shampoos—willow or aloe vera, jojoba beads imported from Madagascar or God knows where.

"Maybe so," he said. "I know you're not the only one who thinks so."

She looked at him mournfully, and he could see her realizing that he was a stranger and sillier man than she'd even suspected. He could see her studying his face, preparing herself to frame the scene in her memory. Then there was a softening and a fading—it was like watching a person let go of a ledge that she's been clinging to for so long that there's a relief in the defeat and an acceptance in the falling.

"The airport, Nina," he said. "I have to go."

"Okay, grib," she said. "I'll drive you."

And so she drove him, dry-eyed now, through St. Petersburg. He slouched down in the passenger seat, wearing sunglasses, and she tied up her hair in a scarf, and they rode along the streets. Vlad sat in the back, glowering and muttering about the security risks and pleading with Aleksandr to call one of the drivers. The city was all deciduous trees this time of year, and networks of shadows skittered across the ground like spiders. Ancient air came up from the Neva and twisted into a welter of flower petals and newspaper broadsheets and brightly colored food wrappers. His wife had just left him, and his staff had just mutinied against him, and yet he felt oddly elated. He reached out and touched the glass, which the staff kept crystalline-clean. The street was choked with taxis, legal and illegal, and luxury cars the size of military tanks. In the car next to him, a woman poked her husband in the shoulder and pointed at Aleksandr.

"Sir," Vlad said. "Sir, you are being very, very rash."

"It's broad daylight," said Aleksandr. "It's the middle of the street."

"You're being dumb. I don't know what's happening to you, but you're being quite dumb."

"I'm about to get even dumber."

Nina accelerated the car. All around them, St. Petersburg thrummed with life—the street vendors, the clotting traffic, the trees going wild in the wind. Motorcycles backfired like gunshots and the canals quivered as if they were terrified. Aleksandr and Nina flew along the gray stretch of highway, Petersburg's ancient skyline receding behind them, and then they turned onto Pilotov Ulitsa toward Pulkovo Airport. At departures, Nina slowed the car but didn't fully stop. "Good luck, grib," she said. Her voice wavered slightly but recovered.

With that, the car—her car now, Aleksandr supposed, although it didn't matter much—was off, submerged into the honking assembly of taxis and limousines. Aleksandr looked at Vlad and told him to run for the ticket counter. They took off, disturbing an old woman with a long flea-bitten coat and a dog the size of a guinea pig, dodging a stern-looking man who waved his cane in consternation.

Somewhere in the sprint, Aleksandr had a moment to enjoy it—the exhilaration of being out in a public place without a route, a map, a

plan for any security eventuality, an entire army of helpers and mind-
ers. In this, there was a minor lifting—not as momentous as a libera-
tion of serfs, or the sight of an army retreating from Moscow, or a free
election in some future unimaginably far—but still, it was something:
this small thing of pushing your own way through the messy world,
stumbling without a spotter, running the risk of taking your own falls.

20

IRINA

Perm, June 2007

Viktor and I had agreed that we would go. I'd called him that night—after he'd spent hours drinking with Boris, listening to him rant and rave and nodding miserably in agreement—and said, "We're still going?" There had been a pause at the other end of the line, but I never felt unsure about how it would end. He said, "How about tomorrow?"

We'd jimmied into the apartment early, before Vlad was in for the day. Viktor had been given a key, it seemed, in those days when Aleksandr knew him well enough to know that he was a decent boy, though not well enough to imagine that he might ever use that decency against him. A network of dew sweated against the panes, and an overgenerous, fractured light came in through the windows. It was the kind of light that seemed to be throwing itself at your feet to beg for mercy. Or maybe the kind that falls down on its own knife in the name of honor.

Nina was strangely kind to me that last morning in St. Petersburg. We'd caught each other in simultaneous sneaking—she clearing out the luxury soaps from the cabinet, me sneaking a hastily written note into Aleksandr's coat pocket.

"You are going, then?" she'd said, and though her mouth was drawn into a fussy, disapproving shape, there was a gruffness to her voice that made me want to trust her. It made me see her, fleetingly, as a different person: younger and rougher, the kind of person who might have had to scurry about to have enough to eat or think about. It made me understand how you might grow up to be someone who spent most of your time flopping around in an enormous silken bed, or fingering the delicate buds of overpriced earrings. Nothing makes a person materialistic like severe deprivation.

(Now, on the plane, that observation alone sends me into raptures of reflection; I parse the differing threads of my own loss, I savor the nuances of this particular disaster. How I will miss my own brand of clutching materialism, the treasured sensory joys of existence. Not only the transcendent, transporting vista or symphony or epic or orgasm, though there were those. There were also—just as much—the humble pleasures of getting enough sleep or eating a really good sandwich. Then, also, there was the possibility of observations such as the one I had made about Nina: the way that the world could tilt slightly sideways, even when you thought all of its potential positions were already known. Then, too, there was the joy of learning the destinies and back-stories of characters and countries, always stranger and more inevitable than the fates conjured by fiction. How I will miss all of this. But then I remind myself of the obvious point—realized again and again but never fully believed even now, on this plane, the country roiling cobalt black below us—that there will be no missing of anything, worthy or unworthy, at all.)

At any rate, Nina was our accomplice that last morning, creeping into the bedroom she would no longer share with Aleksandr and blasting the air-conditioning so that he wouldn't hear us as we ruffled through papers, and nosed through notebooks, and packed up the camera equipment, and stole the credit card that Aleksandr used for film-related expenses. Whatever this film will mean, ultimately—and as a person who will never know for sure, I am increasingly interested in guessing—the country will owe its arrival, partly, to Nina.

Then we were careening through the early-morning city. There were still daubs of darkness on the farthest part of the sky, and the stars were paling like the face of a person who is afraid but has decided to pretend not to be. I smiled at Viktor in the darkness, though he probably couldn't see me.

Here on the plane, I add this to my catalog of gratitude, somewhere between the sandwich and the symphony: the feeling of getting up very early to do something of consequence.

The engine was starting to rumble already when we first glimpsed Aleksandr running across the tarmac. He was going at an improbable rate; from afar, he was portlier and slower—older—than he seemed up close, when he was throwing his hands about in impatience or engaging in various verbal gymnastics. He was stopped by an airport employee bedecked in neon orange, and turned sternly around. We could faintly see the angry arch of his neck, and we cringed to think of what he was saying. But the plane was pulling away, and he was smaller and smaller behind us. And we knew what we were going to do.

He could come the next day, on the next flight. Of course he could, and yes, we knew that. But I'd seen his stack of death threats, and I'd seen the way he looked at them. And I knew that by going this way, we were giving him the chance not to follow us.

On the plane, Viktor and I looked at each other and blinked. I suspect Viktor was wondering what he had gotten himself into—whether he would lose his job; whether in a wiser, more abstemious age, he would come back to look at this bad decision as the one where everything started to go disastrously wrong. I was beyond this kind of worrying. I didn't know how the trip would go, or what it would mean, or whether it would be a mistake. But I did know that I wouldn't look back on it with anything—pride or regret or misery or guilt or misty-eyed nostalgia—from some unimaginable vantage point. Who I was now was who I would always be. And what I did would have to be admired or despised or corrected by someone else.

The landscape below was quickly tapering off into countryside: dull stamps of beige and eggshell; clusters of villages; long patches of phlox and silver grass, sliced by the occasional vein of a creek. I've always loved flying, watching the earth resolve into its most basic elements: clean, subdued colors; starkly geometric designs. When you watch it all from an airplane, it's difficult to take anything too seriously or too hard. From above, the world and its teeming civilizations looked like nothing more complex than a series of cave drawings.

I thought of my flight into Moscow all those many months ago. The person I was before I touched down in Russia, the person who walked around Cambridge and fell in love and played chess with a strange Swede for whimsy—that person felt so thoroughly remote to me that it was as though she were a memory from a previous lifetime, or an identical twin with whom I had a troubled though persistent psychic connection. I could look back on her—and look back on that life—with something approaching indifference. I could recognize that there had been value there, and that there were memories that the other woman had clung to with the tragic self-importance with which we all cling to ourselves and our cherished little souvenirs. But that woman wasn't me anymore. Or if she was, she wouldn't be for long.

After a few minutes on the plane, Viktor twisted toward me and issued a frank and unnerving stare.

"Yes?" I said. "What? Having regrets? Too late now."

He continued to stare at me, long enough that I started to wonder what Aleksandr had told him about me.

"Look, now that we're in this mess together, I need to know some things," he said.

"Okay," I said carefully. I was thinking that I needed to know some things, too, but that didn't mean I ever would.

"Who are you? Who are you really, I mean?" I looked at him. Maybe he'd always wanted to ask that. Maybe he'd been afraid that doing so would offend Aleksandr or antagonize Boris. Or maybe it's simply the sort of question that you ask only once it's too late for a proper answer.

"What can you possibly mean by that?"

"I mean." He sighed and pressed his eyes shut. I could see him trying to frame his interrogation in some kind of civility. "I mean, why did you come here? What was this? Besides running away. Anyone can run away. Anyone can run away from anything, in fact. You don't need to be dying to want to do this. I just mean, why here? Why this?"

All at once I was telling him—telling him things I'd never told anyone, telling him things I hadn't even known I knew until I said them, and they became unequivocally true in retrospect. I told him about my last chess game with my father, how that was simultaneously a benediction and bewilderment; it had announced the arrival of my adulthood as it had prophesied the onset of my father's obsolescence. After my father had substantially disappeared from us but before he had died, I looked back and tried to find some of the clues to who he had been, to what had mattered to him, to how he had made sense of the world, to how he had addressed his own end. Sifting through the morass of information that was left to me was like pawing through a riverbed and trying to figure out which things are fossils and which things are just stones. But I'd pulled out the fragment that was Aleksandr, and I'd squinted at its flinty sheen, and I'd decided that there— there—was a treasured clue, or a missing link, or a splinter left to me by a divine prankster intent on testing my faith.

And then there was the unendurable pressure of having to die gracefully in front of people I knew. There was the childlike suspicion that this thing chasing me was something that could be outrun; there was the sneaking sense, only three quarters ironic, that Huntington's might not qualify for a visa. Even more primal and even more shameful was the fleeting question of whether my father had ever died at all. I'd watched him die from superego down to cells, but even as a child, I'd had the good sense to darkly scrutinize what I was supposed to be taking at face value. How was the man in front of me—the man who flailed and shouted, threw things across the room, shat on the piano— how was this man the same one who had composed choral arrangements for Bach, and had the capacity to carry on simple conversations in a truly unfathomable number of languages, and followed geopolitics like other men follow sports? Even as a teenager, I suspected that the whole thing might be a sham. This man's leprous face was not my father's face; his syncopated animation was not my father's gestures. If this man was not my father, then my father wasn't here. And if he wasn't here, he was somewhere else—perhaps he'd outmaneuvered everybody, as he always outmaneuvered me at the chessboard in the days before he couldn't anymore.

I told Viktor all this. And then I told him something simpler and just as true: sometimes there are things we don't understand even about

ourselves. Sometimes we run out of the time to keep trying to unravel
them, and we have to sit back and content ourselves with a shrug. But
I think there are some things that we'd never understand even if we
had forever to wonder. There are things that—even if we had unnum-
bered lifetimes to think about them—we still wouldn't know.

It was only four hours to Perm, and I slept most of the way. We
touched down and shuffled out and rented our car glumly, with the
air of hungover teenagers who know that, in a burst of inebriated inspiration, they've done grim damage to their future lives. I let Viktor
drive.

We didn't speak as we skimmed along the Kama River. I rolled
down the window and looked at the water—blue as a femoral artery,
running off to five different seas. Somewhere beyond the thicket of
trees lay the ruins of Perm 36, but we didn't have time to go looking
for it. Even if we did, there probably wouldn't have been much to see:
a ghostly archipelago of stones, a husk of barbed wire, and withered
trees. Through the window, the air came at us mossy and dense and
rich with the complicated, metallic scent of industry. The city skyline
was strangely ridged, which made the horizon feel askew: buildings
jumped at us in weird ways as we approached, and off in the distance
we could sense the hulking presence of the Urals, their humped backs
like fossilized ogres guarding the entrance to Asia. And between them,
perhaps: snatches of weak intercontinental light, backlighting the contours and making paper lanterns of the foothills. And beyond that,
seven more time zones. You could squint and almost see it: tens of
thousands of fields of wheat, overgrown collectives where nature had
clotted over agriculture. Unrelenting taiga pocked by the occasional
relic of the odd, enormous universe: a putrefying missile silo, the void
left by a comet. And beyond that: a smattering of volcanic islands and
then America. I could close my eyes and give myself vertigo just thinking about it. I am not ready to die. I'm not. I am not even bored of the
fact that the world is round.

Outside the window, the sun was brutal, bright and horrible as an
exposed organ.

We checked in to a hostel that was similar to my old hostel. I thought of my things back there in the building that had been something like a home—my pile of myriad clothes and books, all the lingering things that I would soon have to grimly assess and stow, like a pathologist at an autopsy. Better to leave nothing behind than to leave behind so little—just enough evidence for people to know that you only made it two thirds through *War and Peace,* and you were overly fond of shirts with collars.

We found our room wordlessly and thunked our bags onto our hospital-cornered beds. Across the room, Viktor turned to face the wall and change. I eyed him with what I realized was a version of lust, even if was a bit bleached out, a bit bloodless. It wasn't particular to him, I didn't think—although he had nice eyes, I suppose. It was just that he was a man, and we were at a sort of hotel, and I was dying. And sex is supposed to put you in contact with the enduring, or the infinite, or whatever, although I wondered if, in this context, it might have the opposite effect. Maybe the smack of skin on skin would remind me only of our stubborn corporeality. Maybe it would make me start thinking about evolution, and genetics, and continuity, and the future, and maybe I would think about how sex was an inherently hopeful act, and maybe the whole thing would leave me in worse shape than I was when we started. And anyway, Jonathan was somewhere else— a life with him irretrievable now, even if I turned around the very next morning and flew home, even if I spent the night clutching at another man's bones.

I had just about talked myself out of it when Viktor grabbed my hip and stared at me hard. He leaned in. And then we were tearing at seams and hair and skin, and I was on top of him, and we wrestled each other as though we were fighting with our own mortalities: it was high-stakes sex, it was execution-day sex. We clung to each other's bodies: unfamiliar because we were strangers in this way, familiar because we were both human and both still blessedly alive. He smelled like basil. We yelled into each other's shoulders, and it was terror, I'm sure, as much as it was joy. It was like shouting into the apocalypse.

Afterward, he tapped me on the shoulder. "Another question," he said.

"Yes."

"All this stuff about wanting to know how to face defeat," he said. "You think you learned something from Aleksandr about that?"

"I'm here, aren't I? We both are."

"And that's it?"

"I think the only way to properly face doom is to be on time."

Outside, bats made shadowy filaments against the sky. I burrowed into Viktor's shoulder and tangled in the scratchy sheets. It was still early, for a certain demographic. Down on the street, the city geared up like a rusty engine, and I heard mirthful hilarity in the streets all night long.

For the conversations with Simonov, we'd booked a hotel room in downtown Perm. The day after our arrival, Viktor and I drove there in silence. Outside the window, the town petered into white fields and enormous white sky. The sun emerged and began sweating tenuous light. I rolled down the window and smelled cold mud and the bloody smell of rusted automotives.

At the hotel, we promptly ordered decadent room service on Aleksandr's credit card. After half an hour, Simonov arrived. He knocked on the door. "You're the film students?" he said.

We let him in. He had a weathered, tumorous face, spackled with a stingy assortment of zinc-colored teeth. A Kalashnikov rifle was hanging from his hand, limp as a dislocated elbow. It was an odd way to hold a gun.

"Thank you for meeting with us," we said, and then we watched Simonov eat and drink and smoke for a while. He poked at his pork and sucked on his shots. We set up the camera, and it stood splay-legged in the corner. Simonov eyed it and began tapping his knee with the wretched repetition of an autistic child. It was possible, I realized, that he had stage fright.

After we'd all done a couple more shots, we started to ask Simonov our questions. We asked him about his childhood, his rise to power, his thoughts on the greatness of the Russian armed forces. He drank. We drank. We turned off the camera, and Viktor made off-color jokes. Simonov laughed. We turned the camera back on and asked him his thoughts on tensions with Georgia. At one point he banged on the table and started yelling about how Russia was the number one exporter of weaponry in the world. We turned the camera off. He got misty about his children, about his wife. "She looks like a potato," he said. "But God help me, I love her." I glanced at Viktor. We turned the camera back on.

"You've been working here at Perm for a long time," said Viktor carefully.

"Yes," said Simonov. He leaned back. "Ten years."

"So you were here in 1999, then," I said.

"That's what ten years means."

"So you were here on September 3, 1999, then," I said.

He stiffened. "Yes," he said slowly. In the silence, it felt as though the camera were emitting its own tiny sound—the barely audible breathing of febrile ground, or of something waiting to capture something else. "I suppose."

"Were you aware of the disappearance of a significant amount of RDX in the middle of the night on that date?" said Viktor.

Simonov laughed, but it sounded like a warning. "That was a very long time ago," he said.

"You might remember it," said Viktor, "as the night before the bombings started."

Simonov's voice went quiet. "Turn off the camera," he said, and Viktor did as he said. Simonov looked at us differently—his mouth hung open, but his eyes were narrowing into an expression that was cold and, implausibly, quite sober. Then he smiled. "Kind of an odd question for students."

I looked at Viktor. He turned his head slightly to the side.

"I know who you are," said Simonov. "I know who you work for."

I started to speak, but Simonov waved his hand at me. "He will not win," he said.

"No," said Viktor.

"Then there's something we can agree on," said Simonov. "And he's making this film. You really thought I hadn't heard of this? You really thought I didn't know?"

He leaned back and looked at us. His gaze was stricken and faltering, as though he'd been waiting his whole life for this moment, and now that it was upon him, there was nothing he could do with it. For a long time he looked at us, his mouth puckering. "Lucky for you," he said at last. "My daughter was killed in Buynaksk."

I leaned back. "She was?"

"She was."

"I'm so sorry."

He looked down. I looked at Viktor. I could tell that he wanted to turn the camera back on, but he didn't. "They announced it two days early," said Simonov. "Gennadiy Seleznyov announced it to the Parliament, that there'd been an explosion in Buynaksk, and I was so afraid for her. But then she called me and said, 'Papa, I'm fine. It was Moscow. It was a mistake.' Two days later she was gone. They must have gotten their dates mixed up." He chewed on his knuckle. I tried to imagine it. It was hard to imagine what that might take from a person.

I leaned forward. "Can you talk to us?" I said.

Simonov stared. "I loved my daughter."

"Of course," said Viktor.

He shook his head. "I loved my daughter," he said again. "But I have other daughters. I have a wife. I enjoy my own life, if that's not too tawdry to say. I cannot talk to you. I'm sorry."

Viktor looked at me a little hopelessly. "Talk to us," he said. "Talk to us now, for your daughter."

"I didn't know what they were going to do with it," said Simonov miserably. "I thought it was for the Dagestan incursion. I thought it was for some business abroad. I swear to you, I did not know."

"We believe you," said Viktor. "We believe you." He leaned forward. "What was her name, your daughter?" This was a little callous, I thought—but then it was also pretty smart.

Simonov looked down. "Valentina," he said finally.

"That's a pretty name," I said. Viktor gave me a look that told me I was pushing it. There was another long silence.

"I can't talk to you," said Simonov. "Though I can't help it if you break in."

Viktor raised an eyebrow and looked at me.

"I can't help it if you break in," said Simonov again. "But if you do, you need to make sure to really break the windows."

We did it at night, when Simonov had told us he'd get the guards drunk. We could hear them carousing off in the corner of the facility, singing some vigorous military songs and slamming bottles heartily on tables. Next to the office building, rows of Gelandewagens crouched half buried in the muck. Snarled bits of equipment poked out of huge squares of blue tarp. We did break the windows, and then we climbed through—first me, then Viktor. I was bleeding from above my navel, a little. The office was small and organized, with short file cabinets squatting darkly against the walls. We didn't switch on the lights, but we didn't need to. Simonov had made it easy for us. On the desk, he'd set out the papers that dryly noted a request by the FSB for one metric ton of the explosive RDX, signed by himself, and dated September 3, 1999.

We grabbed the paper. We threw some other papers off the table, overturned a chair, tossed Simonov's coat on the floor. We made the place look messy, but we didn't do much damage. Then we folded ourselves back through the window—first me, then Viktor. I could feel a welt emerging on my back where I'd caught myself in the window. In the rec building, we could see the yellow party unfolding into ever deeper debauchery. We returned to the car shaking and triumphant, and we cut our lights, and we drove slowly, slowly, out of the facility.

Even then, even at that late hour, I wanted to know how all of it would play out. Even then, when I should have been dragging my feet to slow everything down, to savor each moment as a precious representative of the beloved totality of life. Curiosity persists, when the answer is already on its way—even, in fact, when the coming answer is the removal of the question via removal of the questioner. So even then, in the car, when looking forward to anything was a sort of suicidal impulse, I found myself wanting to know what would happen next.

Out the window, the moonlight was anemic. I leaned back and felt my blood, hot and temporary, run down my spine.

We get back on the plane at six-twenty in the morning. When we drive to the airport, the sky is only beginning to leak its light, which is coming through pinpricks in the clouds in streaming, outreaching arms. This world is stranger and more beautiful than could ever be imagined ahead of time. I am struck with enormous gratitude for having gotten to see some of it.

The night before, Viktor sat at the table in the hostel and video-taped the document. He held it reverentially, as though it were a love letter or a Dead Sea Scroll, and zoomed the camera in on every damning implication. Then he e-mailed the video to Aleksandr, along with what little footage of Lieutenant Andrei Simonov we managed to acquire. Then he scanned the document to Aleksandr for good measure. "And who knows?" Viktor said as he closed down his computer. "Perhaps we will bring him the original."

Halfway to the airport, it looks to me as though we are accompanied by a follower. A white car, hulking as a beached whale, is loping along the lanes behind us, and it seems to be a playing a counterpoint to our movements—slowing and accelerating when we do. I raise my eyebrows at Viktor, but he's several steps ahead of me. He slows down, he speeds up, he pulls over, he changes lanes. Twenty feet behind us, the big white car mirrors our every move.

"They're following us," I say.

He keeps his eyes on the road. "Well, they shouldn't bother. We're going to the airport, obviously. Where else would we be going?"

And this is the thing about being followed by a huge white car: you can only keep driving, even if you know it's after you.

We check in. The sunlight is breaking across the enormous picture windows and skittering cracked and crumbling across the floor. We wait, but now we seem to be alone. On the television screen, Putin is talking about Aleksandr, saying that his candidacy is illegitimate and ridiculous and doomed and not worth talking about, next question, please.

We file onto the plane, and Viktor lets me have the window seat. The plane is almost empty, I'm grateful to notice. The engine heaves, and we are off—we pull up and out, and below me I can see the terrible blue of the Kama, coiling around the city. I look down at this strange, partially discovered place and think of all the others that exist, half formed and lurking, in my mind: the sheets of light wheeling over the Andes; the snaking, sculpted sand dunes of Namibia; the ancient cities cluttered with a millennium's worth of objects left lying around— when the volcano erupted, when the city was sacked, when the plague swept through the streets and crumpled half the population in a week. There are many things I have not seen. But there are a few things that I have. Maybe living in the world for a time is enough, even if you don't get to see all of it. Maybe it is enough. At any rate, it will have to be.

I find myself looking forward to getting back to Petersburg—to the city that never truly felt foreign to me, though I certainly felt like a stranger there, as I did everywhere else. It's not an original observation, and yet it's coming at me all at once—the bitterness and beauty of looking forward to the simple thing of gulping down a different kind of air. And somewhere behind my heart there's a fermata of feeling— a slight lifting, then a falling that somehow doesn't feel like a resolution. I screw my eyes shut, and then I open them and look down at the ground—it gets exponentially farther away with each blink, with each heartbeat and breath. It was how I always felt about birthdays back when I was younger but after I knew the cost of a passing year. How did I let this happen? I'd think. How did I ever let this life get so far ahead of me?

I lean back in my seat, and I feel the hoisting of the plane, its resilience against the whirring cold, the forbidding blue. The pilot banks to the side, and we are casting an improbably detailed shadow on the countryside; we look like the approach of a mythical bird or an avenging god. Beneath us there must be the rifling of grass against soil, the frenzied roiling of pale-edged leaves. But we can't see those things anymore.

I think, although I am not sure, that my hands are shaking more than usual, beginning to thread forward of their own account ever more audaciously. I watch. I put my hands on the pullout tray, and they tremble and jump.

But then again, maybe it's not pathological. It could just be reverential. It could just be the beauty of the sky and the clouds—the miracle of morning, the heresy of aviation.

21

ALEKSANDR

St. Petersburg, Summer 2007–Spring 2008

In the end, he would have to imagine it. He would never know, not exactly, what happened, or how, or what it was like for Irina and Viktor and the others, all twenty-one of them, their names and nationalities printed in tiny letters in the newspaper some weeks later, after the search was called off and the luggage was identified and the passenger list was confirmed. He doesn't know, so he'll have to imagine.

It was a bomb—a small one, manufactured by the efficient people at the FSB, a hissing coil of fiber and flame that could be attributed to technical malfunction. He doesn't know, so he has to guess, that they were most of the way to Helsinki—just off the coast, maybe, the Gulf of Finland hissing and murky below them. They were about to turn back toward the city airport. (That, he imagines, was a mistake. If the bomb had detonated even a few moments too late—or if the flight had made better than anticipated time—there could have easily been a crash over the city, which would have caused a lot more trouble and probably raised a lot more questions).

They thought that Aleksandr was on it, because Misha had made them think he might be; they may have trailed Irina and Viktor in

Perm, and maybe they made a note of the fact that Aleksandr didn't seem to be with them, but they may have thought that he was in hiding, or incognito, or in the trunk. There was reason enough to think he was on it, and so they believed he was on it, even though he never flew Russian airlines, ever, for this exact reason, and even though his name was not on the list. They may have thought he was using an alias. They may have decided to take their chances. And a month later, when Aleksandr got his credit card statement—with its hotel rooms and room service and alcohol, all purchased in Perm, all reflecting his presence there—he stared at it for a long time before calling to cancel the card.

In the end, it was a calculated risk. Failure, they must have figured, would be worth little. And success would be worth quite a lot.

On the plane, Aleksandr imagines, they fell ten thousand feet in ten seconds, and it was the usual scene: dropping oxygen masks and flight attendants shouting at everybody to get down, get *down*. The people clasped hands with strangers, social protocol made suddenly, aggressively irrelevant. They prayed in six languages. They shuddered, cried, threw up. Was Irina scared? Of course she was scared. But the thing was (he thinks, he hopes), she was used to it.

They angled over the water, and there was a horrible silence from the cockpit, and then the plane came undone—a great unraveling of pieces, bits of people's lives coming unhinged along with it. The windows exploded, and magazines and gum wrappers, teddy bears and toothbrushes, eye makeup kits and rosaries and foreign affairs magazines were whipped out and into the water. The bags were drowned, and later, what emerged was absurd and mundane—tennis shoes, self-help books, bras. Nothing as poetic and tragic as a tiny baby shoe, or a wedding ring still in its case, or an unpublished novel. People died with their lives intact, in full swing, not yet ready to be reduced to symbols or eulogies.

And Irina? Did she die praying, or cursing, or cursing herself for praying? Did she hold the frail hand of the old woman sitting next to her, stroke the arm of the girl her own age? Did she go down flirting with a handsome stranger? Did she cry? Did she scream? Did she learn finally, abruptly, whatever it was she'd needed to learn?

We don't know, and Aleksandr doesn't care to imagine that part.

We do know the oceanic light came in gusts. It was sheer white before they hit the water. At the end, in a way—like some sad things, although not all sad things—he likes to imagine it was beautiful.

———

The embassy was notified. The American press liked the story of an American girl who ran away to find an adventure and a fate. Viktor got no mention on any television program, American or otherwise, although *Novaya Gazeta* wrote him a nice obituary. Aleksandr cried over it—partly because that poor young man was dead, and partly because there were so many things that the newspaper had discovered that he had never asked and thus never known.

Interest in Irina spiked and subsided in a week. The final Harry Potter book was released, and the world was momentarily awash with the kind of worldwide goodwill toward men that usually accompanies only the Olympics or international terrorism. A month after her death, her name had dropped back into obscurity, and anyone who remembered her could conjure up only the sketchiest of narratives—the story of some American girl who had run away to Russia and died there for reasons that nobody remembered or perhaps ever knew.

For Aleksandr, there were a few drawbacks to Irina's brief posthumous notoriety. It raised certain suspicions in certain corners, suspicions that never fully went away. But for the most part, his stock rose modestly after the crash, both at home and abroad. Everybody knew who the intended target had been, and even people who hated Aleksandr admitted that he'd been lucky to escape. (On BBC, Misha, who was now a regular commentator, called Aleksandr "almost suspiciously lucky.") Everybody liked the notion of the government trying to kill someone and failing, and some even seemed to regard the whole project with a degree of baffled amusement. Later, on CNN, a geriatric host would compare Aleksandr to a cartoon bird who perpetually outsmarts a malicious wild dog—and for the first time on live television, Aleksandr was utterly nonplussed and did not know what to say.

For weeks, Aleksandr thought constantly, unendurably of Irina and Viktor. Their names were in his ears, in his skull. They were in every synapse in his circuitry. He couldn't shake them out no matter what he tried. And Viktor and Irina were not the only people to whom Aleksandr owed his tenuous continued existence: they assumed their places alongside Ivan, and the three of them gazed at him with unswerving and disappointed reproach. It was too much: there was an entire aggrieved population in his head.

He sat and looked out the window for God knows how many nights in a row. He watched an escarpment of black descend upon the city, over and over and over again.

———

Boris came back almost immediately. He arrived on a sunny afternoon to find Aleksandr still in his pajamas, letting rings of cold coffee seep onto the stacks of newspapers that were piling up around the apartment. Boris eyed him up and down and said, "None of this looks very presidential." Through raw eyes, Aleksandr stared at Boris and thought of the long life ahead of him—the long life of a survivor. It was his penance for being right, or his reward for being scared, depending on how you thought about it.

Then they sat in silence watching Channel One and counting the lies until the sun went down and the only light was coming from the television.

———

It was some days after the crash—maybe seven, maybe ten: Aleksandr would never remember precisely because his brain stopped forming new memories for a while—that he heard a knock at the door. Even though it was foolish to have done so, he'd put Vlad on paid leave, and he was living alone in the apartment, issuing statements to the sliver of free press whenever they called him, writing letters to all the editors in the West, living around the ghosts of the many people who had lately taken their leave. Vlad had told him how stupid this was, and he'd known it was true. But he couldn't bear the thought of living with only his armed guard—he imagined Vlad manning the kitchen with a machine gun while he made spaghetti in his slippers. He couldn't stand it. Not now, especially not now.

The knock came in the evening. Aleksandr had concluded his e-mails and teleconferences for the day and had settled into his new evening routine of reading his death threats and drinking a quarter of a bottle of vodka and sometimes having a hand at the elite online chess forums, though this was no challenge nor, ultimately, much entertainment. It was Boris, he figured, when the knock came again—he'd probably left something, or had a piece of news that could not adequately be conveyed by telephone. Maybe there was something depressing on television that he didn't want to watch alone. Or maybe he was only lonely, only aimless, only bereft and roaming the streets and finding himself back at Aleksandr's—because where else, at this late hour, would he go? Aleksandr felt sorry for Boris, but even so, he did not want to see him. He'd already spent a non-negligible amount of time with the vodka, and he was experiencing a sensation of pleasant indifference: a sneaking suspicion that the pulsing lights of Petersburg out the window were the most important thing, and everything else was quite secondary. He liked this suspicion even if he didn't entirely believe it, and he wanted to hang on to it as long as possible. So when he opened the door, it was probably with a bit of a scowl, and that was probably the first thing that Elizabeta saw when she looked up at him for the first time in twenty-seven years.

His mouth filled with ash; his bones turned fragile, ornithological. For a moment, or maybe longer, he wondered whether he'd lost his mind—whether solitude and sadness and the repeated imaginings of this exact event had ultimately pried apart his grip on reality. It was true that he hadn't thought to imagine this moment for a good long while. There'd been too much intervening grief, and lately, even his subconscious hadn't been indulgent enough to dip into this particular fantasy—there were, after all, so many other, more dangerous, more pressing ones.

"Aleksandr," she said. "How are you?"

She sounded like there was nothing too terribly odd about her asking, as though she'd gone only a few days longer than normal without speaking to him, and she was curious as to how he'd been spending his time. His arm shot instinctively to the door frame. It was possible he was seeking its assistance in staying upright.

"What happened to the dinosaur?" he said. If he hadn't been a touch drunk, he wouldn't have said it, or he wouldn't have said it precisely that way, or he wouldn't have said it before he even said anything else.

"The dinosaur?"

There was a tsunami of oceanic noise in his ears, and he almost had to ask her to speak up. "The official," he said.

She took a slight step backward. She must have known he would ask, but she probably expected to be invited in first. "Yes. Mitya. He's dead now."

"Isn't everyone?" said Aleksandr. Then he said, "I'm sorry."

"You're not. I'm not really, either, though he wasn't as bad a man as I expect you're imagining."

He looked at her and said nothing. His temperature was coming down, and he was starting to believe that what seemed to be happening actually was.

"Might I come in?" she said.

It was strange that he wanted to say no. He wanted to close the door and collapse against it in exhaustion; his apartment was already haunted enough, and if he let Elizabeta in, even for an hour, he wasn't sure he'd be able to keep living there.

"I'm sorry about your employees," she said.

"Yes."

"I saw on the news."

"Yes, you can come in."

He stood aside and held the door open for her, and when she passed by, he was struck by the incredible strangeness of her proximity. There was his body, and then there was hers, and he could reach out and pull her to him if he wanted to, which he always had. But he couldn't tell if this was better, or worse, or, depressingly, exactly the same. He gestured emptily to the chairs in the office. He then realized that they were covered in papers, and he went and swept them onto the floor.

"Do you want anything? Tea or"—he noticed her notice the vodka bottle melting onto the death threats, and he knew what an odd evening all *that* added up to—"or anything?"

"Tea," she said. "Please."

He stared at her helplessly, then went to make the tea. Nina had left her arsenal, and he selected something he hoped was especially bitter and unforgiving—something that tasted like missing a chance and realizing it far, far too late. Didn't she know how relentlessly she'd harassed him these past decades? Was her cruelty not satisfied? It occurred to him briefly that she might be here to kill him—she wouldn't be the first person to try, and she had, after all, been married to a Party official for some time, and he'd probably been intimately linked to the current government in some way. Once a Chekist, always a Chekist, as Putin himself had said. There was also the small matter that Aleksandr had never really known this woman—not really, not at all—and he'd be a fool to be surprised by anything she might do. And it would be embarrassing, it would be mightily embarrassing, to have dodged a fairly expensive and technically involved plane crash only to be murdered a week later in his own apartment, while wearing slippers, while making tea.

He stayed in the kitchen until the kettle screamed, then brought her a cup on a tray.

"Thank you," she said.

He wanted to be monosyllabic and coy, like she was being. He wanted desperately to make her wait excruciatingly for the accusations that she must have known were coming. But he couldn't. The words were out of him before he'd given them a once-over. "I wouldn't have let anybody else in the world into this apartment, you know," he said. "Unaccompanied and without a meeting. Maybe my bodyguard. Maybe some of my staff. I don't think there's anybody else right now."

She took a sip of the tea. If it hurt her, she didn't let on. "You trust me?" she said.

"I don't trust you. It's not trust that got you in here."

She looked out the window. "You don't trust me. That's funny."

He scoffed. It was outrageous that she was here at all—after all the time, and after all he'd gone through on her account, although he supposed she couldn't fairly be asked to know all that. But regardless, he was an important man now, and he'd run important risks, and there was no reason that he had to tolerate unwanted visits from anyone, let alone her. She'd known a different man in a different lifetime, and even that man, only very casually.

"You married an official." He kept his voice flat, as though this were a neutral fact and he was helpfully reminding her. He hoped he was being cruel. He wanted to be cruel.

"I did."

"You didn't love him," he said. He didn't know this. She could have loved him. Sometimes, over the years, in his more generous moments, he had hoped that she did.

"I didn't."

"But you married him." He was surprised that he had to keep pointing this out.

Her face became cloudy then, and he thought with terror that she was going to cry. It would be an incredible thing to see a woman like Elizabeta cry—like witnessing a freak meteor shower or the exhumation of a sea creature that was thought to be long extinct. Even though it would be a spectacle, he didn't want to see it—he didn't want to see it because he never wanted her to cry, ever, even now, even when he thought that maybe she deserved it.

All this was irrelevant, because she didn't cry. She started to cough. It was a hopeless, wretched, horrible cough, and immediately he wished that she'd cried instead.

"Don't feel bad," she said when she emerged and saw him staring. "That would have happened even if you hadn't brought up poor Mitya."

"What's wrong with you?"

She looked at him witheringly. "You mean—generally?"

"Your cough."

She shrugged. "Cigarettes. Never start, Aleksandr. It's a nasty habit."

He didn't remember her smoking in the kommunalka, and he immediately, quietly, decided to believe that this, too, was the fault of the dinosaur.

"You have a nice view up here," she said. She was trying to move them past the coughing, past the dreadful thing that it seemed to suggest.

"Everyone says so."

"You don't agree?"

"No, it's quite lovely. It's a slightly different view when it's all you've got, but yes, it's lovely."

She watched out the window, and he wished he could know what the view looked like to her.

"So," she said. "You don't trust me because I married poor Mitya."

"Essentially."

"Why do you think I did that?" She was standing up and moving closer to him.

"Because it was easy." He stood up, too, just in case there was going to be hand-to-hand combat. He didn't want to die sitting down.

"Partly that," she said.

"Because you were tired of what you did." She was close, and the only thing to do was to stare straight into her face. It was an odd thing, this aging. It was there as a fading around the eyes and a severity around the chin. But the young person—the real person—was so present, so undoubtedly alive. It was as though the rest—the netting across the eyes and the pursing of the mouth—were a shoddy disguise, not meant to be taken seriously.

"Partly that, too," she said.

"Because you were afraid."

"No," she said carefully. "No, not that." She smelled like oatmeal and lilac—and yes, cigarettes, but they were the cigarettes of prewar Paris, the cigarettes of Ingrid Bergman, not the cigarettes of zeks in the gulag or common people anywhere.

"What else?"

She looked at him then with a look that was more complicated than some people's entire hearts or lives. It was a look that was part resentment and part tenderness and part inarticulate fury. Behind that, maybe, there was something else—something he wasn't sure he was in any position to see or to judge or to believe anymore.

"Aleksandr," she said. "Did it ever occur to you to wonder why you weren't killed along with your friend?"

———

She didn't ask to stay, and he didn't invite her, but somehow she was still there a week later, and she was showing no signs of leaving. They took cautious walks occasionally, along the Neva—Vlad trailing them at a prenegotiated distance—and they told each other their entire lives: the parts that had happened before the kommunalka, and the parts that had happened afterward, and the unseen parts that had happened while they were living around each other. He told her that after he'd first met her, he'd gone and lay on his bed, delirious with a new, improbable, striking thing. She told him that after she talked to him in the hallway, she spent the afternoon asking the steward questions about him until she chased Elizabeta from the room and never dealt with the worms in the faucet. She also told him—never directly but obliquely, unbelievably—that maybe she had married to protect him. Not totally, not entirely, but maybe partly. In the days after the discovery of the pamphlet, she'd pleaded with the dinosaur man (who'd been slow, and not mean-spirited, and hopelessly in love with Elizabeta) and he'd agreed to protect Aleksandr, within reason, if Elizabeta would marry him. And so—because she didn't want to be a prostitute forever, and she was poor, and it was a time when everybody, everybody, had done something of which they were now ashamed—she'd agreed.

They talked also, finally, about Irina—the nominal reason for Elizabeta's visit to him in the first place. She told him how the girl had come to see her—funny, to hear Elizabeta call Irina a girl when Irina had been thirty-one and Elizabeta, even now, even when he squinted, could never be too much older than nineteen. Aleksandr saw now that Elizabeta might feel guilty, too—she'd sent Irina chasing Nikolai, which had gotten her summoned to Aleksandr, which had gotten her killed. He saw that Elizabeta might have thought him an unworthy steward of the young woman she had circuitously sent him. He saw, too, that this was something else they might share.

The bottom line was this: he loved her, he'd always loved her, and he couldn't entirely forgive her, he could never entirely forgive her. She knew this, and they could live with it—live with the best years lost, and irretrievable, and unknowable now, always. Then again, maybe they'd traded those years for these—maybe her protection had bought him his whole life and whatever would one day come of it, if anything at all. He didn't know, honestly, if it were a trade he would make again—but then it wasn't his to make. And when she stayed, and kept staying, and he kept waking up to her, there were moments when he could only feel grateful. There were moments when he could almost believe she'd been there all along.

A few nights after Elizabeta's return, Aleksandr finally looked at the material from Perm. The e-mail from Viktor had been sitting in his in-box, crouching sinisterly like a prank left by a poltergeist, and Aleksandr had been half afraid to open it—he feared that it might unleash a duo of swirling, self-righteous ghosts who would point at him with ghoulish fingers and ask him why he hadn't done some things (maybe everything) differently. But when he opened it, it was only what it purported to be. The footage was as damning as anything Aleksandr could have hoped for; nothing short of an audio recording of Putin clapping his hands and giggling about the attacks could have been better for the film. It was the clincher. It was the closing argument. Along with the footage came an e-mail message from Viktor, now three weeks dead:

Sorry we had to do it this way. But I know you understand.

Aleksandr never deleted it. In later years, it moved farther and farther into the recesses of his in-box, but he never let it go. It was a signal, a semaphore. It was a beacon across an incomprehensible gulf, and as long as it was there, Aleksandr felt that somebody was still swinging the lantern.

The documentary came out in the middle of the summer. It was shown in indie movie houses in the United States, in Western Europe. In Russia, it was pirated and passed along on DVD, though it was viewed mostly by the usual people—the intelligentsia with their wire-rimmed glasses, showing the film to their dinner-party guests and clucking over the things that they were going to cluck about anyway. It was available in nine parts on YouTube, and nearly one hundred thousand people watched it. Aleksandr sent it to the Moscow Film Festival just to antagonize the close buddy of Putin's who ran the thing. *Novaya Gazeta* gave it some coverage and wrote a review, giving particular attention to the findings from Perm. The film was never spoken of on television. At the end of August, the page editor responsible for the film review suffered a tragic fall down some faulty stairs. In October, the editorial writer who'd offered a scathing analysis based on the investigation contracted an implausible, incurable disease and died in a state hospital, where his remains were confiscated by the authorities.

Aleksandr would never know (how could anyone know?) whether it was worth it—worth the death of those two, plus an entire airplane of people, not all of whom were dying of terminal illnesses. But there were times when he walked along the river and felt sure that it was not. There'd been twenty-three people on the flight—twenty-two if you discount Irina, who was already on her way out—and then the two newspapermen, and when Aleksandr fully rejoined the land of the living, he spent his first few trips counting twenty-four people from a crowd: a rubbery-faced old woman with a nose like a toe, a dark-eyed young beauty, two well-dressed young men giving each other a wide distance, a mother with a passel of small children of indeterminate genders who tumbled around her like puppies, an entire grade-school class out for a day. It was not worth it. In the world of painful trade-offs—in a life spent calculating risks—it was not a wise sacrifice; it was a rook for a pawn, a bishop for a rook, a queen for a far-off victory, admittedly improbable.

Aleksandr disappeared into work, and he took Boris with him. Through the rest of the smothering summer into the ruddy fall, they worked: they collected signatures, they gave interviews, they brought up the Moscow bombings whenever it was appropriate and, quite often, when it was not. Aleksandr wrote articles for *The Wall Street Journal* to be read only by people who already agreed with him. He spoke to crowds that were not smaller but also not discernibly larger. Putin unveiled his successor, Medvedev—a skittish-seeming man with no appreciable credentials—who immediately announced that he'd make Putin his prime minister if he were elected. The week of his coronation, he polled at 79 percent.

To the crowds, Aleksandr unveiled his best lines yet: here in Putin's Russia, the government is reviving the idea of collective guilt for dissidence. Here in Putin's Russia, we put people on trial in cages in the courtroom. Here in Putin's Russia, commercial airlines are exploded for politics. Do we want four more years, at least, of Putin's Russia? Because with Medvedev, there is no doubting that is what we will get. And the crowds said no, they didn't want that.

At the end of November, one of the rallies got ugly, and Aleksandr was beaten by a small mob. The Kremlin sneeringly reported that he had spoken English to the reporters there. "I spoke Russian, too," he snarled at Radio Free Europe, even though his lip still hurt when he talked too quickly. "I speak Russian quite well, in fact, and I'd be more than happy to debate Vladimir Vladimirovich on national television so that we can see who speaks it better."

In December—after new, marginally promising poll numbers came out—he was detained by police and thrown in jail for a week. He stared out the window into a pallid block of sky. The week was not pleasant, but it was also, he knew, not representative: he emerged well fed and unharmed, and overall, it was a media coup for his side (CNN rolled old interviews, the blogosphere ignited, there were text boxes in *Newsweek* and *Time*). The week afterward his crowd was bigger than ever, and he knew that they knew that the arrest had been a miscalculation, a blunder into blowback.

It didn't matter. In January they would not let him register—of the 2,067,211 signatures endorsing Aleksandr's candidacy, 80,000 were deemed falsified by the authorities. Venues were canceled, permits revoked. Aleksandr withdrew, rather ceremonially, by delivering a blistering speech in blistering wind. And in March, Medvedev won with a staggeringly robust 70 percent of the vote, while Aleksandr watched the returns in a rented restaurant full of miserable people who eventually resorted to throwing things at the television, then shuffled out—depressed, drunk—into a black and snowy night.

Aleksandr stayed at the restaurant, with Elizabeta making curlicues on his shoulders, until after the staff had finished cleaning up.

Even Misha, whom he caught sneering on BBC a few days later, seemed distressed. "I'm no fan of Bezetov," he said. "But the election was rigged. Obviously, it was rigged. There was no election here at all, so you can stop reporting on the results."

They pulled Nikolai out of the FSB and made him minister of the interior and gave him an enormous dacha in the woods outside Mos-

cow. Aleksandr would see him sometimes when the television was
covering some event in the Duma—in the background, he could catch
Nikolai's red-raw face, his portly nest of jowls. He'd been a loyal ser-
vant to the regime. He might have been prime minister one day if he
hadn't been so unforgivably ugly.

————

At home, at least, there was Elizabeta—and whenever he lost his belief
in the eventual arrival of unlikely events, she was there to remind him.
He carried her around the apartment, and he reenacted every single
inchoate gesture and emotion that had been choking him up for the
past few decades. I always wanted to do this, he'd say. I always wanted
to do *this*. They loved each other, and that was enough, although
her coughing was dreadful, and there were nights when they didn't
touch each other at all and only watched old movies while Elizabeta
sat sucking her oxygen through tubes. There were other nights when
Aleksandr—who was not yet an old man but who would not be able to
say that for long—thought about what it might have been like to have
love for a youth, or for a decade, or for an entire lifetime.

————

His first rally after the election was in Moscow, and he thought—
although he didn't have Nina to count for him—that it was a bigger
crowd than ever. Nine thousand, he figured, maybe ten. Maybe they
were angrier, and maybe they were remorseful, and maybe this time
they meant business. They yelled slogans. They waved flags and held
posters, and some of the posters were of Aleksandr's own crumpled
and two-dimensional face. He cleared his throat to calm them down.
He looked out over them, these people, his people, Russians under du-
ress, citizens with objections. It would always be hard to believe the
polling data, it would always be hard to believe the electoral returns,
when all of these people kept showing up and shouting.

   He pulled the microphone toward him. They quieted down,
friends shushing friends, so that they could all hear what he would say.
He wanted to say something spectacular. He wanted to say something
that would justify all the things that required justification—a countless
number, that. He wanted to say something that would strike the perfect balance of rueful cynicism and quiet, enduring hope. He wanted to

say that there was no choice but to despair—and then, afterward, there was no choice but to stop despairing. He wanted to say that even if they didn't see it in this lifetime, somebody would see it in some lifetime. He wanted to say that the historical sweep is a consolation, it has to be a consolation, we have to pretend it's a consolation until it becomes one. He wanted to say that there is honor in being a small turn in a noble game, even if one doesn't get to know the outcome. He wanted to say all this, but there was no way to say any of this, and there were notes to consult. He looked down. They were waiting. He looked up again.

"We have lost this round, my friends," he said. "We have lost this game, to use a terrible chess metaphor. There was a time when I was a young man that I beat an old favorite just by letting myself imagine that I might."

It was a weak comparison, he knew. It took more than imagination.

"Some of you might remember this," he said, "although I expect that many of you are far too young. This was when chess was a more central pastime. This was before the Internet."

There was light chuckling, though he'd made the joke before.

"That's all I ask of you—it's a modest request, after all, for an old man who has been through a lot. I don't ask you to believe that we will win. I ask you to imagine that we might."

And they were. He knew they were. He could feel them imagining— he could almost hear the collective crackling of their most personal wishes, and some of them were what you might expect: a girl wants her brother to return from Chechnya with his limbs and his sanity; a young man wants to vote in an election that doesn't make him throw up afterward; an old woman wants to know what happened to her father during the Terror, and she wants a government that will tell her. Maybe some of them have more modest desires. Maybe some of them want to watch Putin handle a hostile press conference. Maybe some of them want to go abroad without being asked what their countrymen have been thinking for the past century or so. Maybe some of them want a satirical comedy program that skewers all of the politicians, makes a gleeful mockery of all of the institutions, every single night.

"Imagine that we might," he said.

He closed his eyes for the briefest moment, and the crowd was quiet and reverential. Their flags caught the wind, and their posters fluttered away, but they didn't stop them. In that moment, through their united imagining, he could almost see it. And who is to say they were not seeing it, too?

————

He spent hours, days, looking for some sign of his correspondence with Irina's father. He wanted desperately to find it, now more than ever. At the same time, he wanted to prove to himself that he could not. He wanted to prove to himself that he wasn't careless with a young woman's last wish—that he wasn't too absorbed with his own marriage and his own democracy to find the thing that counted. He wanted to know that the thing that counted was not really there. He went through countless stacks of the old pamphlets, the carbon copying bleeding into indecipherable bright blue rivulets. He went through his notes on strategy. He went through his old delivery routes and was surprised that he was ever fool enough to write them down. He found a diary entry about Elizabeta, but he could not give it to her now—not because he was embarrassed (although he was), but because confronting the shakiness of his writing, the exuberance of his love, made him want to weep.

He found nothing from Irina's father. He sat for three days straight, scattering the apartment with paper that was as ancient and fragile as an old man's skin. And then, finally, he told himself that he could stop looking. He told himself that Irina had already found whatever she came for.

————

It wasn't until years later, when he was going through Elizabeta's things, that Aleksandr would find the letter from Irina's father. He remembered then Elizabeta's attempted delivery of it in those weeks before her marriage to Mitya, and he remembered the way he'd rejected it while she stood in the doorway, young and alive and disappearing from him for the first time. He remembered the clawing grief at his chest during those days. He remembered how he'd thought that was the worst thing, and what a thin, marginal sadness it had been, comparatively. And then he sat on the ground, among Elizabeta's boxes and books, and cried a little and laughed a little and stared a little, bemusedly, at the ceiling. And then, for the first time, he read the letter.

———

In the aftermath of the election, the world briefly takes an interest. Aleksandr is flown out to the States to explain everything on television. (This happened every so often—whenever there was an event that demanded translation by an English-speaking capitalist who could talk about enormously complicated political upheaval in terms easily recognizable by any high school civics student.) He rides in a limousine through the frenetic city; he watches the hallucinatory lights of Times Square. The taxi drivers all ask him where he is from, and then he asks them where they are from. He can go whole days in New York that feel as though nobody is a native—the city is a spaceship, and everyone in it is a refugee from some dying planet (second world, third world, middle America). The hysteria of the lights, the flagrancy of the money, the stridency of the music—there is an energy that could remind him of Moscow. On MSNBC, he is asked what he thinks of the future of Russia. "We are not looking to win elections," he says. "We are looking to have elections." For a foreign policy blog, he is asked whether Russia is ready for democracy. Might not years of repression, might not the sheer size, might eons of the systematic subversion of civil society—might all that leave the country unprepared for a democratic system? Each time Aleksandr says no, he points to North Korea and South Korea, he points to East Germany and West Germany. People aren't born with a template for government; there is not an indisposition for democracy encoded on a human being's DNA; there's not a love for authoritarian abuse entangled in a nation's soul. There are only individuals, and then there are the governments that serve or disserve them. Democracy is the least bad form of government, he says. It maximizes the liberty of the individual, and in this world—in this uncertain, claustrophobic, ever shrinking world, but really, in any world—is that not the highest good? Is there anything more important than writing what you think, and saying what you think, and walking along a river at night unsupervised? Maybe he doesn't say that last part. And one day in Russia, he says. One day in Russia, too.

But sometimes, sometimes—if he's honest with himself, which he's working at, because who else can you expect to be honest with you?—he wonders. He really wonders.

———

He is asked to participate in a debate at the Institute of Politics at the Kennedy School of Government at Harvard, and he stays in a green triangle of a hotel above the water (duller, he thinks, less sleek and dramatic than his Neva). He spends the day in the colorful jumble of Cambridge. In Harvard Square, he watches the chessmen at their amateurish, faltering games and remembers that Irina played one of them. He did not know her well, and he did not know her for long, and it is not for her or for her country that he continues. And yet he thinks about her short life, and her unwillingness to spend the entirety of it as a spectator, and he knows that there is something to learn from that, if only he has the patience.

He turns toward the Charles and feels the uncomplicated joy of existing out in the world, where he probably won't be found by all the people who are looking. He can believe sometimes that this is actually what Irina came to Russia to find. He can believe sometimes that this is actually a worthy endeavor.

Walking along the river, he is struck again by the nearness of the future. It's just beyond his vision, but it's there. He knows it is. Its presence follows him—along the green Charles, back to Boston's underwhelming airport, up into the star-pocked sky and over the sea. He skims the oil-black Atlantic, the twinkling beacons of continental Europe. The future is with him, he thinks—at least as much as the past and all the people who live there. He can sense it, like the sketchy suggestion of an undiscovered country emerging from the mist, or the shape of an endgame materializing somewhere deep in his psyche. Below him, the lights of Petersburg shine like that future—cold and improbable and galaxy-bright, but closer with every moment of descent.

Maybe he will see it one day. Maybe he will not. It's a big country. But, if you're lucky, it's a long life.

ACKNOWLEDGMENTS

This book was made possible by the generous support of Stanford University and the Iowa Writers' Workshop. Thanks to all of my brilliant colleagues, in particular intrepid early readers Adam Krause, Chris Leslie-Hynan, and Keija Kaarina Parssinen. Thanks to all of my incredible teachers, especially Sandy Warren at the Smith College Campus School; Lisa Levchuk and Peter Gunn at the Williston Northampton School; Alan Lebowitz and Michael Downing at Tufts University; Ethan Canin, Sam Chang, Charlie D'Ambrosio, Elizabeth McCracken, Jim McPherson, and Marilynne Robinson at the Iowa Writers' Workshop; and Elizabeth Tallent, Adam Johnson, Tobias Wolff, and John L'Heureux at Stanford. Many thanks also to Connie Brothers, Deb West, Jan Zenisek, Christina Ablaza, and Mary Popek, all of whom have endured a staggering number of confused emails from me over the years.

I am immensely grateful to my terrific editor, David Ebershoff, and my heroic agent, Henry Dunow, who have offered me astounding insight, generosity, and patience. Thanks also to everybody at Random House, including Evan Camfield, Susan Kamil, Jynne Martin, Maria Braeckel, Avideh Bashirrad, Erika Greber, Tom Nevins, Annette Trial-O'Neil, Richard Callison, and Clare Swanson.

Thanks to Lauren Albertini, Kimberly Bastin, Prerna Bhardwaj, Dave Byron, Jennifer Cantelmi, Katie Chase, Kate Egelhofer, Bev and

Emily Fletcher, Morgan Gliedman, Cassie Jeremie, Keetje Kuipers, Matt Lavin, Aislinn O'Keefe, Ilana Panich-Linsman, Justin Race, Kate Sachs, Maggie Shipstead, Luke Snyder, Becca Sripada, Patrice Taddonio, Brian Tuttle, Jeff Van Dreason, and Kirstin Valdez Quade. I feel lucky every day to know you.

Thanks to my tremendous family, the most stubbornly resilient people I have ever known. Thanks to my amazing friends, who are an endless source of hilarity and joy. And thanks to Justin Perry, who is the central wonder of my life.

ABOUT THE AUTHOR

JENNIFER DUBOIS attended the Iowa Writers' Workshop and received a Stegner Fellowship from Stanford University, where she is currently the Nancy Packer Lecturer in Continuing Studies.

ABOUT THE TYPE

This book was set in Granjon, a modern recutting of a typeface produced under the direction of George W. Jones, who based Granjon's design upon the letter forms of Claude Garamond (1480–1561). The name was given to the typeface as a tribute to the typographic designer Robert Granjon.